BITE

DZIDO'S LIST

P. CARTER EARNSHAW

BALBOA.PRESS
A DIVISION OF HAY HOUSE

Balboa Press books may be ordered through booksellers or by contacting:

Balboa Press
A Division of Hay House
1663 Liberty Drive
Bloomington, IN 47403
www.balboapress.com
844-682-1282

Because of the dynamic nature of the Internet, any web addresses or links contained in this book may have changed since publication and may no longer be valid. The views expressed in this work are solely those of the author and do not necessarily reflect the views of the publisher, and the publisher hereby disclaims any responsibility for them.

This is a work of fiction. All of the characters, names, incidents, organizations, and dialogue in this novel are either the products of the author's imagination or are used fictitiously.

The author of this book does not dispense medical advice or prescribe the use of any technique as a form of treatment for physical, emotional, or medical problems without the advice of a physician, either directly or indirectly. The intent of the author is only to offer information of a general nature to help you in your quest for emotional and spiritual well-being. In the event you use any of the information in this book for yourself, which is your constitutional right, the author and the publisher assume no responsibility for your actions.

Any people depicted in stock imagery provided by Getty Images are models, and such images are being used for illustrative purposes only. Certain stock imagery © Getty Images.

Print information available on the last page.

ISBN: 978-1-9822-6788-9 (sc)
ISBN: 978-1-9822-6790-2 (hc)
ISBN: 978-1-9822-6789-6 (e)

Library of Congress Control Number: 2021908201

Balboa Press rev. date: 05/03/2021

Contents

BITE - DZIDO'S LIST
1942 - 1944 Nazi Germany

Huey Chang, PHD.............................. Austrian Chinese
Immigrant and
Bio-engineer

Jadwiga Dzido..................................... Polish medical student
at the University
of Warsaw / Nazi
Resistance Fighter

Estella Agsteribbe............................. Jew / Prisoner at
Auschwitz / Gold
medal Dutch Olympic
Gymnast 1928.

Heinz Alt.. Composer / Jew /
Prisoner at Auschwitz

Fabian Dubois.................................... Twin.. Political Prisoner
at Auschwitz – victim
of pigmentation
experiment

Ludovic Duboise................................ Fabien's Twin.. Political
Prisoner at Auschwitz –
victim of pigmentation
experiment

Giuseppe Ricci.................................. Nazi resistance fighter /
Political prisoner at
Auschwitz

1972 – San Francisco, CA

Lori Sanders... Wife of Frank Sanders / Co-owner of the "Bistro" Restaurant and Bed and Breakfast

John Sanders... Bachelor / Retired Korean Veteran / Older sibling of Frank Sanders

1986 – San Francisco, CA

Vaughn Muller... British Immigrant / Retired Banker / Homosexual lover of Huey Chang, PHD

Jonathan Huges.. twenty-nine / Runaway Hustler / Homosexual / AIDS Hospice Resident

Tommy Peck.. Thirty-four / African American / Homosexual / AIDS Hospice Resident

Macias Renaldo.. Portugese American / Homosexual / AIDS Hospice Resident

Fredric Garcia.. Manager Johnson Hardware / Homosexual / Drag Queen / Mulatto 6'2"

Alice Barnes... Clerk at Johnson's Hardware

Ricky Bartholomew............................ Chef at Pearl's 60's Diner

Carol Turley...................................... Server at Pearl's 60 Diner / College Student / Fabien's significant other

Thomas Thorne................................. Bus Boy at Pearl's 60's Diner / High Sophmore / Native American Mudoc Tribe

Jack Thorne...................................... 'Captain' / Mudoc Indian Chief / Widower / Raised Thomas Thorne from childhood

Natasha Burtrel................................. 16 year old female / daughter of Sandy Burtrell

Tanya Burtrell................................... 13 year old female / daughter of Sandy Burtrell

Sandy Burtrell................................... Manager of White Owl Biker Bar

Samuel Stone..................................... Sergeant San Francisco Police Department / 38 years old / Bachelor

Wayne Manis..................................... FBI Agent

Rudi Helbard..................................... Attorney for Thyssen Krupp Estate

Paul Coombs.................................... National Alliance
leader / White
Supremacist /
Owner of White
Owl Bar

Gary Yarbrough................................ Officer of the Order,
a White Supremacist
Organization

Frank Silva...................................... White Supremacist /
Member of the Order

Garmont Silva................................... Son of Frank Silva /
White Supremacist by
association only

William Luther Pierce.......................... White Supremacist /
Leader of National
Alliance / Author of
Turner Diaries

Donald Montgomery............................ Klu Klux Klan Grand
Dragon / Owner of
vehicle repair garage

March 10, 1986
San Francisco

All the poppycock and portentous nonsense weighed heavily on Joey's nerves. He decided to leave his younger sibling's twenty-eighth birthday party at Saint Vincent AIDS Hospice early. Early, as in just after midnight.

His tenants had gathered in the great room, once a bar that served guests at the old family Bistro Bed and Breakfast in San Francisco's Tenderloin district. After the death of their mother, the driving force behind the Bistro, the boys lost interest and customers, and converted it into a hospice shortly after Dylan contracted AIDS.

His brother Dylan's drinking problem was becoming conspicuous. Other than an occasional greeting, or a brief conversation about rent, Joey felt like he was always the elephant in the room. Gone were the usual complaints from patients about room temperature, furniture in need of mending, or wanting to change rooms to avoid the moaning and occasional harrowing scream from another dying tenant. The IV bags, that once kept some tenants hydrated, hadn't been used in months. In fact, Joey's tenants seem to avoid his routine health checks.

"I think you've had enough vodka birthday boy," Joey leaned into Dylan's ear. He attempted the scientific appeal over the failed brotherly scolding. "You know alcohol will exacerbate your already compromised immune system."

"Are you sure I can't call you a taxi?" Dylan responded with a cold patronizing grin.

"I have a monthly bus pass, so piss off," Joey responded crassly, protecting his feelings. If pictures say a thousand words, His tenants churlish facial twitching, spoke volumes. The Hospice tenants didn't wish to be rude, but inadvertently, Joey got the message loud and clear. He had outlived his welcome. Joey had an eerie sense that the real party was about to begin. Unequivocally, not with him. Once his friends, very

1

much dependent on him, now mysteriously ostracizing him. Were they protecting him from something?

Suspicious of his tenant's peculiar improvements to their health, Joey's curiosity was daringly more intrusive. One would normally perceive a Hospice for the dying needing twenty-four-hour care. Inexplicably, instead of beds of lethargic sickness, there was copulation and athleticism. Eccentricities that originated when he rented out his remaining rooms to Doctor Huey Chang and his friends from England five months earlier. Phenomenal progress in the Hospice tenant's health followed. Far be it that he should complain. There hasn't been a vacancy since. Nonetheless, Joey was troubled by an enigma for which there was no logical explanation.

Joey surreptitiously tried to find new lesions on Dylan's body. In fact, he believed that there were none. The patients at the hospice were leaner and sanguinely more active. What happened to the maladies and psychosis that had bedridden the residents a few months ago? Adverse thoughts that his brother would possibly return to his bedridden suffering, kept Joey from picking up the phone and notifying the CDC.

"Well," Joey brushed his silky brunette bangs away from his eyes. "I guess I best be going then, don't want to miss my bus." His sarcastic announcement, released the trapped anticipation in the room.

"Honestly, it would make me feel less concerned for your safety if you allow me to walk you to the bus stop," Jonathan said, looking for an opportunity to share his infatuation with Joey. Jonathan, whom seem to make more progress in his recovery than other tenants, took more than a liking to Joey. Dylan shot Jonathan a disapproving glare. He was more fearful of his brother's involvement with Doctor Chang, than getting mugged on the streets of San Francisco.

"You're too kind, but I'll be fine."

"It's not a bother, trust me," Jonathan insisted with a provocative wink.

"Damn!" Joey complained, rolling his eyes in frustration, "It's hard to read you people."

"I'm going to the kitchen to get a beer," Tommy interrupted. "Anybody else want one?"

2

"No sanks, I'm good," Fabien responded. Fabien, and his brother, Ludovic, were albino twins. Joey loved their European accent and wished they weren't heterosexuals. The only way Joey could tell them apart was a tattoo on Fabien's left forearm depicting his mother. Concealed from Joey, Doctor Chang had fabricated that Ludovic had AIDS to meet tenant criteria. "Vair-is Macias?"

"Upstairs changing into something light," Tommy, Macias's young black lover, answered. Joey was enamored by Tommy's complexion. His lighter mulatto tone revealed not a blemish, pimple, or freckle anywhere. Tommy had checked into the Hospice, a little over a year ago, a wimpy sick kid. Three months earlier, Joey had given him up for dead. He suspected his rebound had something to do with the arrival of Doctor Chang. Why did they purposely keep him in the dark?. Tommy was not only healthier, he looked like Arnold Schwarzenegger's protégé.

"What did you mean earlier when you said the Peckerwood gang made it to Dzido's list?" Joey probed Tommy.

"I'm not sure what you're talking about," Tommy replied awkwardly. To the dismay of the other tenant's disconcerted expressions of censorship, Tommy tried to cover up his slip of the tongue, "Are you sure I didn't say mosquito mist?"

Joey knew he was treading in sensitive waters by the narrowed brow on Dylan's face. "What would mosquitoes have to do with white supremacy? You know the wall to the kitchen is paper thin. You hear things. I'm just curious that's all. Why do I get the feeling you're trying to cover up something? Why is this such a big deal to you guys?"

"The big deal is that you're a busy body and shouldn't be listening in on everyone's conversation," Dylan interjected, torpedoing the conversation from oblivion.

"I'm going to use the head and pick up the mail before I leave," Joey declared, getting up from the sectional. He wasn't going to let on that he was taking it personal. But he always did and loathed their enigmatic need to be covert.

Joey hadn't made it ten feet toward the hallway when a naked Macias, wearing only his tight briefs, came down the stairs stroking a Siamese cat. Long gorgeous black Hispanic eyelashes froze open with alarm, like he'd been caught in a deceitful subterfuge.

"Sorry?" Macias apologized, his voice tinging upward.

Joey paused, awestruck at Macias's sensuous, nearly nude body. "Macias, we've already had this discussion. Dylan is allergic to cats." Joey knew he was fighting a losing battle. "Never fucking mind." He shook his head, tired of being the bad cop. Joey turned back toward the others, "Seriously, is Chang feeding you all steroids? Who do you have to screw around here to be this drop dead gorgeous?" Joey's outburst drew a few snickers, but mostly relief. He abruptly turned and headed toward the bathroom. Besides he'd had too many marijuana-laced brownies to go into his parent ego.

Looking into the eyes of the young man starring back at him in the bathroom mirror, Joey saw a face that he would make love to. So why did he feel so rejected and neglected?

1986, Ronald Reagan was President, Halley's Comet reached its perihelion, the closest point to the Sun, and AIDS, the new pandemic, was being blamed on gay's promiscuous lifestyle. 16,300 deaths have been reported since the Center of Disease Control in Atlanta identified the blood borne pathogen. The disease caused many Gay bath houses to close their doors for lack of business. But not all listened to U.S. Surgeon General's plea to wear condemns for protection and avoid multiple partners. Many defiant believed it was a far-right Conservative plot, and continued to have bareback sex, an expression for unprotected sex. It didn't help matters that the far right fanned the flames of defiance with their homophobic hyperbole.

The faded letters on Saint Vincent's sign on Polk Street, engulfed in weeds and neglected grass, were hardly legible, and in need of fresh paint. Wilted roses, neglected of sufficient water and pruning, lined the perimeter fencing. Before Joey and Dylan's mother passed, the gardens were once the envy of every green thumb neighbor.

"They're back!" Macias broadcast throughout the house. Doctor Huey Chang, his slightly older British lover, Vaughn Muller, and Giuseppe Ricci, a tall Italian with a long chin, entered through the kitchen door from the carport. Ricci was holding up a heavily inebriated juvenile with an acne scared face, shaved head, and wearing a sleeveless leather Jacket. Joey's suspicions surfaced again upon seeing the Peckerwood logo and a swastika tattooed on his right shoulder.

Macias glanced at Joey and shrugged, "Mucho alcohol I guess."

As they walked passed him, it was clear to Joey that the inebriated young man had no idea where he was or where the mammoth Italian was taking him.

"Someone said you had left already," Dylan said, nervously distracting Joey.

"You know I would never leave without saying goodbye," Joey expostulated. "But we need to discuss the Hospice financial situation Dylan." He pointed back down the hall where he had seen the Peckerwood being carried like a bag of potatoes, "And you'll need to explain what the hell that was. Mom and Dad are probably rolling in their graves with the way we're managing the business," Joey finished frustrated and foiled.

"Trust me Joey," Dylan insisted, "Money is not an issue for Doctor Chang. I'll deposit it in the bank tomorrow." He kissed his brother's cheek, "I'd feel better if you'd let me call you a taxi."

"I'll be fine. Love you."

"Ditto!"

April 4, 1973
San Francisco - Bistro Restaurant

Joey and Dylan spent their adolescent years growing up in the four-level house, which many years later would become Saint Vincent's Hospice. Before it became a hospice, it was a thriving restaurant, bed, and breakfast. It was the sole source of the Sanders family income.

Aside from his alcohol addiction, the boy's father, Frank Sanders, was an honest man who had inherited a small fortune from his father. In 1969, Frank bought the old Mulligan Estate in the Tenderloin District, and turned it into a bed and breakfast. Frank and his wife, Lori, had opened an English Krogh style restaurant on the main floor with dining in the infamous gardens in the backyard. Frank attended bar in what was the great room and Lori managed the kitchen. The restaurant, had grown in popularity amongst the locals. The 'Garden Bistro' was opened for Lunch and Dinner. A continental breakfast was served to only guests of the B and B. Frank argued to his last breath, it was Lori's garden that was the signature attraction. Guests of the Garden Bistro stayed on the second floor and the Sanders family occupied the third floor. Frank brainstormed that one day he would finish the basement, but for now it served as storage and a wine cellar.

As the Garden Bistro grew in popularity, seating was by reservation only and the staff had grown to twenty-seven employees.

Guests were seated in the garden grottos, each named after the predominate flower theme on a burnished wooden sign. There was the 'Hyacinth Hideout', the 'Aster Grove, the Columbine Cave, the 'Rose Ravine', to name of few. To their father's discontentment, Joey loved entertaining young male suiters in the provocative 'Cock's Comb Lover's Nest'.

Frank always assumed Joey was a homosexual from his involuntary feminine telltale signs. The flirtatious smiles he shared with young men, especially with one of the male food servers, Roger. Frank detested the Baywatch poster on Joey's bedroom wall exposing mostly naked male lifeguards on the popular TV show. Frank gave Joey, as a birthday gift, another Baywatch poster with female models featured, hoping it was only coincidence.

"Isn't she hot?" Frank remarked as Joey opened his gift.

Joey shot his brother Dylan a disdainful co-conspiracy glare. "If you say so Dad," Joey pretended he liked the gift. It never made it to his bedroom wall. First it was G.I. Joe dolls as a child, which Frank conceded had to do more with the masculine military association rather than the fact Joey just liked to dress them.

"So, you thinking of joining the Navy?" Frank had coveted a yes response.

"Nope," seven-year-old Joey responded matter of fact to his father's disappointment.

Joey installed a lock on his bedroom door shortly after reaching puberty. Days later, Dylan caught his dad trying to pick the lock while Joey had gone out with Roger. Indignation, on Dylan's face, spurred acrimony between father and son.

"What are you doing?" Dylan insisted.

His Father pulled himself together and manned up. "Last I looked my signature was on the mortgage."

"It's about respect Dad," Dylan's older soul often caught his elders off guard.

Frank deliberated, "Yea, you are right," He was suddenly discombobulated and lost for words. "I don't know how to ask you this, so I'm just going to come out with it. Is your brother gay?"

"Really?" Dylan's brow bent inward with disgust.

"Why does he have to lock himself in his room. Is he collecting gay porn or something worse?"

"I don't know," Dylan stood in front of Joey's door, inviting his father to leave and end the uncomfortable conversation. "Why don't you just ask him. Even if he was, that doesn't make him anything less a human being."

Frank looking down disparagingly, "He is going to break his mother's heart."

Dylan sighed, "Mother is much more accepting than you father."

"So, he is. I knew it!" he wiped the stress from his face, "I'm not raising a Queer. I'll get him help."

"Why would you even say that? You're the one that needs help."

Frank was now on a mission, "I will ask him. It doesn't mean I have to like it. I'm allowed to have my own opinions you know."

"As if I didn't know," Dylan sarcastically replied rolling his eyes.

Monday afternoon, April 6, 1973
Bistro Patio

"So, this is where you're hiding," Dylan exclaimed, excited to see his brother. The brothers were taking advantage of the four-day Easter weekend. Dylan discovered Joey alone in the gardens reading at the patio table. Mary and her younger brother, Cory, followed him out onto the patio through the large sliding patio doors.

"Wish you would've come," Mary said, slightly adjusting down the trunks of her two-piece swim suit to cover the little bit of ass that was showing. "It was a lot of fun."

"Hi Mary, Cory," Joey acknowledged them. "Can you stay for a cold orange soda?"

"We gotta get Mom's car back," Mary chagrined. "Just wanted to come say hi." Mary and Cory were toe-head blondes, their tans had a head start on the summer, and they mesmerized fanciers with their narrow blue eyes. They were close in age and often mistaken for twins.

"Ten minutes?" Joey attempted to negotiate some time with them.

"Sorry Joey, I can't make mom late for work," Mary stated. There was simply no wiggle room.

"How about you Cory?" Joey suggested, sneaking a glimpse of Dylan as his posture straightened at the idea. His suppressed smile told Joey all he wanted to know about what he believed existed between them. "I'll drive you home later."

"Love to, but I still have a lot of homework," he resigned. Joey bet himself that Cory was now berating himself for not getting it done earlier. "We better go," Cory nodded toward his sister.

"Bye Joey. See you guys at school tomorrow," Mary said her goodbye's and pirouette like a ballerina then left in a hurry. Joey caught Cory turn his head quickly back to Dylan with a salacious grin and raised brow.

When they were out of earshot, Joey poked fun at Dylan's expense. "I knew it, Cory likes you."

"You're so full of shit." A year younger than his brother, Dylan was athletically gifted, Joey loved romance novels, "Speaking of being discreet," Dylan paused to brace for the fallout. "I caught dad picking your new lock."

"He won't find anything but a couple lines of cocaine, hashish rock, a dildo, couple of boxes of gay porn, and enough condoms to last a life time," Joey rambled unnerved.

"I'm serious," Dylan scolded, lightly slapping him on the back of the head.

"Jesus, I'm kidding. Lighten up will ya? He'll get over it," Joey replied emotionless, glancing at his brother over his book. However, deep down he was drowning in his own unwarranted feelings of shame. "And when do you plan to break his heart brother?"

"What do you mean?" Dylan replied. "I'm not gay. I might have mentioned that I thought some guys are cute. Trust me, I've never thought about having sex with them."

Joey choked on his laughter at the comment. "And that changes everything? You're using Mary to save face."

"Bullshit."

"But I've seen the way Mary's brother looks at you at school. I caught that last exchange between you." Joey smiled facetiously. "And you scold me for not being discreet. You're screwing Cory, aren't you?"

"Nonsense," Dylan rolled his eyes at the notion. "I love Mary."

"Liar!"

"I'm in love with Mary," Dylan insisted unconvincingly.

"And I'm in love with the Anita Bryant," Joey chuckled sarcastically.

The metal chair screeched on the cement patio floor as Dylan got up to leave. He walked around to where Joey sat, still with the same mischievous smile from ear to ear. "I love you brother." Dylan bent down and kissed his brother's cheek keeping with his Mother's Italian ways. "Discreet, please."

"I don't do discreet." Joey went back to his book, 'The Picture of Dorian Gray, by Oscar Wilde. "Mary's brother," Joey said under his breath.

"I'm not screwing Mary's brother," Dylan stated emphatically as he left the gardens. "If mother asks, I'm going to the gym to shoot some hoops."

May 9, 1973
Garden Bistro Bar – San Francisco

"Damn Liberal sycophants!" contended the Methodist preacher, Charley Caples. "Abortion is murder, it's that simple." His less conservative wife, Elizabeth, ten years his senior, rolled her eyes. She kept her dirty blonde hair up in plaits which made her look even younger. Frank, keeping with the impartial bartender etiquette, agreed to disagree. Frank balked silently at the double standards that Lori's Methodist preacher wore on his sleeve. The couple always stopped in for a few glasses of wine after Sunday morning service. Frank never objected to Lori taking the boys to church when they were younger, but it just wasn't his cup of tea. Admittedly he got a few pings of jealous torment, knowing that Lori had referred to Charley as the hottest preacher wearing the cloth.

"I agree with you Frank," the preacher's wife said indignantly. "Roe versus Wade is now a done deal, get over it Charley." Frank shot her a corroborative wink.

"The supreme Court ruling is illogical," Charley continued ranting. "Thurgood Marshall arguments were incredulous and immoral."

"And William Rehnquist is just another 'in your business' conservative judge who puts his Party's politics in front of human rights," she retorted. Frank struggled to keep from arguing politics with clients.

Charley's hairless face contorted like he had just swallowed spoiled milk. "Don't say that Elizabeth, you don't know what you're talking about," His misogynist attitude castigated.

"Frank, do you mind if I ask you a personal question?" The Reverend finally got the nerve.

"Sure"

"How do I get God's message through to guys like you?"

Frank paused to give serious thought to his question. "I don't know Charley. Men of the cloth have it wrong in my book."

"How's that Frank?"

11

"You teach us to fear Witches, when I feel you should be teaching us to fear the people that burn them to the stake."

Elizabeth tried hard to hold back busting a gut. "Jeez Frank, first time I've seen my Husband speechless."

Frank saw that Charley's drink was nearly empty, "One more Charley."

"Sure," he said still sulking and feeling a little ganged up on.

Lori Sander's maternal instinct took note of her son's discontent as he listened in on the conversation. Some of the best rumors got started from the other side of the wall which separated the bar from the kitchen. His face mimicked his disdain for the Preacher's opinions. Lori put her hands over his ears, "We need these potatoes peeled before the dinner rush."

"He's crazy," he mouthed the words to his Mother.

"He's a good man with good intention." Joey rolled his eyes at his Mother's ability to find good in all people.

"Elizabeth is right Ma," Joey spoke purposely louder so that the occupants in the next room could hear him through the wall. "Women now have the right to choose."

"Good for them," Lori smiled at her son indifferently. "Be careful not to cut the potato cubes too small."

"I got asked to Junior Prom," Joey announced to his Mother unenthusiastically.

"I thought the tradition was for boys to ask the girl." Lori knew this conversation was going to happen sooner or later. "What's her name?"

"Marsha Devall."

"Bob Devall's daughter? I thought she was a junior."

"I'm not going," he said, mortified that the other subject might come up.

"I don't know why not," Lori stated, chafed at the thought of Joey wasting his high school years. "Marsha is a very pretty girl. Isn't she a cheerleader."

"I don't want to lead her on. It wouldn't be fair to her."

"No one said you had to go to bed with her," Lori reproved. "Just go and have a great time. Dance, mingle, you only get to go to high school once in your life."

"She hangs around a bunch of brain-dead jocks."

"Hey!" Lori objected, tossing an apple slice that struck him in the back of the head.

"What was that for," Joey complained with a goaded grin.

"Your Dad was a jock, and made the honor roll all three years of high school."

"So?"

"So, you're an extremely handsome boy and just about any girl in California would love to be your date. Your issue is that you're seventeen going on fifty. I don't get it. Why do you want to grow up so fast?"

Joey blushed and put down the peeling tool on the counter and turned to face his mother, absent of his peevishness. "I can't keep going on like this ma. Grandma use to remind us that it was better to be trusted than loved. How can you trust me if I keep lying to you?" He stared into the ceiling for the right words. "I'm…"

"I know," She cut him off. Lori put her hands on her hips and tenderly, in her Italian New York accent, reproached him. "Joey, Joey, Joey, I'm your motha first. You don't think I know things?"

"It's that obvious?" he assented unabashed.

"I've known since the day you reached puberty."

"Really, that long?"

"It wasn't that long ago. A mother just knows." Lori managed a warmhearted smile. "I will love you no matter who you decide to love. And it doesn't matter to me if you were born that way or whether it's a choice. It's your choice to make and nobody else's." She could see that tears were staining his cheeks. "Come here right now and give your mother a hug."

Joey laid his head on his mother's shoulder and held, in his mind, the greatest mother to ever live. "I love you mom. And for the record, I want to be clear. Even if I wasn't born Gay, I chose to be this way."

"I have no doubt," She stated sarcastically at his incredulous statement. "Your father loves you too, no matter how much of a tough guy he comes across."

"He knows?" Joey reacted, suppressing the nervous acid erupting from his stomach.

"Alright," Lori conceded. "It's somewhat obvious." Now, you accept Marsha's offer and enjoy your last year of high school."

Later that night
Master Bedroom

"Doctor Gotler called and he believes the blood test results will arrive tomorrow." Lori's voice quivered nervously. She lay on her back, covers pulled up to her chin, knowing she will toss and turn all night.

Frank sensed Lori's silent hell and didn't want her to face it alone. "Roll over here." He had managed to put on a few pounds over the years, but in all the right places. He wrapped his arm around her, pulling Lori and the bed covers tight against his body. He needed the intimacy as much as she.

Lori sighed, "The lump can be removed if we caught it early enough."

"Honey," He kissed the back of her hair. "Everything is going to be just fine. Besides, you and the big guy in sky have a special relationship."

"How's that?" She snickered and made a face like she had just heard a bad joke.

"You're a major stock holder in his church."

"Maybe I should have donated more," She replied in jest.

"Not to change the subject, but we need to take inventory tomorrow."

"Have you asked the boys to help? Joey may need some extra cash to go to the Prom."

"He asked a girl to the Junior Prom?" Frank seemed surprised as if he had just won the lottery.

She picked up on the slight confusion in his voice. "No, Marsha Devall asked him. She's on the cheer team you know. Not that it matters."

"Isn't that Bob's daughter?"

"Don't be disillusioned," She felt his body relax as his hopes vanquished. "Doesn't mean he can't go and have a good time. It's his last year in high school."

"So, Dylan is still our only chance of having grandkids?" Frank asked as if his lottery ticket was off by a number.

"Frank?" Lori's whisper gave away her despair over her disposition.

"I know, you're scared," His lips closed firmly to hold back any emotion that might upset her. "I am too."

"Hold me Frank," her voice cracked and a tear fell and wet her pillow. "Never let go."

"Never. I promise."

June 3, 1973
Rio Vista - Delta

The Sanders men loved to fish. When the opportunity presented itself, usually during Dylan and Joey's school breaks, they were off to the Delta to catch a few Stripers. Frank's childhood pal had bought a resort on the Sacramento River waterfront in Rio Vista and regularly comped them a cabin for the night. Frank didn't wish to take advantage of his friend's hospitality and always tipped more than the rent.

The Bistro was closed on Mondays and Tuesdays. However, those days were hardly days off for the Sanders due to thorough cleaning and preparing rooms for the next guests. But, when a fishing trip was in the works, Lori sacrificed her time to relax so that the boys could have their boys time together.

Crossing the deep channel of the Sacramento River over the Rio Vista Bridge, Frank's brother, John, sat in the front passenger seat chewing tobacco and occasionally rolling his window down to spit. John had more of their Mother's DNA. His face was round and unlike Frank, wasn't born with his Father's dimples. John had grown a long salt and pepper beard to hide his otherwise feminine features. Dylan and Joey sat in the back seat of Frank's 1970 Oldsmobile 442 metallic blue muscle car. He incessantly bragged of Its 455 cubic-inch V8 engine and 365 horsepower. Tackle boxes and fishing poles between them afforded them little wiggle room. Frank named the car, Katana after a DC female superhero whose sword contained the soul of her dead husband. No reason really.

"Remember Frank, it's not your first left, that's a private road. You want 160, River Road," John pointed to the next exit as they came to the end of the bridge. John was typically the worry wort in the family, but to a fault, that trait inevitably benevolence. Frank would excoriate him for handing what few dollar bills he hand to roadside panhandlers. John inevitably would respond, "I didn't do it for them, I did it for me."

"You boys have your fishing licenses with you?" Frank asked.

15

"In my wallet," Dylan replied.

"Should be in my tackle box," Joey replied uncertain.

"You need to start checking this stuff before we leave Joey," Frank rebuked. Frank was conjuring up a plan to approach Joey to give conversion therapy a try. He read in the San Francisco Chronicles that the Mormon church claimed to have success turning gay boys straight.

"I know Dad, but why would anyone take it out?" Joey rationalized.

"Still, it's just makes sense to check."

"It's there," Joey insisted.

John interrupted the Father Son lecture, "Turn left up ahead near the sign that says 'Cliff House Fishing Access.'"

"I bought a package of sardines for bait if anyone is interested," Dylan offered to share.

"Yea, I might take you up on that," Frank reacted.

"I'm sticking to worms," John retorted. Katana bounced as it left the paved highway, the dirt road to the fishing area became a little rough. "Wish they would fix this damn road."

"There's hardly a breeze this morning," Frank said smiling. "It's gonna be a great day for fishing boys."

Dylan perceived there was something bothering his Father. He didn't seem his jovial self. "Thanks for taking us Dad. I needed this. Midterms nearly killed me." He turned and stared down his seemingly ungrateful brother.

"Dido," Joey replied poker-faced. Then he turned to his brother and rolled his eyes at his pseudo endearments.

"How does this clearing look?"

"Park the damn car so we can catch our dinner tonight." John quipped.

One by one the small fishing expedition grabbed their tackle box and pole, minding the terrain, found their spot on the riverbank and cast their line. Frank and John had packed folding chairs for the occasion after years of complaining of hours of standing. Finding a level spot wasn't easy in the tall grass and weeds.

"Joey, what type of bait are you using?" Frank inquired.

"Jigger," he answered confidently.

"You'll have more luck with live bait," Frank responded. "Dylan! let Joey have some of your sardines."

"I'm fine Dad."

"I got plenty Joey," Dylan assured him.

Joey saw their empathy for the queer kid as an opportunity to make a game out of it. "I'll tell you what, if I catch the first fish everyone uses lures."

"Game on," Dylan conceded. "And if we catch first, you'll use live bait. Agreed?"

"Agreed."

Dylan spied his Father's eyes tear up a second time on the trip. Something ain't right, he thought to himself and debated whether to move his position closer. Whatever it was, Dad would tell him when the time was right.

"Damn thing took my bait!" John exclaimed from his position, thirty yards from the others. He stood holding his anchor up and sure enough his bait was half eaten.

"You know that doesn't count Uncle John," Joey cackled.

"Could have been a snag," Frank suggested from experience.

"No, I felt it on there," John replied assertively. "Dang it!"

"There's plenty more where that came from," Frank assured him. "Be patient."

"I guess that's why I'm not good at this," Joey interjected wavering. "I have no patience."

"All good things happen to those who have patience," Frank said cocksure.

"Tell that to the Rockefellers." Joey differed. "They didn't earn their millions sitting on their asses waiting for it to come to them."

"Touché," Dylan blurted with a supportive grin. Their Father shook his head browbeaten.

An hour of recasting and beer drinking passed before it took Joey's hook and bait. "I have something!" he exclaimed, struggling to keep the angry fish from pulling line from his reel. His pole bent as the fish fought to get unsnarled.

"Good God," Frank said elated. He stood up and hurried to his Son's spot on the bank. "Don't yank back too hard you'll bust your pole. That can't be a Striper. Give and take Joey."

"It's a fifty-pound line Dad," Joey stated.

"But that's gotta be a fifty pounder Son," Frank embellished, standing next to Joey who was taking arduous attempts to reel it in. John had already grabbed the net and made his way close to the water's edge. "I don't think that net is going to do us any good John."

"I told you there was a deep hole here. Must be forty feet."

Dylan patted his brother on the shoulder, "Good job Joey. Keep it steady."

"Holy cow!" exclaimed John who could make out the silhouette of the fish in the deep water. "You just hooked a Sturgeon. Must be four to five feet long."

"Come on don't lose it," Frank coached. "Dylan, there's a towel in my tackle box. Go get it and toss it to John."

John had the towel wrapped over his right hand and the net in his left. "She's a beauty." As the fish got closer to the surface he realized Frank was right and threw the net up bank.

Joey needed both hands to hold up his trophy fish for pictures. But it was a proud moment for him and for his Father. The photo later made it to the wall in the Bistro great room. His mother created a Bistro menu specialty item from Joey's catch, Vinegar-Poached Sturgeon with Thyme-Butter sauce. It was a limited time menu item and was a huge hit with the regulars. After two-weeks they had consumed the entire fish.

Frank opted to go out for dinner, claiming he was exhausted, but his excuse didn't fool John who picked up on his lugubrious demeanor. They drove to the Delta Marina Yacht Harbor and had dinner at the 'Point' restaurant. Frank's Father frequented the restaurant with his family since Jack and Richard Bauman built it in 1960. Its enclosed patio deck dining extended over the deep channel and gave clients a picturesque view of the Delta and the marina.

"How about the table in the corner?" Uncle John pointed out to the maître d', the only restaurant employee not in a sailor's uniform.

"I don't have a waiter working that section, but let's seat you there and see if Ted will take your table." The elderly slim built woman, in a formal professional suit, laid the four menus at each chair. "Someone will be by shortly to take your drink orders."

"You're too kind," Frank smiled taking his seat at the table. "Thanks for accommodating us. This is a special table for my brother and I."

"I know," she winked at him. "I recall waiting on you several times."

"This must have been a while ago. We come here a lot," John smiled at her.

"I've only been back to work two months. I quit eleven years ago. If you remember, I use to wear my hair in a bun."

"Yes!" Frank shook his finger at her. "I remember you now. You were my Father's favorite waitress," he fabricated the story to make her feel good.

"Now you're too kind," she blushed. "You folks have a nice dinner."

John ordered a large bowl of clam chowder soup, Joey the roasted salmon with quinoa salad, Frank seared Tuna and house salad, and Dylan had hamburger and fries. Frank and his brother shared a picture of beer and the boys ordered crème soda.

After much talk about the fishing expedition, Frank felt it was time to share the bad news with his immediate family. It was the perfect time with Lori not present. "I hope this is the right time to tell you boys some bad news concerning your mother."

"What's wrong with mom?" Joey assumed the worst.

"The doctor's found a cancerous lump in her right breast," he announced crestfallen. "We will have the results of a second biopsy hopefully by Thursday."

Their faces filled with pain and disbelief. "Oh my God!" John agonized. The boy's eyes filled with tears and one fell and wet Joey's cheek.

The few seconds of silence seemed like eternity for Frank. "She wanted to tell you herself, but I know your first reaction would be difficult for her. Regardless the results of the biopsy." He hesitated to regain his composure, "Your mom needs you to be strong. Promise me."

"Sorry Dad, I just need some air," Joey said trying to manage his emotions. "I'll be right back. I just need a moment to myself." His chair screeched on the linoleum tiled floor as he rose from the table and exited the side door to the outdoor deck.

Dylan couldn't take his eyes off Joey leaning into the deck railing and envisaged his pain. He started to get up from the table to comfort him, but Frank motioned with his hand for him to sit back down. "He asked to be alone. Let him work it out in his own way."

March 10, 1986
San Francisco – Saint Vincent Hospice

"I won't have it!" Dylan insisted after Jonathan asked his permission to date Joey.

Dylan was very protective of his brother, "I have Dr. Chang's word he will not allow him to become one of us."

"Damn shame," Jonathan chagrined. "You know I believe he has feelings for me as well."

"I said drop it!" Dylan barked at his best friend.

"We're leaving," Giuseppe poked his head into the library where Jonathan had asked Dylan to meet him in private.

"We're done here," Dylan affirmed and grabbed his armored trench coat from the back of the wooden peg chair.

Jonathan looked away, crestfallen and discouraged. But with or without Dylan's blessing, his heart was resilient. He was determined to let Joey know his feelings for him.

San Francisco's fog had settled in. The increscent lights from the Polk street shop windows, dimmed by the fog, intensified Joey's maudlin mood. The fog changed the City's usual electrifying nightlife into eerie trepidation. An occasional siren and shadows of figures appearing from side streets, fed his urgency for the safe comfort of his Church street apartment. He lived across town in the Castro District of San Francisco.

Joey brushed his flaxen curls from his eyes. Trembling with an evening chill, he fastened the top two buttons on his leather jacket. He pulled the brown and green plaid shawl up over his nose to filter some of the putrid stench from the mix of sewer and other urban smells. The hard-disco beat from PJ's gay bar across the street, thumped in Joey's ears.

Joey put the Hospice conundrum from his mind. He debated whether to contend with his anxious pangs of loneliness and give in to his libido, or to hasten his steps toward home and distance himself further from all the many afflictions of the loin. Confident that cruising for a good lay, somewhere in the club's human calisthenics of social coquetry, would not be a challenge. He instead took a raincheck.

His step hastened a little as his mind drifted back to earlier that night at the Hospice. He was starting to have feelings for one of his tenants, Jonathan, who was four years his senior.

Jonathan had shared with Joey that he had run away from home at age fifteen. His father beat him to an inch of his life after catching Jonathan with another young man behind the tool shed.

Jonathan's migration to the City of acceptance, San Francisco, found him homeless and left to barter sex for food. His baby face and chiseled stomach lured in many older men willing to dig into their pockets for a piece of him. But luck wasn't on Jonathan's side and he contracted HIV. He had so many sex partners he didn't know where to start to lay blame, or cared to.

Jonathan had explained to Joey that four months earlier, Dr. Chang found him cuddled up with a blanket under a tree at Golden Gate Park. His hours numbered. No longer attractive due to his sunken eyes and skeletal looking body, Jonathan had given up on seeking help and just wanted to die. "I have no idea why he took an interest in me. There were so many that had succumbed." One of many leisure drives through the park ended abruptly, "Stop the car!" Jonathan's life unexpectedly changed.

But Jonathan had stopped short of explaining to Joey what followed next. Although, it piqued Joey's curiosity nonetheless. What he hadn't explained to Joey was that he woke up in a motel room with Dr. Chang and several of his entourage standing over him. The color had returned to his cheeks. He oddly felt better.

Jonathan's heart was pounding with apprehension and fear, "What did you do to me?" he cried out.

"You are safe with us now. You are one of us," Dr. Chang tried to calm his rage.

"I want out of here now!" He snapped back. He reached with his right hand and touched the needle wounds on his left arm. His anger amplified, "I demand to know what you did to me."

"Let's just say we gave you a blood transfusion of a Type that will reverse your symptoms. "Welcome to the family." They had syphoned the blood of a victim intravenously.

"What did you do to him!" Jonathan demanded, discovering the bald half naked man, with a confederate flag tattooed on his shoulder, face down in the bed next to his. "Is he dead?" Jonathan still unnerved, demanded answers. He attempted to sit up but was met by two impressively strong young men who gently pushed his shoulders back until his head met his pillow. "Who are you freaks? You have no right to hold me against my will! You're all going to jail!" This wrought snickers from the two young men towering above him.

"All in good time." Dr. Chang replied wiping the sweat from his brow. Jonathan quickly brushed Dr. Chang's hand away. Dr. Chang stood above him, with a more serious tone, "You're not ready to understand what has happened to you. But, young man, we just saved your life. You will thank us later. Trust me."

March 10, 1986
Just after midnight

Shaking Jonathan from his mind, Joey arrived at the bus shelter on Van Ness Street, defaced by gang turf graffiti. Two homeless juveniles stared with envious contempt. They were obviously together by the way she leaned into him. His demeanor struck Joey as down-right evil. He was bald with tattoos covering both arms, but none sent a chill through Joey's body as much as did the Peckerwood logo on his right shoulder.

Her mouth resembled a pin cushion riddled with small silver rings. Her eyes deep, skeleton like from meth abuse. Joey had preferred that she had not smiled at him. That typically means they are going to ask him for money. The fog would likely blind any witness if they assaulted him. Joey became anxious. Deciding it was safer to walk to the next shelter and avoid an inevitable confrontation, he made haste. The female called out loud enough for him to hear, "Faggot!"

Debunking the situation, he reminded himself not to risk his safety for the sake of his ego. "Great!" he said under his breath, as he could see that the next bus shelter was in front of 'Mikes', one of many Gay bars in the District. At least he was in familiar territory and unlikely to be confronted by racists and homophobes. But that didn't stifle his fear that the gang bangers would emerge through the fog behind him.

As he got closer to Mikes Bar, his anxiety subsided. Joey took a sigh of relief. Under the mullion windows of Mike's, a male adolescent, too young to make it past the bouncer, and too poor to afford a roof over his head. He sat cross legged with his back against the old red brick building. He held his Giant's baseball cap toward Joey, "Anything will help Sir."

Joey stopped, took a second look at the boy. Most likely seventeen or eighteen. Very cute, he thought to himself. A little lanky and hallowed cheek, but very cute with a lot of potential. But espoused with self-pity for his own lonely plight, his mind began to wander into his usual desire for his Romeo. Lost in thoughts of saving him from poverty's inevitable life of illegal drugs and prostitution. His lover, his life companion, nights by the fire while he studied and Joey cooked his favorite meal.

"Are you OK sir?"

Blinking the rest of the erotic story from his infatuated mind he replied somewhat confused, "What? I'm sorry what did you say?"

"Are you alright," The juvenile said, lowering his cap. "You seem distant, like your mind just went to a different planet."

"I'm fine…I was just…never mind I'll be fine." Joey reached into his pocket and pulled out a wrinkled dollar and a few coins. "Here, it's all I got." He dropped it into the boy's cap which drew a short smile of appreciation from the lad.

"Thanks," he replied, lecherously checking Joey out. "Hey, would you like some company tonight?"

"I don't even know your name," Joey inquired as he noticed the bus lights appearing blurred in the fog. "Look, I got to catch this bus." Joey turned and quickened his step toward the bus stop.

"It's Tom," the boy shouted at him. "I'll be here tomorrow if you're interested."

Joey turned, second doubting his decision to not get involved. When he turned back, the bus had passed. "Damn, I needed that bus!" Joey kept on walking ignoring the kid and cursing at his insipid judgment. "Damn it." Turning his frustration on the boy, Joey faced him from a distance, "Do I look like I need to pay for it?"

He walking briskly. It was getting late. Joey needed to get to the Market Street bus shelter, at least five blocks away. It was the last bus stop closest to Van Ness Street.

"Perhaps Jonathan was right," he berated himself, "Maybe I am just a little desperate in need of companionship." But was he becoming that obvious?

A familiar black Sedan with tinted windows slowed down as it passed him. The heavy base rocked the vehicle and thumped in Joey's ears. The Sedan stopped at the curb mid-block. No one emerged. Joey began entertaining thoughts that he may not make it home for one reason or the other. He nearly convinced himself that a cab maybe the safest alternative at this point. Then the Sedan sped away.

Turning right on Market Street, Joey arrived at the trash inundated MUNI bus shelter. The eerie fog began to lift and he could make out a few stars in the night sky. The aluminum shelter bench sent a brief chill through his buttocks. He decided to stand instead. He checked the time on his watch, then reviewed the time tables on the side panel of the shelter. Thirteen minutes until the next bus.

Thumping heavy base from an approaching vehicle was getting louder again. "Come on, seriously?" Joey complained nervously. He realized it was the same black sedan. This time it passed him without slowing and turned at the next corner. His heart beat returned to normal.

He couldn't erase the encounter with the young man at Mike's Bar. "That little reprobate!" he cursed under his breath. "How will he survive when the glow of his youth wears off?" The realization that he was inadvertently reflecting on himself. He couldn't avoid the self-pity and it dragged him into a melancholy state of mind. Joey was turning thirty next May and still single. He could feel his blood pressure elevate. Had he become that Jaded? Had he still not come to terms with being single and aging?

From his peripheral he took note of a tall dark figure, draped in an ankle length trench coat approaching him. The man had appeared from behind the corner infrastructure. Joey grew anxious over the mysterious person's brisk steps. He could make out a male face and the whites of his eyes that seemed to be glued on him. The trench coat, similar to his brother's, fit like a cape and blew open in the slight breeze around his ankles. Joey's breathing quickened. Trepidation inundated his whole being.

"Jonathan?" Joey was relieved. "Are you on foot?" Jonathan had tied his long black hair into a pony tail that reached the small of his back.

"No," Jonathan replied anxious to see him. "I made Dr. Chang stop. I knew it was you." He grasped Joey by the shoulders as if admiring a painting.

"Who else is with you?"

"There's just a few of us from the Hospice. Do you need a ride?"

He wanted to say yes and put an end to a night gone bad. "No, no, the bus will be here shortly." There was something eccentric about Dr.

Chang that haunted Joey and the further he distanced himself from him the better. "It's late, why are you guys cavorting about?"

"Some of us were craving an after-hour snack," Jonathan smiled at his inadvertent pun. Joey was still feeling apprehensive as to whether he could trust him. "Any way the party was starting to wind down before we were."

Like finger nails on a blackboard, the black sedan's brake screeched to a stop at the corner alley. Joey recognized the long Italian face when the rear window was rolled down. "We don't have time for this! Get your butt in the car now!"

Jonathan shot a contemptuous glare at the Italian boy. "Look Joey I felt a connection between us and would like to see you again. Perhaps on your terms."

The corners of Joey's smile raised, exposing his dimpled cheeks, "I think I would like that."

"Come on!" The Italian insisted vehemently.

"OK! OK!" Jonathan yelled back, not taking his eyes off Joey's elation. Joey saw that there was a small streak of blood at the corner of Jonathan's chin. He pointed at his own chin to demonstrate where it was. "You're bleeding."

"Must have cut myself shaving." He replied as his long tongue swept downward like a lizard's tongue does when it takes Its prey. "Mother always told me to clean my plate. Look, I got to go. I want to kiss you so bad. I promise you, I will kiss you."

Joey nodded, still glowing, "As long as you promise."

"Promise."

The Italian boy became angry, "You damn fool, we need to get the hell out of here!"

Jonathan sprinted back to the sedan and climbed in next to the Italian boy, but didn't take his eyes off Joey as he slowly rolled the window back up. The sedan sped away toward Polk Street.

Joey glanced at his watch. Six minutes until the bus was scheduled to arrive.

As the sedan sped away he spied three people walking nimbly, in an effort to avoid missing the bus. A young man in a business suit and two female kitchen employees. All three likely worked the late shift, were routine riders turned acquaintances. A thick Hispanic woman in her forties, her hair net still holding back her coal black hair. She was trying to keep pace with her coworker, a younger woman in her twenties. Joey felt no threat from them but rather security in numbers.

As the trio passed the narrow alley, where minutes ago the black sedan had emerged, their attention suddenly was drawn by something horrific. They stopped, the younger female froze in her tracks, and let out a blood curdling scream. The male and elderly female raced toward whatever frightened her.

As the young man and older woman disappeared down the dark alleyway, Joey too decided to investigate. "Find a phone booth and call for help!" Joey heard the older female direct the businessman. The young man abruptly emerged behind the corner building, colliding with Joey. Joey grasped the young man's suit coat in an attempt to straighten himself from being knocked to the ground.

There was no apology, "Where's a phone booth?" the young man demanded.

"Just on the other side of the bus shelter," Joey recalled. He continued toward the pay phone without second thought. Joey cleared the corner building and looked down to where the Hispanic woman was crouched over two bodies. He immediately recognized them. A twist of fate. It was the couple that had made him feel threatened at the previous bus shelter. The male skinhead had bled out from an apparent animal bite like wound on his neck. Oddly, there was little blood pooled under him. The female was laying on top of him as if embracing him. The smell of city sewer and death turned Joey's stomach. It was all he could do to not vomit.

"I'm not sure, but I might have detected a pulse," the older woman said, as if she had some medical training. "Help me get her on her back."

Joey grasped the juvenile victim by the shoulder and hip and rolled her onto the pavement, pulling her from the skinhead's frozen grip. He gasped languidly at her porcelain face, seized in the agony of death's uninviting grasp. A cold shiver of horror chilled his spine when he realized that she too had a neck wound. The Hispanic woman leaned over her and removed the halter top exposing her small breasts. Lacing her fingers together, she locked her elbows and began to perform CPR.

Determined to save her life, she pushed deep and fast at the center of her chest.

"Do you know what you're doing," Joey asked. "I just heard what sounded like a rib crack!"

"Trust me, I've broke more than one," she said panting. "Right now, that's the least of her problems. Now shut up and watch me, because you may have to take over." Joey nodded affirmatively.

Joey had many questions concerning the coincidence and timing of the hospice tenants and the two victims. Perhaps the blood on Jonathan's chin wasn't Jonathan's at all. It would explain the Italian boy's need to flee. Joey was desperate to believe Jonathan had nothing to do with this, but he knew differently. He knew. Should he tell the police? "You didn't see anything," he assured himself.

Sirens were faint but getting closer. The young man in the suit waited at the corner to direct the ambulance driver to the scene. The police arrived just ahead of the ambulance and the San Francisco Fire Department. The once quiet street now lit up like a street disco. A small crowd formed at the corner of Market Street, some daring to get a closer look.

A black police officer, approximately 250 pounds of morning workouts, emerged from a police car and shouted back to his partner over the loud sirens of the arriving medical support vehicles. "We're going to need to clear for transport. This is one for C.S.I."

"I'm on it!" said his less intimidating middle-aged partner, still in the driver's seat. He grabbed the handset from the bracket on the console and held it to his mouth. "Car 35 dispatch."

"Dispatch, you're clear Car 35."

"We have two victims, one male, apparently in his twenties 10-54", which is radio code for 'possible dead body.' "One female, approximately between fifteen and twenty years old, receiving basic life support from bystander. No suspects at this time. By their wounds appears to be a 10-72," radio code for 'Knifing.'

"10-23, I show medical and back-up already there. Sending a forensics team."

Medical Technicians kneeled on both sides of the Hispanic woman, who was still pumping hard on the female victim's chest. "We've got it from here mam." She stood up. Perspiration dripping from every pore of her flesh. One technician glanced up at the good Samaritan, "You did good."

"Stand clear!", the second medical technician said holding the pads of the electronic defibrillator together to build a charge. He then shocked her heart hoping to start it. Still the heart rhythm machine remained flat-lined. He repeated shocking her a few more times.

"Stop," the first medical technician said, "She's gone. Time of death, one thirty a.m."

Car doors slammed shut. A plain clothes detective in a light tan and knee length rain coat brandished a badge toward the black police officer and noted the officer's name on his uniform. "What do we have here officer Woods?"

"Two stiffs, female, male, trauma to the neck."

"Stab wounds?"

Officer Woods hesitated, "I don't know detective, this one has me baffled." He pointed at the skinhead's neck. "Puncture wounds look like some kind of animal bite."

The detective leaned over for closer inspection, "My God."

"I told you," Officer Woods said shaking his head. "You seem shocked detective."

"Third type of murder in the last three months. Clean M. O. resembles that of a large animal bite without the evidence of a struggle, which is not typical of a mauling. Any witnesses?"

"None," Woods replied, "We're taking statements from four individuals that were waiting for Muni. They discovered the bodies."

"I need a copy," he demanded motioning for the medical technicians to cover the victims. "Put attention Detective Sam Stone. I need to know if they saw anything unusual."

"Will do."

Nuremberg, January 7, 1947
Palace of Justice
United States of America v. Doctor Karl Brandt
Nazi Human Experimentation
Conspiracy to commit war crimes and crimes against humanity

"Doctor Brandt," The Chief Prosecutor, James M. McHaney, walked toward the three judges of the military tribunal 1. His slender middle-aged face, furrowed by stress, was inflicted by the disgusting naked picture blown up one-hundred times It's original size. It's horrific illustration of a tortured woman, equally disgusted the jury of three. "Do you recognize the women in this picture?"

"No, I've never seen her before," the Nazi General Reich Commissioner for Health and Sanitation defiantly replied from the witness stand. His hair, usually greased to the right side, not as kept, his dimpled chin hidden in the wrinkles of sleepless nights.

"Really?" the prosecutor turned back to face the accused war criminal, sitting unshackled on the stand facing his Tribunal. He walked over to the easel and replaced the picture with that of the same victim prior to the medical experiment. Her leg no longer mutilated and infected. Her face, that of a beautiful young woman, absent the bruises of the first picture. "Does she look familiar now?"

Stoically, the doctor again answered, "I've never seen her before." His defense attorney, Robert Servatius, nodded, confirming he was on track with the pre-rehearsed strategy.

"Strange Doctor Brandt," the prosecutor's voice louder and somewhat angered by the doctor's resilience, "We've heard testimony from witnesses, who were guards in your employ, that this prisoner was brought to your bed on more than one occasion." The prosecutor's face wrinkled inward with contempt as he walked even closer to the accused. "Didn't you and other doctors in your charge working for Hitler, cut her leg open, inject streptococcus bacteria, tetanus, and gas gangrene? A horrific and gruesome crime in the name of science, to see if the drug sulfanilamide would cure wounds of Nazi soldiers. And these experiments were conducted without her permission?" McHaney's voice grew louder and didn't pause nor seemed to place a period at the end of

31

any sentence. A skillset common to prosecutors. There was a moment of silence for his diatribe to sink in. His anger settled, "I want you to say her name."

The Doctor's eyes quickly turned from being glued to the back wall of the courtroom to that of the prosecutor's. His breathing quickened.

"Jadwiga Dzido," the prosecutor slowly stated her name. "Say it!"

"I object," the Counsel for the defendant injected, void the usual passion due to his disdain for the accused. "Where's this going Jim?"

Doctor Brandt turned to face the judges in hopes they would intervene and relieve him of this odd demand.

"I'll allow it Mr. Servatius," the presiding Judge, Walter Beals, nonchalantly stated in an attempt to keep it formal. Beals was getting tired. "Just say the name so we can move on."

"I do not know this woman!" the Reich Commissioner of Health cried out.

The prosecutor stopped about four feet short of the table where the three judges sat. A grin formed from ear to ear, "I would like to call as my next witness Jadwiga Dzido."

Military police escorted her through a side door of the Palace of Justice courtroom. She was not the skeletal figure that Dr. Brandt had remembered tied shackled to the cement slab of his medical lab. The prosecution intentionally asked her to wear short pants to show the scars on her leg. The wounds, as described in the briefing, seemed inexplicably better than one with any medical schooling might imagine.

"You can be seated Dr. Brandt," Judge Beals directed. "Bailiff, Escort Mr. Brandt back to his seat. Ms. Dzido, I hope I pronounced your name correctly." Two military police officers grasped Dr. Brandt by his arms and walked him to the Defense's table.

"It's Polish, the d silent," Jadwiga said quietly.

Judge Beals smiled, pleased with his lucky guess. "Ms. Dzido, the bailiff will swear you in if you will please take the witness chair."

The officer faced the witness chair and held his right hand in the air for her to duplicate. "Under order of this Tribunal and the God which it serves, do you swear before both to tell the whole truth and acknowledge that you have not been coerced by this Court?

"I do, but I do not believe in God," Ms. Dzido pledged. "But I can assure you I only tell truth. My English not good though."

The three judges cackled at her comment. "Your English is just fine Ms. Dzido. But I can provide you with an interpreter if it pleases you," Judge Beals assured her.

"No, I good."

"Your witness Mr. McHaney," Judge Beals stated shuffling through documents on his desk in front of him and distributing copies to the other two judges at the table.

The prosecutor approached the witness stand and smiled at Ms. Dzido, "Thank you for appearing this morning Ms. Dzido, this took a lot of courage."

The witness glanced over at the accused. Anger and contempt for him spewed from her eyes. "I have been waiting for this day."

"Ms. Dzido at any time you need to take a break, just let us know. Are you OK to continue?"

"Yes."

Mr. McHaney glanced down at his notes, "You are studying medicine, is that correct Ms. Dzido."

"Yes, I am student at University of Warsaw," she answered glancing back and forth between Hitler's personal doctor and Mr. McHaney.

"On March 28, 1941, you were arrested by the Gestapo and sent to the Lublin Castle where you were tortured in an effort to derive the names of other members of the Union of Armed Struggle Resistance, or ASR. Is that correct?"

"Yes, I was beaten, but I did not talk. I was tied to post. They raped me many times, this Gestapo. I was," she paused to search for the right English word, "What you say... numb?"

"I am so sorry for what those bastards did to you," the prosecutor apologized and shot a contemptuous glare toward Dr. Brandt. Dr. Brandt looked away, unnerved by his comment. On September 21st, of that same year you were transferred from Ravensbruck to Auschwitz. Is that correct?"

"Yes."

"Where you were subject to the medical experimentation earlier mentioned. Is that correct?"

"Objection," the attorney for Mr. Brandt interjected. "Leading the witness."

Judge Beals looked up from his notes to Ms. Dzido, "I'll allow you to answer the question Ms. Dzido. Jim, let Ms. Dzido tell her own story."

"Yes," she replied, her voice cracking and tears flooded her cheeks.

"Are you OK to continue Ms. Dzido?" The prosecutor pulled his hanky out of his suit pocket and handed it to her.

"Fine, fine, I want to tell my story, please."

"Is it true that while you were a hostage at Auschwitz…"

"Objection!" Mr. Brandt's attorney interrupted. "Calling Ms. Dzido a hostage is misleading. She was a prisoner and these were war times."

"Fine," Mr. McHaney replied annoyed, "While you were a prisoner at Auschwitz, did Mr. Brandt, along with other Nazi physicians, inflict wounds on your body and then infect those wounds with bacteria such as streptococcus, tetanus, and gas gangrene?"

"Yes," answered Ms. Dzido.

"Then to simulate battle wounds did Doctor Brandt's Team rub ground glass and wood shavings into your lacerations?"

"Yes."

Mr. McHaney then turned to the accused, "And to further their egregious experiments, did they apply tourniquets at each end of the wound?"

"Yes."

Mr. McHaney stared derisively, shaking his head, at Dr. Brandt. "Your suffering unimaginable. Dr. Brandt and his co-defendants left you for dead. Believed that the experiment failed and you were cremated along with other victims. What kind of monster would violate another human being in such a barbaric, evil, and inhumane manner? Even in war times? Ms. Dzido, is such a monster in this courtroom?"

"Yes," she said firmly pointing at Dr. Brandt. "But I escaped. I was one of the lucky ones."

"Just to clarify for this tribunal Ms. Dzido, you were a victim of an experiment to test the effectiveness of the drug sulfanilamide in curbing progressive gas gangrene of wounded Nazi soldiers. By testifying today, you have done humanity a great service, Ms. Dzido. You represent the tears of the victims that didn't survive this horrific, inhumane ordeal. Your witness Mr. Servatius." He walked back to the prosecution's bench and sat down.

"Cross examine Mr. Servatius?" Judge Beals asked as a matter of procedure.

"Yes." Mr. Robert Servatius, attorney for the defendant stood at his table. "Did Dr. Brandt, or any of the physicians working with Dr. Brandt attempt to keep you alive?"

Ms. Dzido glanced down searching for the right response. "Yes."

"Can you repeat your answer a little louder so this tribunal will know for certain what your answer is. Ms. Dzido?" The defense attorney's point was unexpected and contrived to create doubt in the minds of the Tribunal.

"Yes." A tear formed at the corner of her eye and wet her cheek. "At first they think I was dead."

The Defense attorney abruptly interrupted her. "Ms. Dzido, I didn't ask you to elaborate, just answer my question."

"Mr. Servatius" Judge Beal interjected. "I'm going to break precedent here. I want to hear what Ms. Dzido has to say. Go ahead Ms. Dzido finish your testimony."

"The fascists beat me, raped me, tortured me, and subjected me to much pain. But I only speak today, not because of this monster!" Jadwiga pointed at Dr. Brant with contempt. "How dare you suggest that. I am alive thanks to only one man. He was my guardian angel. He saved me from the gas and furnaces. It was more than just medicine that saved me. But he was as much a prisoner. He helped many. He ordered the guards to take me to my bunk. Yes, he wore a Nazi medical scrub, but he was not a Nazi in his mind. His gentle voice was my hope. I study medicine and familiar with many drugs. This had to be magic. He explain to me, "This formula will work with sulfanilamide already in my body. It will alter my DNA and metabolize amino acids naturally." I thought, how could this be? Our bodies don't produce amino and folic acids. But I'm here, stronger than ever, my wounds healed very fast. He gave me strength to escape."

Her science made no sense to Mr. Servatius, or anyone else for that matter, except Doctor Brandt. "You stated that this Nazi doctor saved your life. A reasonable person might also argue, since this other doctor worked under Doctor Brandt's auspices, that Doctor Brandt had a pivotal role in saving your life. Can you please describe this other doctor?"

"Blood, Paba free blood." The words accidently slipped unsuppressed from Doctor Brandt's lips. His defense attorney turned toward him momentarily with reproach and shook his head slightly for him to keep quiet.

Prosecutor McHaney was not pleased with Mr. Servatius's line of questioning, and shot him a disdainful glare.

She had promised to protect Doctor Chang and not lead terrorist fascist cells to his whereabouts. "Small Chinaman, they say he was killed during the escape."

Dr. Brandt's demeanor was less cynical and the seemingly impossible exoneration had a taken a turn in his favor.

March 11, 1986
Castro Street Hardware
Store, S.F. CA

The Chronicle Headline, "Serial Killer Strikes Again", enticed Joey
to pick up a copy from the news stand in front the hardware store.
Mondays were usually slow at the store where Joey Sanders worked.
When Saint Vincent starting running in the red, he needed gainful
employment. Joey applied for the job as he planned to enroll at the
University of San Francisco. But the deeper in debt the Hospice put
him, finishing his degree seemed less likely to come to fruition.

He began to read the article, *"Detective Sam Stone told the Chronicle
that the killings matched that of the recent Warf Killings. Stone told this
reporter that all the victims had puncture wounds from an apparent animal
bite. Stone added that there was little or no blood from the wound as you
would typically find at a crime scene. Yesterday's victims have been identified
as nineteen-year-old Shane Laskowski and seventeen-year-old Veronica
Payne. Laskowski had several Arian Nation and Swastika tattoos, and was
a member of the Peckerwood Gang. Stone stated, "It is unknown whether or
not hatred towards fascist gangs is a motive in the killings. Stone stated to
the Chronicle that there were striking similarities between the two murders."*

"Hey pretty boy," Fredric, the tall feminine store manager beckoned,
routinely snapping his fingers high in the air. "I don't pay you to sit
around and read the paper." Joey, deep in thought, ignored him. Joey
and Fredric were good friends and Joey's favorite bar hopping buddy.
Fredric Garcia was six feet four inches tall, a twenty-four hour drag
queen, and went by the drag name, Queen La Fredericka. Freddy, to
her close friends, could turn any dull boring evening into a party. The
Queen could see something was seriously bothering Joey. He wasn't his
usual cute self. "Earth to Joey," he expressed some concern.

Joey starred at Freddy with a distant scowl, "I'm totally confused Freddy." He gave Freddy, the paper to read. "I was one of the four bystanders. I was there."

"You saw the murders?" Freddy exclaimed, shocked by the news. "You must be traumatized honey!"

"No one saw the murders. My stomach has been in knots all morning," he replied seemingly rattled. "My head is spinning from all the drama and crap going on in my life!" He looked to the ceiling and shook his head, frustrated with his situation. "The Hospice is going under. New tenants not paying their rent on time. Utility rates going up. I'll never get my degree, and now this! This guy, Detective Stone, wants to talk to me when I get off work tonight."

"Wait a minute Mr. lives in a bubble," Freddy scolded waiving his finger in front of Joey's face. "Why haven't you come to Queen La Fredericka earlier?"

"I don't know Freddy," Joey looked down disappointed in himself. "Pride I guess. Dad never believed in me. After mom died, my Father just gave up. His drinking got really bad. One night he came home from the bar and punched the wall. I ran in to see what had happened. He glared at me with contempt. What he said next cut me deep Freddy."

"I'm sorry Joey," his frivolous attitude drained from his demeanor.

"After what seemed like an eternity, he said, "You're a loser." He then broke out in an evil laugh, "My Homo Sons. You'll never amount to anything. I thought I had two Sons. Turns out I have two daughters with dicks!" He collapsed on the couch and dropped his bottle. I usually helped him to his bed. Not that night, I ran away to the Castro. He died shortly after of an alcohol poisoning induced heart attack. There's more I haven't told you Freddy."

"Hey, you know your secrets are safe with me."

"At least for twenty-four hours," Joey failed at lightening the moment with humor. Freddy managed a smile. "I think there's a connection with the murders and some of my tenants."

"You have to tell the detective tonight," Freddy demanded. "If you withhold information you could go to jail!"

Joey paused, "It's complicated."

"No, it ain't," Freddy mercilessly interrupted, "Complicated is off the table. No, you have to inform the police of what you know!"

"That's just it, I don't know for sure."

"No, no, no, no," Freddy persisted, shaking his finger at him. "Just tell them what you know. What do you know?"

"I think I'm in love with one of them," Joey said under his breath. Freddy rolled his eyes. "Don't think I'm crazy, but I have to ask."

"You better not be playin me," Freddy shot Joey a brazen stare.

"There's no such thing as vampires, right?"

The door activated bell sounded as a customer walked into the hardware store. "This conversation ain't over, and no there isn't, and no I don't." Freddy walked from behind the counter to greet his customer. "Hi can I help you?" He then shot a piqued glare back at Joey. "Ain't over," he mouthed the words.

Castro Street
Joey Sander's Apartment
shortly after 6 p.m.

The doorbell rang. Joey stopped playing with the letters in his Campbell's Alphabet soup. He swallowed hard, scared of the questions Detective Stone might ask. He looked down at his watch. It was a few minutes before seven. The doorbell rang again. There wasn't a lot of room in his small Castro Street studio. His Johnson's Hardware store uniform lay wrinkled on his unmade bed where he had tossed it. The kitchen sink was full of dirty dishes. The heavy base thumping, from the studio next to his, was faint but the vibrations could be felt under their feet. Your typical bachelor's pad.

"I wish my friends were as punctual as the San Francisco Police Department," Joey said inviting the detective in. "Please come in. We can sit at the table."

Detective Sam Stone took in a panoramic view of Joey's cluttered studio apartment. "Sorry if I interrupted your dinner," Stone apologized.

"No, that's OK, I wasn't very hungry. Sorry about the mess. It's a small apartment."

"You need a wife to clean it for you," Detective Stone humored. Joey didn't laugh at his insensitive remark. He caught the rainbow flag hanging above Joey's bed out of the corner of his eye and realized at that moment he may have offended him. "Sorry, I have nothing against homosexuals."

Joey shrugged his shoulders, "My Mother use to say that a lot." Detective Stone smiled his approval. "I'm not getting any younger Detective. There have been many lonely nights. Sometimes I wish I did have a wife."

"Or a husband," Stone replied, doing his best to seem tolerant and accepting.

"I can tell you're one of the good cops," Joey said. His anxiety draining from his face. "What can I help you with Detective?"

"I like to start by getting to know the person I'm interviewing. Would you mind telling me just a brief synopsis of who Joey Sanders is?"

"Where do I start," Joey sighed pinching his forehead between his thumb and forefinger. "I was born twenty-nine years ago. I have a brother a year younger. We inherited my Father's business, a little restaurant on Polk Street and turned it into a Hospice. My brother Dylan, when he's sober, manages it, and I keep the books."

"Garden Bistro?" Stone interjected enthusiastically.

"Yes."

"No way, I loved that place. Me and my Frat Bros use to go there a lot for Sunday Brunch. Best food in town. Frank and Lori were your parents?"

"You knew them?"

"Hell yea," Stone exclaimed slightly slapping the table. "Use to bump into Frank at the shooting range. Shame about your brother, he could've been an NFL hall of famer. The day I turned twenty-one, your Dad bought a round at the bar. I never paid for a drink all night long."

"That explains why they nearly went bankrupt," Joey replied. They both cackled at his humor.

"They were the greatest. Your Ma took one of her famous cheesecakes out of the cooler and made me blow out a candle she stole from the piano in the great room. Your parents were the best. We laughed all night. I'm sorry go on."

"No no, it's not a problem. I like when people remember them. People have so many stories about them. Sometimes I feel like I hardly knew them. So where were we. Oh yea, so we re-opened the restaurant as a hospice. It was a small hotel as well so it was an easy transition. My brother contracted AIDS and is a live-in manager. I work at Johnson's Hardware store on the Castro. But I'm saving to finish my degree as a Rad Tech and then get a Masters in Hospital Administration."

"Wow, you're ambitious," Stone nodded. "I wish you well. "So, I read your statement you gave, and have just a few questions."

"OK,"

Stone continued, "I believe it's very strange that no one heard Mr. Laskowski or Ms. Payne struggle or cry out for help. Yet you heard a scream from one of the witnesses. Odd, don't you think?"

Joey's anxiety returned. He nodded affirmatively. "I was waiting at the bus shelter when the other three noticed the bodies. It must have happened right before I got there."

"See that's where I have to play detective, because you stated that you had been waiting there at least five to ten minutes, and you didn't hear anything. However, Ms. Payne was still warm when you and Ms. Silva performed CPR. Did you see anyone else other than the other three witnesses?"

"There were a few people walking the sidewalk on Market Street doing their business, but I was the only one at the bus shelter."

"Did you speak with any of them?"

"No," Joey choked down a sudden chill. He had made his mind up that he was going to keep the encounter with the black sedan to himself. "I had missed the last bus on Van Ness and had to walk to Market. Typical late-night traffic for Market Street."

"In your statement, you also stated that you had an earlier encounter on Polk Street with the victims at a bus shelter. Can you confirm what you said in your report?"

"Originally my plan was to catch the bus at the Shelter at Turk and Van Ness, it's the closest shelter to Eddy and Polk where the Hospice is located. That's where I first saw them."

"Them, meaning the victims, correct?

"Yes," Joey replied, his nerves clouding his mind. "They weren't cordial toward me. Staring at me like I was a piece of dog shit stinking up their space. I felt uncomfortable and a little threatened. I had decided to wait at the shelter in front of Mike's Bar. I hadn't got 10 feet from the shelter when the female called me a fag."

"Made you very angry, didn't it?" Stone injected.

"Not really," Joey could see through Stone's line of questioning. "I've learned to cope and avoid confrontation."

"Did they follow you?"

"No."

Stone resumed, "See, I can't figure out how they got from Turk Street to Market and Rose Street. They had to have followed you."

"Maybe they did," Joey tried to blow a hole in his theory. "Maybe they walked down Franklin. It is a more direct route to Rose and Market."

Stone's, I gotcha grin stretched from ear to ear. "Why didn't they just catch the bus at Turk. Unless they wanted to pick a fight with you?"

"No, trust me, I kept an eye on them. They were still waiting there when I got to Mike's Bar."

"Well, one fact we do know is they never got on the bus," Stone said nodding in agreement.

"They're homeless officer. Most likely they were shelter hopping to avoid confrontation with you guys."

"It's possible," Stone conceded. "You ever had an encounter with skin heads?"

"Who hasn't?" Joey had to change his game plan and play devil's advocate.

"I don't believe I ever have," Stone countered.

"You're not in a minority either," Joey glared at him with a stone face.

"Good point," he said looking down and raising his brow in checkmate. "Look Joey, here's my card. If you recall anything that might help me with my investigation, call me."

"I will." Joey took his card and put it in his shirt pocket. "I hope you find your guy detective."

"Oh, I will," Stone said assuredly. "It may take a while, but I have a reputation for not leaving cases cold." They both got up from the table together and walked to the door.

"Sorry I couldn't have been of more help," Joey said opening the door for him.

"No, you've been very helpful," Stone said with a satisfied tone as if he had solved the case already.

"Goodbye detective."

"For now," the smile hadn't left Stone's face. Joey closed the door after him.

August 10, 1973
Los Altos Gun Range

"Five dollars for 100 rounds Frank," The young and attractive Los Altos Gun clerk declared, pointing to the menu on the wall behind her. Frank Sanders was a regular, and learning the client's names was the Los Altos Gun Range customer service policy. "But we're running this special through the weekend, bring a friend and the second 100 rounds is on the house."

Samuel Stone laid a one-hundred-dollar bill on the counter, "Frank's my friend."

"I thought you were doing your shooting at the police academy Sam," she said retrieving two boxes of one hundred rounds from under the counter and placing one box in front of the men.

"Not any more, I graduated," Sam announced with a huge smile of satisfaction.

"Thanks," Frank recognized the young, stalky, square chin, Turkish born man. "Sam, right?" Sam had frequented the Bistro with several other young college age men from Stanford University.

"Yes, no worries, my pleasure. Perhaps you can buy a round of drinks for my friends after Stanford kicks USC's butt this Saturday."

"Gladly," Frank said.

"Sam," she studied his gun case, "You're shooting a Raptor ll right?"

"I am."

"Just making sure I gave you the right amo." She was short and had to hold on the counter to climb back up on the high stool. "You men are in in seven and eight today. Good shooting. There are replacement targets on the table at the entrance. Just help yourself to as many as you think you'll need."

"Thanks Marcy," Sam nodded. "You want seven Frank?"

"It doesn't matter, suit yourself."

They grabbed a hand full of paper targets and headed to the back exit leading to the outdoor range.

"Is that a Smith a Wesson 340?" Sam asked, surprised that Frank would bring an older gun to the range.

"Belonged to my Dad," Frank held it up for Sam to inspect. "Feel how light it is."

Sam held the gun and pointed it at the target. "Five rounds?"

"Yep," thirty-eight Special." Frank attached the paper target to the line and released the weight which sent it flying to its base. "I usually shoot my Glock G22. My Dad's been gone a few years now. We use to come here a lot. Yesterday was his birthday and I have this silly ritual, you know," Frank paused to hide his emotions.

"No, I get it." Sam handed the gun back to Frank.

"How do you like your Raptor?"

"To be honest, I haven't shot it in over a year. I have thirteen handguns. My favorite is a SIG P220 Combat. Marcy assured me this morning on the phone she could accommodate me."

"She's a sweet girl," Frank raised his brow affectionately. "I'm trying to convince my oldest Son to go out with her."

Sam hooked his paper target to the wire and sent it to the target. "You're youngest Son made it in the Sports section a couple weeks back. Golden Arm, the editor called him. You must be proud? O'le Miss, Nebraska, those are good schools to play collegiate football."

Frank couldn't help but smile proudly. "I was hoping Dylan might play for Stanford so I could go to all his games. The football team has begun their two-a-day practices. If he can top the great year he had his Junior year, the kid can pick any college in the Nation."

"Even if it's par, one thing for sure, I see a scholarship in his future."

"Yea, then there's that," Frank didn't seem too excited. "His first game is two weeks from this Friday. Bring a date and join Lori and I."

Sam noted that something was causing Frank consternation and there was no way it could be the fact that his Son was on his way to a great future. "I'd like that. OK, I'm loaded."

"Go ahead." Frank watched as Sam unloaded his first ten rounds. The black bullseye no longer existed. "God damn!" Frank was awestruck. "They teach you how to shoot like that at the Academy?"

Sam grinned humbly, "No, the range I learned on was my Father's Montana Ranch. My O'le man was quite the marksman. Got a lot of County ribbons hanging at the Ranch house."

"Wow, I'd hate to be in a gun fight with you," Frank made light.

Sam retrieved the paper target and pointed to one shot half an inch outside the bullseye and showed Frank. "See, I still need some practice."

Frank shook his head in disbelief, "Whatever."

"Frank?" Sam's sincerity put Frank on edge. "Are you OK? You seem like something is sinking your ship."

"I really shouldn't be here but Lori insisted."

Sam's eyes dropped their focus off Frank and looked to the ground soberly, "Look Frank you don't have to tell me if you don't want."

"No, I trust you kid." Frank stared off somewhere else. "Lori started losing her hair today from the Chemo treatments."

"Jeeze Frank," Sam's face cringed inward with pity. "I didn't know she had cancer. God I'm sorry."

"Thank you," Frank said trying to remain stoic. "Can you keep this between us?"

"Sure, it's safe with me."

Frank loaded his gun. "She told me that it was important for her that everything continue normally. Normally!" Frank guffawed sarcastically aiming at the target to Sam's relief. He fired five rounds hitting the bullseye and leaving a black ring around his mark. "She asked me to pretend the target was her cancer."

Sam's eyes widened as he stared flabbergasted at Frank's accuracy. "Holy shit Frank! I'm most certainly not putting my money on cancer!"

September 7, 1973
First Game

Judge Lowell Howell High Minutemen 20, Galileo High Lions 24. With forty-seconds remaining on the scoreboard clock, the Minutemen had the ball on the Lions 48 yard line. Time out Minutemen.

Dylan ran to the sidelines looking for head Coach, Bill Rathers, a local Stanford football legend. A Radiologist at night, Rathers agreed to take the head coach job after months of courting by the Howell High booster club.

Dylan's sweat soaked hair crimped behind his ears as he removed his helmet. He brushed away the few strands of hair that blocked his vision. "Quarter back draw coach," Dylan plead his case. "They're going to blitz and our line is manhandling the nose guard."

Rathers stroked his chin, not liking the risk. "A field goal is not going to win the game for us Dylan. We have three, maybe four plays before the whistle." Demurred, Rathers shook his head, reluctant to take the risk. He deliberated only a few seconds more, then acquiesced. "This one's on you Son. I trust you."

Dylan smiled, "Thanks coach. It'll work."

"I can't watch!" Lori exclaimed covering her eyes.

"Come on Son," Frank silently coached from the home-team grandstand. Lori adjusted the blanket between her and the cold aluminum bleachers.

"They've gotta hit sideline passes Frank to stop the clock," Sam insisted. His shooting buddy had made good on Frank's invitation, but came solo. "You got this Dylan," Sam cheered loudly.

Dylan joined the huddle. The young men leaned in closer for the play call. "Quarterback Draw. Francis, Johnson, I need you to split your guys out of the way. Look for them to blitz."

47

Francis, the team center, turned up the passion and let out a short growl.

"On three. Let's draw them offsides. Don't jump early." All eleven testosterone overdosed jocks, clapped in unison and ran to the scrimmage line. The referee blew his whistle and motioned for play to resume.

Receivers split wide, tailback and flanker also went wide, keeping a few feet in the backfield. "They're going long," shouted the Lion's team captain and middle line-backer. He pointed for the corner-backs to protect the deep zone.

"Ready!" Dylan bellowed loud to be heard over the cheering crowd.

"Show us what you got hot shot!" The defiant Lion captain attempted to throw Dylan off his game.

"Set!" The defensive outside line-backers shifted up to the line of scrimmage.

"They're blitzing," Frank hollered loud enough to be heard above the frantic cheers.

"Hut!" Dylan was pleased that his intuition called the blitz. "Hut!" The Lions held position. "Hut!" Dylan took the snap from the Center and dropped back into the pocket as if to throw the inevitable pass. All four receivers sprinted toward the end-zone to no avail. Fancis and Johnson moved their assigned defensive linemen outside the pocket, opening a gaping hole. Dylan tucked the ball under his arm. The blitz wasn't without consequences. The left outside line-backer grabbed Dylan's jersey and shoulder pad, jerking him off balance. Dylan spun, regaining his balance and sight of the end zone and the win.

The Lion's had been duped. Dylan had an open field. Coach Rather had mentioned that there would be college scouts. This could be the most important play of the game to show case his skills. The importance of it stoked his passion.

Fingers, reaching around the Minutemen linemen, would come up short as he brushed past them and the line of scrimmage. The clock was winding down, thirty-one seconds.

He came out of Dylan's blind-spot, diving for his ankles. Dylan hurdled the middle line-backer, who slid empty handed on his stomach below him.

"Did you see that!" Sam exclaimed.

"That's my boy!" Frank replied gleaming from cheek to cheek.

Grass flew from under his metal cleats as Dylan re-established his footing and sprint toward the end zone. The Minutemen crowd were on their feet screaming and cheering. The Lion fans sat confused and confounded across from them.

Minutemen receivers had changed course and tried to get between Dylan and their defender in an attempt to block or slow them down. Chuck Martinez, the short, thighs wider than his mid-section, tailback, managed to go to the ground with his defender. But it wasn't as easy for the skinny and tall wide receiver, Marty Snider. The Lions safety, with little or no effort, pushed past Snider, and on a calculated course, hoped to intercept Dylan before he crossed the end-zone line. But the safety's speed was no match to Dylan's athleticism, and Dylan carried the ball and the Lion, still wrapped around him, into the end zone for the win. With only seconds remaining, the Minutemen Crowd erupted into cheers of elation as the scoreboard changed. Minutemen 26, Lions 24.

Dylan's teammates surrounded him in the end zone, engaged in butt slapping and congratulatory hugs. Dylan hid from everyone that he enjoyed the ritual more than winning.

Frank was glowing with pride. That pleased Lori more than the score. "Yes! Yes! Yes!

"What an ending," Sam congratulated his friend.

"It's not over yet, there's still twelve seconds," Frank attempted to check his enthusiasm.

"Isn't that the guy from Stanford we met during the Coach's tour of the athletic department?" Lori asked, noticing that he had spotted them and was trying to get their attention.

Frank made eye contact and smiled back with his thumb in the air.

September 28, 1973
Expelled from School

The Sanders family had three phones on a business account with Pacific Telephone and Telegraph Company. One upstairs in the Great room, one on the bar next to the register, and one in the Master bedroom. Only the phone in the bedroom was not a wall mount. The phones rang constantly, usually guests wanting to make reservations or a Vendor demanding payment. But, as unnerving and relentless as the ringing can be, it was bad for business to let them ring more than three times.

It was already the seventh ring when Lori Sanders picked up the receiver in the bar. "Garden Bistro open for lunch and dinner, can I help you?"

"Mrs. Sanders?"

"Yes?"

"I'm the secretary for your Son's school. Your Son is in the Principal's office. You need to come pick him up. He is being expelled."

"Is he alright? What's he being called in the office for?"

"We assure you that the School is not pressing charges, but he was caught having sex with another boy." Lori lost her breath. The news felt like a punch in the gut. Her heart was pounding in her chest as she tried to wrap her head around the possible scenarios. "Mrs. Sanders are you still there?"

"Yes, I'll be right there." She took a deep breath. "Goodbye."

"See you soon, goodbye."

She leaned back against the wall to make sense of it and make plans for her relief in the Kitchen. The Garden Bistro didn't take a break for personal reasons. Someone had to manage the grille. "Danny!"

Danny was working the Expeditor's position. He hurried into the adjacent bar. "Is everything OK? You look like you just saw a ghost."

"Everything is not OK," Lori regained her strength and composure. "I'm sorry to have to do this to you Danny, can you work the grille and expedite? I have to get Joey from school."

"Lori, you should know me better," Danny assured her. "It shouldn't take you long. I'll inform Frank."

Lori thought it odd he wasn't watching the bar. "Where is Frank?"

"He's fixing one of the tables, a guest was complaining it wasn't level."

"Oh, that's right," she replied somewhat perplexed. "I recall now. Jacqueline asked him earlier to fix it."

"Are you sure you're OK to drive Lori?"

"Oh yea, things just got a little blurred for a moment."

Danny shot her a concerned brotherly stare. "I can tend bar, if you'd rather have Mr. Sanders go to the school."

Forgetting her audience, the thought of Frank handling the situation frightened her more than the actual incident. "No, no, I have this Danny, thank you though."

"You better go Lori. Don't worry about the Bistro it's slow today."

"Thanks Danny." Lori was about to the door when she realized she wasn't going anywhere. "Keys!"

Danny was genuinely worried as he observed her not her usual swift and keen self. "You probably want to wear your beanie there's a slight cold breeze in the air." Lori's hair had completely fallen out from the chemo treatments and she refused to wear a wig.

Lori darted up the stairs, missing one step, stumbled and regained her balance. Danny chagrinned.

"Danny, table seven, hold the cheese," Jacqueline called from the doorway. "Where's Lori?" With the same haste as she climbed she descended, holding both the keys and her blue beanie in her left hand and the right on the bannister. "Oh," Jacqueline remarked.

"I'm covering Lori, most likely for the next hour or so," Danny shook his head knowing that Lori's ability to keep working would soon come to an end.

"Do you think Frank will sell the Bistro?" Jacqueline inquired, also assuming the inevitable.

"Let's just get through today," his brow wrinkled inward with apprehension.

51

Judge Lowell Howell High School

Lori had signed in at the front desk with the student volunteer, a freckled petite girl, more interested in finishing her homework. Smacking her gum, the juvenile occasionally smiled at Lori, who was sitting impatiently. Lori stared with contempt at her lack of civility and good manners.

"Can you please let Principal Scott know that Mrs. Sanders is here."

"His door is closed and unless you have an appointment, I'm not to bother him. Those the rules mam. Long as his door's closed." She delivered the rehearsed message to Lori without looking up at her or acknowledging her anxiety.

"He is expecting me," Lori stated, struggled to remain kind to the annoying child.

"Sorry," she replied nonchalantly.

"This is ridiculous!" Lori stood and walked vehemently to the counter. "Look, you silver spoon fed brat, get Principal Scott!" Lori's impetuous demand wrought sudden fear in the student and she pushed away from the counter in her wheeled chair. "Now!"

The unexpected commotion turned the heads of other staff members working at their desks and could be heard down the halls and behind Principal's Scott's closed door. A round face middle aged man, in a white starched shirt and tie, emerged from the office with the plaque on the door that read, Principal. Initially his face was that of an angry administrator. But soon lightened as he recognized Lori. "Mrs. Sanders!" He recognized her from Dylan's football games. "Jill, don't keep Mrs. Sanders waiting let her in. I'm sorry Mrs. Sanders." The chastened student unlocked the counter door. "Please come into my office."

Lori began apologizing to Principal Scott for her Son's behavior. "I'm really sorry for all the trouble Joey has caused you Principal Scott."

Principal Scott's facial expression wrinkled inward, confused. "Joey?"

She leaned in toward Principal Scott just before they reached his office door and whispered, "The secretary said my Son was caught in a sexual act with another male student."

"I'm sorry Mrs. Sanders if we misled you," He apologized and opened his office door. Dylan sat at a conference table in the corner of his office. Elbows on the table and his hands covering his face in shame. He couldn't look at his mother.

"Dylan?" her mouth dropped to the floor. "What? I don't understand."

"Mrs. Sanders, Judge Lowell Howell High School has a very open diversity policy. A child's sexuality is not an issue here. But lude sexual acts committed on school property is grounds for expulsion regardless of the sex of the child.

"Dylan?" Lori, still shocked at this revelation, plead with her Son.

Dylan rubbed his forehead with his forefingers, "It was stupid Ma. I'm so sorry."

"I thought it was Joey," she stuttered still in shock. "How long?"

"Would you like a private moment with your Son?" Principal Scott graciously offered.

Lori nodded.

"I'll just be outside my door," Principal Scott smiled at Lori with pity in his eyes and then shot a contemptuous stare at Dylan for recklessly hurting his mother who was obviously battling another major problem.

Lori took a chair at the other end of the small conference table. "I have two gay Sons?"

"My life is messed up," Dylan muttered unable to look at his Mother. His cheeks tear stained. His demeanor emulated his Father's tough guy façade. "There's not a college in America that will recruit a gay football player. I can kiss my chances for a scholarship goodbye."

"I don't care Son if you're gay," his Mother attempted to console him. "But where was your brain when this all happened? You couldn't control your libido until you were off campus? Who is this other student?"

Dylan hesitated, knowing it would further complicate things, "Mary's brother."

Lori made a face like she had just eaten moldy cheese. "Cory? Oh my God. Poor Mary. This will devastate her. How long have you and Mary's brother been a thing? Isn't he a Freshman?"

"Sophomore, and only one other time when Mary and her Mother went shopping together." He paused for his Mother to take it all in. "Does Dad know?"

"He will sooner than not."

Crestfallen, Dylan's head fell into his sweaty palms. He couldn't hold back his hopeless disposition any longer and wept profusely. "I'm so sorry Ma, I'm so, so, sorry." He raised his head and begged her forgiveness. "You don't deserve this, the cancer," he paused and tried to regain his composure. "I've selfishly messed it up for everybody."

His Mother walked over to him and put her arm around his broad shoulders. "It's not going to be an easy road ahead Dylan. But I want you to know that I will always love you." A maternal silence followed. Lori stroked his curly blonde hair. "I'm going to get Principal Scott. Let's go home."

March 14, 1986
Saint Vincent's Hospice

"Have you seen Dad's tool box?" Joey asked his brother. The grand stairway creaked under Dylan's heavy foot as he descended. "I thought he kept it in the closet under the stairs."

Dylan shifted his shoulders so that the trench coat fit snug. "You cleaned it out last. Have you checked the basement?"

Joey winced, "I really don't want to go down there. It's so filthy."

"What do you need a tool box for?"

"The bathroom sink is leaking in my apartment."

"I thought that was the landlord's responsibility," Jonathan hollered from the living room. He and Fabien entered the hallway in their trench coats, also dressed for a night out.

"I need it done today not a month from now," Joey chagrinned.

"I'm good with that sorta thing," Jonathan beguiled. "I could fix your plumbing."

"That's not the type of plumbing Joey needs help with," Dylan cajoled with a short laugh through his nose. "You're going to Pearls, remember? While you still have friends."

"Where is everyone?" Joey inquired. He thought it strange that the Hospice seemed too quiet. He was elated to hear Jonathan's voice, but was still on edge knowing he had lied to Detective Stone about Jonathan being at the scene of the murders. The blood on his chin.

Dylan responded, "Muller took everyone to the Old Clam House for dinner. Fabien doesn't care for fish."

"No like crustacean," Fabien replied with a smirk.

"Dylan says this Pearl's Diner has the best shakes around," Jonathan courted. "Why don't you join us?"

"Not putting that crap into this gorgeous body," Joey humored. "I'm on a mission to fix a sink." Joey took note of the fact that Jonathan sober was more tolerable than Jonathan's ostentatious plastered.

"Suit yourself," Dylan said, making his way to the door. "Did Muller's payment hit the bank?"

"Yes, Muller overpaid though, by one hundred dollars," Joey raised concern.

"Don't worry about it," Dylan replied. "I'm sure it was just his way of apologizing for forgetting."

"But."

"See ya," Dylan said saluting, he closed the door behind him.

Joey didn't like being alone in the big antiquated mansion. He recalled as a child, the eerie kettling noises from the basement boiler from lime-scale accumulations. Running into his parent's bedroom, frightened from the whistling of the trapped air in the pipes, he begged to sleep between them. As a child with an over-active mind, Joey was convinced it was the boogie-man warning him of what he might do to him if he closed his eyes.

He missed his mother dearly. What he wouldn't do to feel her comforting arms around him one more time. Her gems of great wisdom that only made sense years later. It seemed easy for Dylan to move on after losing both their parents. Joey was much closer to his mom. No doubt he was mommy's boy.

Through the kitchen, across from the pantry was the door to the basement and wine cellar. Flipping the light switch, located on the casing wall, he opened the door and noticed that the basement light had burned out.

"Shit!" Joey cursed, irritated by the indurate mission to find his Dad's tool box. "Please be in the drawer," he spoke aloud to himself. First thing to go right all night, was the flashlight still where he had placed it last, in the junk drawer. "Thank God."

Creeping down the stairs, one step at a time, Joey shined the flashlight in all directions. Shadows, cast by the three-inch circular light, moved behind their objects like ghosts.

He realized, as he got to the bottom step, that finding Dad's toolbox was going to be cumbersome. There were so many storage boxes and old Bistro Restaurant equipment. Besides it was pitch black.

Shining his flashlight to find a clear place to step, he spotted one of his mother's garishly beaded dresses draped over an open cardboard box. He raised his light above the box to discover that the garment bag, with Lori's expensive dresses, was unzipped.

"God people," Joey grumbled, "Have a little respect." He hastily stepped over a box of old napkin holders and pushed aside a larger one full of table tents to get to the dress.

It froze in Its tracks, more spooked and frightened than Joey. Tiny pink eyes, aghast at this intruder as if Joey were trespassing. He immediately shined his flashlight on the rodent. Joey reacted to the repulsive Rat with an ear shattering scream. The creature appeared rabid with infected mucus discharging around his mouth. Startled, Joey stumbled backwards and dropped his flashlight. Batteries scattered between the boxes after the cap popped off the battery shaft when it hit the floor. The basement went dark, very dark. Joey's breathing accelerated as did his anxiety.

"No, no, no, no!" Joey panicked, his arms flapping about to grasp something solid to pull himself up. But he could only find air as the cardboard box collapsed under him. Panting hard he managed to get back on his feet.

"Flashlight! Find the damn flashlight." Trembling, Joey knelt down and began to feel around on the cold cement floor. Shaking off a few cobwebs and rat droppings, he found the flashlight and one battery. He now needed to find the other battery and the cap. The thought came to him, "Now I know how I'm spending Muller's extra hundred, Exterminator."

After a few minutes of feeling around, he found both the second battery and the cap. Reassembling the flashlight, to his amelioration, the flashlight worked and again he had light. "Focus! Toolbox," Joey reminded himself, flummoxed with fear and apprehension to continue.

Scanning the basement with the light spray of the flashlight, he spied the handle of one of Dylan's old baseball bats and pulled it from the cardboard box. Holding it above his head, ready to strike and kill, he gained a little more of his confidence back. He couldn't help but notice Dylan's sports paraphernalia in the same box that his mother had packed Dylan's stuff, right after Dylan moved out. His old leather baseball glove, trophies, and Dylan's most treasured football, signed by Oakland Raider's quarterback, Ken Stabler. It brought back memories of Dylan and his father quarreling in the Bistro lounge over football on the television. The patrons taking sides, Dad a die-hard 49er fan, and Dylan rooting for whoever played them. Joey believed Dylan just liked to provoke Frank to stir things up. Frank, thought it good for business.

"Focus on the mission, toolbox!" Joey's sights were back to sweeping the basement floor with the flashlight. Bingo! Of course, under Frank's workbench. He realized where he had gone wrong. Someone had pushed all the boxes to the center of the room, clearing a pathway around the boxes along the basement walls. It seemed odd to him that it wasn't the other way around. Typically, storage boxes are stacked against the wall.

Next to the workbench, a large free standing safe, apparently bolted to the studs behind it. Next to it, empty medicine vials and used syringes, meticulously stacked on the workbench table top. Joey's mind was spinning out of control. "Just who is Doctor Chang? Are the hospice AIDS patients being healed legitimately or by some alchemic sorcery?"

Shining his light toward the toolbox, he was aghast by dried up blood spots on the cement floor. Strange that Dad's once tool cluttered workbench was cleaned off and smelled like Pine Sol.

Joey's narrow light followed the blood trail to the workbench where it originated at one end. Frank was proud of his workbench, solid construction supported by four by fours and steel brackets. The table top was a three quarter-inch thick, twelve-foot steel plate. It was unfathomable to Joey that anyone would dare perform heinous cult like rituals on it.

"What the hell!" Joey's stomach wrenched from what he saw in the perimeter of the light. Directing the flashlight towards the leather wrist shackle, he realized that something malevolent was happening on Dad's workbench. Shining the light at each corner, he confirmed his suspicions, matching leather wrist and ankle shackles.

"What to do, what to do, what to do!" his thoughts running parallel to Detective Stone's inquisition and accusations. They hadn't intended for him to find out. But they had to know it was inevitable, suggesting that he look in the basement.

He decided to follow the trail of blood drippings to see where it would take him. Only a few feet to his right, the blood disappeared under the wine cellar door. Joey hesitated, part of him imploring him not to open it from fear of what he would find. It was locked from the inside. There was an outside entrance door to the wine cellar. However, the king was on a ring in the office desk upstairs. If he could find a narrow nail like object, he could rig the lock open. His parents installed the lock to keep the kids out. The Fire Department required prevention standards requiring that the locks have an access pin hole that a nail like tool inserted could open. This was a no brainer. As adolescents, the brothers simply used the prong on their belt to open the door to heist a bottle of wine to enhance their many slumber parties.

Joey, removed his belt and poked the prong of it in the small hole on the door knob and pushed it in. He made contact with the release and opened the door. He kept his light and eyes on the trail of blood spots, taking small calculated steps. He was all too familiar with the wine cellar layout. As the blood stopped at the shelves to his left, designed to hold heavy beer kegs, his nostrils filled with a putrid stench.

Joey slowly raised his head, praying it wasn't a dead rat. He felt himself becoming light headed, most likely from his rapid breathing. He reached out to brace himself against the wooden shelves. The shelfing shook as he Grasped onto a post to steady himself. It jarred an object from the upper shelf which dropped like a pendulum and swung a foot away from his face. He screamed like a damsel in a horror movie. A second scream followed his realization that it was a human arm. It appeared porcelain white, like a doll's. Except, none of his dolls had Mein Kampf tattooed on the forearm above a confederate flag. Mein Kampf, the title of the fascist articles of faith, written by the furor himself, Adolph Hitler. He was shaking profusely.

Taking a leap backwards, Joey followed the arm up to see from whom it was attached. The cadaver's massive arm and shoulder terminated at a black leather vest. Joey derived the man to be in his early forties, bald, the typical white supremacist hair style. Phlegm, mixed with blood, had dried before it began to drip at the side of his mouth. His lips as pale as his bloated face, mostly hidden by a salt and pepper handle bar style mustache. Eyes frozen open to the moment he took his last breath. Shining his flashlight down the body, the mammoth creature was naked except for the pair of cut open blue jeans, stained in blood, and leather jacket.

But what he saw next chilled Joey to the bone. He had seen the same two puncture wounds on the neck of the juvenile victims in the alleyway. A bite mark, not typical of the nomenclature descriptions of the human bite, nor unfamiliar to any text book animal bite.

Surely, Detective Stone would reason, "Aren't you the owner of the Hospice? Isn't it coincidental? How serious is your animosity toward Skin Heads?" He was very much confused, but convinced for his freedom, he wasn't having this nightmare.

March 14, 1986
Pearl's Diner

"Thomas, table seven still needs to be bused," the waitress mentioned to the bus boy at the Prep Station. Carol was a spunky well-endowed sophomore at City College. Thomas, her bus boy, was a handsome sixteen-year-old Native American with a long black thick mane of hair. At work, it was kept in a ponytail as part of California's public health code. "Sooner we get the dining room cleaned the sooner we get out of here. And I still have homework," she complained.

"Carol, did you see a tip on table two?", Thomas asked, already knowing the answer.

"That old guy stiffs me all the time," Carol said infuriated. "I swear next time I'm going to secretly piss in his coffee. Thomas do me a favor and drop this check at Booth Six, young couple with the toddler."

"Sure,"

Pearl's Deluxe Burger joint, at 708 Post, is one of the oldest restaurants in the Bay area. Its 60's ambiance attracted locals. But the clientele was changing along with the neighborhood. The Tenderloin District was becoming more and more indigent homeless youth which were prey for violent gangs.

Dylan had convinced Jonathan and Fabien to treat themselves to Pearl's famous strawberry shake. Although it was late, his sweet appetite was also an excuse to get out of the Hospice and destress.

Jonathan nodded his head sideways toward the door for Dylan and Fabien to notice the three male ruffians entering the Diner. "Keep your eye on that trash," he said to Dylan trying not to be noticed, "Peckerwoods." Peckerwoods were a white supremacist gang.

"I see 'em," Dylan replied shaking his head as the thugs purposely sat next to the young couple at booth six. The father looked anxiously for his tab. "Shit," Dylan exclaimed, "Creeps have their eyes glued to the wife. It's about to ugly."

"That's very nice of you sir to offer to pay for our dinner tonight." The twenty something, bald red bearded bully, smiled facetiously at the average built husband, still in his business attire. Across from the human refuse in the same booth, a skinny white teen with black gridlocks and a swastika tattooed on his neck. It coughed out a laugh, knowing well what was about to go down. Another, more tired looking Peckerwood, twice his girth, nodded with an equally as wicked grin. Red beard sat sideways feet hanging over the edge of the cushion. The thick heavily freckled arm stretched the length of the bench back, which they shared. The red bearded gangster nudged the young father's shoulders. "If you're leavin, I'll be more than happy to hang onto your bank card." Looking over at his wife, he undressed her with his eyes. "Wife is mighty fine lookin Sir."

The young father kowtowed and looked down for courage. "You guys need to buzz off and leave us alone," the wife fired back.

"Well looky here boys," Red Beard tilted his head and pushed his lower lip out. "Look who wears the pants in this family. Hey boy?" he motioned to Thomas, who was heading their way with the check. "Let our waitress know that this fine dude has offered to pay for our dinner."

"Look we don't want any trouble," the young father stated sheepishly.

"Sir do you want me to call the police for you?" Thomas said handing him the check and glaring at Red Beard without any indication of fear.

Thomas's dauntless demeanor, angered Red Beard. He reached up and grabbed Thomas's collar tight in his fist and pulled him down to eye level, "You think you're a tough guy Tonto?" He tightened his grip, choking Thomas.

"Let him go and get the hell out of here, now!" demanded Carol, approaching their booth.

Red Beard pushed Thomas to the floor. Thomas sprang back to his feet coughing. "Bitch, this is no way to treat good customers."

"You heard her shit for brains. Get the hell out of here," Dylan exclaimed in a normal tone. Dylan, Fabien, and Jonathan had crept up behind them without being noticed. Red Beard's accomplices immediately challenged them and attempted to get up from the booth. With organically engineered speed and strength, Jonathan seized and bashed their heads together. They both slumped unconscious back into the booth. Aghast by Jonathan's inexplicable brawn, the small audience stepped back, unsure whether they would be their next target.

Red Beard's eyes widened the size of silver dollars. His nostrils flared like a bull at the matador, and he charged at Dylan. With the same inexplicable speed, Dylan grabbed Red's swinging arm by the wrist and twisted it behind his back, bending him forward. Dylan's free hand grabbed Red Beard by his belt and rammed him through the glass door to the restaurant. Glass shattered everywhere as Red Beard spread eagle onto the sidewalk and rolled into the street. He got back up, sized up his chances of winning the battle, and took off running, abandoning his friends.

"Sorry about the door," Dylan tipped his Trilby hat to the fearless waitress. "You better have someone sweep up this glass before someone gets cut." Though fearful and frozen in her tracks, Carol looked up and nodded nervously.

There was a thump as one of the gang members tried to lift his head off the table. "Tommie call 911," she ordered him, afraid to take her eyes off the dark heroes. Glass crunched under their feet. Their long trench coats swayed in the San Francisco breeze, blowing through the shattered glass door as they disappeared into the night. The strawberry shakes, still more than half full, remained on the table.

"They forgot to pay," Thomas said straightening out his shirt.

Police sirens could be heard approaching the restaurant. "I got their tab," Carol insisted, still flabbergasted by what just happened.

March 15, 1986
Hardware Store

Joey paced the sidewalk in front of Johnson's Hardware store as his co-worker Alice kept her eyes glued on her watch. Alice was a middle-aged computer nerd that balanced the books, paid the bills, and ordered inventory. Her inferiority complex, due to her slight obesity, caused her to over compensate with a larger than life attitude. "Mr. Johnson is going to fire Freddy if he is late one more time," she stated rolling her eyes derisively. "Lord Joey, stop pacing!"

"He still has five minutes," he replied looking down at his watch and then down the street for his friend. "He slept through his alarm again. I know it. Damn it Freddy." He managed a canned smile as a customer stopped and looked up at the "CLOSED" sign. "The doors will open in just a few more minutes mam." She smiled at him and walked back to her car.

"That queen tips the bottle way too much," Alice said shaking her head in disgust. "His liver needs to join the brotherhood of organ survivor's Union, it just keeps on working."

"He's still young Alice. Give him a break."

"All those orgies, drugs, and dancing till the sun comes out," she continued, "If he'd only put the same passion into his job."

"I think that must be my problem."

"You don't party every night like the queen bee," Alice rebutted.

"I know, perhaps I should. I need a change in lifestyle. Hell, I even bore myself," he said equally disgusted with his situation.

"Are you crazy!" she scolded. "You want to die from AIDS? You need to be careful these days."

Keys banging against the glass door as Freddy opened the lock, turned their attention away from Joey's dire love life. Queen La Fredriecca's face appeared to them like a mug shot on America's most wanted. His eyes bloodshot with fatigued wrinkles under both. It was definitely a hard night and he was not happy to be employed today.

"Sorry," he muttered under his breath. "Please don't tell Mr. Johnson, I'm only a minute late getting opened."

"We can't keep covering for you Freddy," Alice rebuked.

"You're fine," Joey interrupted her, "I had you right at nine a.m." He spun around forewarning her, "Isn't that right Alice?"

"Whatever," she said, flipping him off with her finger as she headed toward the employee break room.

"Count in Joey."

"Seriously Freddy," Joey protested. "I was on the register yesterday and the day before that."

"My head is about to burst," Freddy complained of his imminent hangover. "Please Joey, I can't tax my brain on that register today."

"You owe me two days next week." Joey chagrined. "After you get done vomiting, fix your shirt, it's inside out. Nitwit."

The Queen immediately looked around for loathing spectators. "Oh my God," Freddy panicked putting his hand over his mouth to cover his embarrassment. "No one saw me, did they?"

"Only your pride," Joey chuckled. "And you left him at the bar last night."

"Girl," Freddy waived his finger in the air at Joey. "I'm a wicked mess."

"Yes, you are," now go powder yourself."

He looked over his shoulder on his way to the employee breakroom, as his feminine self often does. "And you should know, I left my pride naked and sleeping in my bed."

"Now I need to vomit," Joey scoffed and took the empty drawer out of the cash register.

Customers began to fill the hardware store. Some came with a mission to purchase that one part that caused their machine to quit, others just to look to see if there was something they couldn't live without.

"You need to get yourself a puppy," Freddy suggested as he put price tags on new merchandise.

"I agree," encouraged Alice, also tagging at the counter. "They'll love you unconditionally and you won't have to do their laundry or their dishes."

"Yea but they don't pay rent either," Joey said rolling his eyes. "If I did get a dog, it would be mean looking, loyal, and have a strong bite, like a German Shephard."

"I thought you hated big dogs?" Alice said as her brow wrinkled inward perplexed. "No, you need a cute lap dog you can cuddle with and dress up."

"He can get that at the bars," Freddy said rolling his eyes.

"How about you Alice?" Joey deflected the attention. "Who's new in your life."

"What life?"

"Girl, you are beautiful!" Freddy endeavored to build her confidence. "You just need a Queen La Fredericka make over. Starts with a good base and the right eye shadow to match your hair. Which I would give you the complete Marilyn Monroe doo at no charge to you baby."

"I would kill to see that," Joey endorsed. "Let's make it a night out. What do you say?"

"I say in your dreams," Alice protested.

"Come on Alice," Joey insisted. "You'll have a great time. What do you say we all go out this Saturday night?"

"You better make me up to look better than Margaret Thatcher," Alice acquiesced.

"Thatcher? Yes, but no one can look better than the queen. Speaking of myself of course, the real queen." Freddy spun 360 with his chin higher than his nose. Alice shook her head, annoyed at his untamed feminine masquerade.

"Great, it's a date." Joey exclaimed.

"Honey," Freddy changed the subject to a more serious matter. "Did your tenants catch up their rent?"

"Yea," Joey said with a dichotomous grimace.

"Why you so, not all that excited?" Freddy asked. "Girl, last you mentioned it, you were about to be homeless."

"I don't know Freddy," Joey paused. "Do you remember me mentioning the new European residents?"

"Sort-a."

"Well, get this, Doctor Chang, one of my non-sick tenants, wants to buy the Hospice."

"Girl, you better jack the price."

"I don't want to sell it," Joey said, hoping Freddy would find a good reason to sell. "I promised Dad I would keep it in the family."

"Have you lost your mind?" Freddy scolded.

"I know it," Joey agreed. "I just don't want to let my Father down."

"Honey, you've let your Father down all your life. One more time won't kill him again."

"I don't know," Joey said helping Freddy with the merchandising. "I've dreamt of turning it back into a bed and breakfast. Resurrecting the Olé Garden Bistro. But I'm going to name it Lori's in tribute to my mom."

"Don't be stupid!' Freddy continued to admonish. "You could take that money, buy a nice Condo and pay all of your tuition." He shook his finger at Joey. "Let me be your come to Jesus and you listen to your queen mother. Take the fucking money you moron."

"You're very convincing, but I miss those days," he reminisced.

"Get over it Girl. Those days are dead and gone. Gone! Bye Bye! E-va-por-ated," He repeated each syllable slow and hard. "Those days had their turn." He paused, "I'm being serious now. Think of yourself for once. Please."

"You're right," Joey conceded. The further he distanced himself from the unexplainable abominations at the hospice, the better. Washing his hands of the Hospice would put distance between him and the dead body he discovered in the basement.

"You know I'm right"

Joey grinned, convinced he was about to make the right decision. "You're a good friend Freddy."

"Oh oh oh, I charge honey," he shot attitude back at Joey. "Trust me you'll get my bill."

March 16, 1986
Early the next morning

French twins, Fabien and Ludovic Dubois, spoke little English. Both had penetrating blue eyes. But they were not Albino by birth. The identical twins were born in Bordeaux France in 1923 to a Hungarian father and a French mother. They didn't know their father. Merely two drunken libidos fornicating after the bar closed at a Hotel in Bordeaux. Nine months later Fabien and Ludovic were born. They took their Mother's maiden name only because their mother could not remember the malefactor's last name.

Fabien and Ludovic joined the French underground to defeat Hitler. The boys were captured two days after the Germans invaded France. Because they were twins, they were tapped out of an execution line by Nazi General, Karl-Wilhelm von Schieben. Von Scheiben was aware of Doctor Josef Mengele call for twins for his medical experiments. Mengele believed that if he could genetically alter a person's production of melanin in the melanocyte cell, he could reverse the process. He was successful. Eventually, the twins developed Albinism. This was all part of Hitler's scheme to make the perfect race of white people.

The breakfast crowd, at Pearl's Diner, was winding down and a few were starting to order lunch. But the normal chatter went silent as the four young men, all wearing ankle length trench coats entered the restaurant.

"They're here," Thomas pointed out to Carol.

"Thomas, tell Marcel to put them in my section." Carol was determined to know and understand them.

Marcel, had been the maître d' at Pearl's longer than Thomas had been alive. Thomas did as he was instructed. "Marcel, Carol wants you to do her a favor and seat them in her area."

"You tell Carol that she got the last customers," he said, not looking directly at Thomas as he picked up four menus from the counter.

"She said she was going to call off sick if you didn't," Thomas fabricated.

"Fine," he acquiesced. "You tell Carol she owes me and if she calls off this Friday all her tickets will be non-tippers."

"Got it," Thomas nodded as Marcel smiled professionally at the four young men waiting to be seated.

"Right this way please," Marcel motioned for Dylan, Jonathan, Fabien, and Ludovic to follow him.

Each of the four Hospice tenants folded their trench coats up and stacked them at the end of the booth.

"Carol will be your waitress. She'll be by shortly to get your drink order."

"Thank you," Dylan smiled back at him.

"I like zis place," Fabien stated with his French uvular trill pronunciation of his Th sounds. "I see why you come here many zimes a week."

"Didn't take them long to fix the glass door," Jonathan pointed to the repaired glass door where Dylan had rammed the Peckerwood through.

"Here she comes," Dylan interrupted him. "Let me handle this please."

"Hi, can I get you guys something to drink?" Carol said holding her pen and pad ready to write their orders.

Dylan read Carol's name tag pinned to her red and white striped uniform. "So, Carol, I want to first pay for the shakes and the broken door."

"Please," Carol insisted, "I comped your shakes and the glass was covered by the insurance. You don't know how appreciative we are that you stood up to those gangsters. They had it coming to them. Trust me it was my pleasure."

"Thank you," Dylan grinned from the side of his mouth. "But it is no problem and besides you are a very good waitress and deserve to be tipped." He took hold of her wrist, pulled it toward him and slipped a hundred-dollar bill into the palm of her hand. Dylan then closed her fingers around it with his other hand." She swallowed hard, somewhat aroused by his strong but gentle grip.

She gradually opened her hand. Shocked at the generous tip, "No really, you don't need to do this."

"It would make us very happy if you would accept," Jonathan dipped his chin and stared at her like a school teacher disciplining a student.

"Wow," Carol shook her head, "I don't know what to say. Thank you."

"Your very welcome," Dylan replied. "My name is Dylan."

"Carol," she said, pointing to her name tag.

"I see," Dylan grinned. "And this is Jonathan."

"Nice to meet you again," Jonathan followed up.

"And these are the twins, Fabien and Ludovic."

Fabien quickly extended his hand. Carol reached to shake it when he caressed it and kissed the back of it. "Pleasure iz mine. You are very beau-siful."

"Thank you," she said managing a flirtatious smile. "Is your accent French?

"Yes, is French," he replied still holding her hand.

Jonathan, impatient with Fabien's sudden admiration, rebuked him. "Christ Fabien, let her go so she can take our drink orders. I'll have a small orange juice," Jonathan placed his order.

Carol, fumbled with her pen. "OK."

"Tomato," Dylan added.

"Same," Ludovic nodded. "zat sounds good."

"Water for me," Fabien said, admiring every movement that she made.

"Just drinks today gentlemen?"

"Yes, thanks." Dylan answered, suspect of her line of questioning. "Is that a problem?"

"It's just that I've never seen you guys eat anything, and you've been coming to Pearl's for a while now."

Fabien interrupted her with an out. "You very rude Dylan." Fabien continued coquettishly smiling up at her. "You migh-say, we had very laz supper Ms. Carol."

"Well, OK then, I'll be right back with your drinks."

Carol returned to the waitress station and began reaching into the small cooler for orange and tomato juice containers. "They are so damn hot lookin," she said under her breath. She turned to Thomas who was emptying his bus tub and placing the dirty glasses upside down in the dishwasher rack, "I'm especially fond of the Albino in the blue satin shirt. What do think of him Thomas?"

"I don't know, I kinda like the outspoken one," he blushed.

Donna, a generation older, also a waitress, overheard his comment, "You both need to avoid them. They're trouble," she said with her back to them as she punched the numbers on the cash register.

"You have to get into a little innocent trouble to avoid regrets," Carol responded. "Didn't you ever get into trouble?"

"Once," Donna quipped. "He drained my savings and my dreams. Never again."

"Perhaps you're right," Carol empathized. "I don't ever want to become that jaded."

"You said his name is Dylan?" Thomas asked.

"You're sixteen," Donna lambasted. "It's called statutory rape."

"I'll be seventeen next month. Besides, I'd let him rape me," Thomas grinned wide.

Donna shook her head, "If you didn't have such cute dimples, I'd slap some sense into you."

"Yes, his name is Dylan," Carol answered his question. "But Donna's right, he's a little old for you."

Thomas grabbed the tray with the four drink orders. "Let me save you the trip."

"Hey!" Carol sighed as he disappeared with the tray. "I can't believe he just did that!"

Donna put a hand on her shoulder as Carol stood aghast. "You need to protect him. He's a very cute kid and those monsters aren't the heroes you think they are."

"How do you know they're monsters?" Carol interrupted.

"Trust me." Donna shot a disdainful look at them. "They're monsters."

September 10, 1974 5:30 p.m.
Saint Francis Memorial Hospital

"I actually believe you just maybe a better Chef than me," Lori smiled at Joey, about to take on way too much responsibility for an eighteen-year old high school graduate.

"There's no one better than you mom," Joey replied, with a boyish smile. He moved her water glass, with a flex straw, closer to her. The hospital food tray rotated on a separate apparatus on one side of her hospital bed. She spent the better time of her last few days in the Bistro kitchen teaching him how to cook to the menu.

"Did Dylan get registered for school?"

"I don't know," Joey lied, vexed by his brother's apathetic and irresponsible behavior.

She wasn't fooled, intuitively enlightened by his disgruntled expression. "Promise me you'll look after him."

"Mom," Joey wanted to avoid the discussion. Dylan's capricious new lifestyle had pitted the brothers against each other. He was still angry that Dylan wasn't taking his share of responsibilities at the Bistro.

"It's his senior year Joey. I just want for him to graduate."

"He will," Joey assured with tongue in cheek. But he knew that Dylan had no intention of finishing his senior year. "Dad said he'd be by later to visit you."

Joey was struggling to stay upbeat and strong for his mother. The chemo treatments had caused her to lose all her hair, again. Her pastor's wife had knitted a pink and blue beanie hat. She missed her blonde hair which had begun to grow back after a short Spring recovery in 1973. After her condition worsened, she retired her blonde wig and resigned to wearing the beanie.

"I'm worried about your father's drinking problem." Lori stated. "He needs to pull himself together and manage the business. It would kill me again to know that my kids are begging on the street."

"John won't let that happen mom," Joey countered, "He's too invested in the Bistro."

"Don't get me wrong, I love my brother-in-law," Lori despaired. "But John isn't the sharpest tool in the toolbox. You have better business sense Joey. You're eighteen now, and you have power of attorney if something happens to your dad."

"Why would you say that mom?" Joey softly scolded, sanguinely keeping her from worrying. "John has done well for himself and Dad is going to be just fine."

"Thanks to your grandpa," Lori interrupted him. "And I know my husband. The bottle is his psychiatrist. The Sanders family are drunks." Knowing her days were numbered, self-reproof was her coping method of choice.

Joey, picked up her right hand and kissed the back of it. Not letting go of it, he closed his eyes, fighting back tears. "I'm trying to be strong for you." He paused and took a deep breath.

"I know, I know," She replied tenderly.

"Will we be fine mom?" Joey stated not as a question. "Hell no, we won't be." He sniffed and wiped the tear from his cheek with his shirt sleeve. "I've stopped pretending that some miracle drug is going to save you. The road is going to be so hard without you. I can't promise that Dylan will get his shit together. But know that I'm going to give it my best shot. I can't promise Dad will sober up either. But I'm going to be a thorn in his side unless he does. But, but because of you, we're going to make it. And even if we have to sell and move to a trailer house in wasteland, USA, we'll survive. But I will always think of you mom. I wish I had an ounce of your spirituality, then I'd know that someday I'll see you again. But I don't believe in God. I've always been honest with you mom and I would hope that even on your death bed, you would expect nothing less. I love you so, so much." He raised his head to the ceiling so she wouldn't see his tears.

She squeezed his hand, "Ditto." Lori's cheeks were also tear stained. "You are my world. I have enough faith for both of us dear. Trust me it's not over. But, I don't know if I have enough strength to keep fighting this pain." She pushed the food tray to the side and patted the mattress next to where she lay, "Lay next to me." Joey climbed on the white hospital comforter and put his arm under his mother's pillow. She leaned over and kissed his forehead. They laid together on the hospital bed and finished watching an episode of "Gunsmoke" on CBS network television.

Next Morning September 11, 1974
Breakfast

"Good God Joey," Frank complained as he entered the Garden Bistro Kitchen. He squinted to block out the full complement of kitchen lights contending with his pounding head. Another day of Frank grappling with the body aches and pains of another hangover didn't move Joey to empathy.

"Coffee's made," He reacted insouciantly flipping pancakes on the Industrial size stove. The Sanders men rarely skipped Joey's breakfast at the small corner table that doubled as a prep table before the Restaurant opened. Many major Family financial decisions, arguments, and slapstick moments occurred at that table. John Sanders had taken temporary residency at the Bistro to help his brother manage the Restaurant while Lori was treating her cancer. "Is John up?"

"His light was on." Frank mumbled as he escorted his coffee to his seat at the table.

Joey's stomach was unsettled. Anxiety over his mother's suffering, his Father's declining will to live, and his brother's irresponsible carousing, had taken him to the breaking point. "Can you tell him breakfast is ready?"

"Don't bother," John interrupted, appearing rested and eager to fill the void in his stomach. He slapped Frank on the shoulder and sat kitty-corner of him. The wooden legs of his chair screeched across the tile floor as he positioned himself closer to the table.

Joey dropped two pancakes on Frank's plate from the stack of five on his spatula and the remaining three on John's plate. Noticing the bias, Frank shot Joey a disdainful stare waving his finger between the two plates of disparity. "Really?"

"There's plenty more where they came from," Joey reproved.

John drenched his stack with syrup. "How can you eat those without butter?" Frank reproached, turning his nose up.

"Eat your own damn pancakes, Cruella de Vil," John castigated, chomping down on a cheek full of pancake. "Christ, who fluffed up your feathers today sunshine?"

Frank shook his head as if to shake off the deserving attacks.

"Dylan said he'd cover Lisa's tables so she can cover the bar for you," Joey informed his father, sliding two over easy eggs into a pool of syrup on Frank's plate.

"You're a good boy Joey," John lauded, glancing over at Frank with a castigating stare.

"Yea, yea, thanks Son," Frank disingenuously stated under his breath. John shook his head with disappointment at his brother.

"Dylan!" Joey shouted down the hallway, as if his voice would travel upstairs. "Breakfast!"

A few minutes later, heavy footsteps in haste, thumped down the flight of stairs. Flabbergasted at the sight of the bruising on his head, the men at the table were frozen with forks in hand.

"What on God's green earth happened to you?" John probed.

"You don't want to know," Dylan avoided the question and sat in front of the empty plate on the table. He grabbed two pancakes off the pile on the serving plate. "Still warm, great."

"Answer your Uncle's question and don't be rude," Frank reprimanded. "When are you going to grow up and stop lookin for trouble?"

"When homophobes like you leave us alone," Dylan excoriated. He turned his attention toward his uncle and lightened his tone. "Got jumped by a gang of queer bashers in front of the Sun Club. My friend got eight stitches. Four against two, and they call us pansies."

"Stay away from those places and none of this would happen," Frank continued to berate him.

"Came prepared," Dylan pulled brass knuckles out of his pocket and laid it on the table. "You should see the other guy," he gloated as he stared down his Father. "Why don't you ask San Francisco's finest why they sat in their squad car and watched it go down?"

"That ain't right," John's eyebrows wrinkled inward with disgust.

"You're lucky they didn't have bats," Joey remarked genuinely concerned with his brother's carelessness.

John, troubled by Joey's anxiety added, "Next time, we may be trying to identify you in a cadaver bag."

"Do you want me to cook you some eggs?" Joey asked, trying to change the subject.

Feeling the tension between Father and Son, John tagged on Joey's deflection. "You still pumping the iron?"

"Three times a week," Dylan shrugged. "Sometimes four. It's easier now school is out." He looked good but only for narcissistic motivations to turn gay men's heads and not his overall health.

While Dylan's eggs sizzled on the grille, Joey reached over and squeezed his brother's hard bicep. Teasingly, he winked as he kissed his cheek. "God, if only you weren't my brother."

"Gross," John smirked.

"Jesus Christ," Frank censured. "It's bad enough having to deal with your mother's cancer, but having to listen to this queer shit! Leave it outside! Please!" The boys picked up on their Father's grief amidst the anger and stifled their urges to suffocate him further. Silence followed.

Dylan stabbed his fork into the table, "Fuck you!" He stared at his father with contempt.

"Dylan don't." Joey implored him. "Please, please don't go there."

"I didn't give up a professional sports career because I was ashamed." His face flushed red with anger. "I dropped out because I saw the shame in your eyes. I would have done anything not to have embarrassed you. Let that sink into that thick skull of yours. I am not ashamed of who I am. I am a proud queer." He shot out of his chair and stopped at the Kitchen door. "I'm calling off sick for the day." He shook the thought of returning out of his mind with another dagger for his father. "Fuck that, I quit!" The front door slamming shut was the last evidence of Dylan for several weeks to come.

"There goes a promise to mom I'm going to have to break," Joey sighed, tossing his apron on the counter. "Nice parental skills dad," Joey patronized, shaking his head in disgust at Frank. Frank's lips were pressed closed, struggling to hold back retaliatory threats and make an even bigger fool out of himself.

March 23, 1986
The Sale is Final

The weatherman had forecast more fog. Doctor Chang insisted he pay for a round trip taxi for Joey, from his studio apartment to the Hospice. Joey was grateful, as he was still dealing with the Trauma of the murder investigation.

Dylan met him at the curb and opened the taxi door for him. "Ah brother," Dylan kissed both of Joey's cheeks as he handed the taxi driver his fare with a very gracious tip included. "Thank you."

The driver was the son of an Iranian immigrant. He had a long narrow beard below the chin and wore a blue satin turban. Although he knew the city well, he was obviously not happy to be working the swing shift in the fog. But his attitude changed for the better when he saw the amount of gratuity in his hand. "Thank you very much, thank you, thank you."

"Are we really doing this?" Joey asked his brother still a little apprehensive.

"Doctor Chang is a very wealthy man," Dylan assured him. "Trust me brother, he has the funds to invest in fixing this money pit into something mother and father would be proud of."

"We had so many memories here," Joey sighed. "Who is this guy? He's a mystery to me. How did he come by all his money?"

"He's a Doctor for Christ's sake," Dylan replied annoyed with the incessant questions.

Joey stopped abruptly on the front porch, his countenance more agitated and nervous than seconds before. "Do you know about the body in the basement?"

"Oh my God Joey," Dylan's head was spinning from all the questions. "Just stop! You're not only incorrigible, but now you're hallucinating!" Dylan opened the door and motioned for Joey to enter.

"I know what I saw."

"You didn't see shit, you hear me? There's no damn body in the basement," Dylan stated adamantly. After adjusting to the shock of Joey's admission that he knew, Dylan's face shifted emotionless. "Drop it." Joey pushed passed Dylan, crazed, but inexplicably obedient.

His mouth dropped, somewhat in shock from the interior makeover. It smelled clean. New Wayne's coating mahogany paneling, with regal blue striping wall paper above it, lined the hallway and the great room. New antique furniture replaced the old decrepit pieces. "What the hell!" Joey exclaimed touching the new furniture to make sure it was real.

"It's gorgeous, isn't it?" Dylan's satisfaction gleamed ear to ear, changing his demeanor to move past Joey's bombshell confession.

"This had to cost thousands," Joey said bewildered at how expeditiously things had begun to change before the ink on the bill of sale had dried.

"Ah, Mr. Sanders," Doctor Chang said with elation as he appeared from the office.

Joey turned and mouthed to Dylan, "What's he doing in my office?" Dylan shrugged his shoulders.

"Finally, we get to meet formally." Dr. Chang stood two feet shorter than Joey. He bowed to Joey, as was the Asian tradition for greeting.

"Likewise," Joey falsely professed, smiling awkwardly.

"I hope you don't mind, but I have done a little renovation." Doctor Chang could sense Joey was a little nervous and angst over the unauthorized pre-empted changes. "Can we retreat to your office and discuss the sale? I've had the boys prepare a little supper as well." Doctor Chang had turned toward the office before Joey had a chance to agree.

Joey glared indignantly at Dylan as they followed Doctor Chang into Joey's office. To Joey's satisfaction nothing had changed. His desk still cluttered with invoices and other documents. However, the small conference table in the center of the room had been cleared. A white linen table cloth covered it and four table settings.

As Dylan passed by Doctor Chang, he clandestinely leaned in toward him and whispered, "I thought Giuseppe cleaned the mess up in the basement."

Doctor Chang rolled his eyes with disappointment, "So did I, Damn." Forcing a grin, he directed his attention back to Joey. "I hope you like tataki," Doctor Chang pointed at the adorned raw meat sliced evenly over rice.

"I have no idea what that is," Joey turned his nose upward in disgust. "Is that raw beef?"

Dylan's head dropped, disappointed in his brother's lack of culinary sophistication, "It's like sushi Joey."

"Oh," Joey had no idea what Dylan was talking about. "I don't think I've ever tried it."

Doctor Chang smiled at his charming ignorance, "I think with a little wine you will love it." He then described the rest of the feast. "This is Konnyaku. It's a type of potato. And here we have Tamago, which is egg over rice wrapped in sea weed."

Joey felt his stomach tighten, "And what is in this bottle, it looks like blood? Did you just kill the cow?"

"You would not like that," Doctor Chang continued. "I assure you it is not cow's blood. It is a delicatessen and you have to acquire a taste for it."

Dylan turned his head to hide his sudden stifled urge to laugh. "So, it is blood?" Joey inquired still curious.

"Oh yes, have you ever had blood sausage?" Doctor Chang rationalized with him.

"Stop, I'll lose my appetite."

"Sorry I didn't realize Joey was here," Vaughn, an older man in his late forties announced in his English accent. He stood leaning against the door frame. His salt and pepper hair was slicked back with at least a pound of jell. He wore a white shirt with lacy ruffles in front and on the sleeves. Reflections of light off his polished patent leather shoes momentarily blinded Joey. His narrow face was clean shaven.

"He just arrived dear," Doctor Chang smiled with affection at him. "Shall we eat first and talk business afterwards?"

"Great idea darling," the new owner agreed. "But first let me formally bridge our friendship and shake his hand." He took two steps into Joey's space and grasped his hand firmly, not quickly letting go of it. "Vaughn Muller," his stare as hypnotizing as his strong stature.

"Joey Sanders," Joey replied in almost a whisper. "How are you connected with Doctor Chang?"

"He is my significant other I believe you Americans say. I just refer to him as my husband. Does that offend you?"

"No, no, no, I wish we were as mature in our values here in the States." Joey and Vaughn Muller joined Dylan and Doctor Chang, already comfortable at the table. Doctor Chang poured a little wine in Joey's glass and held it up to his nose to approve.

"Is it satisfactory Joey?"

"I love the sweeter wines," Joey said scooting his chair to the table. Doctor Chang finished pouring his glass.

"Wonderful," Doctor Chang enthused. "Your brother has similar tastes. We have a great after dinner Port from the Douro Valley cellars."

"Why are you interested in the Hospice Doctor Chang," Joey inquired above the clanging of chopsticks and forks against the glass plates.

"Well, Mr. Sanders," he explained, "My family needs a comfortable home with lots of bedrooms to accommodate them. We believe we have found the perfect location."

"Your Family?" Joey asked puzzled. "What about the Hospice patients?"

"They are my Family," Doctor Chang said reaching over and placing his hand on Dylan's back.

Vaughn raised his glass filled with blood, "To Family, however you define it."

Joey reluctantly raised his glass of wine and shot Dylan a perplexed glare. Glasses clanged. "Dylan does seem happier than I've ever seen him. In fact, all of the residents have made inexplicable improvements. I haven't had an invoice for AZT treatments in Months. It's just so very odd. Dylan's lesions are gone. It's like some kind of sorcery."

"What reason would you have to complain then?" Vaughn said with raised brow. "I assure you, it's not voodoo science."

"No, it's great," Joey said shaking his head. "What of the other thousands," he exclaimed in a harder tone. "Do you plan to save them all from this disease? How are you saving them? If it's not voodoo science, then what? Don't you feel a moral obligation to share it with the medical community?"

Dylan stood abruptly. His chair falling over backwards. "Why Joey?" His chin dropped to his chest. "Why can't you just be happy for me and leave it at that?

Doctor Chang reached back and picked up his chair. "It's OK Dylan. Your brother is right to be inquisitive. It looks like you enjoyed the Tataki Mr. Sanders," Chang quickly redirected the conversation. He nodded toward Joey's empty plate. "Are you finished or would you like more?"

Dylan sat back down and Joey took a deep breath. "No thank you, I'm full."

"Let me take your plates and I will return with the sales agreement. I assume you brought the Title Report and Deed with you?"

"My banker informed me that I could sign off on the deed, but he would need the sales agreement signed by a Notary. He also wanted the Title Company to be there."

"I see," Doctor Chang said. "I don't think that's a big problem. We can go over the agreement then and sign it later. When is a good time that we could set up with your bank to finalize escrow?"

"I take lunch from one to two. My banker stated that he could do it then. Are you free at that time?"

"Of course," Doctor Chang affirmed. "We'll be there."

Footsteps racing down the wooden staircase got the attention of the diners. Fabien stopped at the office door on his way out. "I see you later."

"Tell Carol I want to meet her bus boy," Dylan hollered out as Fabien made his way down the hall.

"I zink he would like zat too," Fabien yelled back. The door closed behind him.

"Carol from Pearls?" Joey directed his question to Dylan.

"Not all our residents are gay Joey," Dylan reminded him.

"It's not a good idea for him to go out on his own," Vaughn stated looking at Doctor Chang like a protective parent. "I think Ludovic should shadow him."

With his arms full of empty dishes and glasses, Doctor Chang paused at the door, "I also believe Giuseppe should tag along with Ludovic." Vaughn nodded affirmatively.

"Anyone up for some Port wine?" Vaughn asked, "It's the bloody best."

March 25, 1986
The First Date

"Is diz place proper enough for you?" Fabien asked from across the table. His knuckles drumming the table nervously.

Carol was amused and flattered at the same time. She put her hand over his to qualm the fidgeting nervous fingers. "It's fine," she smiled with assurance.

"Sorry, is just a nervous habit," he responded looking down at his half-eaten chicken cacciatore. After collecting himself he collected her hand with his animated fingers and stroked it. "Would you like more wine?"

"Just a sip more thanks," she said locked in an infatuated stare. "I've never eaten at the Lamplight Grille. I really like the ambiance here. Not too formal, yet, not a dive either. Nice choice Fabien."

"Sanks," he replied with an insatiable grin. "Sis place much like me, simple."

She chuckled at his attempt at humor and reached forward slightly and gripped his forearm. "I don't mean to be so forward," she said with an insincere apology. "Solid, you work out?"

"Sa guys and I go to Charley's Gym. You know zis place?"

"I've heard of it."

"Mondays and zursdays," he continued, happy that she admired his physique. She wasn't alone. His biceps and pecs were screaming to bust through his shirt. "Would you like to go zere with us?"

"Oh no thanks," she shook her head. "I get enough exercise at Peal's." She released her grip and dipped into her lamb stew. "I love this stew, how's your cacciatore?"

"Very good," he replied. Fabien was suddenly distracted by three teenage girls giggling at his expense. The twins had gotten use to the humiliation from the freak show they provided immature minds.

Carol took note that their inappropriate behavior was causing him consternation and might just possibly ruin their first date. "Bitches grow the fuck up!" she spoke loud enough that most of the guests in the restaurant took concern, including the maître'd from behind his podium.

Steve, and his boyfriend, Victor, scoped Market Street for a place to satisfy their appetite after a long day of bar hopping. The University of Utah sophomores paid for fake identification, and against their parents will, ran off to the City of peace, love, and diversity, San Francisco, the Gay Mecca, for a weekend of debauchery. They hadn't spent any of the two hundred bucks they had in their pockets. They were the fresh young meat at the bar and suitors had kept their glasses full. Victor, a little more responsible, knew when to stop. Steve was sure to wake up with a miserable hangover.

Steve and Victor met each other in Middle School, ironically in Mormon Seminary third period. Their conservative families understood them to be just very close friends. In reality, they had been indulging in the love that dare not speak Its name. After the first intimate encounter, the guilt had kept them away from each other for weeks. But their libido was greater than years of indoctrination of intolerance. Once out of the closet they had sex insatiably.

Steve's feminine demeanor, adorned with rainbow earrings and a T-shirt that read "Celebrate Diversity," was sure to turn the heads of a less tolerant straight crowd carousing Market Street bars. Their small physical statures were hardly intimidating by any means. They noticed the Lamplight Grille's lit up neon sign. "There," pointed Steve, still guffawing at Victor's jokes and burping up vodka cranberry.

They crossed at the next intersection unabashedly without care for their safety. Victor still somewhat piqued over Steve's vulnerability, did not want to be the kill joy.

"Get a load of this?" Giuseppe said, left hand on the steering wheel of the parked black sedan. His right hand pointing at the two sacrificial lambs crossing the street. Ludovic followed his pointed finger to the crosswalk where Steve and Victor were about to cross into a small crowd of hoodlums outside the Cactus. The Cactus was a narrow dive bar. It's clientele? Peckerwood bike gangs looking for a brawl.

"Zis no end well," Ludovic looked back at Giuseppe. "Do we blow our cover and gez involved? I mean if Fabien learns zat we stalk him, he will be angry."

"Let's lay cool and hope there's no trouble," Giuseppe said putting his hand on Ludovic's shoulder. Ludovic nodded affirmatively.

"Didn't that boy from Rio have gorgeous eye lashes," Victor remarked, trying to hide his anxiety toward the small crowd of leather vests and motorcycles between them and the Lamplight Grille. The Lamplight Grille was two store fronts down from the Cactus bar.

"I'm not into three ways. But if you want to go for it, go for it. But you'll find your own way back to Salt Lake City."

You're still jealous cuz he asked me to dance, admit it," Victor blew his own trumpet.

"Ok, I was a little jealous."

Feeling one up, Victor shot Steve an exonerated smile, "Lighten-up please, it was only one dance. You heard me tell him I was with you when he asked me what I was doing later."

"You've been reminding me of that all night," Steve replied annoyed. "So, do me a favor and give it a rest."

Crossing over to the next block, it was obvious that the loathing vile stares from some in the crowd, meant inevitable trouble for them. "Just ignore them and keep walking no matter what insults they make," Victor agonized.

"A couple of them are cute," Steve naively raised his brow.

"This is no time for gay shenanigans," Victor reproached. "Trust me these are foes not friends."

The obese one spoke first. His leather vest too small, covered little of his bare chest and protruding stomach. "Hey sweet heart, wanna suck my dick?" He grabbed his crotch. Two other bullies, their backs against the brick wall of the Cactus, grinned.

"After you get him off you can do mine too," added an acne infected Hispanic male, standing next to the obese one.

As they got closer, Victor swallowed his terror caused indigestion. "Don't panic Steve. Just keep walking."

"Let em be," a female reveler demanded. "They haven't done anything to you."

Without warning, the acne infected delinquent violently shoved Victor into Steve. Steve managed to stay upright, but Victor fell to the concrete. Victor looked toward the pain from his right hand and noted blood oozing from the scrapes. Steve knelt behind him, "Leave us alone."

The crowd began to break up. Those not wanting to get involved or implicated retreated back into the bar. Some enjoyed the show. "You're an asshole Frank," the empathetic female yelled at their assailant.

"He spit on my boot, the faggot!" Frank protested fallaciously.

"He didn't spit on your boot Frank," she braved through the testosterone filled tension. "This crap is just going to invite the cops."

Steve helped Victor to his feet. "Look we don't want any trouble," Victor protested.

The same skinny white juvenile from the incident at Pearls moved off of the wall. His hair still kinky with black gridlocks. The swastika tattooed on his neck marked him. He immediately got into Victor's face. "Good, then do the right thing and lick your spit off my friend Frank's boot before I kick the living shit out of you!"

Frank moved his boot out and pointed to it. "I think you'd better listen to my friend here, he's a really bad ass. I'm just afraid of what he might do to you. Perhaps you should get down and lick my boot clean. Now!"

The sound of lips puckering and coughing up spittle, turned every head towards the Albino and his Italian cohort. His aim was on target. Ludovic's slimy green saliva splattered on Frank's extended boot. "Zere," Ludovic taunted, "Now I seez it," he said mocking him.

Giuseppe shrugged his massive shoulders, "That's spit all right."

Frank swung at Ludovic. But with unimaginable speed, Ludovic caught his fist in his palm and twisted it backwards and raised his knee hard into his testicles. The gangster tried to exude a cough, but there was no oxygen left in his lungs.

Ludovic pulled the cigarette from behind Frank's ear, tossed it to the sidewalk and smashed it with the sole of his shoe. "Your momma no explain sis bad for you?"

The obese gangster caught his breath, "I'll kill you, you freak of nature."

"Well zen," Ludovic smiled. "Consider zis, what you say, self-defense." Ludovic spun on his left foot, his trench coat whipped around him like the rings of Saturn. He drew his right foot back, similar to the tension on a bow, and released his kick to the back of Frank's legs. His upper torso fell to the concrete hard as his head bounced off it. He lay still, blood dripping from his ears.

"You Bastard!," the skinny white supremacist screamed. "I think you killed him." He charged at Ludovic but was clotheslined by Giuseppe's sudden outstretched arm. He too went to the concrete. Pouncing on top of the juvenile, Giuseppe swung his trench coat over him, hiding him from view of the crowd. The Nazi screams turned into a blood gurgling cough and then went silent.

Victor and Steve stood frozen in fear. Ludovic walked deliberately up to Victor, "Go home to your mommies children." He then turned to the small crowd that had clustered close for safety. "Siz show is ova." No one dare speak.

A slurping sound from under Giuseppe's trench coat wrought bent faces of disgust from the onlookers. "Lez go," Ludovic shouted at his friend. He raised his head and turned to face the crowd. His lips and teeth were tainted with fresh blood. Giuseppe stood above his motionless prey. The juvenile's eyes were frozen wide with death's fearful acknowledgment. What the onlookers saw would traumatize and scar them for life. Endless nightmares and fear of going out at night for their usual muggings and misdeeds.

Several of the patrons of the Lamplight Grille had put down their eating utensils and ran into the street to investigate the blood curdling screams. The black sedan had sped away North on Market as sirens approached from Macias and Market streets. Fabien and Carol were among those that had left their half-eaten meals to survey the commotion.

"Zis can't be good," Fabien exclaimed holding Carol close to him. Between the heads of the onlookers, he was able to make out two bodies lifeless on the sidewalk in front of the Cactus Bar.

"I wish they would close that cesspool," the master chef and owner of the Lamplight Grille chagrinned. "That bar is really bad for business."

"You may get your wish," Carol interjected unsolicited. "I believe those cadavers maybe connected to the Cactus." Police and emergency response vehicles flooded Market Street in front of the bar. One medical technician placed his index and middle finger on both the deceased's carotid arteries and confirmed they were dead on arrival. Other responders covered the bodies with white sheets. It was now a crime scene and medical teams began to leave.

Victor and Steve walked solemnly toward the Lamplight Grille. "I just lost my appetite Victor. Are you OK?"

Victor was choking back tears, "No I'm not OK," he scolded him. Why would you even ask me that question?"

"Sorry," Steve's festive feminine demeanor had drained from him. "Sorry. I just wanna go home. The Albino is right, this whole trip was a bad idea!"

Still traumatized, Victor stopped. He turned and faced Steve, then fell into his arms and wept. "Let's go home."

Victor suddenly stopped, the fear returned and the color drained from his face. "That's him," his tremulous voice muffled with fright. His finger shaking as he pointed at Fabien, Ludovic's twin. "That's him", he yelled louder for the crowd to hear."

Fabien shrugged his shoulders and pointed to himself. "Why you pointing me boy?"

"You were there," Victor slowly backed away, trepidation shaking him to the core. "You killed them."

"That's him!" Steve took closer examination of Fabien. Why wasn't the Albino running away? Was it possible for him to be standing there when he clearly saw him drive away in the opposite direction. "I don't understand," Steve regained his composure, somewhat mystified.

"No that's him," Victor yelled sharply.

"What's the problem here?" Detective Stone demanded, his badge high in the air. Stone was hoping he had a possible person of interest.

"He did it!" Victor insisted still pointing his trembling finger towards Fabien.

"Him?" Carol interjected. "That's impossible he's been with me all evening."

"She's right Detective," the owner of the Lamplight Grille confirmed. "They've been eating at my restaurant for most of the night."

The owner's apron and Chev's hat gave more credibility to Fabien's alibi. "Why would you think it was this man?" Stone inquired of Victor, acutely critical of his accusation.

"I swear, he's the spittin-image of one of the guys who murdered those bad men," Steve spoke for his suddenly not so garrulous lover. "But they left in a black car going North. I don't see how it would be possible." With a low brow Steve took a more absorbed look at Fabien. "Sir you could be the killer's twin."

"You're nuts kid," Carol chastised.

Stone began to bark orders, "You boys stay put. I may need you to take a trip down to the Station." He turned, "Jack!"

His partner ran up to him, "Yea?"

"I need statements from these folks and the owner." Stone began to scratch notes on his pad of paper. "Anyone at the bar cooperating?"

"They still claim they were all in the bar drinking", Jack sighed perturbed. "They all say they didn't see anything."

"They're liars!" Steve rebuked their stories.

Stone snickered, "They hate cops kid."

Jack had already connected the dots, "Same MO Sam. Neck wounds. Animal like teeth marks. I don't get it. It's like these killers are vampires."

Fabien, who had remained prepensely quiet, suddenly was sure who the killers were. He swallowed hard. He thought to himself, "Doctor Chang had me followed." He felt betrayed, but not surprised. He knew things were about to get ugly for the Creed.

"Are you OK?" Carol asked concerned.

"I sorry. Zis kid upset me."

"I understand," Carol said genuinely.

"I hope you never have to," he replied. Carol was perplexed at his response.

Fabien stopped the car in front of Carol's apartment complex on the corner of Clay and Hyde Streets. He had fallen in love with his 1965 restored Ford Mustang. Doctor Chang bought it for him, contingent on the agreement of loyalty to the Creed. Fabien had hoped to get a job, once they had settle down, and buy it back from him. Although he knew Doctor Chang wouldn't have it.

"Thanks for dinner," Carol said checking to see if her roommate's bedroom light was on. It was. "I had a really great time," she turned and smiled affectionately at him.

"Zis night was special," Fabien replied, amorous of her beauty queen charm. "I wish," he began to apologize for the dreadful excitement, when she put her index finger to his mouth.

"It wasn't about us," Carol stopped him. She refused to allow what happened at the Bar to ruin their first date. "Please come inside, I want to introduce you to my roommate," she said with some excitement. However, her intent had an ulterior motive. They were mature adults and whatever happened next, she was sure would be consensual.

The erection in his pants took precedent over the Creed's restraint policy. All potential intimate relationships must receive Doctor Chang and Vaughn Muller's blessing. "OK, I zink I would like to meet zis roommate," he said with grin from ear to ear. Carol began to open her door, "No, please wait. Stay in za car please." She was encouraged by his manners and immediately shut the door. Fabien got out of the 65 Mustang and walked around and opened the passenger door for Carol.

"Now you're what I classify as a real gentleman," Carol said, encouraged by his respect for her.

"In my Country, za polite zing." He held the door open as Carol climbed out. He offered his hand and she took it. He closed the door as Carol hurried through the open corridor to her apartment door. Fabien followed closely behind. She fumbled with the keys with nervous enthusiasm, found the right one, and inserted it into the lock.

"Come in," she insisted.

Fabien followed her into the apartment. He was pleasantly surprised at the amount of space in her two bedroom downtown prime real-estate quarters. "Wow, you muz pay much for diz."

"That's why I have a roommate. I thought she might be here. Her bedroom light is on. She's probably at the clubs dancing. She likes to party late on the weekends. Her name is Rosie. I think you will like her. Here let me take your coat." Carol hung both of their coats in the closet next to the entry door.

"I'm sure I will like her. She is friend?"

"Would you like a drink?" Carol asked making her way to the kitchen.

"Yes please."

"Make yourself comfortable," She insisted, pointing to the green couch with four light brown pillows encased in knitted shams. Carol opened the lower cabinet door to the alcohol supply. "For wine, we have a red cav or merlot. We also have vodka, brandy, or grand Marnier."

"Small brandy please," he answered, inspecting the family pictures hanging above the television. "You have large family?"

"Three brothers and four sisters," Carol replied pouring brandy into the cocktail glass. "My second oldest brother was killed in a tragic car accident two years ago."

"I'm so sorry," Fabien consoled. "Zay all very attractive," he added, making an effort to say all the T consonants to impress her.

"Thank you," she smiled taking the wine glass down from the glass shelf above the counter bar. The ceiling cabinet separated the living room from the kitchen. "We're the weird exception."

"What mean by zis?" Fabien chortled.

Carol shrugged, "Most families get together and argue and fight." An uninhibited smile embellished her natural beauty. "My family," she paused, delighted, "Let me just say that we're all very good friends."

"Zis is very good," He responded. The memory of his horrific world war two childhood days filled him with melancholy.

Carol took immediate note of it. "Did I say something wrong?" She asked, handing Fabien his cocktail.

He wanted so much to share with her his secret miracle. "How you say, complicated," he managed a short smile and all the Ts. He patted the cushion for her to sit next to him. "Zis drink is very good." Fabien was concerned his reticence would disappear with each drink. Conveniently, the SR metamorphose miracle afforded him masculine youthful features. However in his mind, he was old enough to be her grandfather. His thoughts began to drift. Perhaps this is a huge mistake. There's a great possibility, and risk, if this relationship matures, she could be hurt in more ways than one.

Fabien carefully set his brandy on the coaster next to the vase on the coffee table. With his index finger, he guided her chin close to his. She held her wine glass above and away as not to spill it. Fabien's libido was beyond his control. Their eyes like magnets drew their faces together, lips brushing at first, then pressing hard. His tongue plunged into her mouth seeking out her flavor. Both panting, she pulled away realizing that some of her wine had spilled and stained the carpet. She moved forward setting her glass on the table, sure to leave another stain.

Before he could speak Carol resumed kissing him, entangling her fingers through his silky curly white albino hair. Not wanting to break their lip lock, they both stood simultaneously. Fabien reached around her and drew her slender waist into him. Her hands roamed his muscular back and without concern for his consent, grabbed at the curvature of his opulent rock-hard buttocks. She felt his enormous and excited penis and for a moment of shock, shuddered from the thought of it penetrating deep inside her. She fidgeted with his belt buckle, desperately trying to get access to his sex. It was all the permission Fabien needed and he unzipped her dress from the back, which fell like a curtain in a Broadway show. The leading role to him, her sumptuous perfectly sized breasts, and he wasted no time unhooking her bra. It too fell to the carpet. He cupped one in each hand and sensually pinched and rubbed her nipples until she began to lose control of her senses. Her head arched back as she moaned from the pleasure of her pain. He seized the moment and kissed softly the nape of her neck. With greater enthusiasm, she managed to unbuckle his pants. He stepped out of them. He wasn't wearing underclothing. She was pleased and dropped to her knees. Fabien released his grip knowing his passion would be swallowed and satisfied.

The sound of a car door grabbed her attention. "Shit!," Carol exclaimed. A naughty and somewhat embarrassed grin encompassed her face, "My roommate!" She grabbed his hand and quickly led him into her bedroom, leaving a trail of clothes as evidence that she wasn't alone and didn't want to be bothered.

May 6, 1933
Berlin
Zur Katzenmutter
(The Mother Cat)
Gay Bar 6:30 p.m.

He swung his small leg over the bar stool, and using the bar top as leverage, lifted himself up and sat next to his friend. "It's happening," Doctor Huey Chang, a German Bio-engineer, said in a low voice to the bearded man in his fifties.

"Rohm had no part in it, I assure you," Doctor Magnus Hirschfeld replied shaking his head in disgust.

"He is the head of the SA," Doctor Chang disputed. "He could have stopped it."

"There's too much infighting in the Nazi hierarchy. It would be suicide for him to oppose fascist Ideologues. You don't think Hitler already knows that Ernst Rohm is a homosexual? The only thing keeping him alive is the fact that he and Hitler are dear friends." Doctor Hirschfeld's eyes began to fill with tears. "Did the SA burn all the books?"

Doctor Chang took note of his friend's despondent emotions. "I'm sorry Magnus, all twelve-thousand. There's something else you should be aware of."

Doctor Hirschfeld leaned forward, cupping his face in the palms of his hands, "What now?"

"The SA tore down the "Institute of Sexual Science" sign. It now has a Nazi flag flying over the doors."

"My life's work destroyed in one day. I cannot go back."

Doctor Chang put his hand on his friend's back for support. "This place would be burned to the ground as well if not for the fact that many of Hitler's officers pick up male prostitutes in this joint. You know this."

"I've packed my bags," Doctor Hirschfeld said stoically. "I leave by train for Paris in three hours. I have a speaking engagement there. The University is paying my fare. I'm saying goodbye dear friend. I won't be returning to Germany. You should come with me."

"It would be impossible."

Doctor Hirschfeld placed his hand on Chang's shoulder, "There is a rumor that the fascists plan on passing page 175 into German law making it a crime to be a homosexual. Doctor if this passes they will arrest you and you could be sent to Neuengamme concentration camp."

Doctor Chang hung his head low, "Don't berate me, but I have accepted a post with Doctor Josef Mengele."

Doctor Hirschfeld threw both arms into the air with disgust. "Why? It is common knowledge that he is using prisoners at Neuengamme for medical experiments against their will."

"Mengele has offered to finance my Sulfanilamide Rejuvenation Project," Doctor Chang muttered with palpable shame. "I know right now you think very ill of me. Perhaps that I have sold out to the Nazis. If there was another way don't you think I would have already completed my research?"

"But why use dirty money?" Doctor Hirschfeld cautioned. "Come with me and approach the French government."

"You don't think I already have?"

"And?"

"The French Consulate wrote a very repugnant letter chastising me for playing God. That it was immoral what I wanted to do." Doctor Chang paused, "Besides, it's possible that I can help save lives."

"Doctor Chang, good evening," the young muscular and shirtless bartender approached Doctor Chang. "What are we drinking tonight?"

"Vodka, straight up with a twist," Doctor Chang barked ostentatiously. "And Rocky, make it a double."

Rocky nodded and turned to the rear of the bar to make the Doctor's libation.

"God, I wish I was the mirror in his bathroom," Doctor Hirschfeld chortled. He pushed his empty glass to the opposite edge of the bar. "I've got to run. You be cautious my friend. I will miss you." He stood and embraced Doctor Chang.

"Likewise, Magnus. Please write."

"I will, but I will leave the French Consulate as the return address," He put on his Fedora hat and laid his coat over his arm. "If it gets dangerous please come to France."

"Thank you, Magnus. Have a safe journey." Doctor Chang turned away with a distant stare. He knew it was more than likely he would never see this popular scientist again.

"That will be one Reich mark Doctor Chang," Rocky stipulated, holding his Vodka for collateral.

Two days later – Schutzstaffel Office of Doctor Josef Mengele

"Doctor Mengele will see you now," announced the SS guard to Doctor Chang, who had grown impatient after sitting forty-five minutes in the lobby. The Nazi SS guard escorted Doctor Chang to Mengele's office and opened the door for him. Doctor Mengele was seated behind a mahogany crafted desk with his Iron Cross medal hung on the wall behind it.

"Doctor Chang," Doctor Mengele said, pretending to be thrilled to see him. He motioned for him to take the chair in front of his desk. Doctor Chang had always been enamored by his strikingly handsome features. Thick black mane of hair and full brows above his boyish grin. "Sorry to keep you waiting. I was on the phone with Ernst Rohm concerning my new transfer to Auschwitz."

"Auschwitz?" Doctor Chang's brow bent inward with curiosity. "They have a lab there?"

"They do now doctor," he replied with an indecent smile. "I want to learn more about your Sulfanilamide Rejuvenation research. Do you believe that this procedure is some kind of medical miracle?"

"Without proper pilot tests on live specimens, it's only a theory. I don't know that it would guarantee immortality, but if successful, would greatly enhance the healing process for our wounded soldiers."

"The Fuhrer himself has taken a special interest in your work," Doctor Mengele said matter of fact with a tinge of jealousy in his voice. "I assure you that you will have all the funds and specimens you need to advance your Work. Now briefly inform me of your project."

"In short, Sulfanilamide is a form of sulfonamide antibacterial. Organic and safe, and will synthesize natural folic acid which will be unaffected by PABA inhibitors."

"But Doctor Chang our bodies don't produce folic acid naturally," Doctor Mengele challenged.

"Hear me out Doctor please." Doctor Chang paused, "However, there is still one glitch."

Doctor Mengele leaned forward, concerned, "Doctor Chang?"

"Kidney failure maybe certain without natural steroid chemicals found in non-depleted blood which react with the drug to produce folic acid."

"Isn't Gerhard Domagk testing similar effects from the prodrug Prontosil?"

"Yes indeed," Doctor Chang sighed. "Gerhard and I attended a conference of Biological Advancements in Madrid. I mentioned to him the work of Jacques and Therese Trefouel who lectured on the possible chemotherapeutic properties of this drug. He took copious notes over dinner that evening. He later called me, warning that my results were flawed. He tested the chemical with diethylene glycol and produced Elixir sulfanilamide which he was afraid maybe poisonous. He experimented on apes and he was right. They all died."

"Then why would I want to invest in your work if it is flawed," Doctor Mengele anxiously inquired.

"Because Gerhard's models never used the steroids that I just mentioned," Doctor Chang nodded confidently. "The consequences of the unknowns potentially could kill the specimen."

Doctor Mengele finished his thoughts, "But if these tests are successful?"

"We could save millions of lives," Doctor Chang ended his own statement with concern in his voice that Mengele had other intentions.

"You will come to Auschwitz and I will provide you with the specimens that you need. We will run tests on the prisoners there." He managed a satisfied grin, "How ironic doctor that these criminals may save our wounded and keep our armies strong."

"Ironic indeed," Doctor Chang said without the same enthusiasm.

March 27, 1986
Hospice Meeting, Enforcing the Code

It seemed like forever for the bus to finally arrive. Joey had become numb to the night chill and Paced back and forth to stay warm. A short woman in her mid-fifties, dressed warmly for the inclement weather, glanced at his pacing invidiously from the corner of her eye. Joey envied the down jacket that kept her warm. Too late to go back to his coat closet and choose something warmer than just a light windbreaker.

Joey looked for an open seat as he walked down the aisle of the bus. He managed to find one next to a stout construction worker. His tool chest on the floor between his feet, his sweaty odor Joey relished in long breaths. Joey suppressed a yawn, the store front neon lights flashing, passed him like a flickering television screen as the bus sped away. He was growing tired and wished he was in his bed deep in Delta sleep.

He recognized the Billy Joel tune 'Only the Good Die Young,' blasting in the earphones covering both ears of the construction worker. His mind viscerally living in another world. Dirt caked under his finger nails and work clothes in need of a strong detergent, the muscular, shirt bound young man, slumped down in his seat. His knees braced against the seat in front of him. The cantankerous elderly woman sitting in the seat in front of him, turned and gave him a disapproving glare. He apologized and sat back up in his seat.

Joey's mind began to wander. Thoughts of Jonathan inundated his adulate and deprived cravings. Why was Dylan so against them getting together? His fancy had grown to desire. As eccentric as Jonathan seemed, he wanted to satisfy his carnal needs more than Dylan's warnings.

Avowed to ferret out the mysteries behind the strange affairs of the new Hospice tenants, he decided to drop in on his old clients without warning. He was unnerved by their secrecy and the space Dylan insisted Joey give him. It wasn't normal. Not like him at all. Dylan had become so protective of him, yet more distant. Joey was perplexed by it. He was on a mission to get to the truth.

Pastel colors painted the clouds soft red, blue, and purple, as the last ray of sunlight disappeared into the cement skyline. "Do you think the police have any leads that might connect us to the killings?" Dylan inquired of Doctor Chang. He had notice Dylan standing at the window of his room browbeaten and inundated with more on his mind than just the glorious sunset.

"Mind if I join you? I hear it on good source that you never miss a sunset?" Doctor Chang deflected. "Coastal clear nights are rare and magnificent I would agree."

"You're avoiding my question Doctor Chang," Dylan insisted getting an answer to an unavoidable dilemma that may break up his family for the second time.

"You can't stop the sun from setting," Doctor Chang replied sagaciously. "But I can assure you, it will rise again. It is what it is. We will survive."

Dylan shook his head, frustrated that the Doctor was treating him like a school boy. "What sense am I to make of this?"

"The blood-letting doesn't come without complications boy," Chang grinned. "What will be will be. Fortuitously, you have the convenience of inexperience driving your passion. Our passion is driven from the excruciating memory of the pains of torture at the hands of the Nazis. Leaving here should be the least of your worries."

Dylan's eyes shifted from the sky to the little man standing shoulder to shoulder with him, though a few heads below his. "How can that not concern you?"

"I've put this talk off for some time. It's time."

Dylan's content turned to nervous uncertainty. "The last time I heard those words my mother was trying to make peace between me and my father."

"So, I'm not the first to try and calm the beast? Look, I would only be lying to myself if I tried to paint your father as anything but the man you shared a tumultuous relationship. The Fascists may have eluded your sheltered life, but hate has many faces."

"I'd rather not talk about my pernicious childhood," Dylan warned Doctor Chang with a stiff upper lip.

"Fair enough. But I'm not leaving you without some parting word for the wise." Dylan released a long-held breath. "I want to share an astute Cherokee Indian folklore from a book I read when I was studying to be a scientist. "The Chief, seeing a burning anger in his grandson, petitioned him to hear his demise. "A fight is going on inside me," he said to the boy. "It is a terrible fight within me between two wolves. One is anger, guilt, and self-pity. The other is good, kind, humble, and benevolent. The Spirits have informed me that this fight has the potential to either lead to destruction of my soul or a life of serenity, hope, and joy." His grandson gave in to festering curiosity. "Please tell me which wolf will win grandfather?" He begged. The wise old sage smiled, "The one you feed."

The Doctor's epiphany disclosed the undeniable demon Dylan took refuge behind his anger. His truth manifest in the form of a tear that wet Dylan's cheek. "I'll never forgive him Huey."

"I didn't say you had to," Doctor Chang replied less empathetic. "Just stop feeding it."

The doorbell rang. "I wonder who that could be?" Dylan left the room to answer the door. Doctor Chang followed him. Taking the stairs two steps at a time, Dylan raced to the door, peering through the tiny peep hole.

A sense of relief it wasn't the cops, he opened the door for his brother. "Joey?"

"We have to talk," Joey insisted letting himself in.

"What seems to be the problem," Dylan knew right away that Joey was on to them as pieces of the puzzle came together. "Don't I not get a proper embrace? I'm still your brother."

Joey routinely hugged and kissed his brother's cheeks without the brotherly passion he routinely demonstrated. Doctor Chang stood at the top of the stairs, ease-dropping on their conversation. Joey took a deep breath, "Did you watch the evening news?"

Dylan, still attempting to protect his brother from the truth, replied ingeniously. "I try not to, why? Are you in some kind of trouble?"

Joey caught Doctor Chang standing at the top of the stairs from the corner of his eye. "Can we speak in private?"

"Yes, let's retire to my bedroom."

"Good evening Doctor Chang," Joey said, managing a fake smile as he brushed by him. "I like what you've done to the grounds."

"Thank you Joey. I hope you have time for Dylan to show you the improvements to the gardens."

"I would really like that Doctor," he responded from down the hall.

Once in Dylan's bedroom, he closed the door behind them. "Did Doctor Chang hire a contractor to make over the front yard?"

"Vaughn Muller, he's a master gardener of sorts. You will be very pleased with what he has done with the gardens."

"Dylan," Joey's anxiety returned. "Detective Stone paid me a visit this week. I'm afraid I maybe his number one suspect in the Market Street vampire murders."

"What!," Dylan became angry. "That's absurd!" He pressed his forehead against his palms and shook his head in disbelief. "What reason?"

"Stone is making up shit between the lines of my police report." Joey looked away hiding his tears of frustration. "I'm my own worst enemy sometimes."

"What are you telling me Joey," Dylan probed.

"I admitted to having an encounter earlier that evening at a bus stop with the victims. But nothing happened. I left, the female shouted a few offensive stereotypical labels out at me. And that was it. But he believes that I was the last person to see them alive. I believe Stone doesn't buy it. I think he believes I followed them and in retaliation, killed them."

"What evidence does he have?"

"It's the lack of evidence that keeps me suspect number one."

Dylan put a comforting hand on Joey's shoulder. "He's fishing. Stoking his ego. He has nothing. You'll be fine."

There was an uncomfortable pause. Dylan became infuriated at the realization that his brother was being implicated over the indictment of the Code. Dylan tried to suppress the anger at Jonathan, who convinced the others that night, that those two skin heads were a threat to his Joey. "Dylan, there is something else that I haven't told you or Detective Stone," he said staring at the floor about to release his veracity on him.

"Joey, what are you telling me?"

"Were you there that night in the black sedan?" Joey turned and demanded the truth.

"What night?" Dylan replied, pretending he knew nothing as a cold anxious chill inundated him.

Not getting an immediate answer, Dylan looked away, terrified of what Joey's reaction might be if he came clean.

"Don't worry, Stone doesn't know anything. But, please, don't play stupid. It's no coincidence that the black sedan just happened to be following me. Don't pretend that I'm too naïve to know there's something extremely eccentric about what's going on here. Unexplained AIDS recoveries, nightly prowling. You don't think I see the obvious? I believe I know who killed those two-skinhead scum and it grieves me to believe that you do too. But that's a problem for me because I'm having strong feelings for Jonathan. I just need to know. Am I falling in love with a murderer?"

Dylan continued to stare at the wall, shaking his head. "This is all my fault brother."

Drained of emotion, the pain visible on Joey's face, plead, "Please, I just need to know."

"I should have never agreed to let you attend our parties," Dylan suddenly became protective. "I don't want you to become involved with Jonathan. You can't see him anymore."

"Why damn it! Why are you so adamant? Is it because he has AIDS? You don't think I know how to protect myself? Why?" Joey fumed, standing and stepping away from his brother. "Who the hell do you think you are? I'm an adult. You shall not control me!"

"You need to trust me!" Dylan shouted back indignantly of his Right.

"Trust You?" Joey cried back, vexed at the mere thought. He chortled mockingly, "Trust You? My God, there are people getting murdered by what looks like, and I can't even believe I'm saying this, vampires. It suddenly crosses my mind that Jonathan has blood on his lips, that I'm sure doesn't belong to him." He stopped his rampage. "Am I going crazy brother? I'm so lonely and volatile right now."

"Is everything alright?, Vaughn Muller asked on the other side of the closed bedroom door.

"Yes, yes," Dylan replied annoyed. "We're fine. Please leave us."

"It is getting late," Muller ingeniously attempted to give Dylan an out. Knowing well of the no win dilemma Dylan was finding himself. For the sake of the anonymity of the Code, he also was prepared to end their brotherly conversation. "Will you allow me to show your brother the improvements to the Gardens?"

"Can you give us a few more minutes," Dylan conceded. "I am anxious for my brother to see the Gardens."

"I'm afraid I can't do that Mr. Sanders," Muller charged. Calling him by his last name was his way of putting Dylan on notice there might be consequences. "There's just enough moon light."

"I'm sorry brother, I have no choice."

Joey nodded taking note of Dylan's apparent fear in his eyes. Perhaps it's better that he didn't know anything anyway. "I can't wait to see what you've done with my Mother's Garden Mr. Muller."

Muller opened the door, "Shall we go then? I'm sure your Mother would be very pleased." As Joey approached the doorway, Muller shot Dylan a disdainful glare.

"I didn't get to explain to him about the changes in the Garden yet," Dylan replied, staring at Muller with the same contempt. The Garden was a rehearsed metaphor used by the house guests to clandestinely refer to the Code.

"Wonderful," Muller sarcastically approved, "Not all the flowers are in bloom, yet."

Pearl's Restaurant earlier the same night

"Ricky!", Carol protested to the prep cook behind the counter. "Ticket seven says no cheese."

"Watch me," the older chef said exasperated with her incessant complaining. "You lift the bun and you remove the cheese. Do you think your precocious little fingers can manage? Good God, kids these days."

Carol's brow wrinkled inward in disgust, "I'm not touching other people's food Ricky." She rolled her eyes. He tossed her a pair of tongs onto the high food holding counter which then bounced off the heat lamps onto the lower table next to her. "Really Ricky." She dismissed him, picked up the tongs and removed the top bun and tossed the slice of cheese into the trash.

"He should retire, the old buzzard," Thomas snickered as he stocked clean glasses in the drawer of the side-station. "How did your date with Fabien go?"

"Amazing," she replied with a fulfilled smile.

"Is he big?" Thomas indulged inappropriately.

"Thomas!," Carol scorned insincerely. She grinned, "Oh yea!"

"I need details," Thomas kept prodding.

"Why am I having this conversation with a sixteen-year old?"

"Seventeen next month."

"Still," Carol shook her head, "Thomas can you take this to table eleven?" Carol handed him a catsup bottle.

"So, do you think Fabien would give you that Dylan guy's phone number?" Thomas stood anxiously waiting for an up or down answer.

"Table eleven!" Carol reiterated in her best protective parental tone.

"I'm going to be a senior! Everyone treats me like a child," Thomas protested.

"Hmmm," Carol pointed her index finger to her forehead. "Maybe that's because legally you are still considered a child."

"I'm not a virgin you know," Thomas continued to debate the matter.

"I don't care," Carol pointed toward table eleven. "Table Eleven, catsup, now!"

"I hate you," Thomas stated disingenuously.

"They're roommates," Carol acquiesced. Thomas smiled and took the catsup to table eleven.

April 28, 1942
University of Warsaw

Jadwiga Dzido sat in the second chair on the third row of the lecture hall next to her best friend, cohort, and aspiring pharmacist as well, Eina Weyssenhoff. Eina and Jadwiga, bonded because of the many coincidences that they shared. Pharma major wasn't the only interests they had in common. They discovered they were both avid cooks, passionate readers, both turned horny campus boy's heads, and both were members of the Union of Armed Struggle Resistance Fighters. Jadwiga had convinced Eina to join the fight against the Nazis.

"Note textbook references to today's lecture on the upper right-hand corner of the board class," stated the guest lecturer from Copenhagen, Denmark. "My name is Niels Bohr, I've been invited to speak on fundamental solutions of linear hyperbolic partial differential equations."

"I fail to see the relevance," Eina whispered to Jadwiga.

"I'm starving," Jadwiga mouthed her complaint.

Doctor Bohr took note of their inattention from the corner of his eye. "I'm proud to say that I was a friend of the greatest Polish physicist of our time, Doctor Myron Mathisson, the father of L.H.P.D.."

"Campus Bakery?" Eina continued under her breath staring clandestinely toward the lecturer.

Jadwiga nodded.

Doctor Bohr paused, turned to face Eina and Jadwiga. "Young Lady, row three chair one, what is your name?"

"Eina Weyssenhoff," Eina replied with a smirk.

"And your classmate sitting next to you?"

"Jadwiga Dzido," Eina answered, still with a disrespectful smirk.

"Well Ms. Weyssenhoff," the lecturer stated matter of fact, "I apologize if I'm wasting You and Ms. Dzido's time today and that you both deem it unnecessary to understand how L.H.P.D. is an important topic in today's medical research."

"I'm sure it's important," Eina replied embarrassed at the unwelcomed attention of the other forty-six students.

"May I continue without further distraction then MS. Weyssenhoff?" the Doctor inquired, stroking his chin between his thumb and index finger.

"Please," Eina replied feebly.

"Great!" the Doctor stated with mocking enthusiasm. "I take it everyone has initialed the attendance log?" He held it high for them to see. "If not, see me after class." He put the sheet of paper on top of the podium. "Please note the first posted reference in your text book, autobiography of author." He paused for the commotion of students thumbing through pages to get to the mentioned page. "Doctor Mathison's theories added several terms to the nomenclature of medicine as we know it today. He was my friend, and I, along with many other known scientists, mourn his sudden loss last year. But the benefits of his discoveries have set a foundation for many of you attending today's lecture, whom are studying bio-engineering."

"I don't know what bio-engineering has to do with being a pharmacist," Eina whispered loud enough for Jadwiga to hear.

Doctor Bohr paused and looked toward the door to the lecturer hall. He did not wish to be competition to the thumping footsteps approaching in the hallway that was distracting his student's attention. A brief silence, then a hard knock on the door. Doctor Bohr nodded at his student aid sitting in the front row to investigate. The Aid walked briskly to the door and cracked it open just enough to expose his face.

"You're interrupting an important lecture. Can it wait?" the intern asked with authority and disdain for the Nazi brigade awaiting in the hallway.

The Schutzstaffel SS guardsman held his indictment up to the young intern's face. "We're here on official business of the Reichsfuhrer."

the Polish student grimaced. "It can't wait?"

"I would advise you to move out of the way boy or be arrested for obstruction of official government business," the guard barked. His stern countenance wrinkled on his middle age oval face, shrouded with unshaven stubble. The Intern moved out of the doorway as the gang of SS Troopers stormed into the lecturer hall. "Jadwiga Dzido," the burly guard announced. "You are charged today with high treason. Turn yourself in now." He pulled a picture of Jadwiga from his pocket, studied it, then inspected the faces of the students.

Jadwiga's adrenalin was racing through her veins. She slouched in her chair and looked down at her lap, hoping not to be recognized. But instead it drew attention to her.

"You!" the SS guard pointed at Jadwiga. "Stand and identify yourself!" He suspended her picture in the air adjacent to where she slowly stood, chin still touching her chest. "I said identify yourself!" She refused to speak. He motioned for two SS guardsmen to follow him. Jadwiga slowly scanned the hall for an escape route. But he was on to her intent, "You run and I will have you shot."

"Eina!" Jadwiga cried grabbing hold of her. Eina stroked her hair.

"What is her crime?" Eina demanded. "She has done nothing wrong!"

The Nazi commander grabbed Jadwiga's hands and pried them from Eina. "She is a National Spy and therefore faces charges of high treason." He pulled Jadwiga's arms behind her and handcuffed her wrists together.

"Eina, please take care of my puppy," Jadwiga knew there was a very high risk of her not returning to her studies. "Eina, please."

"Yes, yes," Eina watched as they dragged her out of the lecturer hall. "They've made a mistake Jadwiga. I will obtain an attorney for you. I promise," She cried out loud as Jadwiga disappeared out the door.

May 6, 1986
Pearl's Restaurant

Thomas's shift didn't end until one a.m.. He had been raised by his grandfather and had very little recollection of his alcoholic mother, whom ran off with a stranger when he was six. His grandmother died of cancer the following year. His grandfather continued to smoke despite knowing the cancer sticks claimed his beloved Martha. The "Captain" was a nickname that he was known by his co-workers at the Mint. He was named after the famous Modoc Indian Chief Captain Jack. Thomas referred to him as simply Jack. Jack's face was chiseled from the sun. He never went outside without his black stocking cap and cigarettes. His long nose and fingers were callused and weather-beaten. Jack attended all of Thomas's little league football games. He quietly stood at either end of the field as he hated crowds and avoided conversation. But Jack loved to show off his green 52 Chevy Model 3100. The California Department of Transportation had threatened to take away his license due to his failing eye sight. He still kept his bi-focal specs in his front pocket instead of on his face as his license required. Thomas was Jack's pride and joy. But Thomas kept his homosexuality a secret from Jack, afraid it would kill him.

"Carol, you shouldn't walk home this late at night," Thomas said concerned for her safety. "If you can wait an hour, Jack will give you a ride."

Carol slipped into her knitted sweater, "You are so sweet Thomas, but I'll be fine. Besides I need my sleep. I have a calculus class at seven in the morning."

"For once this kid makes sense Carol," Chef Ricky, normally her nemesis, exclaimed from behind the service window. "You're playing Russian Roulette with the creatures of the night."

"You underestimate my girl power Ricky," Carol winked at him and exited through the back door.

"Stupid kids," Chef Ricky chagrinned.

She couldn't afford a car on her college budget. Carol's parents were middle class wage earners themselves. Her father worked a part time job and set up a bank account just for her college. Every dollar went toward tuition. Her paychecks from Pearl's covered her rent and board and left her little for entertainment which took a back seat to her studies.

The thunder of throttling motorcycles startled her. She glanced behind her to see three Harley Choppers, all with ape hangers, pull away from the curb. Two riders in full leathers, and one bald red bearded and bare-chested rider wearing only a leather vest. One thing Carol was convinced, they had her in their sights. Their faces full of anger and malevolent intent. They discovered her routine orbit from work to home, and had been waiting like vultures for her to leave work. Carol was their chip in a plot to get revenge for the murder of two of their fellow peckerwood gang members. The peckerwood subculture had mixed with the white supremacist skinhead gangs. The origin of the peckerwood gang started in, not surprising, San Quentin State Prison 300 miles northwest of Kern County.

She decided to change her routine and turned down Washington Street instead of Clay. Carol quickened her pace. Looking back over her shoulder, adrenalin pumping hard through her veins. She could hear the choppers getting close to the corner. Washington, as was most of San Francisco streets, was a steep uphill climb. A solid wall of four-story brick apartments and homes with girded entrances. Adjacent to each resident, locked single car garages that looked like prison walls. Her defense mechanisms began to kick in. If they approached her she could scream and someone would hear her. It was just after midnight and there were no signs of life on this Nob Hill residential street. She began to tremble, but not from the chilly night air. "Oh God," she cried between deep breaths.

The choppers did what she prayed they wouldn't. They turned onto Washington. Side by side, they took up the entire street and reduced their speed to a crawl. Red Beard was flanked by the other two peckerwood white supremacists.

Tears swelled in Carol's eyes. She knew this wasn't going to end well for her. She began to run, not looking back. An engine roar and a flash of black leather streaked past her and stopped about fifty feet in front of her. Her assailant unmounted his iron horse and began to run toward her. She stopped, turned only to see the other two gangsters running at her from the other direction. She was trapped mid-block.

It was time to scream. The air escaped her lungs but was met by a black leather glove which firmly cupped her mouth and nose with such pressure she believed her jaw had been broken. Nothing came out. She couldn't breathe. Her arms trapped to her side by the behemoth's arm which pinned her against him. Panic consumed her every pore. Eyes wide as fear could force them. She recognized her attacker as the long frizzy red bearded character that attacked Thomas at Pearl's last week.

"This is for Donald," Carol was fully conscious only until the succor punch to her face. Everything went black.

An hour later
Pearl's Diner

Thomas tossed his backpack from his shoulder to the front seat as he climbed into the passenger side of Jack's truck. "Hi."

"Do you have homework?" Jack inquired. He was not happy with Thomas electing the late shift during school months. He backed the truck out of the parking berth in the employee-parking lot in the rear of the restaurant.

"Yea, but it's not due till Friday." Thomas answered. "I'm off tomorrow. Piece of cake."

"You're going to have to quit this job if your grades go down this semester."

As Jack was about to pull away, Thomas spied what looked like two feet protruding out of the large green dumpster in the back corner of the lot. "Grandpa, pull over!" Thomas shouted for Jack to stop.

Jack trusted his grandson unequivocally and hit the brakes on the old truck. "What is it Son?"

"Pull over, hurry!" Thomas anxiously bounced on the truck seat and grabbed the door handle and opened it before the truck came to a stop. "The dumpster grandpa!" he exclaimed terrified.

Jack could see what looked like small feet with silver painted toe nails hanging over the end of the dumpster. "Thomas, let the police handle this!" Jack cried out for his grandson to stop.

"Grandpa, bang on the door and tell Ricky to call the cops!" Thomas hollered back. "Tell him to call an ambulance too."

The dumpster came mid chest to Thomas. But what he saw next tattooed a grotesque picture in his mind that will have an indelible effect on him for life. Carol's beaten, cut, and naked body tossed like a sack of potatoes on top of the pile of garbage. She was left for dead. "No! no! no!" he screamed, pulling himself up and climbing into the dumpster. His weight pulled him further down into the trash as he attempted to roll Carol over face up. Her face swollen, hardly recognizable. Carol's vagina was covered in coagulated blood from being repeatedly raped. "Help me!" Thomas screamed holding Carol's blooding body close to his.

Jack arrived at the dumpster, "Rick is calling 911 Son. Help is on the way. Can you help me get her out of there?"

"Yes! Yes!" Thomas gathered his emotions and lifted her over the front of the dumpster into his grandfather's arms. Jack laid Carol on the pavement. He took off his shirt and wrapped it around her waist. He then gathered his jacket into a roll, lifted her head and rested her head on it. "Son, give me your shirt!" Thomas unbuttoned his shirt and handed it to Jack. He covered her breasts. He placed his face over Carol's mouth and nose to feel her breath on his cheek and to watch to see if her chest would rise. "She's still alive. Her breathing is shallow. Hang in-there little girl," Jack said shaking his head despondently.

The back door of the restaurant flung open and Ricky came charging out. "Help is on the way," he shouted out. "I'm going out front to direct them back here."

"OK," Jack said waiving him off. Sirens could be heard from a distance growing louder.

"Why didn't you listen to me, why?" Thomas wept profusely.

Early morning hours following day
Sutter/CPMC Cathedral Hill Hospital

The Hospital elevator doors of the fourth floor slowly opened. Seven piercing sets of hollow eyes full of the fury of angry men appeared. Like crusaders marching into battle they emerged from the elevator car. The long trench-coats, which draped around their lean statures, swayed about their feet. Crisp shimmering silk shirts helped define their broad-shoulders and pecs. All seven men wore black leather ankle boots that clacked in unison with each stride. Their entrance into the hallway of the Intensive Care Unit, turned every head, including the nurses and doctors.

"I hope this Hospital has security," Jack said to his grandson, sitting on a bench outside of Carol's room.

"Dylan!" Thomas exclaimed in a low voice, standing and waiving to one of the lead men. "She's in here."

Jack also stood, "You know these guys?"

"The Albino looking guy in front is Fabien, Carol's boyfriend."

Jack relaxed his posture, "The doctor was firm. She can have no visitors."

"They're the good guys grandpa," Thomas reassured him.

Fabien recognized Thomas and quickened his pace toward him. "Thomas, how is she?"

"Not good Fabien," Thomas declared painfully. The other six Hospice clan caught up to them. "She's in a coma. They beat her up really bad."

Fabien's chin dropped to his chest as he fought back tears. "Who did this?"

Thomas paused and looked around for signs of law enforcement. "This may help." He pulled a blood-stained note from the front pocket of his jeans and handed it to Fabien. "I found this shoved in her mouth."

"Thomas, why didn't you give that to the police?" Jack admonished.

Fabien unfolded the note and read the elementary hand writing. "Fag lovers, Eye for an eye, tooth for a tooth. White power." He took a deep breath and handed the note back to Dylan to read.

"I think it would be wise to turn that note over to the police," Jack insisted.

"Are you Thomas's Father?" Dylan approached Jack.

"His grandfather."

"You're right, would you mind," Dylan reached out his hand with the note for Jack to take.

Jack hesitated, nodded affirmatively, and retrieved the note. "I'll see they get it."

"I'd like to see her," Fabien demanded.

"You can't. Carol's in isolation at Doctor's directive," Thomas informed him. "But at that second window you can get a glimpse of her through a gap in the curtains."

"Show me," Fabien requested.

"Sure, follow me."

The group of supporters followed Thomas to the second window looking in on Carol's room. "There's not much of her to see," Thomas depicted. "She's pretty much bandaged head to toe. The attending nurse said that she is lucky to be alive. If grandpa and I," he paused, choked up and unable to continue. Dylan pulled him close to console him.

Fabien turned to Jack, "Sank you, sank you. You save her life."

Jack shot Fabien a reassuring smile. "She's not out of the woods yet young man. But I will tell you she's a fighter."

Fabien nodded and turned back to the window. "Why her face bandaged?"

Jack continued to answer his questions. "They broke her jaw. The doctor had to wire it shut. They also broke her right arm and she has several shallow surface wounds, the detective told me they most likely tortured her while raping her. The obstetrician was here about an hour ago to see how much damage they did down there."

"Bastards!" Fabien muttered under his breath.

Jack could see the anger racing through Fabien's veins. "Best leave this up to the Cops Son." Fabien took note of Jack's hand on his shoulder. "These skinhead gangs are violent freaks."

"I've seen enough," Dylan said straight faced. "Did you wish to stay?" He looked at Fabien for an answer.

"Zhere's no need," he replied and glanced up at Jack. "I'll come early in the morning. Sanks again." Fabien turned to the other Hospice tenants, "I very hungry now. No?"

"Starving," Dylan said with a vengeful grin.

"I'm going with you," Thomas declared. He knew they were scheming to even the score.

"I don't think you should go Thomas," Jack was adamant. "You have homework and chores to do." Jack knew that Thomas could get seriously hurt if he participated in whatever these young men were conniving. "And you've been up all night. You can't miss anymore school."

"Grandpa, I'll be all right," he assured Jack. "Besides, they're just going out for breakfast."

Dylan was growing very fond of Thomas and by the lascivious looks they had exchanged, it was mutual. "We'll get him back safe and early so he can get his chores done. I promise you."

"I agree with grandpa," Jonathan challenged Dylan's libido. "I think we should have a meeting at the house before we go to breakfast." He glared at Dylan with slight contempt.

Dylan walked over to the nurses' desk and helped himself to the note pad behind the counter. The nurse behind the desk raised her brow in objection. She rolled her eyes as he searched for a pen. Reaching in her drawer she located a pen for him. "Please, would have got you there sooner."

Dylan tore off a sheet from the pad and jotted down his phone number. He walked away from the desk without acknowledging the nurse. "Here's my number Thomas," he folded the small sheet of paper up and placed it in Thomas's palm. "Call me," he paused, then corrected himself. "Us, if anything changes."

Thomas stared at his palm as if holding a thing of great value. "I will, you can count on it."

Dylan looked back at Jonathan with disdain, "Now let's go have our meeting. Shall we?"

May 7, 1986 –
Johnson's Hardware Store

"Joey, can you put a few hours of overtime in this afternoon?" Freddy asked, taking inventory of the plumbing section.

"Sure," Joey replied from the tools section. "I can't stay too late though."

"Anything you can give me would be appreciated. Mr. Johnson wants inventory completed by Friday."

"Wow that is pushing it," Joey exclaimed, cutting open the boxes of deck screws. "Why did we order so many boxes of deck screws? Do we have a special order?"

"We did," Freddy explained, "But Oliver Construction cancelled their order for the track project at half moon bay. The project is being held up in court by some pissed off conservationists. Mr. Johnson wants to keep the order just in case they win. He believes Oliver will win it."

"Crap!" Joey chagrined. He spied Detective Stone entering the Hardware Store. "What does he want now?"

"Do you want me to lose him?" Freddy said, snapping his fingers as if he had magical powers.

"No," Joey replied, "I'm going to have to answer his questions sooner or later. Might as well get this over with."

"You're not in any trouble are you?" Freddy asked sincerely.

"I don't know," Joey's demeanor exhibited fear.

Detective Stone caught Joey in his peripheral, "Awe there you are." Stone changed directions toward the tools section. "I figured you might be at work. We'd like you to come down to the Station to answer some questions."

"I'm on the clock detective."

"I understand," Detective Stone acknowledged nodding. "Where's your manager?"

"I'm right here," Freddy replied stone faced. "This matter can't wait?"

Detective Stone held up his badge, "Official police business. I'm afraid not. This should only take about an hour."

"I guess we don't have a choice, do we?" Freddy stated rolling his eyes.

"I guess not," Stone raised his brow sarcastically.

"Do I need an attorney Detective Stone?"

"You're not under arrest," Stone shrugged.

"Let's just get it over with," Joey resigned. "Lead the way." Joey followed Detective Stone to his car which was parked in the loading zone in front of the Hardware Store.

Tenderloin Precinct Interrogation Room

Joey sat in the corner with a small desk between himself and Detective Stone. The room was rather small and had a weak scent of bleach. Aside from the desk, the only other furniture were five folding chairs, three of which we leaning against the wall.

"Joey this is detective Roberts," Stone introduced the forensic psychologist. "He's with Forensics. Forensic psychologist, Best in his field.

"You think I need a shrink?" Joey groused. "Please."

"He may be of some help. Don't be closed minded."

"Let's get on with it," Joey replied shaking his head somewhat appalled.

"OK, let's do," Stone continued. "In your police report, you stated that there was a short encounter between you and the victims. Can you elaborate a little more by what you meant by encounter? What was said, or did it at any time get physical?"

"Like I previously told you Detective, I just felt uncomfortable waiting in the shelter with them. They were giving me some pretty loathing stares. I felt if I stayed it might get ugly. As I was leaving, the female called me a "fag". Joey paused and glanced up at both men. "And that's it. I made my way down to Market Street. That's the last I saw them until they were discovered by the three-people mentioned in my report."

"Just to be clear, the female victim was still barely hanging onto her life. Is that correct?"

"That's correct," Joey answered Detective Stone.

Stone relaxed back into his chair as Detective Roberts leaned toward Joey to give his assessment. "Odd, don't you think that you were at the Market Street Shelter, and, well, let me read from your statement. "I had been waiting about five to ten minutes for the bus, when I heard a scream from a young woman. I turned to see three people looking down an alley." There's still a whole bunch of missing time." Roberts leaned in toward Joey approximately a foot between their noses. "Ten, even five minutes, is a long time to bleed out and still be alive. But during that time you didn't hear a commotion, scream, nothing. If I have to be honest, here's what I believed happened." Detective Roberts grinned facetiously, "You had enough. Let's just admit everyone has a snapping point. I can't imagine how many times in your life you get called a queer, fag, homo. It's gotta weigh on your nerves. Am I right?"

"You have no idea detective," Joey stoically stared into Detective Robert's eyes, not blinking or showing panic. He felt betrayed that Stone didn't stop Roberts.

"Give me a chance here. Then you notice them following you. You're scared. You look around and find a two-prong kitchen fork."

"A what?" Joey protested

"Stay with me," Roberts drilled. "You hid in the enclave next to where the victims were found. Then you seized your opportunity, snuck up behind them and stabbed them in the neck. Am I pretty close to the truth Joey?"

"You haven't even got off home base dude," Joey protested. "I am not a murderer Detective." Joey looked over at Stone with contempt, "I think I need a lawyer."

"Weighing these cases Joey, it's my job to seek out persons of interest. You had an adverse interaction with the victims. You were near the scene of the crime and you have motive. If you confess, we'll work a deal with the District Attorney's office and get the charges lowered to manslaughter under duress. By chance you wouldn't know any albinos?"

"I'm done Detective," Joey stated adamantly. "No more questions without my attorney present."

"As you wish kid", Stone shrugged. He leaned in toward Joey with grave intent, "I wouldn't leave town if I were you. This matter is before the grand jury. I would strongly advise you to get an attorney."

"I need to get back to work," Joey insisted and stood up ready to leave.

"I can take you back," Stone offered.

"No thanks," Joey shot Stone a cold contemptuous glare. "I don't accept rides from strangers, let alone my enemies."

"Suit yourself," Stone said with raised brow of indifference.

May 19, 1941
Auschwitz-Birkenau German Concentration Camp

Feeling weak from near starvation, Jadwiga Dzido was most thankful that she didn't have to join the other prisoners for roll call, which could take up to two hours. Many of the prisoners who collapsed from fatigue or fainted during roll call, were rushed away by Commandant Hoss's SS guards, and never seen again. What she was less thankful for was knowing there was a reason she was told to remain in her block, block 10. She was shivering uncontrollably, her vagina painfully on fire from the incessant rapes.

The blocks were not heated and unsanitary conditions caused many to fall ill with fevers. However, no one dare complain to the Nazis, as doing so meant your immediate demise. No one ever lived to tell of the medical treatments they received to get well. Healthcare just didn't exist.

Jadwiga lay on her hard-wooden bed. She heard small clatter of feet about her head. She opened her eyes to see a four-pound rat staring at her from the edge of her bed. Rats carried a multitude of deadly diseases. The rat was hoping that she was dead meat. With all the adrenalin left in her, Jadwiga swiftly grasped the wool cap off her head with her right hand. She slept on her side and used her right arm for a pillow. Swatting at the Rat, she captured it inside her cap. Trying to escape the Rat got Its head stuck in the wool knitting. Jadwiga swung her cap violently and relentlessly against the wood post of her bed until the Rat ceased squealing. She could feel her heart beating fast and hard in her chest. She tossed her bloody hat in the trash bin near the entrance to her block.

Jadwiga was now afraid to close her eyes. "You!" demanded an SS guard appearing at the door to her block. "Stand." She swung her legs off of the bed and sat at the edge of it. "Come on, quickly!" he barked directives at her. She was near giving up. She stood staring at the floor thinking her life was about to end. "Major General Hoss will see you now. Move faster." The square faced, slim youth, seemed to enjoy his new authority and grew impatient with her. She considered jumping this little creep and filching his rifle. But she was too weak to succumb him in what would normally be a simple feat, right out of her combat training.

Losing patience with her, he rushed to her and grasped her arm. She decided it would be in her best interest not to resist. She struggled to match his pace.

"Why are we going to the infirmary?" Jadwiga muttered timidly. "The officer's quarters are the other way."

"Shut up!" he barked.

He marched her past the infirmary entrance and to a garage Just behind it. Parked in the garage were a Hearse and an ambulance. How ironic that neither had never been used with so many people dying. He stopped her and turned her back to a post supporting the I-beam above it.

"Take off your clothes!"

"Why?", Jadwiga objected.

"Do it now!"

She stepped out of her striped prison pants and lifted her shirt above her head and let it drop to the cement floor. "Please, show some decency," she begged.

"Shut up!" He stepped behind her naked body grabbing both her wrists and tying them behind the post. She felt a similar bristly rope about her ankles. He pulled the rope tight. For a moment, she lost her balance and began to lean forward. The sharp pain from the tight fetters pinched at her wrists and ankles. Anxiety raced through her veins as he covered her eyes with a handkerchief he pulled from his pocket. The world was black and she could no longer rely on her sense of sight. "I will be back."

Minutes seemed like hours. Jadwiga was becoming numb to the pain. It was so cold.

She heard footsteps enter into the garage. She listened keenly, attempting to calculate how many. "Gag her," a male voice ordered in a strange casual way as if it was a common daily activity.

Footsteps to the side and behind her. "Open your mouth wide." She refused. "Don't make this difficult." Jadwiga resisted steadfastly. Fingers pinched her nose tight. She couldn't breath and gasped for air. At that moment, a rope was thrust into her mouth and tightened behind her head, followed by an oily rag. She coughed incessantly and believed she would vomit. Her nostrils filled with the stench of petroleum.

There was a moment of complete silence. Her heart pounding in her chest. It was one cold hand on her breast and then two, three. They pinched at her nipples. She lost count of the many hands that roamed her naked body. Fingers entering every orifice. Men's penises grinded against her. One by one they mounted her. Tearing at her already wounded vagina. Jadwiga screamed with each thrust. Puffs of air muffled under the oily gag.

"Take her down and hand her over to Doctor Mengele. This interrogation is over," Major General Rudolf Hoss said with an ingeniousness grin. His denigration was followed by short laughter from the other men.

Both guards had pulled Jadwiga's arms around their shoulder to support her near lifeless body. They walked out of the garage transporting Jadwiga between them. Her feet, dragging behind her, had left a trail of evidence that had no forensic justice.

The Medical Lab holding room was an improvement from her old block 10. There were benches and a toilet in the corner of the room.

Shivering profusely, Jadwiga's naked body was coiled in the fetal position on the cold cement floor. Her body fighting to survive the trauma she had just encountered. As she regained her senses, she realized that her thin prison rags had been tossed on the floor next to her.

"Miss, can we help you off the floor?" Jadwiga opened her eyes, still somewhat out of focus. She saw compassionate and piercing blue eyes and wavy blonde hair of a young gentleman crouched over her. Jadwiga understood the French language, but was still struggling with some words. Still living in the moment of her rape, she wanted to scream. Distrust, of the opposite sex, caused her immediate angst. The young men moved out of her space. "We're not going to hurt you. Please let us help you," he implored.

Jadwiga turned her head, eyes searching for the 'we' he referred to. Standing over and behind her was the same man. She believed she was losing it. Was she seeing double?

"This is my twin brother, Fabien," Ludovic's empathetic soft voice reassured her that they were friends not foe. They had draped her prison garments over her to respect her privacy. She motioned with her finger for them to turn away so she could slip back into her prison garments.

Paley screams of torture could be heard from the adjacent lab. There was a gun shot and the screaming ceased. The faces of all three prisoners, waiting their fate, were stricken with fear. Subjugated hope of surviving, vanquished by the new silence.

May 7, 1986
The Hospice - Temptation

Thomas and Dylan climbed out of the black sedan. Dylan had asked Jonathan to let him out by the front gate. Thomas felt a connection to Dylan and was confident it was mutual. Thomas was apprehensive of Jonathan's disdain for him and wasn't comfortable remaining in the Sedan. He felt like a wort on a prince's forehead from the condescending glances from the others in the car. He was just as sincere about getting revenge and settling the score. But there was the other thing. The butterflies in his stomach when Dylan's eyes scanned lasciviously over his body at the hospital. Thomas kept quiet during the ride as not to rile more objections to his tagging along. He kept berating himself for lusting after Dylan when his friend was near death at the hospital. Was he a risk as Jonathan had mentioned? Why? He wanted to look and dress like them, be as crazy strong. What possible reason did they conceal that he was unworthy?

"This is where you live?" Thomas asked with nervous excitement climbing the steps to the front entry.

"This be the place," Dylan replied fumbling with his key ring for the house key.

Thomas took note of the Saint Vincent Hospice sign still shrouded in tall weeds. "Is this a hospice for AIDS victims? Thomas become apprehensive that he might now understand the risk that Jonathan was so concerned with. He couldn't help wonder whether Dylan is concealing the fact that he has AIDS.

"Use to be," Dylan replied mendaciously. His conscious was playing the guilt fiddle in his mind. It kept playing Joey's admonishment to be thoroughly honest about the fact he had AIDS. Had Doctor Chang's Steroid cocktail and several blood-lettings cured him? He meant to get tested but Doctor Chang had warned that tipping off the healthcare industry would have catastrophic consequences.

A male operatic voice was belting out the song Ave Maria from inside the Hospice. "Do me a favor," Dylan asked of him.

"Sure."

"Stay in the sitting room until I come and get you," Dylan glanced back with an unyielding straight face.

Thomas felt a nervous stomach flare up his throat, "Sure. Will you be long?"

"No." Dylan held the door for Thomas to enter. His first impression of the house decor was that of an ancient regal palace. The wallpaper and furniture were from the Victorian era. Muller was sitting on the sofa reading the San Francisco Chronicle. He peered over the paper with a censured glare at the young arriviste. "What an unexpected surprise Dylan," his voice gave a hint of his disapproval of Dylan's infelicitous guest. "Welcome young man. You sure are a handsome boy."

"I assure you I'm not a boy," Thomas excoriated Muller, "But thank you for the kind words.

Muller stood and held out his hand for Thomas to shake. "My name is Vaughn, Vaughn Muller. I like your confidence."

"Thomas, Dylan's friend."

Dylan wasted no time with small talk. "We need to retreat to the library."

"Where's the others?" Muller demanded in an angular manner.

"Parking the car."

"Have a seat Thomas." Dylan requested as rehearsed. "I'll be back to get you shortly."

Thomas was not sure whether the ornate elephant king armchair was for show only and decided to walk past it for the floral pattern, less expensive Carolina Rustica arm chair. "It must be fifty degrees in here," he complained.

"Here," Dylan tossed Thomas the Yousa throw, with the Union flag print that was tossed over the elephant king armchair. "Sorry, we like it cold."

"I hadn't noticed," he replied sarcastically.

Dylan paused at the arched entrance to the sitting room and grinned. "Of course, you're speaking of the temperature of the house, right?"

Dylan's eyes pointed to Vaughn, whose hospitality toward Thomas was a little on the cold side.

"Of course," Thomas smiled licking his bottom lip as a sign he wanted him to hurry.

Books, neatly shelfed and categorized alphabetically by author, filled three walls floor to ceiling. The library also served as an office where Creed business was conducted. Wingback chairs, some with end tables, lined the walls facing the mahogany desk below the large picturesque window. Dylan never liked to sit and stood near the doorway. Jonathan was the next to enter and took a chair next to Dylan. Muller greeted them in his tweed suit, minus the tie, and a rolled-up map in his hand. He took his usual chair closest to the desk. The big chair behind the desk was always reserved for Doctor Chang. The twins followed next in freshly laundered silk shirts. Giuseppe Ricci, shirtless with blue suspenders, that held up his blue jeans, entered next, holding a bottle of beer in one hand.

"I have great news," Doctor Chang announced as he passed through the door and straight to his reserved chair behind the desk. "I received a phone call from Istanbul just a few minutes ago, and Heinz and Estella have decided to join us here in the States."

"I'm the new kid," Jonathan said, not sharing in the elation. "Who are these people?"

"Sorry, we often forget," Vaughn Muller apologized. "Heinz Alt was a great Jewish composer who met his wife, Estella Agsteribbe, a member of the 1928 Summer Olympics Dutch gold medal gymnastics team, at Auschwitz. Estella's husband was also Jewish, the Nazis murdered him and their young son. She was twelve years Heinz's senior."

"They became inseparable," Giuseppe chimed in.

"He finished her sentences," Muller continued.

"They're presumed murdered by the Nazis, their choice," Doctor Chang sighed and shook his head. "Dylan, I need you and Jonathan to secure a room for them. I believe that we can use room fourteen. Fourteen is conveniently next to the second-floor showers and wouldn't be a huge project to connect to the plumbing. Convert fifteen into a bathroom and large closet please."

"I'll call the contractors tomorrow," Dylan nodded at Jonathan who nodded in agreement.

"Do we have an arrival date?" Jonathan asked, knowing if left up to Dylan he would procrastinate until the last day.

"May tenth," Chang answered quickly.

"We have a few days," Jonathan reacted and began to massage his own neck. His ineffectual relief for whenever he became nervous.

Doctor Chang unfolded the map and laid it on the desk before him. "Let's get to this other matter." He removed his glasses and stroked his forehead as if he had a headache. "Vaughn has been very diligently researching out possible culprits who have motive for torching the Synagogue on Mission Street. He and Ludovic drove by a bar frequented and operated by members of the Peckerwood white supremacists gang, 'The White Owl'. It's a hole in the wall bar and somewhat secluded. It's located in San Mateo on thirty-third avenue near railroad tracks."

"Iz East of za tracks and is hidden between large concree warehouse walls of adjacenz buildings," Ludovic added. "Of course, zay cheap for CCTV surveillance which makes za perfect strike." Ludovic paused momentarily and looked to Doctor Chang for permission to break the other great news to the house. "We believe sis is za gang zat attacked Carol."

Muller broke in, "During our stakeout, we saw Red Beard leave the bar and talk to one of the gangsters who was present during the attack on the gay kids."

"Vhen?" Fabien asserted.

"We need pictures taken," Doctor Chang insisted. "I want this to be clean. There can be no evidence left behind for San Francisco's finest."

"How long will zat be," Fabien protested.

"We'll be ready by this weekend at the latest," Doctor Chang assured him.

Fabien's voice grew louder. He clenched his fist to absorb his frustration. "We need to sake care of business now. zay need to pay for whaz zay did to Carol."

"Do you know why there are more starving Hyenas than Lions in Africa Fabien?"

Fabien looked down at the hardwood floor, not in the mood for one of Doctor Chang's lessons. "Please indulge me."

"Strategy," Doctor Chang continued regardless. "A Hyena will attack the herd, while a Lion patiently waits for the weak ones to fall behind. The Hyena's risk is met by an angry mob of Impalas that gang attack and wound it and often cause it to retreat. The Lion easily traps its prey, and quite frankly does the herd a favor. The steroid cluster can't save you if you take a bullet to the heart. These skinheads are armed and very dangerous." He paused for it to sink in. "So what is it Mr. Dubois?"

"Why up to me? It looks like you have zis all planned out."

"Good," Doctor Chang smiled unsympathetically. "This will be a blood-letting so there can be no survivors and no mess left behind." His voice getting louder at the end to emphasize his disappointment in the media coverage of the latest blood-letting events.

"So, when are we going after them?" Thomas asked impatiently on the edge of his chair.

"You're not, and it won't be today," Dylan replied matter of fact.

"Why?" His heart had been racing on adrenalin.

"Come with me, I want to show you my Mother's garden," Dylan reneged on his promise to involve him.

"But what about Carol's dignity?" Thomas remonstrated.

"Something about a Lion and a Hyena," Dylan amused himself. "You have to trust me. These creeps are going to pay dearly."

Thomas was disappointed, but had no problem believing in Dylan. He had seen his abilities to handle difficult situations up close. "Fine," he relented and looked coquettishly at Dylan. "Now what's this about your Mother's garden?"

As Thomas followed Dylan through the upgraded dining room and into the rear gardens, his libido was charging. Was this his chance to get intimate with Dylan. He was tormented with desire for him. And the feeling was mutual. It was like a maze of shrubbery. So many places to get lost and hide. "My Mother had a green thumb. She passed away, cancer."

"I'm sorry," Thomas consoled.

"It was a bed and breakfast in the beginning. After my Father died, my brother Joey, and I, turned it into an AIDS hospice with my uncle John's help. Doctor Chang then bought it from us. The B&B was well known for the Garden Restaurant my Mother operated. However, Muller has to take credit for much of the restoration. Us Gay folks are born with strong genes for design and gardening, but somehow I missed that gene."

But Thomas was suddenly anxious about something Dylan said. "Are you," he hesitated apprehensive to suggest that Dylan might have the virus.

"Positive?" Dylan completed his question. "No." To go into detail of his healing would tip him to what was sacrosanct and strictly prohibited from public disclosure. "You?"

"Oh no," Thomas abruptly replied. "I haven't even kissed a man. I hope this isn't a game changer, but I'm still a virgin." It didn't matter as Thomas could see that Dylan was excited by the fact and breathing hard. The large bulge in his corduroy pants was evidence.

Dylan led Thomas deep into the gardens to a patio bench tucked in a Japanese like grotto of bonsaied boxwoods, a small fountain behind the bench, and a lantern near the entrance. Thomas went to sit down on the bench, but Dylan grabbed his wrist and pulled him backwards into his space and wrapped his arms around him. He felt a little uncomfortable with being caressed with his back to him. Dylan's hard phallus pressing against his firm butt dissolved him with pleasure and uncontested trust.

"Are you OK with this," Dylan's voice rough, as if it didn't matter whether he consented or not.

"Oh yea," Thomas sighed, chilled with intense erotic pleasure. Dylan's hands went under Thomas's shirt and moved up and over his chiseled stomach, pausing to enjoy Thomas's athletic work outs. He found Thomas's belt and loosened it and unzipped his jeans. His hard, bulging sex, anxious to be free, pushed out and into Dylan's playful hands.

"Nice," Dylan whispered into his ear and kissed the top of his long black silky hair. Thomas's jeans fell to his feet. He immediately stepped out of them. Dylan took notice of his smooth Native brown strapping thighs and calves. The raw unleashed desire to taste his lips, his tongue, and youthful skin crazed Dylan. He turned Thomas like a top and pressed his mouth against his, forcing his mouth open and plunging his tongue deep into his mouth. Thomas didn't fight it and grabbed Dylan's sex, still caged behind the corduroys. Thomas's legs quaked at the thought of his Titanic hard penis penetrating him.

Dylan had underestimated his thirst for blood until he tasted Thomas's mouth. He was losing control, licking his face, kissing him profusely, and sucking on his neck. His masculinity overpowering his feminine empathy aroused him into an insatiable desire to taste him, drink him, have him.

Unexpectedly, Thomas felt the sharp point of Dylan's scissor. "What are you doing?" He attempted to break his firm grasp. "Stop it you're hurting me." Dylan was even more caught up in the moment. He opened his mouth wide, panting hard as sweat drained down his face.

But Thomas benched Dylan's weight and wedged his hands between them, pushing Dylan away with every ounce of energy left in him. "I said stop!" he screamed at him while climbing back into his pants. "What's wrong with you?"

Dylan regained his senses, "I'm so sorry, really," he was still panting trying to catch his breath. "I don't know what got into me." Would he have bitten through Thomas's skin simply to satisfy his urge? He stared at Thomas with shame for what he had nearly attempted. "What have I done?"

"Were you going to kill me?" Thomas, still unforgiving, felt his neck for blood. There was none.

"Look, I'm sorry I didn't realize I was hurting you," Dylan's voice cracking with sincere regret, knowing he wasn't being truthful. He lost control and that would always be the elephant in the room. "I would never kill you."

"Do you have some weird vampire fantasy? Because if you do, I'm afraid I'm not into it." Thomas was still shaking.

"It won't happen again, I promise."

Thomas paused for composure staring at the cement patio floor. "I really like you Dylan." He raised his head from a brief deliberation of what just happened and formed an anguished concerned wrinkle in his brow. "I wanted for you to like me as much. I was so hoping you would be my first." A sharp pain where Dylan's teeth had nearly punctured his neck, caused an immediate reaction. It was tender to the touch. Sure to bruise, he vented, "Shit! How will I explain this?"

Dylan was too embarrassed to speak and simply nodded and held out his hand for Thomas to take.

Thomas hesitated. Dylan kept his hand extended. Thomas cautiously reached for it and held it. Neither wanted to let go. Gently Dylan drew him back to him and pressed his head against his chest and began to weep. "That won't ever happen again I promise you."

"I need to feel safe with you Dylan," Thomas became the adult.

"I know, I know."

Dylan hadn't taken part in a blood-letting for some time and he partly blamed his lack of judgment on his body's craving for a blood-letting.

"I would like to see you again," Thomas gazed into Dylan's gorgeous blue eyes that melted him like butter. "But you scared the hell out of me, and I'm not sure I can trust you." Dylan tilted Thomas's chin upward and softly kissed him. "I'm just too confused to continue right now, but I do want to see you again. Friday night?"

"I'm committed Friday, business," Dylan answered with disappointment. "How about Saturday night?"

"I would really like that." Thomas was gaining his libido back after Dylan's kiss. He would have picked up where they left off, but he still hadn't resolved the unwelcomed fear and apprehension. "I think I should go. I need to process this whole day. You know, Carol's rape and beating and all. I'm just emotionally drained."

"You don't need to apologize," Dylan managed a slight smile. "I'm the one that owes you an apology. I just don't want you to believe that I took advantage of you because you are young. I am really attracted to you and," he hesitated to corroborate the right words. "And I want you. Not just as a one-night stand, but I need to love you, touch you, take care of you, and yes earn back your trust."

Thomas formed an elated smile and kissed Dylan long and hard.

Later that afternoon
Johnson's Hardware Store

He always asked for Joey because he explained things better, and did not suppress his secret crush on him. Retired at age sixty-seven, Joseph Winters, a.k.a. Junior, was on a fixed income and relied on himself to repair and remodel. "I will need channel lock pliers, don't you think?"

"There," Joey pointed to one of the items in his basket that he had located for Junior.

"Perfect," Junior said going down the instructions Joey wrote out for him. "Plumber's putty?"

Joey pointed to the putty. "Now Junior, don't forget to drain the trap."

Junior searched his list. "I don't see it on here."

"I forgot to put it on the list, but it's very important. It's located under the sink usually at the lowest point of where the elbow turns."

"Here let me just add it at the top of the list. Can I borrow your pen?"

"Certainly," Joey smiled, took the pen from his shirt pocket and handed it to Junior.

"You've been extremely helpful young man. To show my appreciation, I would like to have you over for dinner one of these nights when you are free."

It was common for Joey to get hit on by his male customers. The Castro was the gay district and Joey had made quite a name for himself and not solely based on his intellect. He often wondered what plumbing his customers were really interested in. But Junior was the real thing, lonely and starving for conversation. Joey had a lot of respect for him. "I am free tonight."

"Six-thirty?" Junior was elated. "Do you like Salmon?"

"I'll eat anything you cook for me," Joey smiled mannerly. "Take this stuff up to the counter and Alice will ring you up."

Junior tore off a corner of the channel locks package and wrote his address on it and handed it to Joey. "Six-thirty."

Freddy was curious, stocking shelves an aisle over, and moved in on their conversation. "Junior are you flirting with my staff?" He snapped his fingers above his head and gave his usual in character roll of the eyes. "Shame on you. Though I can't say I blame you he is damn cute."

Joey blushed. "Princess, don't you have shelves to stock?"

"Princess? Excuse me, I'm the queen mother."

Junior cackled at Freddy's humor. "I'm going to check out. See you tonight Joey."

"See you tonight Joey?" Freddy gave Joey a curious glance.

"Bye Junior." Joey's skittish fun with Junior and Freddy drained from his face. Overtaken by trepidation. His eyes fixed on the front of the hardware store. "Oh shit. Now what does he want." Junior and Freddy turned to take in what was causing Joey's consternation. "I may have to take a raincheck Junior." Detective Stone, followed by two uniformed police officers entered the hardware store. Stone searched the store and an officious grin spread across his face when he located Joey.

"Are you in any trouble dear boy," Junior looked concerned for Joey.

"I don't know," Joey replied.

"Turn around," Stone demanded standing next to Joey. "Joey Sanders, I have a warrant for your arrest for the murders of Shane Laskowski and Veronica Payne."

"I didn't kill anyone. Based on what evidence!"

"Bastard!" Freddy glared with contempt at Detective Stone. "You've got the wrong man."

"Move out of the way before we charge you with obstruction," Stone barked at Freddy.

One of the uniformed officers grabbed Joey by the arm and pulled it behind his back, followed by the other arm. He then handcuffed Joey.

Detective Stone read Joey his Miranda Rights. "You have the right to remain silent. Anything you say can and will be used against you in a court of law. You have the right to an attorney. If you cannot afford an attorney, one will be provided for you. Do you understand the rights I have just read to you? With these rights in mind, do you wish to speak to me?"

Alice covered her face behind the counter and wept. Junior's mouth was still frozen open from the initial shock. Freddy, like most black men, had experienced unfair and racist treatment by the cops and never flinched the disdain he had for them.

As they marched Joey out of the hardware store, Freddy heckled them. "Stone, you run out of black suspects so you have to pick on the gays now?" Stone swallowed hard, trying to ignore what he wanted to say and remain professional. He knew he didn't have solid evidence enough to convict Joey. But he was not a racist.

"Freddy stop, you wouldn't survive a day in jail," Alice squawked at him.

Freddy migrated to the counter observing out the large store windows as the arresting officer pushed Joey's head into the back seat of the squad car. "Alice, we have to do something."

"Like what?" she replied with tear stained cheeks.

"I don't know," his voice cracking as he cogitated a plan. "I have to inform his brother Dylan."

"You go, I'll close the store," Alice encouraged him. "Does he still live in the AIDS hospice?"

"He does. Thanks Alice." He searched for his coat and found it where he had thrown it earlier in a box under the counter.

May 9, 1986 Coeur D'Alene, Idaho Aryan Nations Gathering – Produce Warehouse

The late spring storm had snowed another two inches in Coeur D'Alene Idaho over-night. Jadwiga Dzido picked up her 1985 Jeep Cj7 Renegade rental car in Spokane, Washington. It would be a two-hour drive to the Motel six in Coeur D'Alene, Idaho. Fortuitously, the storm had subsided, and she had about a three-hour window to beat the next one. The Washington Department of Transportation snow removal trucks were out in force. It was Jadwiga's intent to rent an all-terrain vehicle with four-wheel drive in the event of encountering icy road conditions. But fortuitously, I-90 was well groomed. That is, until she crossed the Idaho border.

The White Supremacists group, the Order, had their routine Rally tomorrow night in Coeur D'Alene. She played over in her mind, during the short two-and-a half hour drive, the events of the last two months. Jadwiga had been tracking the murder case of Liberal talk show host, Alan Berg for two years. Berg was the youngest lawyer to pass the Colorado State Bar at twenty-two years of age, and became a political voice for human rights activists. Being Jew, Berg had spewed anti-fascist propaganda on his National syndicated talk radio show. Jadwiga had befriended Berg and admired his war on fascism.

After escaping Auschwitz, Jade, as she was known by friends, spent several years researching fascism and the organizations that promote Its evil platforms. She produced a hit list of current fascist and related white supremacist movements. Against Doctor Chang's advisement, Jade distributed the list, which became the infamous 'Dzido's List', to members of the Creed. To some, Dzido's list was just that, a retaliatory hit list. To less political members, it was simply a grocery shopping list.

"Tomorrow, I avenge your murder dear Alan," she whispered under her breath. "Damn tailgater!" Jadwiga amplified her voice to match her angst for bad drivers. She could see his bearded face in her rearview mirror and decelerated, hoping he would just pass her.

She was not satisfied with how prematurely the case was investigated and closed by the FBI. Agent, Wayne Manis, had been the lead Agent on the case and for many years all matters related to white Supremacist hate crimes. Manis infiltrated the 'The Order', a white Supremacist group founded by Walter Mathews in Coeur D'Alene, Idaho. Mathews burned to death in a house fire ignited by incendiary flares, the result of a raid by Manis and the FBI. Manis was satisfied with the convictions of Cult members, David Lane and Bruce Pierce, and closed the case.

Jadwiga had intentionally sat next to Gary Yarbrough during the trial, The Order's number two guy. During a break, Jade made it known to him that she was intent on joining the National Alliance. Yarbrough was impressed that she had read the 'Turner Diaries," America's version of Hitler's Mein Kamph. Not only did that get Yarbrough's attention, but he was impressed with her ability to quote the author, William Luther Pierce. Leader of the largest US white supremacist organization, "the National Alliance." Pierce and Mathews were members of the Klu Klux Klan and had a mutual admiration for each other.

After the guilty verdict was read, Yarbrough begged Jade to celebrate with other supremacists in the presidential suite of the Marriot Hotel. His motive was less political and more to get into her pants.

He promised her that Luther Pierce would be there. She pretended that she was ecstatic and couldn't wait to meet him. A doorman, robed in the uniform of the Klu Klux Klan, greeted them and asked to see identification and membership card. Yarbrough pulled out his NA card for the doorman and pointed back at Jadwiga, "She's my guest." She was introduced to other fascist members of the 'Order', Frank Silva, Randy Evans, and David Tate, each holding a Champaign glass ready for Luther to make a toast.

Jadwiga was perplexed by the notion that they were about to toast to one of their own being convicted of a hate crime. But that wasn't the case. They were toasting the one that got away with the murder. She wondered whether the FBI had the right indictments. A small group of about thirty men, and one other female, held their Champaign glasses in the air. Luther stood on a small step ladder so that he could be seen above the small crowd. "I propose a toast to Bruce Pierce and David Lane, two martyrs for the promotion of clean-living white folks everywhere."

"Hear! Hear!" they chanted and took a sip of Champaign. But just a sip because they anticipated more celebrating toasts to be made.

Luther cajoled, "But just until we can break them out." His humor was followed by loud laughter and chatter. "We also drink to the death of that repugnant Jew and Communist Liberal, Alan Berg. How about my legal team? Manslaughter! The Kennedy's only wish they had this caliber of legal talent. They will have them out on good behavior and technicalities in a few short years."

Yarbrough leaned closer to her ear and whispered, "They weren't the only ones there when that son of a bitch was killed. The guy who shot the fatal bullet will be a guest speaker at our next meeting of the Order in Coeur D'Alene. You should try and make it. His name is Paul Coombs." He got closer to her ear. "I like you a lot, but I will hunt you down and poor hot tar all over your body until you are unrecognizable if you tell anyone our secret."

Jade played out in her mind what Yarbrough had revealed to her, she was distracted by her anger and lost track of how fast she was driving. She noted on the Jeep's speedometer that she was speeding at ninety miles per hour. "Shit," she snapped, releasing the gas pedal and allowing the vehicle to regain posted speed, all the while checking her rearview mirror for highway patrol.

"Twenty-three miles to Coeur D'Alene," Jade read as she past the road sign. She had written down directions to the motel on the back of a napkin from the table of a restaurant in Spokane.

It started to snow lightly, but not enough for her to turn on the windshield wipers. Finally, she saw the 'Welcome to Coeur D'Alene' sign and sighed with relief that she had beat the pending storm. Fumbling through papers on the passenger's seat, she located the napkin with directions.

"Right on exit to highway ninety-five. At the exit off Macias Marina Drive, take a left. Drive to end of peninsula to motel." She read the scribbling on the napkin over the steering wheel. As she crossed the Spokane river the sun began to set behind her.

The scraggy older motel clerk doffed his ball cap to her as she entered the office and brushed the snowflakes off her shoulder. "I have a room under Dzido."

Finger scanning his calendar, the amiable clerk found her reservation. "Ms. Jade Dzido?"

"That's me," she replied pulling her knitted gloves off her fingers and stuffing them in her coat pockets. "You should have me down for three nights."

"That's correct. Will that be cash or check?" He looked over his wire rimmed glasses.

"Cash." She pulled her wallet from her pant pocket. "How much again."

"That will be thirty-three dollars." She counted a twenty, a ten, and three ones, and laid them on the counter for the clerk to verify. "Fine, you're in room sixteen. Drive to the end of the parking lot and your room is around the corner." He smiled and shifted his reading glasses further up on his nose. "Here's your key. Enjoy your stay."

"I'm sure I will, thank you."

Jadwiga lifted her luggage from the car to the motel room, trying not to slip and fall on newly accumulated snow. She detected that the luggage seemed heavier. She needed to take her steroids. However, she first needed a blood-letting in order for the steroids to acclimate properly in her body. Paul Coombs was her target. She was convinced that he had changed his name after the murder to further distance himself from the crime. She called the Coeur D' Alene operator who adamantly insisted there was no Paul Coombs living in the County. She was going off a hunch from Yarbrough who referred to him as part of the Coeur D'Alene boys. Tomorrow was their Monthly meeting at the produce warehouse. Her body was telling her she was close to desperate for a blood-letting.

Pausing at the bathroom mirror, Jadwiga ran her fingers through her long black hair. Not a gray streak anywhere. She was enjoying her immortality. "Your mine Coombs," She said aloud with a vaunted grin.

May 8, 1986
San Francisco – Hospice

Freddy pounded relentlessly on the front door of the Hospice. "Please someone answer the door," He vociferated with anxiety. It didn't cross his mind to use the doorbell.

Giuseppe opened the door just enough to show his face. "Yes?" Freddy thought it an odd greeting.

"Hi, I'm Freddy, Joey's friend and co-worker, I need to speak with Dylan. It's very important."

"Can I tell him what it's about?" Giuseppe probed.

"It's very personal. Please it's very important that I speak with him. You can tell him it's about his brother."

Giuseppe nodded, seemingly unconcerned and opened the door and let Freddy in. "Stay here, I'll go get him."

"Thank you."

"Wow what a transformation," Freddy said scanning over the renovations of the Hospice.

After waiting, what seemed like eternity, he confirmed by his watch, that he'd been waiting only a couple of minutes. "Jeeze Louise," he complained aloud.

Dylan appeared from down the hall followed by Jonathan and Vaughn Muller. "Freddy," Dylan seemed excited to see him. "Giuseppe said this is about Joey?"

"Detective Stone just arrested him for the murder of those transient kids."

"What?" Dylan became visibly upset. "Joey is harmless. I need more Freddy. Did Joey ever mention this to you?"

"Stone is hell bent on pleasing the Mayor and getting his man."

Muller interrupted, "Look, why don't we take this into the sitting room and discuss it sitting down." He motioned for them to join him. The four men followed Muller into the sitting room and sat within whispering range.

Freddy's stopped panting and relayed what had been explained to him with normal breathing. "Joey told me that Stone is convinced that he that committed the murders, because of something Joey said in his police report. Joey stated that there had been a verbal confrontation between him and the transients just before the murders, somewhere at a bus stop on Polk Street. Stone believes that is motive enough to arrest him."

"That's crazy shit!" Dylan barked.

"Oh my God," Jonathan's face became white as a ghost. "We need to discuss this in private. Do you mind Freddy? Sorry."

"Why can't Freddy hear what you have to say?" Dylan asked perplexed and unfastening the top button on his red silk shirt.

Jonathan looked at Muller for his support, "I don't think Doctor Chang would approve."

Muller nodded, and turned to Freddy. "No offense Mister... ah," he paused for Freddy to inform him of his last name.

"Garcia," Freddy finished his sentence.

"You're Hispanic?"

"My Father is Hispanic my Mama is Black."

"If you wouldn't mind waiting in the lobby I sure would appreciate it." He stood to escort him. Once Freddy was in the lobby, Muller lifted the hook and keeper latch of the Victorian style wall door and lifted it out with his finger. Pulling the door from inside the wall he closed the room off from the lobby. "Mulatto child," he smiled coquettishly. "So, Jonathan what is your concern that we had to be rude to our guest?"

"Do you recall the night Joey came over to conduct an inspection on the Hospice and ended up staying for one of our parties?"

Dylan squinted, vaguely recalled the evening. "That was the evening that you wanted to screw my brother."

"I didn't get to home base, but I did steal second."

"Let's get back to what happened," Muller castigated.

"It was after midnight and I was concerned that Joey wanted to take the bus. So, Giuseppe, Ludovic, and I, convinced Doctor Chang to do a drive-by just to make sure he was safe.

"You followed him?" Muller gawked at the mussed story.

"We attempted to, but Dylan's brother is swift on his feet and got a good head start. We spotted him at the Polk shelter, where Freddy stated Joey's encounter with the two skinheads. We had planned to approach him, but he immediately left the shelter. There must have been a confrontation, just like he claims. We circled the block, but Joey turned down a side street and we lost him again. We became very concerned when we noticed that the male skinhead and his female side kick were headed the same direction as Joey. The male creep had a tire iron in his hand. We hadn't had a blood-letting in weeks and Doctor Chang agreed that these fascists needed to contribute to the cause."

"This is a huge problem," Muller said suppressing his vexation.

"So how are we going to fix this for Joey," Dylan demanded.

"This is our fault!" Jonathan appealed. "We have to figure out how to get him out of jail. I'm going to turn myself in. It's the right thing to do."

"No!" Dylan insisted. "Joey would be in a body bag had you guys not been there." Dylan's face grew angry. "Christ, this douche-bag had a tire iron! Those bastards had it coming!"

Muller put his hand on Dylan's shoulder to calm him. "We need to find out what his bail is. We can start with that. In the meantime, why don't you give, what's his name?"

"Freddy," Jonathan supplied.

"Freddy, a ride to where he needs to go."

"What about Joey?" Dylan said anxious to get him out of jail. "I don't think he has that kind of money."

"You let Doctor Chang and I worry about that. This involves all of us."

"Thank you," Dylan's tears were tears of gratitude. Vaughn Muller embraced him and kissed his silky dirty-blond head.

"We're all one body. We must support each other if the Creed is going to survive," Muller said, void of emotion.

Strategy

Vaughn Muller stood in front of a blown-up map of a small bird's eye view of the White Owl bar and adjacent buildings on Third Avenue in San Mateo, California. Railroad tracks ran down the middle of the map.

The blood-feeders met regularly in the library for meetings. But today's gathering wasn't the conventional health and wellness check. This was a convocation of strategy on a level that they hadn't dealt with since world war two. It was possible that their way of life could be threatened. Anxiety overtook their appetite for revenge. As Muller went over the plan a second time, it was clear to him, by the fear in their eyes, they were growing apprehensive and not as dauntless.

"Here's the White Owl bar," Muller pointed with his laser pointer. "North. Macias street runs East and West and the railroad tracks run North to Macias. The White Owl is this building on the East side of the tracks. Across the street, Kentucky Fried Chicken. To the West, Century Theater. To the East of the bar is a gas station slash auto shop. But we will be occupying this building just North of the Owl, an abandoned warehouse. The frontage road, between the White Owl and the tracks, is how we access the warehouse. There is a small parking lot to the rear of the Owl and a garage that is actually attached to the warehouse. Even though the parking lot belongs to the warehouse, the Peckerwood gang members park their motorbikes behind it. The executions will take place in the garage. The Bart commuter rail train passes by every thirty-minutes. It's so loud you can't hear your own voice. We will wait for Red Beard and hopefully the two other assailants Carol identified in the pictures of owl patrons leaving the bar." Muller pinned up three pictures of gang members on the map. One, obviously Redbeard. A second picture he attached was that of a clean-shaven man, corpulent and bald. Finally, the third picture of another Peckerwood sporting a knotted goatee which made his face even more pointed. "We pick them off one by one or all together. But there can be no witnesses."

"I thought we were just going to torch the place and get rid of the scum once and for all," Jonathan objected.

"Your anger shadows your better judgment," Doctor Chang chimed in. "Waste not want not." He stood up and walked up to the easel and stood next to Muller. "We need the Innocent to see us as vigilantes, not a militia."

"It wasn't easy taking these pictures," Giuseppe interjected as Chang walked up to the map. "It's not as secluded as we first thought."

"Even at midnight there's a lot of traffic," Doctor Chang added after taking a sip on his dry martini. "Mainly due to crowds leaving the theater." Giuseppe and Ludovic had taken detailed notes and pictures from staking out the Bar for the last two nights.

Doctor Chang took over the meeting. "Three human bodies, although definitely not a gourmet meal, should suffice are feeding needs. And!" his voice raised and pointed to one of pictures, "We know that Red Beard and this peckerwood animal attacked and raped Carol." He pointed to the bald Peckerwood gangster.

"How you know zat!" Fabien agonized. "Zere are no witnesses. Zay all guilty by association!" But Chang, being a hard pragmatist was not affected by his emotional whooping.

"Dylan, bring in our source," Doctor Chang requested flicking the brim of his hat. Dylan motioned to Giuseppe to assist him. The young men disappeared down the hall to the kitchen and into the basement. The muffled cries, from the tied and gagged young fascist, they had worked over, grew louder as they ascended the basement steps.

Too poor to afford a motor bike, the slender freckled face nineteen-year-old, still acclimating his body to alcohol, stopped to vomit behind the theater. Some of the spittle dripped on his leather vest, but he was too inebriated to notice. Fate couldn't have written a better non-fiction character for them to target. The black sedan turned into the truck loading area behind the theater and pulled alongside the staggering youth. Giuseppe rolled down the driver's side window and asked the sick lad if he wanted to get high. Covertly, Dylan had gotten out of the vehicle just prior. With the stealth of a wild cat, approached the fascist from behind and rendered the Peckerwood unconscious with a chloroform drenched rag. "I guess that is a yes," Giuseppe quipped with a grin. Giuseppe got out of the car and opened the rear door as Dylan easily handcuffed his hands and tossed him in the back seat.

Giuseppe's right arm was draped under the juveniles handcuffed arms, wrenched behind the Peckerwood's back, grasping Dylan's shoulder for support. Dylan did likewise with his left arm. The prisoner's feet never touched the floor. Red and bruised, from hard slaps at wrong answers. The Peckerwood lifted his battered face and with his one eye, that wasn't swollen, scanned the library.

"Gentlemen," Dylan said somewhat proud and flamboyant, "Meet Edward." They dropped him on the floor. Unable to block his fall, he landed on his stomach with a hollow thump. Saliva dripping from his mouth, he moaned.

Edward had lost his resilient and resistant attitude from the night before. "Please let me go," he plead for his life, barely able to spit out the words.

Fabien got up slowly from his chair. His face red with contempt. "Do you zink we should show you za same mercy your Peckerwood friends showed Carol? I mean sis only fair, do you zink?"

"Turnabout is fair play," Muller nonchalantly shrugged his shoulders. "I agree."

Fabien placed his boot on the side of Edward's face, pinning it to the floor. In one final plea, he begged, "I told you who did it. What more do you want from me. They'll find out I told you. I'm already a dead man. You said you would let me go if I told you." Sympathetic ewes and awes slipped spuriously from those in the room.

"Well, perhaps we should do you a favor and prevent you from having to face such a horrific gang bang," Doctor Chang said mockingly. That was the cue they all were waiting for. They rose from their chairs and approached their prey lying handcuffed and half naked on the library floor.

Fabien lowered to his knees next to Edward's battered head and brushed back his long hair exposing his ceratoid artery visibly pulsing in his neck.

"Please, what are you doing?" Please! "Edward wept like a traumatized child. But Fabien, a little turned on by the boy's helplessness, firmly placed his hand over Edward's mouth. He attempted to scream with what little adrenalin he could muster. But it was not enough. Fabien's mouth opened wide exposing razor-sharp canines. He bit lightly on the boy's ear and jawbone. The boy began to kick and tremor. But he was not a match for Fabien's powerful embrace. Licking clean the pulsating target, Fabien's bite was capable, sophisticated, and erotic. Crushing bones and ripping flesh, like a surgeon his lips found the offering jugular, creating a vacuum.

"Don't drain the dear boy entirely," Vaughn scolded. "Please do share."

May 10, 1986
Coeur D'Alene, Idaho –
Produce Warehouse
Meeting of the 'Order'

Jadwiga left the motel a couple hours early, hoping not to rush her dinner. Jade gave herself a few extra minutes in the event she had a difficult time finding the produce warehouse. She liked quaint Ma and Pop joints. She hated crowds and usually ate by herself. Her English had improved and her accent hardly detectable.

Sherman Avenue would take her to Lakeview Drive and finally to Fernan Road where the warehouse was located a half a mile from that turn. The storm had passed and the sun had finished melting what ice and snow the plows couldn't cut through.

Coeur D'Alene not only made it to her list of Fascist hot spots, but top ten most beautiful Cities to visit. Traveling East on Sherman she caught glimpses of Fernan Lake between breaks in the tall pines. Before the Interstate Ninety on ramp, was a gas station where she filled her gas tank. Jadwiga had less than a quarter tank and she had a personal rule, never let the tank get below halfway. Billie's Grille and Bar was adjacent to the gas station and she was pleased with the convenience of a one stop shop.

Billie needs to hit these hinges with a little WD-40 Jadwiga chagrinned as the heavy wooden front door of the Restaurant Bar screeched loudly. This brought unwelcome attention from a couple of drunks leaning over the bar starring into their beers.

"Find a table, I'll notify the waitress for you," the grungy bearded bartender instructed her. "What can I get you to drink."

"Arnold Palmer," Jadwiga replied. She saw the puzzled look on his wrinkled face. "Half tea half lemonade."

"Don't have that."

Her brow raised letting this Lenard Skinard type understand that his establishment was a little out of date. "OK, how about a sprite?"

"I can do sprite. I'll have it right there little lady." She rolled her eyes disgusted with his misogynistic demeanor and comment. Then she reminded herself, she's no longer in civilization, different societal rules, have patience.

A corpulent middle-aged waitress, hair tied back in a bun, and smacking her gum as she talked, laid a menu down in front of her. "Did Gill the bartender get your drink order hon?"

"Yes thanks."

"Do you want to take a few seconds and decide what you want or would you like me to come back?"

Jadwiga, knew it would take an act of congress to get her back so she opted to place her order now. Opening the narrow food stained menu, she located an item she liked that the cook couldn't screw up too bad. "I'm ready. I'll have the mac and cheese, with cheese toast."

"OK dear, I'll turn this into the cook and your order will be right up." The waitress tore the top sheet off her order pad and returned to the kitchen.

Billie's Restaurant and Bar walls were made of raw spruce logs and the diffused lighting gave it a rustic ambiance. An Elk horn chandelier above her table was further confirmation that she had entered killer nation. Then she forged a grin at the oxy-moron that they were now the hunted.

She noted that her glass had a lipstick stain on the rim. She pushed it aside. Perhaps the Idaho Board of Health was afraid to step foot in this town, let alone inspect the food handling procedures. It reminded her of when she was locked up in Auschwitz and complained to the Nazi guard of finding rat piss on her soup spoon. "You should be lucky we even feed you, Pollock whore," he responded, sharing no concern for her safety.

The memory of her experience in the concentration camp fueled her disgust for the neglected glass. As the waitress returned with her mac and cheese, Jadwiga let go on her with all the brunt of her anger. "I need a new glass!" she complained. "Do you not inspect the silverware and dishes before they're placed on the table?" She reigned in her anger after noting that nearly all the staff and clientele were giving her negative vibes. "Don't mean to be a snoot, but cleanliness should be first priority." She shook her head and ignored the deprecating disdain of strangers.

"Sorry miss," the waitress said with a forced smile. She snubbed her nose at her and stating each word profoundly slow. "I'll bring you a clean glass."

Jadwiga had completed most of her meal when she heard the sound of gravel under several vehicle tires outside the restaurant. There was laughter and an indecipherable conversation right before three men entered and sat at the bar. She recognized one of the men as Frank Silva, a person whom Gary Yarbrough had introduced her to. She debated whether or not it would be advantageous to approach Silva to see if he remembered her.

The subdued man sitting on the stool next to Silva, was sixty something and with white hair and trimmed beard. Next to him a younger good-looking man sporting a ducktail haircut. "Gill can we get three tall draft beers?"

"Sure," he replied pulling three frosted mugs out of the cooler. "Nice to see you brought your pops Frank. How ya doing Stanley?"

"Fine."

"I like your suspenders Stanley. Your wife make those for you?"

He snorted, "Right! They're store bought. Got em at Meyers."

Frank took note of Jadwiga in his peripheral. "Hey, aren't you Gary Yarbrough's friend?"

She smiled back and nodded. Suddenly the tension in the room subsided. If Frank Silva befriends you, you must be good people. Folks in Coeur D'Alene kowtowed to the men of the Order, including law enforcement and politicians. Bad things just seemed to happen to those that opposed them. Silence was the antecedent to survival.

"Come join us," Frank invited her to the bar.

"Thought you'd never ask."

Fortuitously she had finished her meal. She draped the used napkin over her plate, grasped her glass of sprite to take to the bar. The glass of water was untouched, just to get under the waitress's skin.

Jadwiga took the empty stool next to Stanley. "So, I overheard the bartender refer to you as Frank's Father?"

"Stanley, nice to meet you."

"Jadwiga, you can call me Jade."

He extended his hand for her to shake. She did so with a fabricated smile. "You know Frank obviously, and this is my younger Son, Garmont." Garmont gave her a reticent void of emotion nod, coquettishly inspecting her head to toe. She smiled approvingly.

"I have relatives in Spokane, thought I'd take Gary up on his offer to attend the Order's monthly assembly." She had become skillful at concocting safe stories to protect her real identity.

"He'll be pleasantly surprised I'm sure," Frank added. "You and Gary a thing?" His question got Garmont's attention. "After the trial, he kinda boasted about you."

"No," she replied with an embarrassed grin. "Just an acquaintance." For the first time Garmont smiled. "But that's very nice of him."

Stanley raised his brow and rolled his eyes in disgust, "Mr. Yarbrough is anything but a nice guy."

"Why would you say that Dad?" Frank took exception to his vitriol comment. "You don't know Gary like Jadia and I."

"Jadwiga," she corrected Frank. "You can call me Jade."

"Sorry," Frank apologized.

"That's all right. It's not the easiest name to remember."

Frank downed the last third of his beer, "Well, I guess we'd best be going if we're goin to be on time huh?"

"It was nice to meet you miss," Stanley said extending his hand again.

She grinned, "Pleasure's been mine." She remained at the bar until she heard their vehicles drive away.

"Do they always travel in separate vehicles?" She asked, looking at Gil for a logical explanation.

"Stanley doesn't like the Order. Never goes to their meetings." Gil paused from cleaning glasses, "Can't say I blame him. They're a little too radical for even me."

"That's a shame," she castigated, staying in character. She finished the last drop of sprite in her glass and sat it on the bar. "Thanks."

May 23, 1942
Auschwitz-Birkenau German Concentration Camp

Living quarters, at the Medical Research wing, was a step up from the blocks where the main population of prisoners slept. Jadwiga was thankful to have a pillow and a thin blanket to preserve some of her body heat when the sun went down. But there was no largesse the Nazis could do for her to relieve her anxiety of the inevitable. Persons taken to the M.R., never returned to the main population. They may have just as well delivered Jadwiga her last meal.

Jadwiga shared her block with fifteen other prisoners. Each unique to a specific laboratory experiment. She had no inkling of the torture she was about to endure. It was apparent that the Dubois twins were being injected by chemicals that messed with their skin pigmentation. Jadwiga was aware of a Study in France to give Albinos the necessary body chemistry for pigmentation using Cycad plants found in the ancient forests. But the Nazis for some nocuous reason were removing that protection from their bodies. Turning them into Albinos. Her best guess was in line with Hitler's dream of creating a perfect race of Germans. Fabien had a bad reaction to chemicals being injected in his body. The first night he came back from the Lab he screamed all night from the excruciating pain. Jadwiga demanded of the guard, standing watch, that he ask Doctor Mengele to provide him morphine. He replied dispassionately, "I have my orders."

May twenty-three, nineteen forty-one, started out non-eventful. The dispirited prisoners had given up on hope and slipped into a melancholy state of depression. The twins laid awake on their beds staring into the ceiling. A troubled Catholic Priest paced the floor. Jadwiga sat on the edge of her bed unable to think. Two male homosexuals crouched in a corner embracing and numb with fear. Homosexuals were identified by a pink triangle sewn on the breast of their prison garb, the habiliment of prisoner identification. The triangle was the shape of a German traffic warning sign and was the model used. A golden double triangle, one inverted over the other resembling the Star of David, identified Jews. A red triangle represented political prisoners, including social democrats and communists. A purple triangle was identified with other religious zealots, including Catholics. But Jadwiga wore an un-inverted red triangle identifying her as a spy.

The sound of boots pounding the turf grew louder. Normal sounds, usually inconspicuous to one's consciousness, became pestiferous. Anxiety raised their blood pressure. Each praying it wasn't their turn.

The SS guard backed away from the door as it flung open. Two SS guards were dragging, like a sack of potatoes, a tall maltreated Italian man, and in their usual presentation, tossed his near dead body on the floor and left. That is when they all realized the last person extracted from the group, the prior evening, was not coming back. The Italian guy would inherit their bed.

"Wait!" the Priest called after the SS guards as they left. "Why are homosexuals in my block? I demand you remove them immediately!"

The older alpha male held the younger homosexual's head close to his chest. "God end this nightmare, please!"

Jadwiga purposely bumped the Priest's shoulder hard as she went to assist the Italian prisoner, "Sit your pompous ass down before I knock you down." They exchanged scornful stares.

The left side of Italian's face was bruised. Dried blood stained his upper lip. He lifted himself up on his elbows to take in his new environment. His eyes squinted as if this were the first time he was exposed to the sun. "This isn't block eleven?" He began to weep. "Thank God."

"Do you need help getting on your feet?"

"I haven't eaten in days," he was exasperated with each syllable he babbled. His lips were calloused and split from thirst. "Do you have water?"

"Leave him!" the SS guard ordered.

"Can someone please get me some water!" Jadwiga lambasted.

Ludovic scooped a tin of water out of the wash basin and handed it to her. "It's all there is."

"I said leave him!" the SS Guard became angry pointing his Jager rifle at her.

Jadwiga ignored his orders and held the tin cup to the Italian's cracked lips. "Go ahead and shoot me you bastard. You might be doing me a favor." He had heard the other SS guards speak of General Rudolph Hoss's bragging of his sexual conquests, and Jadwiga was his favorite. He was more afraid of Hoss.

She held his head up and gave him small sips of water. "What happens in Block Eleven?"

He swallowed hard and tears of gloom and despair wet his cheeks. "You can't lay down. They put you in a four by four room with no windows. No food. No water. I'm not sure but I think I was there for three days. Not sure."

"Sick Fuckers" Jadwiga protested. The SS guard shot her a disapproving look. "Help me get him to the empty bed." Ludovic helped him to his feet and wrapped his arm around his neck for support.

The SS guard guffawed, "You allow a female to give you orders? Ludovic ignored his comment which pissed him off even more.

Footsteps, leather rubbing against leather, the door opened. In the threshold stood a small middle-aged man with thick arms and chest draped in a white physician's gown. He was flanked by two SS guards who towered above him and stood inattentive to the doldrums of their job.

"You," he pointed to Jadwiga. "Come with me." The other prisoners looked on her with pity and a moment of gratitude that it wasn't their turn. The SS guard, keeping watch on their block, had a facetious grin standing at attention.

The fear she felt this time was different than the morose despair of being a prisoner. Was this her final hour? Insatiable anxiety filled her entire body and deflated her spirit. Her breathing accelerated. "Take slow deep breaths," her childhood physician would tell her. She couldn't remember when her anxiety was worse.

They led her into a steel framed building behind the medical lab. There was a strong odor of bleach. Some rooms she passed had a stench she remembered from the cadavers in medical school.

"In here." The physician directed. "Remove your garment and lay down on the table." The aluminum table was center floor of the small clinic. Typical hospital instruments lay on shelfing above a large sink as well as surgical tools used in emergency rooms such as, scalpels, retractors, lancets, rasps, trocars and surgical scissors. She understood the purpose of each tool. But unfamiliar was an ax hanging on two nails driven into the wall. "Was this how they disposed of the bodies?" The morbid thought raised her heart beat even more. The inattentive guards became aroused as she exposed her soft youthful unblemished flesh. She climbed onto the table and lay face down to cover her private parts.

"Roll over!" the physician demanded. She obeyed and he immediately secured the leather manacles around her ankles and wrists. He then walked to the head of the table out of her view and pinched her nose shut. At the second she opened her mouth to grasp for air, he compressed a one-inch metal pipe into her mouth and tied the straps attached at each end behind her head. The attending physician perceived, by the change in their breathing pattern, that the SS guards were getting sexually turned on. "Out!" He pointed to the door.

"What is your problem?" the furry faced SS challenged him. "Mengele has never denied us a little extra compensation for our service."

"As your ranking officer I'm ordering you out of here. I will bring your behavior up with Doctor Mengele. You can count on it. Now get out."

The guard looked lasciviously at Jadwiga's breasts. "Shame though," he said stopping near the table he cupped her left breast, closed his eyes and tightened his hold on it. He removed his hand and exited the room along with the other SS guard. Jadwiga was too emotionally numb to react to the sexual abuse she had suffered. She didn't blink through the ordeal. But she was thankful that it stopped.

"I have the extra vile of sulphonamide," a male voice announced entering the clinic. She couldn't make out who this person was as the first physician had placed a rag over her face.

"Five out of eight survivors, still too risky to ask the Health Minister for approval." She recognized the voice of the first physician.

"Four out of eight."

"Damn!" There was a short pause. "We waited too long to administer the drug after infecting the wound. Perhaps it is unrealistic to add lead to the wound. What if we only infect the wound with dirt and bacteria?" He shook his head confounded, then answered his own question. "No, most wounds are caused by some form of shrapnel. The sulphonamide has to be administered sooner to be effective. It's time to try adding the steroid," Doctor Huey Chang suggested, taking a deep breath.

"But the inhibitors," the assisting physician warned. "How will you introduce unaffected plasma?"

"The Field Doctors will need to have the drug with them on the battlefield. I believe you're right, there is a direct correlation between the lapse of time between infection, treatment, and the recovery." Jadwiga was ascertaining her plight in her mind as the doctors described the experiment. "Is it plausible that the Field Doctors can treat the infections within an hour?"

"Possible but unlikely."

"So, we save one in four soldiers. Mengele will agree those are still better odds."

"OK, one hour. Let's get started." She could hear their footsteps as they maneuvered around her. Clanging of small metal tools on the aluminum table as they prepared to operate. "You will want to bite down hard on the metal bit. This is going to cause you significant pain." It was at that moment she realized the inhumane truth, they were not going to knock her out with anesthetics? She tried to scream but it was muffled by the metal bit in her mouth. "Try to miss the Femoral artery this time Doctor. It took me three hours to clean up the blood from the last one."

"No problem," the ghost physician replied. The first incision was three inches into the left leg and her bicep femora cramped. The excruciating pain was beyond any she had ever known. She screamed out all the air from her lungs and became very nauseated. "Bite down!" He then drew the scalpel down her leg to just above her knee. Nothing could compare to what she was about to endure.

"Bacteria is in," the first doctor stated.

"Now infecting with dirt and gravel." Her pain meter flew off the charts as the doctors inserted metal pieces, small pebbles, and dirt into her wound. Her teeth began to bleed from her gums from the enormous pressure of her bite on the metal pipe. Their fingers pushed debris further into her wounds.

"That should do it." They bandaged the wound and made a tourniquet above it, similar to the treatment wounded soldiers would receive on the battle field. The contaminated tools were dropped into the metal sink and washed in a saline solution. Jadwiga wished at that moment someone would fire a bullet into her brain and end the unbearable pain.

The temperature had dropped to forty-six degrees. They had decided to delay Joey's bail until after the blood-letting. It was the smoking gun evidence that would give Joey's story credence. It wasn't a solid alibi, but blew holes in Stone's theory. After all, how could Stone link Joey to the serial murders when he's locked-up in jail.

Dylan brushed away the cob webs from the dust caked window with a broken two by four that was laying on the garage floor. With the back of his hand, he scrubbed away the dust making a clear spot on the window to view anyone going in or leaving the White Owl bar.

Muller held one of three CB hand held radios that Doctor Chang had purchased from the hardware store. Jonathan staked out the entrance to the Owl from the back seat of the black sedan that was parked in the Southeast parking lot across the street. Nobody came in or out without being visually inventoried. They had been holding in the vacant warehouse since 11:00 p.m. Their twitching and pacing was beginning to annoyed Muller. He worried that they were growing too impatient.

"One zer-tee," Fabian stated, impatiently staring at his watch. Many of the guests of the White Owl had left. The carbon exhaust, from the Peckerwood's motorcycles seeped through the cracks in the windows.

"It's him," Dylan's voice a near whisper. "And he's alone."

"Red Beard?" Ludovic asked moving closer to the window. "Zat is him."

There were three cycles still parked in the rear parking lot. Fortuitously, Red Beard's was closest to the man door entrance to the garage. Dylan cued Giuseppe that Red Beard had turned his back to them. "Now."

A few of the small rocks slipped from Giuseppe's grip. He cracked the door slightly and tossed the rocks at Red Beard's cycle and stood behind the door. A few made contact with his bike, scoring small scratch marks on his fender and gas tank.

Red Beard was furious, "Son of a bitch!" Turning to inspect his bike, and from where the rocks had been thrown. He saw that the garage door was open a tad. "Bastard juveniles! Consider yourselves dead!" He didn't pause to take a closer examination of the damage. Red Beard charged toward the garage door in a rage. Pushing the door with brute force, he stepped inside the garage. It was dark except for the shadows cast through the windows by the Club's neon lights.

Stunned by the dark figures of the Creed, he stopped abruptly in his tracks. His anger was stifled by the fear of the dire realization that he was out numbered. Not by juveniles, but by the subject of his nightmares, vampires. Blood sucking vampires.

Giuseppe, who stood behind the door, quietly shut it behind him. Red Beard abruptly turned to see who had caged him in and was met with Giuseppe's right hook. It connected on Red Beard's chin, knocking him off balance. He stumbled backwards. Dylan swung the two by four at Red's knee caps, as if the bases were loaded with two outs. Red Beard fell backwards, wailing in pain. His head hit the cement floor hard. Suffering a moment of unconsciousness, he came to, looking into the merciless, angry faces of blood thirsty retribution.

"I know you," Red resigned with regret, identifying Dylan and Fabian. Immediately he understood why he was being ambushed. A facetious grin inundated Red's face, he would get in one last jab. "Ah! The bitch's boyfriend. Pretty little thing. Amazing what you can do with a beer bottle," He vaunted and closed his eyes knowing he was a dead man.

Fabian drew his hand ready to strike, but it was stayed by his brother. He reminded himself of Doctor Chang's reproach to control his emotions and not compromise the blood-letting. Fabian so wanted Red Beard to feel the pain he put Carol through.

"Squealed just like a little pig while its belly's slit open," Red continued dauntlessly.

Red Beard needed to know that today, Carol would be vindicated. "Wait!" he demanded holding out his hand to stop Muller from placing the chloroform-soaked rag over his nostrils. Muller backed off. "Zis one is for Carol." Dylan and Ludovic nodded that they were with him and pulled his legs apart, just as Fabian had previously schemed. Stepping between Red Beard's legs, he kicked his pointed boot with crushing force into Red's groin. At that moment, as he opened his mouth to exhume the large volume of oxygen in his lungs, Muller pressed the chloroform rag into the cavity of rotten and missing teeth. Red Beard choked on his own saliva.

Tilting it to the side, Giuseppe kneeled on his head, exposing Red's jugular. Wiping Red Beard's neck with a disinfectant, then with another dry rag, Doctor Chang prepared their meal. The Creed waited patiently behind Muller for their rejuvenation. Using his tongue to feel for a pulse, he positioned his razor-sharp canines over the carotid, like a surgical scalpel. The familiar sound, like teeth ripping into the meat of an apple, queued the others that the blood-letting had begun.

Muller could not contain the amount of blood trapped in his mouth by his inability to keep pace with Red Beard's panic stricken pulse. Blood seeped out from both sides of Muller's mouth. He quickly covered it with the alcohol-soaked rag. "Make it quick," he turned and faced Ludovic, who was poised to be next. "His heart is beating faster than a race horse."

California laws require clubs and bars to stop serving alcohol by 2:00 a.m. The owner, Paul Coombs, had driven with one of the bartenders to Coeur D'Alene Idaho for what he described to Sandy, the club manager, as a business trip. She had kicked the last guest out at 2:20 a.m. pulled the cash from the register and went into the office. Bundling the paper currency and rolling the coin, Sandy then counted down her till, reconciling it with the night's receipts. Zipping up the bank pouch with the day's deposit, she locked the safe and office door and made her way to the rear exit of the bar. Sandy would never have made it to Sports illustrated magazine's swim wear edition, but swore if she ever had plastic surgery on her larger than life nose, she was center fold material. She worked out at the Gym regularly and had no problem man handling drunks and their sexual advances.

Fumbling with her keys, Sandy struggled to find the one to the rear door of the White Owl. In the dark shadows of her peripheral vision, she made out two male figures sitting on their motorcycles side by side. She clutched the bank pouch between her left arm and her body and considered going back into the bar and calling 911. She was mortified with fear that they were waiting for her. She pulled out the flashlight from her tweed coat pocket and shined it on them. "I have a gun!" They did not respond or even wince. The stream of light from the flashlight stopped on Red Beard's neck where she could see the scab of congealing blood. "Oh my God," she mumbled in disbelief. "Jesus Christ Red!"

She scanned both of the Peckerwood gangsters head to toe and realized that their hands and feet had been wired to the handle bars and foot pedals. Someone had propped their bikes up with two by fours. Their heads were also wired to a metal pipe that ran down the back of their leather jackets and kept them from falling off their bikes. But she knew why and what happened when her flashlight shone on the sign nailed to the chest of the one Peckerwood she detested most. Sandy had thrown him out of the bar more than once for stepping over the line. She only knew him as Red. Ease-dropping on a conversation pinning Red as the guy that beat and raped a woman, thought to be associated with the vampire vigilantes.

The sign was written with the blood of the victims, "Casus belli." The expression is a Latin term Hitler used meaning an act or event that provokes or is used to justify war. Sandy had no doubt why these murders occurred, but not who committed them. She reasoned that by their handy-work, the murders were well orchestrated, engineered, and a very well orchestrated hit job. Her stomach knotted up from the gruesome sight of it all. But it wasn't odd to her that she felt no empathy for either of them. Pulling the keys back out of her pocket, Sandy let herself back into the White Owl and called the 911 operator. Needless to say, she was pissed-off. Not because of the murders, but knowing that she may not get any sleep this morning.

May 10, 1986
Meeting of 'The Order'
Coeur D'Alene, Idaho

Jadwiga set the letter from Yarbrough, with the directions to the warehouse, on the dashboard of her rental car. The sun had started to disappear behind the mountains and she began to feel the cold change in temperature. Trying to focus on the road, she located the heater switch on the Jeep's control panel. The slight distraction caused the vehicle to careen slightly off the road. The front right tire bounced over a small snowbank but she was able to steer the Jeep back into her lane.

"Left on Lakeside," Jadwiga spoke the next direction as if carrying on a conversation with herself. She slowed down so that she could read the street sign. It was Lakeside. No one was behind her, but she signaled left anyway, not knowing if there was a traffic cop incognito.

She traveled about a quarter mile before her next coordinate, Fernan Lake Road. It had become dark and she could only make out the few house lights on the other side of Fernan Lake. Fernan Lake Road had only been plowed once and ice had begun to form on the road. Driving on Europe's winter roads prepared her for driving in inclement weather conditions. Jadwiga saw a turnout, about two hundred feet down the road, and slowly pulled over. She got out of the vehicle and crouched in front of each wheel, turning the axel dial to four-wheel drive. She understood quite well from experience that four-wheel drive won't stop you from skidding but will help a driver gain traction.

Back on the road she became a little nervous that she would miss the warehouse as the only beacon was the occasional porch light and the skip marks within her headlight spray. But after driving about a mile, Jadwiga was grateful for the simple directions she got from the motel clerk. Jade was relieved to see the sandwich board sign at the edge of the paved entrance to the warehouse. It read, "National Alliance." She turned into the parking lot which was lit by one street lamp loosely hanging by its wires atop a utility pole.

Jadwiga counted at least twenty-five vehicles haphazardly parked. In her rear view mirror a set of headlights turned in the parking lot behind her. By the frozen steam like breath, leaving the lips of men in conversation, she knew it was bitter cold outside. Most took shelter in the warehouse.

She parked near a restored 1948 Ford F-1 pick up with wooden bed rails. Jadwiga scoped out the property. Befriending Yarbrough was nothing but luck. Jade was banking on the dividends she hoped he would produce for her. Top of her list was Paul Coombs. Yarbrough mentioned that Coombs would be supplying the booze from a bar he owned in the bay area? She was hoping that he was delivering the alcohol in person.

Jadwiga was stoic by nature, but for the first time in her life since Auschwitz, she felt unnerved and afraid. She was outnumbered by a male hate machine in a remote area of the woods where there was no support system to fall back on. One mistake would be her demise.

As she stepped out of her vehicle, she immediately drew the attention of the men standing between their vehicles laughing, no doubt at some racial joke or conquest she guessed. She had over dressed for the occasion. However, her classy dress suit was a front that perhaps would convince them that she was, or knew, someone of political importance. Their eyes followed her to the man door entrance into the warehouse.

Jade found it odd that chairs were set up in a large circle. A makeshift bar of empty pallets surrounded by men toasting and spitting chewing tobacco into brass spittoons. She wanted to meet the man behind the bar, prying open cardboard boxes filled with bottles of booze, and pouring attendees glasses.

"Jadwiga!" Gary Yarbrough saw her standing by the door looking somewhat lost. He waived for her to approach the bar where most of the attendees waited for the meeting to start. As she got within ear shot of Gary he reached out to shake her hand. "I had this feeling you'd show." He seemed delighted and deep within his lecherous thoughts of exploring every orifice of her body. "I would like you to meet Joseph Voss."

An oval faced professional looking businessman, with an open blue silk shirt and pleated dress pants, also held out his hand for her to shake. "You look stunning."

"Thank you," Jadwiga blushed.

"Gary told me he met you at the Berg trial."

"I'm a big fan of the Turner Diaries, and thought it a great opportunity to meet like-minded people." She turned and smiled gratuitously at Gary, "I couldn't have been more fortunate to have met this amazing guy."

Gary took her compliment with enthusiasm, "Trust me the pleasure was all mine." He turned to the average built man tending bar. He had jet black hair and mustache, and looked back at Jade. "What are you drinking sweetheart?"

"Beer is fine."

"Particular brand?"

"Does he have malted beer?"

"Paul, the Lady would like a malted beer. Do you have that?"

Bingo! Jadwiga celebrated to herself. This had to be Paul Coombs.

"Somewhere here I have a box of Dark Ale by Angel City Brewery. It's a little bit stronger alcohol content than most sweet beers, but I think your gorgeous guest will be pleased."

Jadwiga chortled and nodded her appreciation of his craft. "Wow, I'm very impressed. A man that knows his beer."

"I've been in the bar business way too long."

"You own a bar?"

"the White Owl in San Mateo California. Have we met? I don't believe I've seen you at these functions."

Yarbrough's jealousy pushed in on the conversation. "Sorry Paul. Let me introduce you to Jadwigo." He paused. He could never pronounce her last name.

"Dzido," she injected holding out her hand for Paul to shake. Gary was not happy at the length of time he held it before letting go.

Gary interrupted, "Jadwiga, did I mention that Joseph here was the chief financial officer for Torkid Rieber?"

She became concerned that she should have known the name. "Really? That's very cool," she felt safe with her response. She debated whether it might have served her better had she admitted she didn't know who Torkid Rieber was. "I'm new to the Alliance and recall reading his name somewhere."

Joseph's fascination with her drained from his face. "Texaco?" His brow raised, suspect of her alliance. "It's only one of the most celebrated National Alliance backers. His company secretly supplied oil to Franco during the Spanish civil war."

"Yes, of course," she saved face. She had always wondered how the fascist movement got their weapons and oil. She suppressed her sudden anger. She had lost several of her friends who had joined the government to fight off the fascists in Spain. But the government was overwhelmed by the lucrative support Franco received and succumbed to the coup. She wanted the night to end. She wanted to get busy planning a trip to San Mateo, California.

Jadwiga felt an on and off again pain in her feet. It typically started with the feet and legs, but if a vampire goes too long without a blood-letting, it can progress to the organs and if left too long, it can be fatal. How long is too long? Immediately after their rescue in Auschwitz, Doctor Chang had schooled his human experiments on the critical nature and process of the blood-letting. "Five or six days without, and your body's nervous system will start giving you signs. fifteen days without, and you will start feeling weak and more frequent pain. Thirty days and your organs begin to feel their age, if you know what I mean." The blood-letting reversed the aging process. However, some rare blood types didn't respond to the steroid cocktail. She only had one encounter with a rare blood type and it made her sick for two weeks. It was like her body was trying to catch up for lost years. Too much oxygen, during the blood-letting, and airborne particles create an unhealthy host body. For that reason alone, Chang's vampires use the ceratoid artery in the neck. The vampire like sucking was convenient and avoided having to use large sophisticated medical equipment, like the device developed by the Nazis.

"But why wait," she thought as she looked over the Nazis assembled at the meeting. This is a vampire smorgasbord. A mélange of narcissistic white elitist fascists. "Why wait for San Mateo?"

Gary Yarbrough had invited her to sit next to him in the circle. Across from her sat Frank Silva and his handsome brother. She caught herself licking her upper lip as if she had already tasted his blood. The Texaco accountant sat next to Gary. Women conventionally weren't allowed to sit in the circle. Wives sat in chairs against the wall next to the make-shift bar. Jadwiga was the only female sitting in the circle which earned her catty and indignant stares from the wives.

Paul Coombs walked to the center of the circle holding a worn, leather-bound copy of the Turner Diaries. "Considering the weather, which most of you locals aren't affected by, I want to thank you for attending this Quarterly meeting of the Order. Especially those that have traveled long distances." He glanced at Jadwiga as he made the comment. He paused and then held up the Nazi rag. "Our Aryan Brotherhood can sleep easier tonight. Alan Berg, our Nation's most revered communist liberal, has been executed and sent to hell." Everyone stood and clapped. Some whistled, some shouted racist terms, "Death to liberals," "Jews and Niggers die." Trying hard to stay in character, Jadwiga clapped, turned and smiled at Gary. He smiled and nodded back. It was extremely hard for Jadwiga to hide her indignation, but her safety depended on her ability to improvise convincingly.

Coombs waited for their excitement to de-escalate. "However, there's another front we must wage war." You could have heard a pin drop as he peeked their curiosity. "I received a call from an employee this morning that two more Aryan brothers were brutally murdered outside of the White Owl. One of the victims was a dear friend. A kind soul and a true fighter for Aryan Nation Rights. His name is Red. In the last six months twenty-three of our brothers and sisters in the Bay area have been brutally murdered by an albino misfit and his friends." Jadwiga swallowed hard, overwhelmed with alarm. She would call Doctor Chang the minute she got back to the motel. Coombs's speech went on for the better part of an hour. They loved him. He was well versed in all things fascist and spoke of the progress of National

Alliance movements all over the world. Jadwiga was on tenterhooks throughout the entire meeting hoping it would soon end.

A few times she exchanged flirtatious glances with Garmont, Frank Silva's brother. She noted a reciprocal annoyance with the whole cult thing. Most likely Garmont attended the meetings to be on good graces with his brother. She was formulating a plan to entice him to her motel room. He was extremely attractive and perhaps he was the one she needed to end her vertiginous moments of hunger and female urge to copulate.

"Before I go I want to remind everyone to pay their dues on time next month. Mr. Pierce thanks you. And if you can join the march for segregation in Birmingham in July let me know. There's still a few seats we need to fill on the bus. Finally, I understand that a tribe of Niggers are planning on moving into Chattaroy." Grumbling chants of disdain echoed throughout the warehouse.

"Over our dead bodies," A salt and pepper haired wife cried out from the corner.

Paul shot her an affirmative smile, "Well then, Gary is lookin for anyone interested in helping him make sure that we keep Chattaroy pure. If you know what I mean."

Gary leaned toward Jadwiga's ear and announced, "Nigger works at a sawmill near Spirit Lake. The sawdust there is about to turn black."

Coombs paused and grinned at his phlegmatic self, "Finally, I want to end on a humorous note. Why are liberals like assholes?" He paused but didn't acknowledge the few attempts at humor. "No matter how much you wipe them, they still stink." Bad joke Jadwiga laughed at her own understatement.

"God he's funny," Gary whimsically muttered between chuckles.

"Be safe driving home. Good night." Paul Coombs was full of himself as the group cheered and clapped.

"Gary, where are the restrooms?" She had been holding it throughout the meeting and now it was becoming painful.

He pointed to the corner of the warehouse where the owners had framed in an office. "You'll see the restroom once you pass the office. It's one of them unisex toilets."

"Thank you." She saw that an elderly slim built man with a hunched back, was slowly making his way towards the toilet. She knew that he would take forever and it was imperative that she beat him to the door, or she would pee her panties. Quickening her pace, she passed him about ten feet from the restroom door. He shot her a brazen look of contempt. She tried the door handle but it was locked. "Shit!"

"It looks like someone beat you to it," the elderly man said with a saucy grin.

She managed an insolent smirk, "Looks like it." A small line had begun to form behind her. Second to the old man was Garmont. He smiled coquettishly at her and she returned the favor. This was the opportunity she coveted to nonchalantly invite him to her motel room.

"Sorry," a large middle-aged man, who most likely lived on fast food, emerged along with a lingering stench from whatever he flushed down the toilet.

Amidst the turned-up noses of those in line, the old man combatively fanned off the smell from his face with his hand. "What the hell Horace, did you have beans for dinner?" the old man stated pugnaciously and unapologetic.

"Fuck you Leonard," Horace responded unabashed but embarrassed.

She was next. "Just empty your bladder. Don't be puttin on your make up on dear," Leonard scorned without shame.

"You have no filter, do you?" Jadwiga admonished entering the restroom. The others in line laughed at her comment. Once inside she locked the door. With her legs straddling wide over the toilet to avoid the diarrhea stains on the toilet seat, she let it flow with a sigh of relief. With her bladder drained she stepped back into her pant suit and pulled her wallet from her bra. She searched for the motel card. At last she found it. She then took out her lipstick pen and wrote her room number on the back of card. She left the restroom.

"About damn time," Leonard reproached.

Jadwiga stopped by Garmont and reached her hand out to shake his, "Jadwiga, we met at the restaurant." He looked down at his hand as he felt her clandestinely slip him the card.

"Yes, I remember."

"It was nice meeting you. Perhaps we'll meet again soon."

"I'll make a point of it," he serendipitously accepted her offer.
"Perfect," her wish fulfilled.

11:30 p.m. Saturday Night

"Hello, Vaughn Muller speaking,"

"Hi Vaughn," she held the motel pay phone close to her ear and scanned the parking lot from the phone booth. She could not afford to miss Garmont. "It's Jade."

"Are you in the States?"

"Idaho, place called Coeur D'Alene."

"Why the bloody hell would you be in Coeur D'Alene?"

"It's complicated Vaughn," She scanned the parking lot again.

"Do you need money?"

"No, I'm good. Have you been watching the news?"

There was a brief hesitation. "Why?"

"You must be following the murders at the White Owl Bar?" He didn't answer. "I'm coming to the Bay area I need to talk with Doctor Chang. There's going to be trouble. I need to warn him."

"We'll meet you tomorrow at the Palace of Fine Arts, six p.m. sharp." There was a click. He had hung up on her. Muller didn't seem his jovial self. Why was he short with her, not a good omen? Perhaps Muller suspected that authorities had tapped their line. She slammed the receiver down on the phone saddle and pushed the double expanding door open.

Jade undressed and slipped into a silky black night gown that accentuated her perky breasts and long sexy legs. She poured herself a glass of red chardonnay in the complimentary plastic wrapped cup on the vanity. She took a sip, "Nasty shit," she repined. "Where is he," She impatiently complained to herself looking at her watch. It was getting close to midnight and she had to get up early to make it to San Francisco before six p.m.

Headlight spray brightened her room through the thin curtains which were drawn closed. She smoothed out the wrinkles in the bed spread, put down her wine, and went to peek through the curtains. It was Garmont. The truck engine stopped and the headlights turned off.

The truck door swung open and his snake skin cowboy boot hit the pavement first. His baby face was irresistible. Clean shaven square chin and dimples, blond mustache, and a curly mane to match. To his brother's chagrin, he liked it long under the black cowboy hat. It was obvious that he didn't work out, but he had large bi-ceps and a narrow waste line. He was tall and filled his tight jeans to her liking.

Garmont tapped lightly on the door, in an attempt to be respectful of her neighbors. Jadwiga unlatched the chain lock on the door and stuck her head out the door. Jadwiga surveyed the sidewalk and parking lot for potential witnesses. "Did you think I wasn't going to show?"

"Come in," She grabbed his hand and pulled him in closing the door behind him. She pointed to the end of the bed. "Have a sit and make yourself comfortable. Can I take your hat?"

"Thanks," he lifted it off with all four fingers and thumb from the top.

"Why don't you set it on the cadenza. I know men are particular about keeping the shape of their hats."

He obliged her and took a deep breath as he took all of her in with his eyes. "You sure are pretty mam."

"I prefer you can call me Jade." She smiled taking his hand. It was youthful and almost as smooth as hers. "Do you mind if I get a little personal."

"There's not a lot to know about me," he replied timorously. "Go ahead."

"How old are you?"

"Twenty-two."

"Twenty-two?"

"Yes mam." She could tell he was nervous.

"Jade, remember? Call me Jade, I'm not your mother." Although she was old enough to be his grandmother.

"Sorry mam."

"Tell me, is this your first time?" Her grin still ear to ear. He looked down embarrassed. "Hey, that's OK, every young man has a first time. I feel honored. You are one charming young man."

"Thank you."

"I'm going to the bathroom to get another glass of wine. Do you drink wine? I do have half a fifth of Jack Daniels in my suit case."

"Whisky please I haven't acquired a taste for wine yet."

"Whisky it is." She touched his lips with her forefinger. "Why don't you get out of those cowboy clothes and I'll fetch us our drinks."

He wasted no time disrobing. He unbuttoned his shirt and flung it over the chair next to the night stand. He struggled somewhat with his cowboy boots. Jadwiga thought it amusing and cute. His cowboy belt buckle was large, silver, and round. He threw his jeans over the same chair. He left his white boxer briefs on and sat back down on the bed. She couldn't help notice his firm butt with profound perfect dimpled cheeks and the white briefs tucked deep between them. She licked her teeth licentiously feeling aroused by his hairless youthful body.

"Shall we make a Toast?" She stood in the bathroom doorway naked, holding her wine in one hand and his Jack Daniels in the other.

He turned his head, "My God your hot." His breathing was slow and he shivered a little from the eroticism. Reaching down, he tucked the tip of his rock-hard erection back in his boxer briefs. He tried to pull the pee flap closed but his erection was nine inches and wanted out.

"Come here," she demanded like a Dominatrix controlling her slave. He stood up and slowly walked toward her. "Nice." She complimented his aroused penis which poked through his boxers. "Drop your shorts." He obeyed, but stumbled a bit trying to climb out of them. Garmont was really enjoying being submissive. Her body was smooth but firm like a man. Jadwiga had taken the steroid mixture. She had one hour to have her long overdue orgasm and to perform the blood-letting. There was about a foot between them. She placed the palm of her hand on his chest and moved down his torso until she was on her knees staring at the pulsing erection. She wrapped her hand around it, leaned into it and kissed it.

Garmont took a swig of whisky, sat the bottle on the night stand, and sighed with pleasure. "Oh my God, that feels so good." She swallowed his aroused member deep into her mouth, her tongue playing with it. He closed his eyes and placed his hands on the back of her head to take control of motion. She swiftly grasped his wrists and pulled his hands behind his back. He was shocked at her strength and became a little unnerved as to where this was going. Jadwiga slowly stood, licking his stomach, all the while keeping a grasp on his wrists. "You're going to wish this never ends," she spoke softly into his ear. She nibbled on his ear lobe and licked inside its cavity. Garmont moaned with delight and gave himself up to her without inhibition. Pressing her mouth hard against his, she bit softly on his lips. He believed that she was going to suck his tongue right out of his mouth. He was ecstatic with pleasure.

She began to walk him backwards, still wrapped around him in a lustful embrace, until his buttocks pressed against the bathroom counter top. She released his left hand and reached into her open duffle bag and pulled out a set of handcuffs. His libido meter went off the charts. He began to sweat as his heart beat was off to the races. Garmont didn't fight her, didn't complain, didn't care, he was in erotic heaven. Fastening each of his wrists in the handcuffs, she grasped his erect penis. She ignored his groaning and pulled him by his penis to the bed and pushed him backwards on it. His long blonde curly hair had fanned around his head. He wasn't handsomely masculine, but cute in the adolescent appeal. She licked the inside of his thighs. The salty sweet taste of his skin on her tongue. She straddled him on the bed and slowly lowered herself guiding his erect penis into her vagina. His body quivered. Gyrating her hips like a piston, she exhaled long.

"Fuck, that's incredible," he closed his eyes and opened his mouth, releasing an erotic, "Yes, oh ride my cock. Please. Yes, yes." Her rhythm became more and more rapid, until both had orgasmed. She rolled off him and lay limp, in sensual bliss.

"Let's take a shower together, clean up, and maybe round two," Jade initiated plan A.

"Can you please take the handcuffs off?" He implored. "They're starting to hurt my wrists."

"I will," she teased. "But not until after our shower."

She could see that he was aroused again. Jadwiga had a long drive ahead of her and needed to get this over with. She could feel her nerves starting to burn and was in need of an immediate blood-letting. She led him into the bathroom. She grabbed both shoulders and gradually turned him around away from her.

"What are you doing now?" he asked unconcerned as if he already knew the answer.

"You'll see," she replied with deviant aberration. Reaching again into her duffle bag, Jadwiga pulled out a blindfold she normally used to block out sunlight when she took afternoon naps. She placed the blindfold over his eyes and fastened the Velcro straps behind his head.

"Is this necessary?" But she could tell by his erogenous grin everything she did to him had an aphrodisiacal effect. "Is there going to be a code word for stop?"

"How about the word more?"

"But what if I want more?" Garmont's titillating words were carnal, and humorously dirty. His flesh tingled with insatiable desire for a fetish he had only read about in pornography magazines.

"You need to shut up." She held a gag in front of his mouth. "Now open your mouth wide." He obeyed without protest. "I'm going to lead you into the shower. There's a tile seat built into the shower that I want you to sit on so you don't fall. Nod your head if you understand." He nodded affirmatively.

He detected that her voice was more serious and less amorous. How could he say the code word with a gag in his mouth? She could see he was growing a little nervous. She fondled him and kissed the lobe of his ear, "You have to trust me." He got aroused again and nodded that he was still in the game. "Now walk slowly with me into the shower. Be careful there's a tile lip at the door. Step up." The shower floor was dry and keeping his footing wasn't difficult. She gradually sat him down onto the tile ledge. His entire body shivered from the cold tile on his buttocks.

She ran her fingers through his hair and began to kiss the nape of his neck. He tilted his head giving her total access. He groaned lasciviously through the gag in his mouth. Licking the stretched muscles in his neck, she gradually moved her lips over the pulsating ceratoid artery. At first, she sucked at the skin as if she planned to leave a hickey. She stopped, opened her mouth wide, then with brute force bit down hard through the fibers of youthful flesh, severing the artery. Drinking from him the sweet nectar of life. Her body welcomed the Paba inhibitor free blood.

Garmont seized, went into momentary shock, feet extended and shaking violently, then limp, giving up his ghost.

Jade released her bite and stared at his pale beautiful young face, eyes frozen wide in shock. His body resting up against hers. She began to tear up when she realized that she really liked this kid. It was great sex and Jadwiga couldn't admit to herself she nearly fell for him. Besides, she got a vibe Garmont was indifferent to the Order. But he identified as a Nationalist, a fascist, and they had tried to end her life. Now the tables had turned. The romance evaporated with her referendum of revenge.

A small amount of Blood dripped from his wound and down the middle of his chest. It soaked his crotch and finally fell onto the tiles and into the floor drain. Reaching up, Jadwiga turned the faucets to their fullest and then adjusted the hot dial to a warm temperature. His heart stopped beating and the blood quit oozing from his wound. She took the shower spray handle out of its cradle and rinsed the blood from Garmont's naked body and down the drain.

Feeling refreshed and rejuvenated, Jade felt the stamina to run ten Iron Man contests. She would need the extra strength for the most difficult part of her plan, disposing of Garmont's body.

She searched his pant pockets for the truck keys. Finding them, she tossed them on the night stand. Dragging him, like a bag of Idaho potatoes, his head hit the lip on the shower and thumped on the tile floor. She took off the manacles from his wrists and dressed him. Pulling him to the front door, she opened it and scanned for eye witnesses. She did not need the inconvenience of a second victim. Fortuitously, her room was around the back of the motel and obscured from the road. It was awkward getting under him to lift, what would have an hour ago, felt like a hundred and fifty pounds. After the SR rejuvenation an easy ten pounds. At the Gym, Jadwiga had pressed two hundred fifty pounds on a normal day. But after a blood-letting she could easily lift twice that weight.

Garmont's pickup truck was in need of a tune up. Trying not to flood the engine, she pumped the gas a little and got it to start after several attempts. Siphoning some of the gas from her rental, Jadwiga had filled a vase from the motel room and secured it between her legs.

East Fernan Lake Road was like a meandering river with switch backs and curves that would challenge even the most accustomed local driver with a few beers in their belly. Spring run-off was a few days away. The Lake was low.

She could see in her head light spray the upcoming switch back at the top of a small cliff. Jadwiga stopped the vehicle, set the parking brake, and shifted the transmission into neutral. She acted quickly, hoping to avoid any unwelcomed traffic. Opening the driver's door, she stepped out onto the street. Pulling Garmont by his belt towards her, she was able to get him positioned behind the wheel. She doused him with gasoline and dispensed the rest throughout the cab of the truck. Her lungs filled with the smell of petroleum and she had to take a moment to cough it out.

Striking a match, Jade tossed it into the cab of the truck and then pulled on the parking brake release handle. The cab was consumed in flames as the truck rolled down the grade and disappeared over the cliff. A second later, an explosion and a cloud of smoke barely visible in the moon lit sky.

Saturday, May 10, 1986
San Francisco County Jail

"You're free to go Mr. Sanders," the jail guard said matter of fact. He was a scrawny thin man with black hair and spectacles. Joey couldn't help judge the guard as the most unlikely to fit the job posting credentials. He unlocked Joey's cell and held the barred door open for him. "The District Attorney wants me to remind you that bail doesn't alter the charges against you. In other words, don't leave town."

"Did someone post bail for me?" Joey probed, for it seemed somewhat of an enigma. He knew of no one with a million dollars that would arbitrarily fork out that kind of money for him.

The district attorney argued to the judge to wave bail, given the seriousness of the charges. The judge shook his head and over ruled, stating that, "Given Mr. Sander's clean history, and the weakness of the evidence, bail will be set at a million dollars. And I want him sequestered to County boundaries. Do you understand Mr. Muller?"

"Your rich friends are waiting for you in the lobby," the guard pointed to the exit.

Joey passed by the cells of criminals who had committed serious crimes. Some looked upon him with envy as he walked passed their cells, a free man for the time being. Others with contempt and evil stares that made the hair on his arms stand up. One creepy bald-headed Caucasian, with multiple tattoos, smiled, winked, and grabbed his own crotch. "I'll be waiting for you sweetheart." Joey took a deep breath and continued past his cell. He proceeded through a hallway of offices until he saw the sign above the door, 'Visitor Waiting Area.' The jail guard, who escorted him, instructed, "Through there. Go to your left and see the clerk at the window for your clothes and special effects. Do you understand?"

"Yes."

He was anxious to see who cared that much about him to invest a million dollars into his temporary freedom. He pushed open the

Regency double aluminum swinging traffic doors and scanned the lobby. It was a large lobby with bullet proof glass installed in clerk windows to his left and padded cushioned chairs to his right. Toward the exit door he saw Dylan with a cute Native American youth standing next to him Dylan was flanked by Joey's heart throb, Jonathan and Vaughn Muller. Joey had referred to Vaughn as the arrogant guy with the English accent. But, all ill intent toward him, vanished with the realization that he was his ticket to freedom.

"Joey!" Dylan called out his name.

Joey hurried his steps toward Dylan and Dylan ran toward Joey. They embraced.

"Is that your boyfriend?"

"His name is Thomas."

"Kinda young, don't you think?"

"I don't think about it. But he's not only hot, he's very smart, sensitive, and kind."

"And hot," Joey reiterated with a superfluous smile.

"And hot," Dylan blushed. "Come on, let me introduce you."

"First, tell me where you got a million dollars?" Dylan stopped and walked back to him, already knowing the answer.

"Doctor Chang fronted the money for me." He paused tongue in cheek. "Can we discuss it later?" He grasped Joey at his shoulders. By Joey's resolute expression, he wanted answers now. "Look, you're my brother and I love you. You have to trust me. Vaughn Muller is a licensed attorney in California and has volunteered to represent you. He's very good Joey. He reviewed the DA's weak evidence and was confident he could win this case. If he wins he gets his money back."

Joey's lips turned up with a satisfactory grin. "Let's go meet your friend."

He started with Thomas, "This is Thomas. Thomas, Joey."

"Hi, it's nice to finally meet you," Thomas flattered Joey and reached out and shook his hand.

"You know Vaughn Muller and Jonathan."

"I do." Joey looked into Jonathan's eyes with a dallying smile.

"How are you?" Jonathan asked in a non-trifling manner.

"I wish I could say I was all right, but you know the circumstances."

Vaughn Muller reached out and shook Joey's hand. "You're going to be just fine. The evidence is not as corroborating as the DA believes it to be."

"Thank you so much for taking my case. I just can't thank you enough." Joey doted his appreciation as he fought to hold back the tears of joy swelled up in his eyes.

"Well I'm not free," Muller amused. They all laughed at his humor. "But expenses will be included in our counter civil suit."

"Excuse me," Joey turned to his brother. "I have to check out at the window and get my things. I'll just be a few minutes."

"We're not going without you," Muller avouched. He pointed to some empty seats in the lobby. "We'll be waiting for you over there." Joey thought it a little odd and somewhat annoying that Muller always seem to speak for everyone. He never thought his stubborn minded brother would ever succumb to anyone in this manner. It was like a peonage and they were his peons. But he was never going to challenge it. He had benefitted greatly from his generosity.

The clerk was busy processing out a prisoner ahead of him in the line. There was a lot of licit documents that had to be signed.

The elevator door across from the lobby opened and to his chagrin, Detective Stone stepped out of it and began walking toward the lobby doors. "Shit what does he want now?" Joey muttered under his breath. "I'll ignore him and perhaps he won't see me." Stone had been informed that Joey was being released. He had a second office on the third floor of the County Jail.

"Mr. Sanders," Detective Stone said, besieging his space.

"I'm not talking to you Stone," Joey said with ironclad resistance. He refused to turn and look at him. "Now on, go through my attorney."

"You have an attorney?" Stone asked with a spurious grin. "I need the name of his Firm."

"Sounds like a personal problem." Joey was trying not to lose face or get angry.

Detective Stone's officious grin drained from his face and filled with aggravation. "That's how it's going to be?" he stated unctuously. "Just don't leave town, because I will find you. See you in Court loser."

Joey did not respond.

Joey's Apartment in the Castro District
Castro Street and Market Street

"This is it," Joey pointed to the three-story corner apartment building on Nineteenth and Castro Street in the Castro District. "I can't thank you enough Mr. Muller."

"It's been a while since I've argued a case, but I promise this is a no brainer." He spoke from the back seat of the black sedan with confidence. Joey loved Muller's British accent. It had a sense of authority to it that Joey couldn't explain.

Thomas sat in the middle of the front bench seat with Dylan's right arm draped over his shoulders as Dylan steered with his left. "Are you sure you don't need company? Dylan asked aggrieved at Joey's determination to be independent. "I just don't think you should be alone." He pulled up to the curb on Nineteenth Street and turned on his hazard lights.

"I'll be fine," Joey reaffirmed.

"I agree," Jonathan chimed in. "I'll stay with you. I can sleep on the couch."

"It's a studio," Joey smirked.

"No problem. I can sleep on the floor." Jonathan had exited the car before Joey could comment.

Joey didn't fuss and shook his head with auspicious surrender. "I guess that's a yes."

Dylan began to demand that Jonathan get back into the sedan, but Thomas put his hand over his mouth. "Just let it be." It was apparent Dylan wasn't happy with Jonathan. It just seemed weird to him that his brother might sleep with his best friend, even though he knew Jonathan no longer had HIV.

"Joey, why don't you swing by this evening and we can go out for dinner," Dylan suggested.

"I don't think I'd be good company. I'm a bit tired. I haven't had a good sleep since my arrest."

"Then you'll join us tomorrow for Sunday brunch," insisted Vaughn Muller.

Joey had one foot on the curb and looked back into the car. "I'd like that. What time?"

"Is ten o'clock too early?"

"I'll see you guys at ten o'clock," Joey said pleased. Closing the door of the sedan, he turned toward Jonathan, expecting a bodacious grin. Instead Jonathan was looking crestfallen at the sidewalk in despair.

"What's wrong?" Joey asked. "Why do you look troubled?

"We have to talk," Jonathan tried to find the word

"About?"

"Not out here," Jonathan explained, nodding his head at the busy pedestrian traffic.

"Sure," Joey agreed and reached out to take his hand. It was warm and languid. He gripped it tighter. "Let's go inside." Joey led him up the second story stairs and into a hallway. The proprietor had made over the three-story home into an apartment building with four flats on each floor. Joey's studio apartment was the second on the left.

The door to the apartment across from Joey's was wide open and party-goers, remnant from the night before, were still playing loud music. However, fragments were standing in the hall struggling to carry on normal conversation in an inebriated state, while others were visibly passed out on the couch and floor.

"Thank God they only party on the weekends," Joey griped in ear shot of the guests in the hallway. Many were shirtless and not wearing shoes. He liked his neighbor Roger, a younger gay City College freshmen whose parents had to be arrantly wealthy. Roger's bodacious fit body attracted the same ilk and he spared no cost at throwing extravagant parties with hard liquor and caviar. By Joey's long licentious stares at the gorgeous men, causing him to fumble a little with his keys, Jonathan wasn't buying any of his platitude.

"Sorry, it's a bit of a mess," Joey apologized as he managed to get the door open.

"No worries." Jonathan stepped across the threshold realizing that Joey was a little unorthodox. Polar opposite of the meticulously clean gay stereotype. No, he broke the mold. Worn clothes draped over chairs and piled on the floor, dishes stacked up in the sink, and cob webs in all corners of the ceiling. Joey rushed about apologizing incessantly in damage control mode. Picking up clothes and tossing them all into one corner and clearing half full glasses off the end tables next to the unmade hide-a-bed couch, that's most likely never been a couch. "Look, don't bother on my account. You need to rest."

"It's never been this filthy," Joey extenuated.

"Stop," Jonathan pleaded. "Sit down. We need to talk." Joey put the last dirty glass in the sink and sat on the edge of the hide-a-bed next to Jonathan.

Jonathan paused, fiddling with his thumbs in his lap and tearing up. "Has your brother ever mentioned anything about me?"

"Like?" Joey's brow bent inward with curiosity.

"Like, did he ever mention that I had AIDS?" Jonathan asked waiting for a reaction.

"No, but then nobody ever had AIDS," Joey corrected him, making emphasis on the word had. "There's no cure. You either have it or you don't." He was well informed about any medical breakthroughs. "Do you?"

"No," Jonathan responded. "I mean I did have it but now I don't."

"Wait, I'm confused," Joey ran his hand through his neglected long hair and shook his head. "If you had it, you still have it." Joey's mind was full of perplexed thoughts. He couldn't help think about the miraculous improvement and strides his brother had made with the disease. "Are you trying to tell me that you tested positive at one time and now you have a negative result to prove it?"

Joey's insolent demeanor had Jonathan worried. Was this not the right time? "Yes, that's what I'm telling you."

"This is insane. Is my brother negative?" Joey stood up and began to pace. "I mean if this is true, and I have to admit my brother's symptoms have gone into remission, why, why, not share it with the medical community?"

"You have to trust me." Jonathan looked worried that he may have just messed everything up and endangered everyone at the Hospice. "I really, really, like you Joey. But I need you right now to trust me."

"Trust you?" Joey challenged. "I admit I'm equally infatuated, but I hardly know anything about you."

"Will you let me explain at least?" Jonathan pleaded.

Joey took a deep breath and covered his face with both hands. "Yes, please explain."

"I need to know that I can trust that you will keep this between us." Jonathan sighed looking for the right words to placate his concern that he may not be able to trust Joey.

"You want me to keep a secret?" Joey asked perplexed.

"A huge secret."

Deliberating, Joey sat back down on the bed and rested his chin on the top of his closed fist. "I just don't want to get hurt."

"Please, I'm asking you to take a leap of faith," Jonathan implored of him.

Joey nodded affirmatively, "OK, OK, I'll probably learn it all sooner than later."

"I'm serious," Jonathan became firm. "This absolutely must not leave this room. Will you swear to that?"

Joey looked deep into Jonathan's strikingly handsome hazel eyes and into his soul. "I promise on one condition."

"OK"

"If somehow it implicates criminal activity, all promises are void. I'm in enough trouble already."

Jonathan knew he was now caught in a catch 22. "Never mind Joey. I can't go through with this. This was a bad idea. I'm sorry I involved you. Just forget it." He smiled as if to change the subject to something less problematic.

"No!" Joey became besieged with rage. "No! you don't get to lead me on and then hang me out to dry."

"I'm sorry Joey, but it can't be hinged on conditional."

"At least tell me just how seditious is this thing you want to tell me?" Joey was keen to ascertain the facts.

"I'm sorry Joey," Jonathan could not risk the security of the others for his romantic scheme. "If you can't trust me enough to swear to this, I won't divulge anything."

Joey's hunger for the truth, supported by the irrefutable evidence that the Hospice patients were healthier than most Olympic athletes, gave credence to Jonathan's story. He had to trust him. "I will give you my word, no conditions, and I will not share this with any one. I swear on my dear Mother's grave."

Jonathan's desire for Joey was enfeebling. "Do you believe in vampires?"

"Oh sure, and ghosts and goblins too," Joey could only reply with winsome sarcasm. "Are You serious right now? Vampires?" Joey rolled his eyes. "Have you lost your mind?"

"You didn't kill those Nazis," Jonathan said unnerved.

"I know that."

"I did," Jonathan said void of guilt.

Joey recalled the female juvenile's pale complexion and being repulsed by the animal like puncture wound on her neck. "This is crazy!" He also recalled the newspaper article linking previous murders to a cult like vampire ritual. All the murders had puncture wounds at the neck and the victim's blood drained from their bodies.

Jonathan tried to make sense of it for him. "Doctor Chang was part of Hitler's team of physicians who performed medical experiments on prisoners. He was also part of the resistance and portended that his experiment failed. But I am living proof that it didn't."

"So how successful is it really if you have to kill people and drink their blood to survive?" Joey made a repulsive face. "I can't believe we're discussing this."

"Tommy, Dylan, and a guy named Macias, were all patients at the AIDS Hospice. Doctor Chang rescued me from Golden Gate Park. I was two breaths away from death. The others were survivors of Auschwitz medical experiments." Jonathan could see Joey was having a hard time ingesting all that he was telling him.

Joey was rubbing his temples trying to put the pieces together. "So, what happened to Tommy and this Macias guy? I remember them."

"Hungary, Macias has relatives there. Tommy agreed to go with him after they became an item. They're preying on members of the Arrow Cross Party, an active fascist cell in that country."

"So, you kill Nazis?"

Jonathan nodded affirmatively. "Before they kill us, you, anyone who doesn't agree, look, or think like them. But there's more than just us. Look, we're just equal opportunity haters, we hate haters."

"And why do you need other people's blood?"

"Something to do with frolic acid depletion and Paba inhibitors. Cells rejuvenate, adrenaline reaches new levels in the body and Doctor Chang's steroid cocktail is the magic. I really don't understand it. But I'm living proof it works."

"So, there's really no correlation between Bram Stoker's vampires and Doctor Chang's?" Joey couldn't hold back a grin from his cheap shot at humor.

"Aren't you hilarious." Jonathan was not amused.

"Sorry, it's just way, way, out there in la la land for me to wrap my head around it." He took Jonathan's hand. "I have just one more question and I have to get some rest."

"I'll tell you what I know."

"Where is Chang and Muller getting all their money? I mean who would post a million-dollar bail for a complete stranger."

"As it became evident that Soviet troops were approaching Auschwitz in 1945, Doctor Chang's work became more and more valuable to Hitler. Imagine a super army, whereby wounds healed instead of succumbing to necrosis and bacteria, such as gangrene. One of Hitler's Cartels, ran by a guy named Krupp, who had supplied Hitler with steel for artillery and armaments, was directed by Hitler to give whatever Chang needed. Krupp should never have trusted Chang. We're not talking about a few million, more like close to a billion. The Krupp family trust is tenaciously hunting for Chang. Which is one of the reasons he and Muller came to the United States."

Joey looked even more perplexed. "Your secret is safe with me. But I've always known that you were somehow involved with the skinhead's death. I mean, you guys just happen to show up about the same time they are killed and Giuseppe is frantic to get out of there. The blood on your chin. But I couldn't divulge that to Detective Stone. I'm glad they got killed. Does that make me a bad person? And I have to say, I'm starting to have serious feelings for you."

Jonathan took hold of Joey's hand. "I really like you a lot. I mean you're all I think about lately as well. I want to be with you."

Joey leaned into Jonathan, resting his head on his chest. "So, what now?"

"I don't know," Jonathan protracted the inevitable. His lips softly kissed Joey's hair. But the interminable life had its flaws. He was indifferent to whether or not it was in Joey's best interest to subject him to the blood-letting and all its complications.

Joey looked up into Jonathan's brawny and stalwart face. "Just hold me."

Jonathan pulled him in close and affectionately stroked his arm. Jonathan had a great pair of lips that he painstakingly kept moist with lip balm and the fragrance made Joey wild with lust. He leaned down and lightly connected their lips together. Joey suckled on the moist soft flesh and pushed his tongue deeper into his mouth. The metallic taste of his saliva was more defined than other men that he had Frenched. Oddly, fell lasciviously into a hypnotic state, but Joey showed no indignation for it.

They kissed hard for a few minutes. Joey rested in Jonathan's arms. He was exhausted and sleep deprived. Having a difficult time keeping his eye lids open, Joey finally succumbed to sleep. Jonathan kissed his forehead fraternally.

Joey was relatively light for Jonathan to carry. He managed to get his arms under Joey's knees and picked him up like a baby and laid him down on the bed. He removed his shoes, propped a pillow under his head and covered him in the blanket that was discarded on the chair next to the bed. Jonathan stood over him for a moment in adoration of his exquisitely handsome features. Cautiously, Jonathan laid down next to him. Joey approvingly reached for Jonathan's arm and wrapped it around him, spooning in him. Jonathan's dignity meant more to him than a night of insatiable pleasure. He let him sleep.

Saturday Evening, May 10, 1986
Vallejo to the Palace of Fine Arts in San Francisco, California

"I'm running late," Jade exclaimed from the phone booth. She had to yell into the receiver to be heard above the noise of the traffic.

"That's fine," Muller answered from the library phone. "Where are you?"

"Vallejo."

"Don't rush. Take your time. We'll simply adjust our plans and have dinner first. We're about a twenty-five-minute drive to the Palace of Fine Arts. Call when you get to Berkeley."

"I understand."

"Jadwiga, drive safely."

"Thanks Vaughn."

"I'm very much looking forward to seeing you again."

"Same."

"See you soon."

"Goodbye."

"Goodbye dear."

Forty-five Minutes Later

Jadwiga had folded the map and stashed it on the dash above the steering wheel of the rental car. She was Southbound on Interstate 80 looking for where the 101 merges. She recalled that the map indicated that she should stay to the right, and there it was. Veering right, the sun was now in her eyes. Traffic was backed up at the traffic signal on Market Street as the Central Freeway came to an end. A young transient couple held up a sign on the corner, 'Homeless Need Help.' The male had a messy man's bun haircut and the female's braided hair was adorned with beads. But their clothes were obviously miss-match items from Saint Vincent's thrift store. Jadwiga had a weak spot for the homeless and struggled to get a five-dollar bill out of her wallet. She rolled the driver's side window down and held the bill out the window so that they could see it. The light had turned green as the young man ran between her car and the truck in front of her.

He snatched the bill from her hand and smiled gratuitously at her, "God bless you." The sudden horn blast from behind startled her. In her rear view mirror an impatient elderly man, already traumatized by the heavy traffic of the city, was pounding on his steering wheel and cursing at her.

She nodded and forced a smile, "Please hurry the light is green." He grimaced and briskly walked back to the curb. It wasn't the first time she had been criticized for her small philanthropies. Jade believed that charity benefitted her self-esteem and added to her integrity. That in the end it really had nothing to do with the benefactor.

She turned right on Market Street and cancelled her turn signal. Changing lanes to the far-left lane, she turned left on Van Ness Street and was pleased with her navigation skills. Van Ness would end at Fisherman's Warf where she would follow the marina to the Fine Arts museum.

Parking was scarce and expensive in the city, but Jadwiga found a parking berth at Broderick and Marina Boulevard, a couple of blocks from the Palace. Although she was particularly proud of her navigation skills, she was embarrassed by her parallel parking skills. But, after a few attempts she managed to get the rental car somewhat in the space.

The alluring harbor reminded her of a small port town in Italy. Yachts of all sizes buoyed in the inlets and older couples playing bocce ball under the lights at Crissy Field park. Red and blue pastel colors accentuated the blazing sunset through the cables of the Golden Gate bridge. Muller couldn't have picked a lovelier place to meet.

Under the Rotunda and through the magnificent tall, sculptured, and gilded arches, she recognized her old friends, Doctor Chang and Vaughn Muller. She was jubilant to see them, but felt a little languid from the long journey. "Vaughn! Doctor Chang! It's so good to see you again," she exclaimed, kissing them both on the cheek. "You both look great."

"How was Coeur D'Alene", Muller asked with the same enthusiasm.

"It wasn't the Alps, but very beautiful. It snowed." Both men loathed the cold and turned their noses up at the mention of it.

"How was the drive?" Doctor Chang interposed.

"Longer than I expected," She said rolling her eyes.

"You must be starving," suggested Doctor Chang.

"I snacked a little along the way, but yes, you have no idea."

"We had an arousing suspicion as such," Muller interjected. "We cooked cranberry apple pork and we'll warm you a dish of it when we get back to the house."

"I'd like that very much. I have a predilection for cranberries."

"Let's retreat to the pond." Doctor Chang pointed to the exit to the pond. "We didn't want to discuss your situation at the house. You never know who's in earshot of your conversation there." She nodded and followed them to a cement park bench overlooking the large pond where a family of swans paddled away to the other side. "So, tell us about your adventures in Coeur D'Alene."

She sat on the end of the bench looking into their inquisitorial expressions. "Do you remember hearing about the Alan Berg murder?"

"Horrendous!" Doctor Chang said indignantly.

"I hit pay dirt at the trial. I was befriended by a White Nationalist by the name of Gary Yarbrough, who invited me to the after party. It is there that I met high ranking members of the white supremacist group known as 'The Order.' I also learned that the FBI had the wrong guys."

"Wasn't their leader Mathews who later was fried in a house fire during an FBI standoff?" Muller recalled.

"Yes, and now they look to a guy named Paul Coombs, he was the guy that pulled the fatal trigger. He disclosed to me that he lives right here in San Francisco. I swear listening to him address the small group in Coeur D'Alene, was like listening to one of Hitler's speeches on the radio. It was frightening."

"So, do you plan to take issue with this Coombs bloke here?" Muller asked officiously.

"I do. He owns a bar called the White Owl." By their awestruck expressions and agape mouth drops, she realized they too were familiar with Coombs. "You know him?"

"Our boys have been there," Doctor Chang interjected.

"The White Owl?"

"Carried out a blood-letting Friday on two Fascists that roughed up and raped a young lady that Fabian had been going out with," Chang continued.

"That was your Operation that Coombs talked about in his speech at the Rally last night." Admittedly, Jade wasn't dumbfounded by the coincidence. "I shared with him that I was in town. He wants me to meet him for a drink at his bar. I have his number."

"Well, you won't have to do it alone," Muller insisted.

"No, I do have to do it alone. I cannot bring suspicion to the Operation. These are really bad asses Vaughn," she replied slightly indignant. Deep inside she loved these men and felt a strong debt to them for giving her a new life. She did not want them to get hurt. But obviously they had become involved.

"You don't think we know that," she piqued Muller's nerve. "You're bloody right about this gang of thugs. This is personal. Berg and I were dear friends. Coombs is mine. The word on the street is that a group of albinos are starting a genocide on White Supremacist gangs," Jadwiga explained.

"How do you know this?" Doctor Chang asked.

"Coombs. I believe that the twins could be in real danger. I have to stop this guy before this becomes a war."

Muller sighed despairingly, "Too late I'm afraid."

"Speaking of the twins, I believe they will be elated to see you again," Doctor Chang said with an endearing smile.

"I promise you, I can handle Coombs," Jadwiga assured him. "I'm meeting him Tuesday night at the White Owl."

"I'm not sure that's a good idea," Muller candidly injected his discordance. "You should take a raincheck. Allow us to do some research on the Peckerwood Supremacist organization." He wasn't sold on her plan of rapprochement. "As we have learnt from dealing with the Nazis, infiltrating may get you some gains, but more than not, it will also get you killed."

"I'm aware of the risks Vaughn," She answered irreducibly determined. "I'm not taking on the Peckerwoods. This fascist is not getting away with Berg's murder. I'm sorry."

"Eliminating Berg was a huge win for the Nationalist Alliance," Doctor Chang interposed his usual scrupulous and calculated reasoning. "You both make a lot of sense of a seemingly irrational dichotomy. But xenophobia will never be defeated, but we must keep it from winning again." The tolling of the Ferry Building Clock Tower bells could be heard across town in the Embarcadero. It was eight o'clock. "Let's get you to the house, you must be famished."

"You're preaching to the choir Doctor. I want to share with you my years of research on global fascism. Ironically, it can be summed up on one page." She pulled a folded piece of paper out of her front pocket. This represents a list of Fascist movements that I have dedicated my life to wiping out. One by one." Jade choked up with emotion, "It's been a very lonely life. You're all the family I have left," she smiled with tears of gratitude and kissed both of the men on the cheek endearingly.

"We will always be here for you," Muller nodded and smiled. "Where are you parked?"

"Two blocks away, not far."

"Huey will ride with you so you don't get lost."

"Thanks."

May 11, 1986
Sunday Brunch –
Saint Vincent's Hospice

Early Spring morning dew glistened on the rose pedals in Saint Vincent's garden. Muller had pulled three of the garden tables together and covered them with a white Polyspun table cloth. Each place setting had a crystal Champaign glass for Mimosas and a crystal water glass for water, a bread plate, salad plate, and a dinner plate. Atop the dinner plate Vaughn had folded, in the Bishop's hat style, red cotton napkins. After setting the table he went back to pruning the roses.

Doctor Chang's blue dragon embroidered satin kimono robe, clipped on the side with a large flower shaped bun, tightly around his mid drift. "Table looks fabulous dear," he praised his lover, calling out to Vaughn from the covered porch.

"Fair dinkum mate," Vaughn replied not losing sight of his pruning.

"I don't think I've seen this many settings ever at our table."

"Did you forget we have three guests coming."

"I know of two, Jade and Joey," Doctor Chang acknowledge with a puzzled look.

"Remember, I told you last night while you were brushing your teeth that Dylan invited that cute Native American lad. Bloody, what's happening with your memory?"

"Was his name Danny?"

"Thomas," Thomas announced, entering the patio. "Like Danny Thomas the actor. Only not Danny" Both men were surprised to see him and chuckled at his humor. "Sorry, I'm a bit early. I thought there would be more traffic."

Doctor Chang got up from the table to welcome him. "It's Sunday dear. There's no traffic on Sunday." Grabbing his shoulders, Doctor Chang pulled him closer and kissed both of his cheeks to Thomas stiffed apprehension. "Giuseppe has taught us the proper Italian method for welcoming friends to our abode. Hope you don't mind."

"Not at all."

"You know you smell as delicious as you look. Love your cologne."

"It's a musk my papa Jack gave me for Christmas."

"Won't you have a seat at the table? The others will be here shortly. The twins are in the kitchen cooking our brunch. Brunch will be ready soon."

"I saw that. It smelt great!"

"There you are!" Dylan said excited to see him and holding the Sunday newspaper in one hand. He looked disheveled as if he just got out of bed. His white undershirt was wrinkled from being slept in. "Giuseppe said you were out back."

"Hi," Thomas kissed his cheeks keeping with his newly taught Italian ritual.

"Wow, wasn't expecting that." Dylan stepped back looking surprised as both Muller and Doctor Chang chuckled. Amused at Doctor Chang's off the hip scheme to kiss the kid. He then leaned into Thomas and kissed him on the mouth. "I'd slip you the tongue but I haven't brushed my teeth yet." His comment drew more cackles.

"Hi handsome," Doctor Chang greeted Dylan, his chair turned from watching Muller perform his gardening. "Is that for me?" he asked starring at the newspaper in Dylan's hand.

"Oh yes, sorry," Dylan apologized and handed him the San Francisco Chronicle Sunday Edition. "I let my brother in and saw it on the porch."

"Well, where is he?" Doctor Chang anxiously inquired.

"In the Library with Jonathan."

Vaughn Muller's brow raised as did his finger as he reprimanded plangently so all could hear, "Please inform Mr. Jonathan Hughes that Joey is my guest not his. He is not to monopolize on Joey this morning. After all, I invited him to brunch." His farcical demand drew laughter from all within ear shot.

"I heard that!" Jonathan announced from inside the kitchen where he and Joey had migrated.

Eventually all the settings were taken up by residents and guests at the new Saint Vincent Hospice. At both heads of the merged tables, Doctor Chang and Vaughn Muller.

"Can you pass the hash?" Jade requested.

"Sure," Dylan handed the bowl of corn beef hash to Fabian who, handed it off to Ludovic who, held the bowl as Jade dished a portion on her plate.

"Thanks," Jade expressed her gratitude.

"Thomas, how are your studies going?" Vaughn Muller inquired after taking a sip of hot herbal tea.

"Except for math, pretty good."

"You should ask Jade to tutor you," Doctor Chang interposed, picking his teeth with his fingernail. "You know she has her doctorate from the University of Warsaw."

Thomas looked perplexed, "What State is Warsaw in?"

Dylan swallowed hard, as did many at the table at Thomas's naivety. "Poland."

Thomas was digging himself in deeper, "There's a State called Polland?" To which the clinging of utensils on the glass plates stopped, many eye lids raised, and some choked on their food and coughed.

Dylan attempted to save face, "Are you sure math is your worst subject? Poland is a country in Europe."

Attempting to find synergy, Muller injected, "I'm sure Jade wouldn't mind tutoring you Thomas if you asked her."

"I don't mind at all if I'm still in the City," Jadwiga's furtive suggestion surprised Muller and Chang.

"We were hoping that you would be here for the long term," Doctor Chang replied with angst.

"Surely Jade you'll stay a while and let us enjoy your company?" Muller cut in. Vaughn Muller had developed a Father-daughter relationship with Jadwiga from their post war home in London. Jadwiga had stayed with them for several years after finishing her degree in Warsaw. She was afraid to return to Poland as the persecution under the Russians wasn't much better than when the Nazi's occupied Poland.

"My List, remember?" was the only answer she felt would suffice.

"Look, I'd be glad to tutor you as well," Joey offered.

Both Dylan and Jonathan shot Joey a jealous glance at his offer.

"Tell us about your list," Thomas insisted. His question peeked everyone's curiosity.

"It's a personal matter," Vaughn attempted to shut the subject down. "It's a Fascist hit list that…"

Slamming his palm on the corner of the table, "Not everyone here is privy to this conversation," Vaughn dutifully and vehemently interrupted. Some of the light silverware jumped out of place on the third section where Vaughn was sitting. Aghast and startled, the mood of the beau monde shifted out of joint as well.

Doctor Chang broke the silence, "Come on everyone, finish these hash browns." He held the bowl up for someone to grab.

Monday, May 12, 1986
The Turning Point

It was another rainy maudlin Monday morning. Cocaine had kept him up most of the previous night. An evening of sushi and debauchery that began at the O'Farrell, an adult cinema theater near San Francisco's Tenderloin District. Starring out the large neon lit window of the White Owl Bar, Paul Coombs took a sip of coffee and considered walking over to the Kentucky Fried Chicken across the street. He believed that greasy food would work wonders for his hangover. A ritual he and his late wife Amanda would indulge in before going to bed. He missed her.

"Paul, you have a phone call," Sandy, the bar manager informed him as she opened the till and inserted the starting bank and separated the bills in the drawer.

He rubbed his aching forehead, "Can you take a message Sandy."

"I can, but he says the matter is very urgent business. Says he represents the Thyssen Krupp Company."

His Uncle Werner was a corporate officer for the Krupp company in Germany and supervised the Iron mill in Esson for Gustoff Krupp during the great war. Werner left Paul one point five million dollars in his will. The other half of Werner's assets went to Paul's cousin Erik who resides in Munich. "Can you please take his number and I will call him back?"

"Sure." Sandy was a single mom of two teenage girls and was hired as a favor to his friend Don, Sandy's Father, and fellow Supremacist from his younger days in Mississippi. Paul had treated her more than fair, often paying for expensive medical treatments that her children needed and once flipping the bill for a trip to Disneyland. In turn, she turned a blind eye on Paul's regular patrons grabbing her ass and playing along with their misogynistic jokes. But more importantly she had an eagle eye on managing Paul's bar against employee theft. She had earned his loyalty on more than one occasion.

She went back into the office and then re-emerged with the caller's indignant response. "He said it can't wait and to wipe your ass and come to the phone." She tried to hide her amused grin at the caller's jocose response.

"Son of a bitch." Feeling dissed, Paul picked up his coffee from the table, went into the office, closed the door, then picked up the phone. "This is Paul Coombs."

"Mr. Coombs, my name is Rudi Helbard and I'm a private investigator for the Krupp Family Trust."

"I know the company well. Are you calling from Germany?"

"I'm in San Francisco staying at the Double Tree Brisbane Suite 402, but my Firm is located in Chicago. I'm endeavoring to locate two men who embezzled more than a half billion dollars from my Client. We have done our research and believe these two men, along with a number of other individuals, might have migrated to San Francisco."

"I'm sorry, I don't see how this involves me," Coombs interrupted somewhat aggravated.

"I'm hoping we can help each other."

"Sure, if you want to donate a million to the National Alliance, otherwise you're wasting my time."

"Your cousin gave us your name and shared that you are involved with the Alliance in San Francisco. Trust me, I just might be saving your life."

Coombs sat up in his chair and was suddenly keen to ascertain where this was going. "Is this some kind of extortion plot,' Coombs responded indignantly.

"You seem like a smart man Mr. Coombs, I'm sure you've read the news concerning the albino serial killer?"

"OK, now you have my attention."

"Good." There was a short pause. "We believe these killings are the first major lead to finding our Client's money. I'm going to read some names to you. Let me know if you recognize any of them."

"Go ahead."

"Doctor Huey Chang?"

"No."

"Fabien and or Ludovic Dubois?"

"Never heard of them."

"Giuseppe Ricci?"

"No bells going off."

"Jadwiga Dzido?"

"Goes by the name Jade?"

"It's possible. Do you know her?"

"It's possible." Advantage Coombs. "I don't understand the connection and how that somehow puts me in harm's way."

"They kill Fascists."

Coombs swallowed hard and became anxious over the intel Rudi was disclosing. He seemed less incredulous. Was she a Mole?

"Mr. Coombs have I lost you?"

"No, I'm still on the phone." It was all coming together for him. The Berg Trial, her fake alliance with the Order. Red Beard's ritual like murder. And what if Garmont's death is somehow related? Who's next? "We need to talk in person."

"I've already arranged for a limousine to pick you up. How soon can you be ready and shall I have them pick you up at the White Owl?"

"As soon as possible, White Owl."

"They're on their way Mr. Coombs."

"I'll need a Bloody Mary." There was no response as Paul heard the phone click before he got the word Mary out of his mouth. "What are you up to Jade?" He shook his head, disappointed that he may have to kill her. Perhaps Garmont suffered the same fate.

Double Tree Hotel – Brisbane, CA

It hadn't been ten minutes, since the Krupp Attorney hung up the phone on him, that the limousine pulled into the yellow painted loading zone in front of Coomb's bar.

"Sandy my ride is here," Paul Coombs sucked the last inch of Bloody Mary and left the glass on the table.

"Wow, some ride," Sandy took note of the fancy limousine parked in front of the bar.

Paul handed her a note with the address of the Suite number at the Double Tree Hotel in Brisbane. "Hopefully you won't need this information. But then you never know."

Sandy read the address on the post-it note and placed it in her pocket. "Those guys don't look too friendly," she said directing Paul's attention to two behemoth suits leaning against the curb side of the limousine. Private security personnel wearing suits and sun glasses, with the intent to look intimidating.

"Don't worry, I'm armed."

"Be careful Paul," Sandy beseeched as he exited the front entrance of the bar. She watched as one muscle-man walked around the front of the limo and got into the driver's side door. The other shook Paul's hand and opened the rear door for him. After shutting the door behind Paul, he climbed into the front passenger seat. The Limo sped away.

Paul Coombs kept a visual memory of where he was going through the one-way tinted side window. The limo got on the 101 Bayshore Freeway and merged off onto the Sierra Point Parkway off-ramp. It made a quick right onto Shoreline Court and another quick right into the Double Tree Hotel parking lot.

Stopping at the main entrance of the Hotel, the suit in the passenger side got out and opened Paul's door. "Mr. Coombs follow me." Coombs purposely didn't make eye contact and maintained body language that gesticulated that he would not be intimidated by their physical size. The limo took off after Paul's door was shut. He was left standing at the curb as his escort walked to the main entrance doors and held one open for him. Paul followed him into the elevator and up to the top floor suite 402.

It was a very large suite with panoramic windows looking over the bay to Candlestick Sports Arena. Sitting at a round coffee table thumbing through legal documents, Rudi Helbard stood and greeted Paul. "Mr. Coombs, welcome." He pointed to the empty chair across from him. Paul was impressed that he had a fresh Bloody Mary on top a bar napkin in front of the empty hotel chair.

"I'm impressed. You remembered," Paul Coombs sat down at the table and took a sip from his complimentary libation. "I like you already."

"That was the idea Mr. Coombs," Rudi replied elated. "Thank you for coming on such short notice."

"You said the magic words on the phone," Coombs stated with some incertitude.

"I assure you we both will benefit greatly from this meeting."

"That's why I'm here."

Rudi wasted no time getting to the matter at hand. "The individuals, whose names I ran by you earlier, heisted a very large chunk of my Client's money."

"The Krupp Family?"

Rudi nodded affirmatively, "Thanks to your cousin Erik, we were able to locate you."

"I still don't understand how that involves me," Paul winced.

"It doesn't." Rudi paused and leaned back adjudging whether or not Paul Coombs would be a risk or would corroborate with his plan. "We need Doctor Chang alive, but he is surrounded by some very dangerous individuals with," Rudi paused for lack of a logical description, "Inconvenient superpowers."

Coombs leaned forward, chin to chest, his pupils starring at Rudi from the top of his eye sockets. "Superpowers, like superman?" He snickered with cagey hesitance.

"I can't explain it Mr. Coombs, but the individuals that I previously mentioned to you, and there is likely more, were part of a Nazi bio-engineered experiment that we now know was successful." Coombs's face contorted incredulously with each unfathomable claim. He pushed a copy of the 'Illustrated London News' in front of him. The bold headline read, 'Vampire Serial Killer Strikes Again?' Below it was a close-up illustration of a Victims neck with teeth marks encompassing two distinct puncture wounds. Coombs skepticism drained from his face as he studied the illustration.

"This is insane," Coombs uttered unexpectedly, spooked as he scanned the article. He couldn't refute the resemblance of the murders to the same method of execution used in the San Francisco murders.

"Let me shock you even more," Rudi announced sliding another newspaper in front of him. It was a copy of a 1947 edition of the New York Times article continued from page one. The story header read, 'Nazi Medical Experiment Victim Testifies.' Below the title was a picture of Jadwiga Dzido.

Paul Coombs brought the paper near his face for closer inspection. "That's her, but," he paused for lack of words to describe the phenomenon.

"But she still looks the same. Hasn't aged," Rudi completed his thoughts.

"That's impossible, she'd be an old lady by now," he stated disconcertedly. "How's that possible?"

"If I knew Paul, I'd be more interested in the medicine than the money." Rudi retrieved the Newspapers and tossed them to the floor. "Do I have your attention now?"

Coombs put both elbows on the table and rested his forehead in the palms of his hands pressing his fingers into his scalp nervously. "What's your plan?"

"I need intel and manpower. But I need you to be selective, this job requires loyal muscle and not fainthearted bozos. Do you get my drift?"

"Not a tall order. But what about compensation? I mean now that I'm aware of the risks, perhaps I do it my way. My men have put two and two together and frankly they won't even go to the toilet without someone watching the door."

Rudi reached into his suit coat inside pocket and pulled from it a thick envelope with ten thousand dollars, all one hundred-dollar bills. "Perhaps this may change their minds."

Paul Coombs accepted the envelope, inspected the contents, then grinned ear to ear. "Now you're talking my language."

"Ten thousand dollars up front and ten million total payment when you deliver Doctor Chang alive and still able to sign his name."

"That's a lot of money Mr. Helbard," Paul gloated. "You have a deal."

"Alive Mr. Coombs or the deal is off." Rudi insisted and shot him a disdainful look.

Tuesday, May 13, 1986
The White Owl Bar

Jadwiga parked across the street in the rear theater parking lot. The 501 jeans were an uncomfortable tight fit, but she had to dress down to acclimate to the callow bar crowd. Normally she wore her hair in a bun with dovetail braids to the nape of her neck. But she had let her hair hang loose on her bare shoulders. The air was chilly and she was now regretting wearing the ribbed halter top from her limited travel collection.

She had spoken to Paul Coombs early that morning and confirmed their date for six thirty. She had arrived early to canvas the area for a parking spot. Parking was a premium. She had rented a room at a Motel 6 in San Mateo, about two miles from the bar, trying to distance the Creed from her mission. Once back at the motel she would execute Coombs and set the bed, where his dead body would hopefully lay, on fire. Jadwiga had paid for the room with cash and registered the room under his name. "He's my husband," she told the curious motel clerk. That was plan B. Plan A entailed Coombs inviting her to his place where she would carry out the execution and cremate Coombs and his abode.

It was a typical slow Tuesday night at the Owl. Three Peckerwood gang members were shooting pool at the far end of the Bar. Leaning over the table, the slim, pinwheel mustache, bald, and shirtless Peckerwood, turned his focus from the cue ball, to Jade entering the bar. He liked what he saw. She raised her brow and smiled flirtatiously back at him.

Sandy was tending bar and waived her over. "You must be Jade?"

"Hi," Jade acknowledged her and reached out to shake her hand.

"Just a sec," Sandy said wiping her dish soap covered hands with a bar towel before grasping Jade's extended hand. "I'll let Paul know that you are here." She disappeared through the back door to the office. Jade mounted the bar stool and scoped the bar out. Other than the three pool jocks, an elderly biker sat at the end of the bar staring at his tall lager which he had barely touched. At a table next to the North window sat a young couple, obviously naive of what type of patrons frequent the Owl. It was convenient and they stopped in to have a drink. Fortuitously for them, they were Caucasian. Sandy was protective of the civilian clientele. She called them the 'Unawares.' "Their money spends too," she reminded her regular clientele.

Paul Coombs emerged from the back office pretending to be excited to see her, "Jade!" He took the stool next to her. "What are you drinking?"

"Rum and coke."

"Sandy, Rum and coke for Jade, and I'll have a whisky sour. Did Sandy introduce herself?"

"We shook hands. It's nice to formally meet you," Sandy smiled at her.

"Likewise," Jade stated with slight smile.

"Sandy manages the Owl for me. Don't know what I'd do without her. When did you get in town?"

"Yesterday. I'm staying at a motel a few miles away from here."

"I don't like motels in the City, maids aren't required to check for bed bugs," Coombs wrinkled his nose in disgust. Jade couldn't help but recall the incident with the rat in Auschwitz and thinking how sheltered Americans were.

"You look particularly handsome tonight," Jade coquettishly remarked.

"Ah, it's the black silk shirt," he replied modestly.

She pinched the shirt tail between her thumb and forefinger then rubbed her forefinger over his chest. "You're right it feels good."

"Anything else you'd like to feel?" he baited her.

"Get a room you two," Sandy gibed, setting bar napkins under their drinks. They seemed to ignore her remark meant to humor them.

In her peripheral view she noted that the three pool sharks had left the bar. "So, Paul tell me how you hooked up with the Order?"

"I didn't, they contacted me. I attended a National Alliance rally to hear Bill Pierce speak. That's where I first met Walter Mathews. Of course, you're familiar with Walter's situation?"

"Of course," she recalled the name but couldn't remember where or why she was familiar with Walter Mathews. She became somewhat anxious and wished he had not asked the question.

"I'm going to visit him this Friday."

She interrupted, "Do you mind if I go I'd really like to speak with him."

Coombs looked confused, "Speak with him? I was referring to the cemetery where he is buried."

Jade swallowed hard. Had she blown her cover. "I'm eccentric, what can I say. You don't believe in spirits Mr. Coombs?"

His condescending stare sent a few shivers down her spine, "No, no I don't. You talk to dead people?"

She pointed to his glass that was still untouched, "Here drink up. Let's talk about something more positive." He could see by her goosebumps on her arm that she had become nervous. She grasped her own drink and raised it to her mouth. "Here's to Walter, cheers!" He raised his glass and tapped hers, then took a sip.

"So, Jade tell me, why did you become involved in the Alliance?"

She wanted nothing more than to change the direction of the conversation. "My grandfather was murdered by the Red Army. They raped my mother and drove them from their home. When they returned a Jewish family was occupying our home. My mother joined the new fascist movement in post war France and vowed to rid the world of Communists and Jews." She could tell by the distrust in his face he wasn't buying a word of it.

Paul Coombs smirked and pulled out a Glock 19 9mm Compact Semi-automatic pistol, that he had tucked under his belt and hid by his shirt. Secluded in his lap and under the bar top, he pointed the gun at her. "Why don't you tell me the real reason why you're here Jade?"

She struggled to stay in character, "I told you my reasons. Now put that away."

"Perhaps I can refresh your memory as you seem to be a little shaky on the details. You grew up in Poland during the 30's, got your degree at the University of Warsaw, and joined the resistance fighters."

"What are you talking about? I'm a proud Aryan Nationalist," she remonstrated angrily. Her anxiety turned to fear as Sandy tried to explain to the naïve couple at the table that there was an emergency and she had to shut down the bar. The older Peckerwood member sat still looking at her with malevolent disgust as if he were in on it.

Paul waited until the couple had left the bar and Sandy had locked the entrance doors and drew the shades. "I don't believe you, Jadwiga Dzido." He pronounced her full name slowly and by each syllable. "In fact, I have it on good intel that you and your friends," he paused as she straightened up with a rueful expression. "Oh yes, I know about the good Doctor's operation here."

"You're making a big mistake. Call Gary he'll vouch for me."

Coombs laughed at her remark, "Yes, let's do. Trust me, Gary's aware of everything. Gary believes you may have something to do with Silva's younger brother's death."

"So, what's next? Are you going to kill Me?"

"Not right away. You're more useful to me alive than dead. I have some very rich friends who have a beef with Doctor Chang." She became horrified. "And you are going to help deliver him to them."

She grimaced and cackled, "I'm not helping you do anything!"

He slowly dismounted the bar stool keeping the gun's aim on her. He then shouted at her, "Stand up! Now!" She obeyed. Rudi's claim that these bio-engineered freaks had super powers haunted him. Would a bullet even kill her? Would she attack him and break his neck? He could not hold the gun steady as he led her to the rear parking lot and into the empty warehouse.

Thursday, May 15

Vaughn Muller had been pacing the Hospice for two days, concerned about Jadwiga's disappearance. "Bloody hell! You should have insisted that she not go!" Muller berated Huey. The house guests could hear them argue in their bedroom through the thin plaster walls.

Fabien knocked on the quarreling lover's bedroom door, "We're leaving now."

The door cracked open enough that Fabien could make out the right half of Doctor Chang's face. "Please don't take long, we need the Creed to meet soon."

"Zis won't take long."

"Thank you," Doctor Chang looked defeated.

Thomas's grandpa Jack, had given Dylan an earlier ride to Sutter Cathedral Hill Hospital and met up later with Fabien and the other Hospice guests in the lobby.

"Zay have released her, yes?" Fabien asked.

Before Dylan could respond Carol emerged from the elevator with a female nurse escort. She moved slowly, not quite acclimated to her crutches. The swelling had gone down, her left eye was bandaged, and her wounds still held together by stitches.

"Carol!" Fabien shouted to get her attention. He hustled his steps toward her. She looked frantic as if she didn't know him.

He was immediately taken back by her inability to identify him. "Iz me, Fabien."

"She suffered major head injury sir. She may or may not get her short-term memory back," the nurse ruefully interjected. "She doesn't remember you."

"You must be someone I know," Carol probed.

"Yes!" Fabien stated with a pang of anguish knotting in his stomach.

Carol took notice of Thomas with the others, "I know that boy."

"Good," the nurse said encouragingly. She waived for Thomas to come over. "What is your name?"

"Thomas. Carol and I work together at Pearl's restaurant."

"Pearl's? I'm a waitress there. Where is my family?"

The nurse reminded her again, disappointed that she didn't recall their earlier conversation. "Two of your brothers are flying in with your mother on Saturday."

She examined Fabien from head to toe and grinned, "I certainly have good taste in men." Fabien grinned ear to ear. He so needed to hear those words.

"It's encouraging that she is starting to remember people and things," the nurse continued. "It's possible she'll get it all back."

"I'm right here you know," Carol chastened the nurse.

"She's also a little feisty which is a good sign she's recovering," the nurse handed Fabien her physician's release, medical follow up documents, and a small sack containing her prescriptions. "Make sure she takes her medication and follows the doctor's instructions." She hugged Carol, "Don't forget your doctor's appointment on Monday."

"Thanks for everything you did for me." The nurse smiled and walked back to the elevator.

Dylan parallel parked the black sedan at the curb in front of Carol's apartment. Conversations were awkward during the trip from the hospital and for the most part it was a quiet ride. Fabien didn't want to frighten her off and held back on any small physical gestures.

"Can you hold zese?" Fabien handed Carol's crutches to Thomas and assisted Carol out of the rear seat.

Carol's welcoming back party followed her to her apartment door.

"Look, I've got it from here," she forced a smile of gratitude. "I just need some time to myself."

"I will bring some dinner for you tonight," Fabien insisted.

"Thank you," She conceded without complaint. "I could use some company."

"Keep your door locked," Dylan drilled. "And don't hesitate to call us if you need something."

"I will, trust me."

"Are you sure you'll be alright?" Fabien worried.

"I'll be fine. I can't thank you enough. I really need to rest."

That was their queue to leave.

"6:00 o'clock. I'll have dinner," Fabien reminded her.

"I'm looking forward to it."

June 2, 1942
Auschwitz-Birkenau German Concentration Camp

"She's coming around," Giuseppe Ricci barked to the others. He knelt at her bunk and held her hand. "Miss, you're going to live." Jadwiga managed to open one eye and her face contorted with disappointment at his prognosis. She really had hoped for death and an end to the torture.

The Dubois twins stood over Jadwiga, taking special interest in their new friend. The pigment in their skin already showing signs of albinism. The Nazi's medical experiment to stop the production of melanin in their bodies was working. Fabien's once blonde mien had already turned a Christmas white.

Doctor Huey Chang had the Sonderkommandos cover her naked body and hide her leg wound from the curiosity of the others in her bunkhouse. Sonderkommandos were professional Jews the Nazis granted extra food rights. They performed unwanted gruesome tasks such as, disposing of the dead, using pliers to rip out the gold teeth of the corpses, and sweeping the ashes from around the human furnaces in the crematorium. They were also known as the Geheimnistrager (secret keepers) by the Nazis and were considered a security risk and were killed and replaced every two to three months. Their demise paled in their minds to the pain of starvation.

"I prayed that God would take her," the Catholic Priest cried at his bunk, face buried in his palms.

Fabien turned sharply toward the Catholic Priest, "Shut up! How is sis you be man of God?"

The ten other prisoners sat silently on the edge of their bunks. Emaciation starting to show on some of the weaker prisoners. One of those, a tall slender man in his forties, who claimed to be an ex-lawyer of Hitler, was softly jabbering apologies to Hitler for his behavior.

Unexpectedly, the SS guard at the door, stood at attention, "Stand!" he shouted. The door flew open and the bunk house filled with SS guards. Behind them emerged two high command personnel, General Rudolph Hoss and Klaus Barbie, otherwise known as the "Butcher of Lyon".

"Doctor Chang confirmed that she survived the experiment," Hoss exclaimed, pleased at the life-saving implications it meant for wounded German soldiers.

"I want this available yesterday," ordered Barbie, a high-ranking Gestapo officer.

"Get out of the way!" Hoss demanded of the three prisoners standing at the side of Jadwiga's bunk. All three shot Hoss a disdainful glare and stepped out of the way exposing a wakening medical breakthrough.

Hoss removed the blanket covering Jadwiga, exposing her stitched wound and her nakedness. "You can see Klaus, even with the debris still embedded in her wound there are no signs of gangrene or other infectious types."

Barbie gave a closer inspection of the wound and noted out the corner of his eye that Hoss's eyes were elsewhere. "I see you have taken a liking to this one," he grinned at Hoss.

"Can you blame me?" he retorted.

"Doesn't it seem odd to you that her wound looks better than one would expect? I want Doctor Chang to deliver the full report to the Chancellor before his next address to the Reichstag." He stood and gave an anxious confused look at Rudolph Hoss. "You said earlier you had a token show of appreciation?"

"You will not be disappointed, I promise." Hoss turned to the ranking SS guard. "You know what to do. The Hauptsturmfuhrer and I will be observing from the tower. "No mistakes!" Hoss had previously reviewed the show with the SS leader. "Come Hauptsturmfuhrer Berger, we have the best seats in the house."

As the Gestapo leader and the General walked out of the bunkhouse, the lead SS Guard began barking orders. "Line up," he shouted at the inmates, who begrudgingly attempted to form a straight line. Nudging them with the barrel tip of their rifles, there became a resemblance of a straight line. The seven SS guards flanked the inmates as they were lead out of the bunkhouse and toward the pit at the edge of the forest. This was the place referred to as the "Dark Gates of Hell," by the residence of Auschwitz.

To their left, about 300 yards, new inmates were being unloaded from open train cars and lined up in front of the barbers and the cleansing tanks. Due to endemic typhus, a louse-borne disease that could not only affect the residents of the concentration camp, but the nearby civilian population, the tanks were filled with a delousing solution. New arrivals were shaved head to toe including arm pits, pubic, and butt hairs. The barbers used dull clippers. The open razor wounds burned as their naked bodies climbed into the tanks and ordered to completely submerge their entire body. The screams were allowed to have a psychological effect on the residents for a sobering compliance to perform unthinkable acts without complaint.

To their right, leading up to the pit, were weaker prisoners, forced to carry large rocks about 100 feet. The prisoner would be forced to pick up another rock and carry it back to the original pile of rocks. An occasional gunshot meant that a prisoner had dropped his or her rock. The Sonderkommado would load the dead body on a cart and dump it in the adjacent pit.

"Stop!" shouted the lead SS Guard. In front of them was a ten-foot square wire fenced cage. It was obviously designed to see into but also to keep small rodent type animals from escaping. The metal cage was enclosed, not only on all four sides, but top and bottom as well. Wood framing was cemented into the ground at each corner. On the far side of the cage, a framed in door. But what caused their hearts to race was the row of ten smaller cages holding large angry rats that had been starved long enough to take them to a level of desperation.

"You two Schwul scum, (German slang word for homosexual), take one step forward." The husky SS officer shouted. The more feminine one began to cry profusely.

"You must be brave Axel. Please stop crying or they will kill you," his lover Hackman plead with him.

"Good! I want to die Hackman," he screamed.

"Please Axel," Hackman sternly insisted. Tears streaking his cheeks.

Giuseppe looked up at the guard tower. He loathed the two Nazi Leaders seemingly enjoying the spectacle. The SS Guard didn't seem to care much about the traumatic conversation and waved to the Sonderkommando standing next to the cage door. Knowing the drill all too well, the Sonderkommando retrieved a blood-stained burlap sack from a hook near the door. The sack was just large enough to fit over a person's head. Another SS Guard pulled Axel's hands behind his back and handcuffed them without any resistance. He then pulled down Axel's prison pants and told him to step out of them.

Fabien knew what was going to happen next and stared angrily at the ground. This did not go well with the SS officer, wanting his mission to go perfect for General Hoss. He stepped in front of Fabien raised his rifle and struck the side of his head with the stock of his rifle. "You will watch or you will die," his lip quivering as his shouted the order at him. Fabien regained his balance and shot the SS Guard a contemptuous stare.

The burlap sack was placed over Axel's head and the woven string pulled tightly around his neck. The Sonderkommando led Axel through the cage door and locked it behind him. Axel, unable to see, stood two feet from the door and didn't dare move. "Please don't do this, please," Axel screamed.

"Please I beg you, don't hurt him," Hackman pleaded with the SS officer.

The SS officer looked up at the tower waiting for the commencement waive from General Hoss. Hoss raised his hand, signaling the Lead Guard to proceed. A nod of his head and the Sonderkommando pulled the string which released the doors on the small cages. Ten famished Rats, educated from past experience on their next meal, circled Axel. The rodents inched closer to their prey. Shaking profusely with fear, he stood frozen, unable to see the approaching creatures but aware of how his life would end. One rat squealed and attacked, biting hard into Axel's right calf. The blood dripping from the wound on Axel's leg, set off a chain reaction of attacking rats, lunging, climbing, and biting into Axel's flesh. Axel tried kicking and turning sharply to shake them off. A few lost their grip. He lost his balance and fell hard, screaming. He rolled, shaking off a few more, but they resiliently attacked again. Axel struggled to stand and began to run. But blinded, he crashed into the cage fencing and fell to the ground. The rats had feasted plentiful on the left leg, exposing his femur, now appearing as bloody hamburger.

"Please shoot me!" Axel screamed as one rat had reached his shoulders and tried to bite into his face.

"Do it!" Hackman demanded of the SS officer.

Pushing the barrel of his rifle into Hackman's left temple, he took a hand gun from his holster and handed it to Hackman. "There's one bullet, miss and the rats finish him off."

"No, please, I can't," Hackman protested.

"Do it!" The officer screamed at him.

Hackman pointed the gun at his lover, his hands shaking violently. His mind flashing back to the days before the fascists changed his perfect life. Waking up in bed with his arm over Axel after a night of debauchery and great wine. He never would have imagined in all his wildest dreams that overnight such evil could turn his world upside down. The security of Axel's unconditional love, gone. The laughter on the dance floor, inebriated and feeling indestructible, never again.

"Steady or you'll miss."

Axel screamed with excruciating pain as the determined rat bit into his soft cheek through the torn burlap sack. Hackman steadied his hands. "I love you Axel!" he cried loudly as he pulled the trigger. The bullet entered the burlap sack. Axel went limp. The rats ran from the sound of gun fire. They regained their confidence and returned to finish their meal.

A very angry Hackman turned and attempted to shoot the ranking SS officer. "You bastard!" But there was only a clicking sound of an empty chamber.

"What? You didn't believe me when I said there was only one bullet?" With Instantaneous and calculated speed, he seized the gun from Hackman, shoved the stock of his rifle into his gut. As Hackman bent over in agony, the SS officer struck him at the head with the same gun. Hackman hit the ground with a thud, unconscious.

"Nice work General Hoss," Barbie remarked with a smirk from the tower.

"I'm glad you found it entertaining Klaus."

Saturday, May 17 1986
Judge Lowell Howell High School - Gym

"What's wrong?" Thomas noticed Dylan's apprehension as soon as he turned into the school parking lot.

"This is the Gym you were talking about?" Dylan swallowed hard, staring at the goal posts of the high school football field above the fence.

"Yea, I go to Howell," he replied as if Dylan should have known it all along. "You went here too, didn't you?"

Dylan's gaze drifted from the football field to the dashboard of Jack's truck. "Freshman to Junior year."

"Where did you finish your senior year?" Thomas wanted to know all he could about the man he believed he was madly in love with.

Dylan grew uneasy and turned his attention out the passenger window, "Can we just change the subject. I'm trying not to feed those memories."

"Sure," Thomas felt indifferent to Dylan's aloof disposition. Disappointed he either didn't trust him enough to share, or that he had resurrected painful thoughts.

The momentary silence seemed like forever. A thin Hispanic youth named Jorge (horhay) Lopez, recognized Jack's truck. He left the small group of young men and ran toward his friend.

"Thomas!"

Thomas smiled at Dylan, "This is my buddy Jorge. You'll like him."

"I'm sure I will," Dylan was trying to be rational and put time between his nightmare and the moment.

Thomas and Dylan got out of the truck and met Jorge near the radiator. Thomas and Jorge chest bumped. "I wasn't sure you'd make it," Jorge said energized.

"I don't recognize those guys that came with you," Thomas asked, knowing that most likely they'd be playing on the same team.

"Those clowns are my cousins," Jorge explained. "The super tall one is Roberto. His family is visiting from Mexicali. You've already met

Francis, and the ugly one is Alberto. Just call him Al, he lives with my grandparents in San Jose."

"He's cute!" Thomas remarked lasciviously. Thomas's comment raised a tinge of jealousy in Dylan that he camouflaged instantly.

"Not my type," Jorge lampooned. He noticed Dylan's awkward embarrassment. "Don't worry, I don't have a problem with the gay thing or with keeping it private. With me, you're good. But my cousins, I'm not too sure. But, it's none of their business unless you decide to make it their business."

"I like you already," Dylan announced to Thomas's delight. "It looks like we have a team. How is Roberto's shooting? He must be six feet eight?"

"Come on, you can ask him yourself."

They finished introductions as they made their way to the Gym entrance doors. The Gym was also utilized by the National Guard on the weekends. But their training had moved to the football field on that Saturday to the pleasure of the youth in the Tenderloin. There were six baskets. The four side units, normally retracted to the ceiling during the regular season games, were lowered to allow more Youth to participate.

Two volunteer teachers, one of which was the assistant basketball coach, would organize the teams and placed them at one of the six courts. They announced for the participants to fall into twelve groups on the bleachers adjacent to the court. Trying to keep it fun for the participants, they allowed friends to form alliances. Jorge's group was assigned team Three.

The assistant coach blew his whistle, "Alright, shut up for a minute. We have rules and expect that you each follow them or be asked to leave. They are, One, no dunking or hanging onto the baskets." That brought a few disgruntled boos. "Second, there will be six games played at the same time and there's only two of us. So, you will police your own fouls. We will call the ones we see. But, we expect that you will use good sportsmanship and impress us with a high level of integrity. Third, any unsportsmanlike conduct, like intentional blows, and you will forfeit your right to play here indefinitely. Shirts will get the ball first mid court. Any questions? Fine. Team One, skins, you'll be playing Team Twelve on court one." He pointed to the mentioned basket. There was a clatter of feet on the wooden bleachers as they were anxious to get started. "Wait!" he roared aloud. "Please wait until after I'm finished to leave. Thank you." He announced Team two, they were an older group. "Skins." He sized up the remaining groups and found one comparable in age, "You'll play team nine, court two." His attention focused on Team three. Jorge's group straightened up. He suddenly became fascinated with one of the players on Team three. Dylan. Dropping his clipboard to his side, he stroked his chin in deep deliberation. "I know you," he said pointing at Dylan. Dylan shrugged, hiding his sudden heartburn. "I was a Senior your Junior. I've put on a few pounds. But you look as fit as when you played quarterback here. Dylan Sanders, now I remember your name. Broke nearly every record your Junior year. Daryl Hawkins, I played wide receiver. It's a real pleasure."

Dylan smiled respectfully at him, "Likewise." Flashback! This was the second-string wannabe that complained I never threw the ball to him.

"You were a football star here?" Thomas abjectly stated. The subterfuge was weighing heavy on the trust he had. This eccentric person was becoming even more a stranger.

But the assistant coach wasn't the only one in the room that recognized Dylan. "I hear he preferred tight ends." The unwelcomed comment from team twelve drew everyone's attention to the early thirty something skin head sporting a Mohawk haircut. He was sitting amongst other like-minded youth. It drew scoffs and laughter sporadically through the groups.

"A comment like that just earned your team a forfeit!" Demanded the second volunteer, a salt and pepper, business cut, athletically built civil worker. "We're not going to tolerate inappropriate behavior. Get out!" He pointed to the door.

The skin head gangster stared at the civil worker with an ingenuous smirk. "Dude, I didn't mean to offend the guy. Chill."

"I'm not offended let him stay," Dylan calmly interjected, sequestering his rage. "Perhaps to show good faith, team three challenges team twelve."

"What are you doing?" Thomas mouthed his words, protesting. "Are you crazy?"

The second volunteer looked to the assistant coach for approval. "Are you fine with that?"

"Sure," he remarked with a small amount of reprisal in his voice. "Team three, skins!" He wrote notes on his clipboard then pointed to the basketball court, "Court three."

The pairing was complete. The loud pounding of feet on the wooden bleachers dwindled as they chaotically intermingled to get to their assigned court.

Team three huddled under the basket as their skin head opponents were passing the ball back and forth at the foul line. They removed their shirts. Dylan's huge athletic physique drew admiring stares throughout the gym and hidden intimidation from his opponents.

Dylan wasted no time implementing his inherent skills, "Zone coverage or man to man?"

"Alberto doesn't speak English," Jorge answered. "But I think we should play zone. I'm too short to get stuck under the basket."

"Good," Dylan surmised in agreement. "Roberto, you're a few inches taller than me. How are your rebound skills?"

"I can play center," he confirmed.

"Alright!" Dylan's determination to make his new team a winning team was building confidence in the others. "Thomas, you and I will play forward. Jorge, explain to Alberto that he and Francis will join you as guards. They only have five guys, so you rotate them." Dylan was pleased with the determination on their faces. "Let's do this."

Francis volunteered to sit out first as the five took their positions. The older skin head walked over to Dylan and extended his hand for him to shake. Dylan's reluctance to shake his hand turned his elated mood sour. His eyes narrowed with contempt, "Ready to get your asses kicked?"

"I don't know. I don't know what that feels like," Dylan shot him a contemptuous grin.

"You're about to find out."

"Shirts have the ball first," Dylan didn't break his stare. "Here's your chance."

Mohawk Man turned and tossed the basketball to a short white kid, with a long face and a bristly blonde goatee, that earned him the nick name Goat. Goat dribbled the ball to the back of the half court and behind the temporary, blue painter's tape, out-of-bounds line.

The second volunteer's intuition didn't place much prospect of a fair game, and took a special interest toward making it one. He drifted toward court three, whistle dangling on his nylon, zebra striped, referee shirt.

"Hands up and stay with your man," Dylan vociferated like any good coach would. And like robots their hands raised immediately.

After a few seconds of trying to find a player free, Goat managed to get the ball into Mohawk Man who wasted no time dribbling to the basket. Roberto planted both feet in front of him. Mohawk Man plowed through him, taking a shot at the basket. Chang's steroid charged adrenalin pumped through Dylan's veins. No one could comprehend that a human being could move that fast and could jump that high. Dylan's pupils turned a pinkish red as he leaped effortlessly above Mohawk Man and topped the ball with his right hand. The ball, Roberto, and Mohawk Man came crashing to the hardwood laminated floor with a loud thud. Thomas managed to grab the ball before it got loose. Heads of nearby teams turned in amazement of the abysmal block. Dylan's block maneuver was more than just skilled athleticism that the assistant coach recalled of the younger athletic star.

An angry Mohawk Man rose to his feet, ready to fight. His younger teammates cried foul. Volunteer number two stepped into their court. "Foul," he stated firmly. This announcement brought smiles of satisfaction on the faces of team twelve. "Charging. Team three's ball."

The smirks drained from team twelve's faces, "Charging?" Mohawk Man got into his face and pointed at Dylan, "He fouled me. Are you blind."

The volunteer matched his tone and pointed to Roberto, still on the floor. "His hand only touched the ball as you ran this guy over."

"That's what we saw," corroborated two players from team four on the adjacent court line.

Tempers settled as they resumed play. Thomas handed Jorge the ball as Jorge positioned himself to throw the ball in from under the basket. Jorge paused with confusing bewilderment as he caught a glimpse of Dylan's blood red eyes.

"Throw in the ball spic," Mohawk Man said under his breath, unable to control his agitation, he didn't want the volunteers to hear.

"Screw you gringo," Jorge taunted him and bounced the ball inbounds to Thomas.

Mohawk Man moved into Thomas's space to his left, as did an average height youth with an athletic body and mesmerizing eyes. His teammates referred to him as TJ. TJ didn't identify with the skinhead gang. He only agreed to join his brother Smitty to qualify a full team. Besides he loved the game.

Spontaneously, TJ and Mohawk Man went for the ball. TJ easily stole the ball from Thomas, who had hesitated, trying to bounce it back to Alberto. Alberto had his back to the mid-court volunteer as Goat slammed his left elbow into his sternum prior to taking a bounce pass from TJ. Alberto bent over in excruciating pain, which left an indefensible easy three-point swish from Goat.

"Aren't you going to say anything?" Thomas plead with Dylan, who seemed to ignore the elbow. "He elbowed him."

"Three zip," Mohawk Man announced with a sleazy grin. "Nice pass TJ."

Thomas glared at Dylan with disbelief and disappointment. TJ also shook his head with the same disappointment with his teammate's unsportsmanlike conduct.

TJ walked passed Smitty to his zone position. "Hey Smitty, I thought we came here to play basketball?"

Dylan ignored Thomas's berating and walk briskly toward Jorge. "Toss the ball high at the basket." Jorge nodded. He turned to Goat, "Nice shot. If that's how it's going to be, turnabout is fair play."

Goat grunted, "Loser!"

As instructed, Jorge tossed the ball high toward the basket. Dylan planted his left foot hard on Smitty's right foot, crushing his toes. Leading off, in the same stride with his right foot, pushed high into the air about two feet higher than Mohawk Man and tipped the ball at the backboard which circled the rim and fell into the basket.

"Unsportsmanlike conduct!" Smitty yelled, trying to hold back tears. He rocked on the floor trying to get his right shoe off. "You son of a bitch, I think you broke it."

"You shouldn't have tried to trip me," Dylan remarked with a cavalier attitude.

"That's what happens when you play dirty," TJ scorned in his ear.

"Whose team are you on anyway?" Mohawk reproached him with a sullied lack of trust.

Smitty had removed his sock. The volunteer referee hustled over to him to inspect his foot. "Wiggle your toes for me." Smitty cringed as he demonstrated that they were still in tack. "Can you play? You only have four players. If you can't manage to stay in the game your team forfeits."

"I'll be fine," Smitty replied dauntlessly.

"Good."

"What about the unsportsmanlike conduct?"

"He said you tried to trip him." The volunteer smiled callously. "Hearsay."

Smitty managed to stand, but could only walk with a limp cursing with each step.

"Walk it out," TJ demanded unsympathetic.

Smitty to Goat from back court. Goat dribbled around Jorge. Goat bounce passed to TJ in the corner. Thomas maintained position forcing TJ to shoot. All air, at least two feet above the rim, struck the corner of the backboard. Roberto had a clear shot to get the rebound, but was not a match for Mohawk's size. He was physically projected off the court as Mohawk went up for the ball over his back. Mohawk came down with the ball and curled his body around it, elbows swinging.

Mohawk hesitated as Dylan planted both feet between him and the basket. They were about the same height, but Dylan's body mass index, more muscular than Mohawk's layers of yellow fat cells, was not budging. Simultaneously, both men leaped to the basket. Mohawk Man raised his left elbow to strike injury to Dylan's face as he attempted a hook shot with his right hand. Instead, Mohawk's left elbow struck Dylan's iron chest with invalid results. Dylan effortlessly had two feet of height over Mohawk and blocked the shot to Jorge. Jorge took an unchallenged shot from the corner and scored. Four to three, Team three.

But the score wasn't the only damage. Mohawk lay curled, rocking in agony under the basket in a fetal position holding his groin. In the opposite corner, TJ turned away from the game to hide his, Serves-you-right grin. "That Fag kneed me," complained the skinhead."

"I'm pretty sure it was my foot," Dylan apologized with slapstick humor. "Sorry, sometimes I don't know my own Queer abilities. Look, chalk up a foul on me and you can throw in the ball. Oh, never mind we scored," he said looking down at him sarcastically. "It is your ball anyway. The way I see it, you have two choices. Your first choice is to put on your mature adult panties and join the game. Or, your second choice is to continue being an insecure asshole and they carry you off the court in a gurney. The freak in me is secretly hoping you make the second choice. Because I'm starving." Dylan's facial muscles tensed, his pupils appeared again as the blood moon in the night sky.

Attempting to stand and catch his breath, Mohawk shot Dylan a disdainful glare, "What kind of freak are you?"

Dylan grinned hauntingly, "You really don't want to find out."

TJ took the ball to back court and as he passed his brother, stated under his breath, "He had it coming." Smitty shook his head, disappointed in his brother's bleeding heart for the super homo.

Mohawk Man, and his band of red necks, team twelve, soon caught on that the muscle of team three wasn't the straight boys, but the behemoth gay iron man. Dylan had proved he wasn't putting up with their epithets, and they were nursing their wounds to prove it.

Other than a few unintentional hard bumps, the mood of the game changed to serious basketball. Dylan knew he easily had the power to control the score and allowed team twelve to make a few earned baskets. But when the volunteer blew his whistle after an hour of play, team three had easily handed an embarrassing loss to team twelve, 48 to 19.

"Mind if I hang out with you guys," TJ asked with unwarranted apprehension. The parking lot had filled with sweaty basketball players trying to get to their cars or to the bus stop.

"Sure," Jorge answered for the group, which hadn't broke stride.

"Sorry about my brother and his pricks for friends."

"No problem," Roberto reassured him. "It turned out to be a good time."

TJ pointed with a nod of his head at Dylan, who had gotten more than a few steps ahead of them, "Who is that guy? He could play pro."

Jorge replied disenchanted. "You know the trophy case we passed by in the gym hallway?"

"Yep."

"His name and picture was on the All State trophy. Most of the trophies were from '73' or '72', I'm sure Dylan was a major contributor. Never figured it out until Coach Hawkins acknowledged it. Oh, it's him all right. I always wondered who this Sanders guy was."

"Now you know," TJ shook his head in awe.

"Wonder if he played college ball?"

"I believe I can guess why his career ended," TJ interrupted. "Because of people like my brother and his Nazi friends." However true, Dylan berated himself for the poor choice that ended his fairytale story.

"Excuse me a sec," Jorge relayed to his cousins. Quickening his step, he caught up with Dylan and Thomas. "Thomas, you and Dylan want to join us? We're going to catch a bite to eat at Pearl's." Dylan and Thomas paused their stride and turned to chat.

"No thanks, Gramps needs his truck. I promised him I'd get it back on time."

"Fine, be that way," Jorge soft punched Thomas's shoulder. "Thanks, it was fun."

"It was," Thomas acknowledged.

"Thanks Dylan," Jorge reached over and shook his hand. Dylan smiled back. "I would have succor punched you too, but I've seen what happens to people who piss you off." They all laughed.

Captain Jack's Tenderloin Home

"Get in early," Jack called from the coat closet near the front door. After pillaging through the pile of old coats and hats on the floor, Jack resigned that his favorite cap was not in the closet. He chagrinned at the fact that there were only three coats still on hangers. "Thomas have you seen my hat?"

Thomas and Dylan lounged in front of the old Magnavox television tube, enjoying a rerun of the cringe comedy, Gilligan's Island. "Did you check the kitchen table? That's where you typically toss it."

Dylan raised his brow affectionately as Ginger brushed up against the Professor in her movie star glamorous way. "Lucky bitch, I think the Professor is hot."

"Russell John?" Thomas cringed. His nose wrinkled upward, "Not my type."

"Thomas! Can you do me a favor and cleanout the closet before you leave?" Jack located his hat, grabbed his keys from the kitchen counter, where he had haphazardly tossed them, and listened for Thomas to respond. "Are you deaf Son?"

"I heard you grandpa."

"See you later."

"Have a great time and take a taxi home please," Thomas plead.

Jack pulled his sliver and grey hair back and secured it in a ponytail with an elastic band he found in the junk drawer. "I'll be fine." The screen door slammed shut behind him.

"I like Jack," Dylan remarked.

"Yea, but I worry about him," Thomas expostulated. "It's starting to concern me. Alcohol doesn't mix well with our kind."

"I think that's just white man's racist propaganda." Dylan continued to lecture, "My Father wasn't a Native American and he could be a mean drunk. And toward the end of his life he really pounded them down."

"What stopped him before?"

"My Mother." Dylan took a deep breath to avoid another emotional reaction. "She kept us all balanced."

"How did she die?"

"Cancer."

"Sorry."

Dylan leaned over and kissed Thomas atop his silky and shiny long black hair and attempted to change the sudden melancholy conversation. "I think this is where Gilligan dresses up in Ginger's two piece."

"Shouldn't they have been here by now?" Thomas asked impatiently.

"They'll be here."

"I hope so, I took the night off to party with you guys." Secretly, he was hoping to spend the entire evening alone with him. He would find out all he needed to know about the man of his insatiable infatuation. His secrets, the ones he wasn't too ashamed to tell. And maybe, just maybe, the truth about the mystery concerning his eccentric behaviors. His abnormal strength and seemingly immortal appearance and history. The more he learned about Dylan, the stranger he became.

Dylan took note that Thomas wasn't laughing at the sitcom but was looking off with a distant stare. "Hey, a penny for your thoughts."

"You can't tell me, can you?" Thomas bemused, knowing Dylan would most likely filter and not give up the unadulterated Truth. "That's OK though. What I know about you, you are a good person. But if you can't tell me, That's fine. But don't believe that I'm some naïve kid that you can hide things from."

"Don't I know that for sure." Dylan looked long and hard at his twitching thumbs. "When I first saw your adorable cute face, I just wanted to get in your pants and avoid any emotional attachment. The family, we refer to as the Creed, especially, Doctor Chang, told me you were too young. He emphatically assured me that I was making a huge mistake and would come to regret it."

"But there's more to their fears, isn't there?"

Dylan nodded affirmatively.

Thomas sat up from his comfortable position. He took slow deep breaths to qualm his nerves that were tingling throughout his body like a million tickly fingers. "Does pain ever turn you on?" He reached with his right hand and turned Dylan's face toward him.

"No, I'm not into that shit," Dylan stated, staring at Thomas with an acrid expression.

"Our first time alone together in the garden, there was a moment I thought you were going to hurt me. Then you actually did hurt me. When I turned, your eyes were red, I saw a demon looking back at me. Honestly, it scared the shit out of me. I know this sounds crazy, but now I have fantasies almost every night. Sometimes I get so into it, I have to masturbate just to go to sleep."

"Sorry, I'm not into whips and chains," Dylan excoriated.

"I guess what I'm leading on to is." Thomas paused to breath. "I don't care about the pain. I want to succumb to you, be part of you, be you. Whatever you were going to do to me, I want you to do it."

There was an awkward silence of indecision. "No, you don't. Not like that anyway." Dylan stood and began to pace. He fought back his sensual desire to seduce Thomas and make an immortal creature who would share his bed into eternity. But it wasn't his decision.

The passion turned to fear. Afraid that he had just pushed Dylan away. "Look, I shouldn't have said anything. If you can't tell me, I'll respect that."

"Your tuition serves you well, Thomas. And honestly, nothing would send my libido through the roof than to share that fantasy with you. But the reality is, those are two entirely different realities. My truth can get precariously ugly, if not dangerous. Perhaps someday. But that day is not today. You have to trust me. But that doesn't mean we can't experiment with the pain in your fantasy," he grinned lasciviously at him.

Thomas smiled back, satisfied with Dylan's admission. His suspicions were on target. Dylan was a vampire. "When did you find out that you were gay?"

Relieved that the topic had changed, Dylan sat back down on the couch and pulled Thomas next to him. Coddling him. "There was this young guy who had a crush on me. I was a Junior, he was sophomore. It was complicated. He was my girlfriend's brother."

"Ouch!" Thomas said rolling his eyes.

"Pops was so proud of me back then. He loved to brag to his bar clientele of all the colleges that were interested in offering me a football scholarship. I was a student mentor in this kid's Gym class. We made it a point to wait until everyone had showered to take a shower together. That way it wasn't obvious. One day we were both caught up in our lust and decided we needed to do more than just stare at each other. The door to the adjacent janitor's closet was left open. We should have known it was open for a reason."

"The janitor walked in on you?"

"I dropped out of high school in the late fall of my Junior year. Dad wanted to enroll me in a private school in Santa Rosa where his brother

John lives. Mother wouldn't hear of it. My Father would have jumped off the Golden Gate Bridge if my Mother asked him to. Mother was battling cancer and wanted to spend the last few Months of her life with me in it. Pops wouldn't look at me. I began to hate him. But more importantly, I began to hate myself. After Mom died, we both began to drink. Like I said, Dad could really hammer them down and it got bad between us. I left home and moved in and out of boyfriend's apartments to keep a roof over my head. There was always a full glass of beer in front of me from some guy hoping to get a piece of my ass. I turned into an alcoholic and, if I'm being honest, a real slut. But the Polk Street and Castro gay bars got boring and I started frequenting the bath houses to satisfy my insatiable sexual appetite. Sex seemed the only thing that made me happy." Dylan hesitated, afraid what he was about to tell him would alienate him. "The Baths satisfied my cravings, but didn't fill the void caused by my father's rejection.

"Is that where you contracted AIDS?"

Dylan nodded affirmatively. "But who knows, I had sex with a lot of men. Let me finish. The Bistro went down-hill fast after Mom died. Had it not been for my Uncle John we'd been homeless. John convinced me to move back home. That he would shield me from Frank. But John had his own aspirations, and running a bar restaurant was not in that picture. My health deteriorated and Joey and John thought the best thing for the Bistro was to be repurposed into an AIDS Hospice. It hasn't been the most lucrative business. Our books fell into the red column. And the healing cocktail medications, that kept some of us alive, stopped working for me."

"Enter Doctor Chang, and just like that, everyone is healed," Thomas finished his story with skeptical sarcasm.

"It's a little more complicated than that, the science and all. I'm really not at liberty to say much more."

Thomas continued to finish his story. "Doctor Chang purchases the Hospice and turns it into a home for immortal creatures." His heart beating fast and hard, but not from fear.

"Hey! Doctor Chang was, is, a legitimate Physician and Bio-engineer!" Dylan responded adamantly and getting annoyed at his persistence. "Look, I've said enough. I don't wish to talk about it any further."

"I want to be part of it!"

"No, you don't Thomas," Dylan insisted. "You have no idea. Don't you still have to clean out the closet?"

"It'll take a second," Thomas answered, somewhat annoyed that he was avoiding the direction of the conversation. "Don't pretend Dylan. You need to believe in me."

"I do believe in you. I do! Just give me some time to digest this, OK?"

"OK," Thomas acquiesced for now.

"Are there extra hangers? I'll help you."

"That's OK, I got it," Thomas declined his offer and reluctantly got off the couch and tended to the disheveled closet.

"They're here!" Thomas exclaimed. The black sedan headlights shone through the glass plated door.

The rear of the stretch limo partially blocked the traffic lane. It drew a few horn beeps from angered motorists that had to going around. "Hurry, we're blocking za road," Fabien called out. He was standing outside the open side door waving for them to hasten their pace. His English had improved somewhat.

"Wow, how come the limo?" Dylan asked Fabien as Thomas climbed in.

"Zis vay need only one car."

Dylan and Thomas took two of the empty seats in the front, facing the rear of the limo. A full stocked bar near the side door. Fabien took his seat next to Joey and Jonathan. Joey was enveloped in Jonathan's arm and resting his head on his shoulder. "Hi bro," Joey greeted, seemingly happy for the first time in a long while.

But Dylan wasn't as happy with the new romance and didn't acknowledge Jonathan. "I didn't know that you were coming Joey." He then looked past Jonathan to the ugliest drag queen he'd ever seen, sitting cross-legged next to Jonathan. "Are you going to introduce us to your Diva girlfriend?"

"Queen La Fredericka, this is Dylan my younger brother and his boyfriend Thomas."

Fredric's eye shadow had smudged a little, which brought a facetious grin to Thomas's face. Queen La Fredericka's eyes roamed both hunky men. "This night just keeps getting better," she said lasciviously with raised brow.

The twins flanked the Queen, inadvertently leaving an empty seat between them, which became the coat closet.

"How's Carol," Dylan asked, hoping for a positive response.

"She's weak, but much bettah," Fabien answered.

The front bumper scraped the curb as the limo backed out of Jack's driveway. The passengers chagrinned at the scraping screech of metal that would inevitably appear as damage upon inspection. "Not my fault," the voice of Vaughn Muller explained from the driver's seat.

"Muller!" Dylan was pleased his dear friend had joined them. "I'm so glad you could join us. Where's Huey?"

Muller hesitated, "Against my better judgment, he and Giuseppe are scouting out the White Owl. We haven't heard from Jade in over a day now. She's disappeared before, but it's not like her not to give us some clue where she's going. She did mention she was going to the Owl to settle some score with the owner."

"You won't believe who's joining us tonight," Jonathan broke his uncomfortable silence.

"Haven't a clue," Dylan replied straight face.

"Tommy and Macias," Fabien answered for Jonathan. "Zay will be delighted to see you."

"I thought they were in Budapest," Dylan inquired, somewhat surprised. "That was a short trip."

"Macias's father is very sick," Muller stated. "We're picking them up on Forty-seventh Avenue at Macias's sister's house. Why don't you boys pour yourselves a cocktail. There's also beer in the fridge."

"Isn't that North of Golden Gate Park?" Jonathan asked.

"Yes," Muller said picking up on his question from the rear of the Limo.

"Mind if we drive by Lindley Meadows?" Jonathan was suddenly filled with a reminiscent desire to share with Joey the place where Doctor Chang found him numb with death. "This place is very special to me."

224

"If you don't mind Vaughn," Joey's stirring excitement poignantly pierced his desire to feel more apart of him. "I would really like that." Jonathan's satisfaction with Joey's deep interest didn't sit well with Dylan who rolled his eyes at the suggestion.

"Those bastards!" Muller bellowed angrily. He made a sharp right turn onto Twenty-sixth Avenue causing Joey to spill his red wine on his only clean pair of levis.

"What the hell!" complained Joey. "Are you high Muller?"

"Muller! where are you going?" Thomas turned in his seat to make sense of his sudden erratic driving.

"Bloody hell, they have semi-automatics. They're going to attack the Synagogue!" Muller explained frantically. He sped to the next block. "I'm circling back."

"What Synagogue?" Dylan pressed closer to the side window. The tinted film on the windows made it difficult to distinguish the world outside of the Limo. Muller's mind was focused on getting back to the Synagogue as quickly as possible and was not attentive to Dylan's confusion.

"Three, possibly four Peckerwood gangsters on bikes jumped the curb onto the sidewalk in front of the Synagogue. They're armed with semi-automatic machine guns," Muller set up the battle for them.

"We should stop somewhere and call the police!" Joey insisted. He felt the hairs raise on his arms from anxious uncertainty of the moment.

"Zere's no time!" Ludovic nodded to the immortals. There was a serious yet inflamed apoplectic confirmation as their pupils flushed with blood. There was going to be an unannounced blood-letting tonight.

Jonathan kissed Joey's mouth, "You and Thomas stay in the car."

"I think we should call the cops." Joey tugged on Jonathan's trench coat as he got out of his seat. "This is crazy Jonathan! They have guns for Christ sake!"

There was no place to park, even the government USD parking lot across the street looked full. Tefillah was most definitely in session. They were about to walk in on an attempted mass killing. But they would not face the Peckerwoods unarmed. Thomas thought it just an eccentric fashion statement that the hospice residents wore long trench coats, even in the late spring. But the long, leather, outer clothing, served a purpose to their madness. Reaching into the inside pockets of their trench coats, the four super vigilantes pulled out what appeared as small pocket knives. With a thumb click, the small metal objects open into spiked boomerang like weapons. They couldn't have reached the side steps to the main entrance faster had they been shot from the barrel of a cannon.

"You underestimate my boys," Muller extolled. "Please stand ready. In about two to three minutes, be ready to close the Limo doors behind them."

Both large heavy wooden main entrance doors had been forced open. The metal parts of the interior workings of one door knob lay on the floor in pieces. The horrified congregation of the Chevra Thilim Jewish Synagogue, all turned to seek out the loud destruction behind them. Facing them were four behemoth armed intruders, outlined by the pastel orange rays of the sun at dusk.

"Jewish scum, today you're all going to hell where you belong!" Shouted the filthy perpetrator left center. He raised his machine gun and blasted several shots aimlessly at the ceiling. A chandelier shattered and glass rained down upon the congregation. There were a few screams. Children crying, clenching onto a parent. The Rabi standing at the pulpit, took cover behind it.

As the smoke cleared from the barrage of gun powder, there stood four avengers, silhouetted behind each gunman. The loose caped ankle length trench coats were blowing about their dark figures by the outside breeze. Jaws were agape, as the congregation deliberated whether the men standing behind the Nazi skinheads were friend or foe.

For a split second the screaming stopped and curious children began to point. But the Peckerwood holocaust squad had no time to be confused. As they began to raise their guns for the execution, all four avengers released their hand-held weapons with immense force and velocity toward the right calf of each Peckerwood perpetrator. The spinning metal ripped through the fabric of their pant leg and lodged deep into their flesh. The war changed hands and the hunters became the hunted. The pain was excruciating and the wounds debilitating. Two guns dropped to the tile floor, one discharged, striking a male member of the congregation in the shoulder. He cried out from the pain as his wife got off her chair to help him.

What started out as a mass shooting, traumatizing the congregation, took a different turn. What they witnessed next would leave an unspeakable and indelible memory that would haunt the Jewish congregation for life. Their eyes moved quickly to capture the four, spontaneous, blood-lettings. It would challenge their faith and put into question their reality. To some, these Angels of the night, so they believed, were sent by Jehovah.

Fabien sucker punched and stunned the youngest Peckerwood who dropped his weapon to the floor. Clenching a fist full of the gangster's hair, Fabien yanked his head back. The semi-conscious Peckerwood's eyes opened wide, dazed and frightened. Fabien didn't hesitate and bit down hard on his jugular. The young man's scream was muffled in his own gurgling blood. He was the first lifeless body to drop to the floor with Fabien still feeding.

Dylan grabbed the collar of his prey and pulled his shirt over his head, then slammed him down to the tile floor. Holding the Peckerwood's thick hands above his head, he crouched over him and sank his fangs deep into his carotid. The perpetrator went limp as Dylan feasted.

Face marred by thick acne, the third bald, overweight Peckerwood, struggled to free himself from Ludovic's powerful bear hug. Kicking his legs out from under him, Ludovic fell with him to the hard floor. His trench coat flared out and hid the blood-letting from view. A few seconds after the Peckerwood's screams ended, Ludovic emerged with a blood-stained chin.

The blood-letting wasn't much of a challenge except for Jonathan's prey. He was a muscle bound, middle aged man, with a crewcut. He managed to gain control of his gun and avoid Jonathan's saliva dripping fangs.

"You're a dead mother-fucker!" He riled.

But there was a mismatch of strength and Jonathan easily wrestled the gun away from him and tossed it out the main entrance. Jonathan's right jab to his jaw was effective and powerful, and the spokesman for the Peckerwood killing crew dropped unconscious to the hard floor with a thud. Standing over him, Jonathan's face flushed red from his strong beating heart, begging to be fed.

"You're in a house of God," Jonathan censured sarcastically. "I'm going to have to teach you some manners."

Falling to his knees, his prey between them, Jonathan lifted the gunman's chin. Thick neck muscles made it difficult for Jonathan to reach the blood source. He was forced to take a deeper bite. Smaller veins dispersed blood everywhere. Hearing approaching sirens, Jonathan sucked hard to fulfill his minimum need. He knew he had to release his bite early. He backed away quickly to avoid being splattered with pulsing red discharge, now spraying like a lose fire hose.

The distant sound of sirens meant it was time to get out of dodge. "Lez go now!" Ludovic demanded. The slurping stopped. With conclusive blood evidence dripping from their mouths, the four vigilantes disappeared through the Synagogue doors.

Joey reached out and grabbed the Limo side door handle and slammed the door shut as the last avenger ducked in and found their seat. Before Joey could manage to close the door, the wheels of the Limo were turning and throwing loose pavement as the spinning wheels gained traction. The limo sped away.

"OK! OK! Take me home!" An anxious Queen La Fredericka insisted in his masculine first person. "Don't axe me to shut up. No way I'm bein implicated in what jist happened back there."

"What did just happen back there?" Joey demanded staring at Dylan grilling him for answers. "We all heard gun shots and there are zero bullet holes in anyone of you!"

"Thank God," Thomas sighed, pleased with the results. But unlike the other mortals, he understood the odds.

Dylan leaned toward Joey and sternly scolded him, "Just drop it, because it doesn't concern you." He then turned his attention to Queen La Fredericka, whose makeup had begun to run down his cheeks. The Limo air turned humid and hot from the sweaty body heat given off by the vigilantes. "You need to calm down right now! Fix your god damn makeup, get a grip on your fucking girdle. You're going to have the best time that your fake tits have ever had or by God I'll rip your high-heels apart and shove them up your ass. Do you read me?" Dylan's face was flushed red with anger and his blood red pupils kowtowed them both into silence.

Queen La Fredericka's ballistic anger drained from his face and his demeanor reverted to second person feminine bitch. His eye lids raised along with the corners of his lipstick covered lips. "My, my, my, you done pushed all my turn-on buttons mister Dylan. That was sexy as hell." The Queen always had a way to cut the ice. The twins busted a gut laughing.

The Rabbi covered the four dead bodies with table clothes from the multi-purpose room kitchen and escorted a very scared and traumatized congregation into the mess hall. Families managed to stay together as parents attempted to comfort and explain away the inevitable children's nightmares that would haunt them until the day they died.

Twenty Fifth Avenue had been taped off at both ends of the street and emergency response and press vehicles were only allowed past the taped off barriers. The wife, and two young Sons, followed their wounded father, now being transported on a gurney, to a waiting ambulance. His shirt was removed by the medical technicians and his shoulder was wrapped in layers of dressing. It was now a crime scene.

Detective Stone arrived shortly after the first responders, and began gathering information from the investigating officers. He flipped his badge to the detectives standing next to the dead bodies. "Lieutenant Sam Stone." He lifted the cloth from the head of one of the victims and felt apoplectic and sickened by the sight of the familiar bite wounds. The very MO of the serial killer he was assigned to arrest. But he was making no progress. "Are these the only victims?"

"Yes Lieutenant, except for a gunshot wound victim being escorted to Saint Francis Memorial ER."

Stone, pulled a creased and worn picture of Joey Sanders out of his pocket. He held it in front of the balding, round-faced detective, who was nearing retirement and more than happy to turn the case over to San Francisco's finest. "I need to see if any of the congregation can identify this man as one of the killers."

"Let me introduce you to Rabbi Price. Right this way."

Stone followed the sergeant to the grand Hall. Jewish leaders were consoling and distributing blank police report forms for any person over eighteen to complete.

Rabbi Price was being interviewed by several members of the press corps. Four elders of the Synagogue stood behind him outside the door to his office where he agreed to address the media's questions. A Channel Two News cameraman, and field reporter, had center stage, flanked by other media representatives.

"How many gunmen entered the Synagogue Rabbi Price?" the local Fox News reporter asked. She then positioned the handheld mic amongst the others.

In the rear of the crowd of reporters, Stone listened intently to the Rabbi's responses. His answers to their questions were much more guarded than those provided to law enforcement. Stone noted that amidst the media conglomerates were logos from international power houses, like NBC, CNN, and BBC, to name a few. He leaned toward the sergeant and in a clandestine whisper chagrinned, "Christ, now the FBI will be getting involved."

Rabbi Price directed his answer to the female reporter who asked the question. "Yes, there were four anti-Semitists."

The new kid on the block, a CNN reporter challenged the Rabbi's claim. "What evidence do you have that the shooters were anti-Semitists?"

"Following their forced entry, one of the gunmen, who appeared to be the leader, began shouting anti-Semitism hate speech. They were on a Jew killing spree."

The Rabbi then pointed to a familiar female reporter for ABC who regimentally kept her hand raised. "What, if anything can you tell us about the four subjects, whom you referred to as guardian angels."

Her question enraged Stone. He turned to the detective, "Did she refer to the killers as Angels?"

"Oh, it gets better," the detective amused.

The Rabbi started to answer but swelled up with emotion and paused. All who observed waited anxiously for him to respond. "It's difficult to express my, our, humble gratitude to whoever, whatever, these true heroes were. I wouldn't be standing here addressing your question if this miracle…" he stopped as tears drenched his cheeks. His voice broke, "They are nothing short of being our Guardian Angels."

"Holy shit!" Stone turned to the detective, who was trying to suppress a heartfelt grin. "Did he just call the suspects Guardian Angels? Every bleeding heart is going to take to the streets now to protest any conviction."

"Seriously Stone," the detective said with raised brow, "They did save their lives."

Then the question that crashed the party. A seasoned CBS male journalist had the nerve to ask it. "Can you clarify the method the alleged vigilantes used to stop the potential mass shooting? We've had it on good sources that the four gunmen were killed by vampire like puncture wounds to the neck. To your recollection, can you confirm that?"

The Rabbi took a deep breath and swallowed hard. His mind racing to find words that wouldn't discredit him. "Look, I'm not a forensic scientist. I'm just not qualified to answer your question."

The CBS journalist was adamant to get some kind of confirmation. "Can you tell us if you, or any of your congregation, saw them strike, stab, or even bite them at or about the neck?"

"I can tell you that no blunt object was used to inflict their mortal wounds. They moved, well, it appeared as if they moved on their targets with unfathomable speed. But let me be clear, the death toll could have topped the records for mass shootings in America. Thank you, that concludes this press briefing." The Rabbi immediately moved through the crowd of badged reporters toward his congregation, sequestered at the other end of the Hall.

Stone stopped him midway, "Rabbi, Sergeant Stone, San Francisco police." He flashed his badge for proof of authenticity. "I need to ask you some questions. Can we go somewhere private?"

The Rabbi shook his head, exhausted and not happy about being interrogated over and over. "Sure, let's retreat to my office." He made an about face and Stone and the Sergeant followed. He closed the door behind them and walked around and sat at his desk. "Fire away."

Stone held up his photo of Joey Sanders. "I need to know if this guy was one of the killers?"

231

"No, but then I was some distance away behind the pulpit."

"That's fine," Stone continued. "Any of the killers appear to be albino looking?"

"Again, I wasn't close enough to really get a reliable description of any of the vigilante's faces." Of course, the Rabbi knew it was, what he justified, as a white lie. A logical and justified sin that Jehovah would forgive him of in the next life.

Stone stared at the Rabbi indignantly, "Let me be straight with you Rabbi, this is a homicide investigation. There were four people murdered."

"Homicide? Is that what you think? Let me be straight with you Sergeant," he rose from his desk and leaned toward Stone. "There's not a single member of my congregation that will buy into your sick synopsis. Those men saved our lives in an act of self-defense. Now, I'm no lawyer, but I understand the law enough to know that an act of self-defense is not a crime."

Stone leaned closer to the Rabbi, "Then let me, as someone, who does have an in depth understanding of the law, explain it to you. Unless your Angels were being threatened and could not be consider perpetrators, the District Attorney will win the self-defense argument in court.

Rabbi Price was inflamed at the insinuation, "Get out of my office and my Synagogue. You want to talk to me, or any of my congregation, you better have a warrant."

"Let's go detective, we're not getting anywhere." Both men excused themselves knowing it was a crime scene and they rightfully, by law, could complete their investigation. But it was not in their best interest.

The next morning the Chronicle's headline read; "Vampire Vigilantes Foil Mass Shooting." This was publicity most certainly unwelcome and dangerous to Doctor Chang's Operation.

Auschwitz
June 4, 1942

The Reichsbank opened Its doors promptly at nine o'clock. Doctor Huey Chang was first in line. Chang took out his neatly folded hankie and wiped the sweat from his brow. The mid-spring morning sun quickly raised temperatures into the seventies. But it was nerves, not the hot sun, that caused him to sweat. He was never certain that he wasn't being followed. He didn't trust Doctor Mengele. However, his celebrated medical breakthrough won him unprecedented trust and latitude by the Fuhrer himself, Adolf Hitler.

He had traveled thirty-two miles from Birkenau Auschwitz to Krakow unescorted. Now only one more hurdle and he would be a very wealthy man.

"Good morning Doctor Chang", The Reichbank clerk greeted him at the teller's window. "The branch manager is waiting in his office for you with your transaction." The Polish female teller smiled professionally at him. Her graying hair line wrapped around her aging features to a large bun pinned atop her head.

"Thank you." This was his second such visit to Krakow in a matter of a few days. He had convinced Doctor Mengele that he had to transfer funds to a lab in Lyon, France, in exchange for the steroids he needed to produce the amount of SR mixture to meet frontline troop demands. What he didn't disclose was the extravagant amount.

She reached around to the front of her window and turned her "OPEN" sign to "NEXT WINDOW PLEASE". "Follow me Doctor." She emerged through a waist high swinging gate in a hip tight green ankle length dress and a keyhole bow tie. She motioned for him to follow. As they walked the short hallway to the manager's office, he scoped adjacent offices for SS Gestapo. Hitler's largest financial backer, the Krupp family, had agreed to give Doctor Chang the banking codes to access the Birkenau Auschwitz Account. However, they were unaware that he had planned to transfer five hundred million Reichspfennig currency to his personal Deutsche Bank Account, two and a half miles away. The largest non-coercive heist of its time. He was fifty percent sure, the manager would demand General Hoss's signature. He was more afraid of the consequences of getting caught making the transfer of funds, than he was his planned escape to France. He hoped to join his friend Doctor Magnus Hirschfield. Hirschfield set up an account for Doctor Chang at the Deutsche Bank Branch in Lyon, France. Doctor Chang would then buy that amount in Gold Bars to transport out of France to a bank in Geneva, Switzerland, approximately 70 miles East. It was very complicated.

"Ah, Doctor Chang," The young executive, fitted in a Gabardine suit vest and yellow tie, stood behind his mahogany desk. Chang had a moment of hopeful intuition that inexperience accompanied his youthful charm. "Lech Dabrowski, how are you?"

"Fine, don't bother standing," Doctor Chang collegially insisted and reached across the desk to shake his hand.

"Starting to get a little warm finally," Lech struggled at making conversation.

"Can't say I'm not glad winter is over. Winters in Poland are very cold."

"Yes," he chortled in agreement. "I spoke with General Hoss this morning on the phone."

"You spoke with Hoss?" Doctor Chang asked apprehensively.

"Yes," Lech dipped his brow in confusion and suspect. "Should I not have? I don't believe the bank would agree to that large amount being transferred otherwise. He was fine with it. No worries. One hundred million in Reichspfennig notes, correct?"

"That is correct."

"Great," he handed Doctor Chang the note already made out. "I have checked the Birkenau Account and your signature is listed." He pointed on the note to the empty line underneath his signature. "Just sign right there to authorize it and we're done here. I notified my friend Aleksy at your Deutsche bank in Krakow, and he is aware that you are dropping a substantial amount in his bank. I don't believe I've ever seen a larger transaction."

"Did Doctor Mengele call you this morning as well?" Doctor Chang set his plan in motion.

"No," He replied as he witnessed Doctor Chang sign the Note of Transfer. "Is there a problem?"

"No, he wasn't sure there was enough to cover this transfer."

"That's odd," he shot him a suspicious glance, "The Krupp Family Trust has over nine hundred million dollars in the Birkenau Account alone."

"There must be a misunderstanding," Chang assured him. "I will clear that up with him when I return to the Camp." The young apprentice played right into Doctor Chang's plan. "The project is going to cost us much more than he originally had asked for."

"What are we talking about Doctor?"

"We actually need at least five times that amount," Doctor Chang chagrined. "Look this amount will be sufficient to get the project off the ground."

"General Hoss mentioned your project would save thousands of our brave soldier's lives."

"It's true."

"Look, Hoss was adamant he was onboard with this withdrawal." He took the note out of Chang's grip. "Here let me make this note for the amount you need. How much do you really need?"

"Can I make a phone call to Doctor Mengele?"

"Sure, it's over there on the credenza."

"Can you give me a private minute?"

"Sure," Lech said and stepped outside his own office and closed the door. Doctor Chang walked over to the phone, finger dialed his own office number on the base of the candlestick phone, then picked up the receiver from its side saddle and began to mimic a mock conversation with Doctor Mengele. He spoke conspicuously enough that someone listening through a wall or door might make out specific parts.

"Doctor Megele?" Pause. "Everything is going well. Mr. Dabrowski has been extremely helpful." Pause. "There's more than adequate amount to fund the project." Pause. "Can you tell me how much you believe we need? Pause. "I see." Pause. "I know the Fuhrer is anxious to implement it." Pause "I will call you back then when I get to the Deutsche Bank.

Goodbye." Doctor Chang informed the young bank manager that he had finished his conversation. "I need you to leave the amount blank. Doctor Mengele needs time to check with vendors and will give me a final amount when I speak to your friend, Alecksy."

"Blank?" he replied perplexed. He knew it was not protocol and went against his better judgment. But he knew that the transfer was being blessed by the Fuhrer and he was well aware of the wrath of the Gestapo. "Do you have a realistic estimation?"

"Somewhere between one-hundred and three-hundred Reichsmarks, roughly,"

He acquiesced and wrote out the blank Note and handed it to Doctor Chang. "Do you need an escort Doctor Chang?"

"No Mr. Dabrowski, you've been very helpful. I will be sure to put in a good word for you to the Fuhrer."

The young banker swallowed hard. "I would be very grateful."

Sporting a more casual look than his friend at the German owned bank, the Deutsche Bank manager's mouth dropped to the floor at the amount on the Bank Note, "Eight Hundred Million! Dabrowski did mention it was an astronomical amount."

"How soon can you wire this to your Lyon, France branch?" Doctor Chang nervously inquired. "The war effort depends on it."

"I'm not sure it can be done, Doctor Chang. Banks don't usually have that much gold in their vaults." Aleksy picked up the receiver of the candlestick phone on his desk and asked the switch-line operator to connect him with the French Branch. A weak female voice answered. "Please connect me with the Branch superintendent. Thank you." Pause "Are you the Branch superintendent?" Pause. "This is Aleksy, the Branch manager in Krakow. I need to wire your Branch a very large sum of funds." Pause. "Eight Hundred Million Reichsmarks Sir." Pause. "Yes, indeed I did say millions, not thousands." Pause. "Don't be too excited. I'm being told by a high-ranking German official that there will be an entourage of German officers that will come into your bank to exchange the amount to gold for international purchases. Can you cover it?" Doctor Chang's adrenalin and nerves were off the charts.

"Perfect." Pause. "I know that Lyon is South of the Demarcation line, but the Armistice protocol." Pause. "Sorry, I didn't mean to lecture you." Pause. "They will be in this afternoon at the latest. Please have the gold ready as I'm being told that war effort depends on it." Pause. "Yes, thank you." Aleksy Gronkowski hung up the receiver. "It's done. I'll have the amount wired to the Branch before you walk out of my office Doctor."

Chang smiled and reached out and shook Aleksy's hand. "Thank you Herr Gronkowski. You are now part of a monumental piece of German history."

"I'd rather keep my name out of it if it suits You Doctor Chang."

"Very well. Is there a private office that I can call Herr Hitler and assure him the medical purchases will be made?"

Aleksy's cavalier attitude drained from his face at the realization that Chang's rank was much higher than previously assumed. "Uhh, certainly! You can use this phone." He pushed the phone across his desk toward Doctor Chang and was excited that he would be observing an actual phone conversation with Adolf Hitler.

"Privately, I have other official matters to discuss with him."

Disappointed, he rose from his desk, "Certainly, I'll be just outside my door when you're finished."

"Thank You."

He waited until Aleksy shut the door behind him and dialed in to the switchboard operator. "International call Lyon, France." Pause. "Thank You." Long Pause. "Magnus?" Pause. "Unbelievably without a hitch." Pause. Doctor Chang snickered. "Where did you get the costumes?" Pause. "You'll need a covered transport vehicle." Pause. "I knew I could count on you." Pause. "Give it at least two hours." Pause. "If everything goes as planned, I'll see you in a couple of days." Pause. "Feeling is the same." Pause. "Yes, goodbye Doctor Hirschfield."

Auschwitz l Bunk House Ten

"If you don't take me with you, I will inform the guard of your plans," The malnourished Catholic Priest whispered from his lower bunk within earshot of Giuseppe Ricci, who was wide awake and anxious, on the top bunk above him.

The Priest's threat enervated his excitement to get out of his nightmare. "You stupid old man. What are you talking about?"

"I heard Jadwiga ask the Chinese doctor where Andorra was," he answered maintaining his muffled voice. "Ravensbruck is nowhere near Andorra. He is breaking you out of here. I've figured it out."

"His patients are being transferred to Ravensbruck Camp for further research. You are not his patient. You're speaking nonsense."

"There's a reason why I'm being ostracized. You people talk privately amongst yourselves. Any time I approach or inquire about your conversation, you shun me."

"How do you know we're not being transferred to Birkenau to our deaths?"

Loud gun fire coming from the black wall, between blocks ten and eleven, disrupted their conversation. The SS Death's-Head's execution of prisoners became more frequent and unnerving.

The priest began to weep, "I can't take it anymore. I'm losing my damn mind."

Giuseppe's intolerance toward him softened, "Look, you have to try to keep it together."

"Please take me with you," the priest began to beg louder.

"Shut up!"

"Keep it down over there," the SS guard barked from his door post.

Brakes squealing could be heard outside Block Ten. "The bus is here," Jadwiga announced, standing next to her bunk. The other prisoners, approved by Doctor Chang, also stood by their beds. Although Doctor Mengele didn't question Chang's fabricated plan to transfer his clients to Ravensbruck, General Hoss was suspicious of it.

The door to Block Ten swung open. Through the door, they witnessed a flat-bed trailer, with naked bodies of men, women, and children, executed at the black wall, being tossed aimlessly on top of each other.

A cyclopean single brow SS guard stepped into the room. He unwrinkled a piece of paper and began to read. "Following prisoners step forward, claim your travel garments and report to the waiting bus outside. Jadwiga Dzido, Fabien Dubois, Ludovic Dubois, Giuseppe Riccie, Heinz Alt, and Estella Agsteribbe. Quickly!"

The Priest began to shake and mutter nonsensically. "I'm going with them." He began to move toward the door where three Sonde kommandos were sizing the prisoners with travel garments.

"Stop, or I'll kill you!" the SS Guard ordered, pointing his gun at him.

"Please check your list for my name. I'm sure there's been a mistake."

"You are not on the list! Get back to your bunk or I'll will shoot."

He stopped, his face blushing with anger, "They're planning to escape," he announced with no shame. "You must warn General Hoss."

Jadwiga glanced at Giuseppe, who was noticeably getting pissed off at the priest's selfish comments. She slightly shook her head to warn him to ignore the situation.

"What are you waiting for, stop them!" The SS Guards broke out in laughter mocking the Priest's insane desperation.

The unibrow SS Guard grew tired of his annoying complaint and walked aggressively toward him. "I told you to shut up!"

The priest cowered backwards, stumbled and fell. "You must listen to me. Give me my freedom and I will share what I know."

"You're a crazy old man. You know nothing!" He grabbed the Priest's prison garment at his shoulder and dragged him to the door.

"Please, they're not my friends," The Priest struggled to get to his feet but didn't have the strength as the SS Guard pushed him out the door. His head split open as he hit the small brick retaining wall, then rolled down five steps and lay sprawled on the cement pad.

Jadwiga turned and surreptitiously nodded to the others to continue changing clothes.

There was a gunshot, and the smoke from the SS Guard's handgun, as he re-entered Block Ten, finished the story. Stepping graciously to avoid getting the Priest's blood on the soles of their newly issued shoes, the chosen ones made their way to the awaiting bus. Estella's stomach wrenched when she saw the Priest's life-less body draped over the executed prisoners on the flatbed trailer. His head hung down, mouth and eyes wide open, blood still dripping from all orifices.

Doctor Chang had warned them to constrain any temptation to use their inconceivable new strength they had experienced from the

Sulfanilamide Rejuvenation process. Rather beseeched them to portray a frail but recovering specimen.

A day earlier

Chang had schemed to initiate the final phase of his plan. He endeavored to keep it clandestinely hid from the Nazis.

Administering the steroid with new blood, gave the SR process a chance to avoid an amino acid tainted system. His life work came down to this critical experiment. If it failed, his infirm victims would likely die, let alone survive an attempted escape. It would all be for naught.

Drawn and nearly quartered atop the metal lab table, the succumbed SS officer struggled to free himself of the leather fetters. A used surgical sponge served as a gag to silence him.

"I'm sorry, I can't do this!" Estelle turned despondently away and into Heinz's arms.

"Why won't a conventional transfusion work?" Jadwiga challenged. She was the only one with any medical training in the small group of prisoners.

Doctor Chang had little time to explain. "Paba."

"Para-aminobenzoic acid, used in the synthesis of the vitamin folic acid which targets harmful bacteria." Jadwiga finished his sentence to prove he couldn't deceive them one more time. "Oxygen destroys the acid."

"The body recognizes the drugs and the frolic acids protect the cells from them." He was growing anxious and frustrated at the same time. "Look, you're just going to have to trust me."

"This is insane!" Heinz protested. "You must be crazy."

"Your lives depend on it." Doctor Chang, knowing they would loathe the blood-letting, knew he too would have to fall victim to his own science. "I too have been taking the drugs," he revealed to their shock. "I will go first. Pay close attention. His heart must still be pumping as you penetrate the skin and form a suction over the artery." Hearing Chang's description of his fate, the SS guard tried desperately to escape his fetters. "Drink about a pint or fill your mouth with his blood twice before switching partners. Don't hesitate, or you might as well kill your friends." His warning got their undivided attention. "Close your eyes and imagine biting into a very rare steak. Your natural carnal desire for the taste of flesh will overtake your senses. Like licking the skin of your first kiss. Your instincts will drive you. Trust me."

The first blood-letting saw immediate, categorical, and positive, results.

But this charade was becoming difficult to cloak from a curious Doctor Mengele, who played a game of deception of his own with General Hoss. To Hoss's draconian law, they were criminals who deserved a death sentence. Mengele knew that in order to learn all the short and long-term reactions to the drugs, they had to be kept alive. He was in favor of transferring them to Ravensbruck Camp where Doctor Gerhard Domagk was not having much success with the antibacterial effects of the drug Prontosil. Perhaps, Doctor Chang's skillsets could aid Domagk.

They arrived at the Oswiecim Train Station. One of the two SS escorts moved to the front of the bus, his rifle angled in front of his chest. "You in the front will wait here until it is your turn to board the train." He exited the bus.

Large thirty-five-gallon metal drums filled with Zyklon B, the poisonous gas the Nazis used to carry out the genocide of minorities and political prisoners, was being loaded in a rear freight car. Produced nearby at the I.G. Farben chemical and pharmaceutical plant, Zyklon B Gas, was being shipped to the growing number of death camps.

Thirty other prisoners were picked up from various Blocks and sat at the back of the bus. "How did you get those clothes?" a thirteen-year old Roma Gypsy girl leaned forward and questioned quietly. Scared that the SS guard at the back of the bus might not approve.

Heinz Alt, sitting in the seat in front of her, slightly turned his head and softly spoke, "We're boarding that train to Ravensbruck. Where are they taking You?"

"To work in the new munitions factory in Brinnlitz."

"I've heard of that place."

"Do you think Herr Schindler will give us nice clothes too?" she pouted, coveting her normal life before the fascists.

"Don't lose hope Fraulein. Perhaps Mr. Schindler will be a good person." She smiled and sat back in her chair. Heinz gave her an empathetic smile and returned his face to the front of the bus. He wanted so badly in his heart to save her innocence. Young girls turning her age were often the victims of sexual abuse. Their parents slaughtered and the perverts finding ways to keep them close.

The SS Guard boarded the steps of the bus, "You in travel garments, follow me."

As Heinz alighted the bus he turned to the adolescent, "Good luck." She nodded and smiled.

"Shut up! No small talk." The SS Guard addressed Heinz Alt. Estella squeezed his hand and beamed a simple grin of acknowledgment of the gentle giant she had bonded with. The two had developed a metaphysical relationship of support after the Nazis murdered her husband and child at the black wall. Had it not been for bad publicity, and Hitler trying to propagate a positive image of Fascism, this Olympic gold medalist would have met the same fate. Nearly starved to death in Block Eleven solitude, Estella Agsteribbe agreed to the severe torture of Doctor Chang's SRP as the lessor of two evils. A decision she would not regret.

The State ran railroad was called the German Imperial Railway. During the war, the private Deutsche Reichsbahn railroad became property of the State ran GIR. The DR Class A2 transport car was used to transport prisoners. It had no windows and resembled more of the 2 axel freight cars. There were no seats and prisoners were tightly pushed into the rail-cars. Prisoners could see through small cracks between the wooden slats of the rail-car walls. The large sliding side door was locked from the outside to ensure no escapes.

The heavy steel reinforced wooden door was slammed shut and a one-inch thick bolt inserted into the lock. Jadwiga motioned for the group to gather at the car's center. The six prisoners bunched in close to keep their conversation somewhat private.

"We have to work fast once the train rounds the corner from the Station," Jadwiga stated emphatically. "Since the blood-letting, I've found incredible strength within myself. But that doesn't mean we're invincible. The wooden slats of the car wall are thick. This could get complicated."

"It's one board," Giuseppe Ricci assured her, "I counted seven boards from the top of the door. The dead bolt is about one and a half feet inside the perimeter of the door." He nodded to the others, "I can do this. I just need someone to push on the board to give me enough space to get my arm through."

"Yes, I can do zis," Fabien affirmed.

"Great."

Jadwiga looked concerned, "We're counting on you Giuseppe." He took a deep breath. "The Vistula river bridge is one mile from the Oswiecim Station. Once past the first curve we unlock the door. Estella, we need your eyes to inform us when we get to the midway point on the bridge."

"No problem," she assured her.

"The Vistula river is about twelve feet deep directly under the bridge. We drop into the water and swim under the bridge to the North bank. Once the train is out of sight, we hall ass along the river bank side into the trees, about four hundred feet. Don't forget there are approximately seven SS Guards riding in the last car. Swim under the bridge quickly and stay out of sight or you'll risk the entire escape. At the end of the trees we head directly North. Across an alfalfa field there will be a Messerschmitt Me 261 Airplane waiting on an abandon dirt road. Doctor Chang and a resistance pilot will be on the plane waiting for us. Are there any questions?"

"Where did Doctor Chang get a plane?" Heinz looked flabbergasted.

"The pilot is a despondent Austrian airplane mechanic at one of Goring's Luftwaffe hangers in Krakow. There is a growing conflagration between loyal Austrians and the Nazis. A few dauntless resisters are receiving emoluments from the Ally Resistance movement to undermine Nazi operations. We have to be resilient. Wait for Estella's queue."

Car to car propagation caused a jolt which set them off balance as the train slowly accelerated. "Here we go," Estella warned. She managed to get her balance and moved to the small crack between two slats of the train car. Giuseppe and Fabien took their place next to the door. The others crouched, ready to leap to freedom.

Same time
Office of General Hoss

"I'm curious Herr Gebhardt, are you aware of the Fuhrer's keen interest in Doctor Mengele's work?

"But," Gebhardt eluded.

"Don't speak!" Hoss scolded, cutting him off. Gebhardt kowtowed.

You're Platoon leader, this soldier standing before me, failed to report an accurate death count in order to hide an execution that I didn't approve. Is that correct?

"He had been pumped with a mind-altering drug," Doctor Mengele stated angrily. "We were observing the prisoner at the time of execution."

"Why would you dare under-mind one of Mengele's experiments?" From behind his desk, General Hoss stared at the report prepared and delivered to him by the Director of camp labor, SS-Unershcarfuhrer, Heinrich Oppelt. Herr Oppelt and Doctor Mengele stood to the left of Hoss's desk. Doctor Mengele visibly angry at the insolent and arbitrary action of the Platoon Leader.

Battalion Commander, Max Gebhardt, stood next to the accused. A goliath of a man with a striking uni-brow, standing at attention and unable to make eye contact with Hoss. Fearing swift punishment for his Turkish subordinate, the Battalion Commander begged the General for clemency. "It won't happen again General."

Hoss nonchalantly pulled his handgun from the desk drawer, aimed it at the accused forehead and delivered a fatal shot. Blood flared in all directions from the entry wound. Some splattered on Gebhardt's face and uniform. The Turkish guard's lifeless body hit the floor with a thud. "There's no room for mistakes in this army, am I clear Commander?" The tyrant placed the smoking gun back into his desk drawer with the same effort he would a writing pen.

"Yes sir, very," Herr Gebhardt responded without contempt or hesitation in his voice. He removed a handkerchief from his uniform pocket and wiped the blood from his face.

"There's another matter General," Heinrich Oppelt stated, visibly agitated.

"Doctor Chang's prisoners are on a train to Ravensbruck," Doctor Megele completed his statement.

"I'm aware, I signed off on it against my better judgment. Commander Koegel confirmed, but wasn't all that aware that Gerhard Domagk was working with Chang on the same Sulfanilamide experiment." Hoss fist pounded his desk, "There's something very inconsistent with Doctor Chang's request. Were you aware of that Doctor Mengele?"

"I am aware of Doctor Domagk's experiments with sulfanilamide. Huey mentioned last night that the Fuhrer gave him carte blanche to fund tests in Ravensbruck. Chang did get my approval to take his affected specimens with him."

"Yes, I'm also aware," General Hoss interrupted. His contempt for Doctor Chang had reached a boiling point. "Herr Himmler spoke of it. They expect me to maintain order but leave me out of the communications!" He shook his head with frustration, tormented by the lack of consideration. "What else?"

"The Priest, Commander Gebhardt's idiot shot, was trying to tell Heinrich's Battalion Leader of an alleged escape," Doctor Mengele aggrieved. "Doctor Chang has been acting very peculiar these past few days. We should have interrogated my patient before killing him."

The tension in the room had everyone, except the General, fearful that they would meet the same fate as the Turkish guard. But the Nazis nearly jumped out of their skin, when suddenly three hard frantic knocks on the office exterior door interrupted Doctor Mengele.

"General Hoss! Doctor Mengele!" two frantic soldiers, assigned to guard the Research Lab, thumped again on the office door.

General Hoss nodded to Oppelt to let them in. They entered the office dragging a dead SS Guard behind them and dropped him on the floor in front of the General's desk. The cadaver had ghostly white skin, except for two small black and red wounds at his neck where the blood had coagulated. The bite like incisions on his neck, shook the men in the room to their core. The guard hadn't been dead long as death's stench had not set in.

"What is the meaning of this?" Hoss angered. "How dare you drag a stiff into my office!"

One of the soldiers apologized and pointed to the neck wounds, "You had to see this to believe it. We found him hidden in Doctor Chang's chemical closet covered with several used syringes."

General Hoss's cheeks flushed red, burning with anger. "I want that train stopped! Now Commander!"

"I am on it General," Commander Gebhardt reassured the General. He turned to leave his office.

"One more thing Commander," Hoss barked.

He stopped to face the General, "Yes?"

"If I don't have Chang and his six prisoners in my office alive by the end of the day, you'll meet the same fate as your Battalion Leader." Gebhardt swallowed hard at the draconian declaration. "One more thing."

"Yes?"

"Get these stiffs out of my office before they start to stink."

"I'll get right on it Sir," Gebhardt abruptly left. He was on a race to stop a train and save his own hide.

DR Class A2 Transport Car

Estella Agsteribbe had to crouch to see through the quarter inch gap separating the wood slats of the train car wall. She was part of a Team again. Struggling to keep her eyes intently focused on the limited view of the geography passing by. Her mind drifted back to the one Olympic Event that sealed her reputation. She recalled the gut-wrenching anxiety as she faced the mat. Her nerves stimulating off the charts. Aerial twist, an acrobatic flip that incorporates a 180-degree rotation. She had only nailed it once during practice. Her Netherland Olympic Sisters looked on with Team Gold Medal dreams, all riding on this one scored maneuver. If she missed it, the Germans would get the Gold. "Anybody but the Germans," they kept reminding her. But her memory of the 1929 Olympics, where she gold medaled, paled in comparison to her seemingly simple task of locating the Vistula River. This time it wasn't a medal at stake, it was her life and the lives of her Team.

How she missed her life in Amsterdam. She would give anything to hear the squabbles of her children, two-year old Alfred and six-year old Nanny, selfish indulgences over toy ownership. They occupied her mind constantly. God! she missed them so much. As soon as they were herded like cattle off the train, the Nazis separated the children from her and her husband Samuel. Poor Samuel, "My poor Samuel," she whispered, holding back tears.

"Hey," Jadwiga demanded her attention. "Are you all right. You can't go all emotional on us. We need you to stay alert."

"For God's sake! Heinz berated Jadwiga. "Give her a break."

"Please, I get it," Jadwiga contended. "Estella, is your head still in the game?"

"Strange," Estella said with awkward confidence, "My coach, Gerrit Keerekoper asked me the same question right before I won the gold medal."

"We believe in You," Ludovic said reassuringly.

"We're past the curve and out of sight," Jadwiga advised.

Giuseppe didn't hesitate and stood opposite the bolted side of the door. Recounted the slats from the top of the train car, he punched with all his might through the board. Impressively, his unexpected strength surprised him. The slat broke in two. "Wow! Did you see that?"

"How's your hand?" Fabien asked, also awestruck at his iron strength.

"Fine," Giuseppe confirmed, inspecting his knuckles. "At least you won't have to push the board open for me. What kind of creatures has Chang turned us into?"

"Can you feel the bolt?" Jadwiga asked keeping them focused.

"Feel? I can see it."

"Good, now pull the damn thing out."

"How fas you zink zis train moving?" Ludovic asked, playing in his mind whether he was going to survive the jump.

"Juz mizz za rocks," Fabien baited his lighter side. His twin brother was always the Lady's man and not so much the athletic type.

"I can see the tree line. We're getting close to the river!" Estella moved her head about trying to see closer. A moment of epiphany. Giuseppe wasn't the only client of Doctor Chang to go through the transition. She took a step back and punched through two boards.

Splinters and large pieces of wood scattered, leaving a gaping hole. "Now, that's better, I can see the whole valley."

"Just make sure no one can see you," Jadwiga shouted as the wind, created by the new holes in the car, whipped through them.

"We're about a quarter mile away from the bridge," Estella said projecting half her face through the large whole.

"Open the door and wait for my word," Jadwiga demanded. She stepped to the side of the door to get a better view of the ground directly below them. She wasn't too happy with Chang, who put her in charge. It made her very uncomfortable to be ordering around adults a little older than she. Jadwiga could tell from the often-resentful jibes and facial expressions, that they didn't like it much either. But that is what Doctor Chang wanted and Chang gets what he wants.

Jadwiga rehearsed the calisthenics of the jump one more time. "The timing has to be perfect. Don't hesitate. Keep your jump tight to the bridge. The river is narrower at the bridge. It's about a thirty-foot drop to the water."

Five of the escapees lined up in single file at the door. Heinz made a point of being last. "Are you OK?" Estella asked benevolently, noticing the apprehension on his face.

"I can't swim."

"You're a quick study. I'll give you the same advice Johnny Weissmuller gave me at the 29 Olympics, "Take a deep breath and hold it until you surface. Take another deep breath, turn on your back and I'll take over from there." She shot him a reassuring smile, "Got it?"

"Do I have a choice?" She raised her brow for lack of words. "You knew Johnny Weissmuller?"

"On my queue!" Jadwiga held her hand out to stop them from jumping too early. "Now!" With blind faith, no sooner had one left the car's platform that the next prisoner dropped less than a foot away. Heinz hesitated for a split second. Estella quickly wrapped her arms around him and pulled them together off the platform. She pressed her palm over his mouth to avoid any uncontrolled screams that might alert the Nazis in the rear caboose. The guards were most likely engaged in a game of cards.

Commander Gebhardt raced passed his Wehrmacht military issued Stoewer, M12 RW, four-seater, Kubelwagen, parked in front of General Hoss's compound. Three confused staff members, carrying their rifles over their shoulders, were ordered to follow him. Across the street, in the administration compound, sat his own private 1939 Horch 930 with a V8 engine. Much faster than the Kubelwagen.

"Get in!" Gebhardt instructed. Unconventionally, Gebhardt jumped into the driver's seat and cranked over the engine. It hummed like a well-maintained vehicle should. Even faster was General Hoss's Mercedes Benz parade car. If he survived this ordeal, he hoped to trade his Horch for a used one that he saw for sale in Krakow. He popped the clutch and accelerated. Kinetic force pinned them back in their seats, feeling the strain on the necks from the whiplash.

"Where are we going Commander so urgently?" asked the young SS Guard in the passenger seat, dimples embedded in his beardless cheeks. His chin speckled with stubble which started growing on his sixteenth birthday.

"To meet the Ravensbruck Train in Bierun Nowy," Gebhardt took another deep breath as he was exasperated from running. "I've called ahead to the Wehrmacht Battalion there. The train will be stopped before it gets to Wawelska Road.

"That's about six miles from Auschwitz One," declared the acne scarred, bronze browed, middle-aged soldier sitting behind the Commander.

"I'm taking the Warszawska highway. It's paved and runs parallel to the tracks. We may even beat the train to the barricade. Our mission is to bring Doctor Chang back to General Hoss alive. If the others resist, shoot them."

The dirt road leading to the Warszawska highway had its share of pot holes that were hard to avoid. Consequently, the guards in the back seat were tossed around like rag dolls. Once onto the better paved, Warszawska highway, Gebhardt pushed the pedal to the floor-board and sped toward the town of Bierun Nowy.

"It appears they've stopped the train Commander," The young SS Guard broadcast, pointing off to the right.

"This is good. Doctor Chang must be shitting his pants right now." Gebhardt made a sharp right on Wawelska Road as the white knuckled SS grabbed onto anything that wasn't also turning from the centrifugal force.

A large military flatbed trailer sprawled the tracks and the cattle guard approximately fifty feet of it. Once the Engineer saw the barrier on the tracks, he put the train into emergency stop and had to engage the brake whistle to notify the Porters to apply the car brakes. There were porters traveling in crude shelters on the Tender, one freight car, and the caboose. A burnt-metallic smell permeated the area from the overheated brakes.

SS and local German Army personnel surrounded the train. Gebhardt spotted the Stabsgefreiter, or Lance Corporal. He was speaking to a small band of enlisted rank. Gebhardt pulled up alongside him. "Herr Koch, good morning."

"Good morning Commander," Corporal Koch answered with a tense demeanor.

"Where are the prisoners?"

"I'm afraid they have escaped," Koch continued. "It's been only a few minutes since we stopped the train."

Crestfallen, Commander Gebhardt took a deep breath to control his anger, "What do you mean they've escaped?"

"Follow me Commander," Koch turned and hastily double stepped toward the right side of the train. Gebhardt, and his three SS Guards, followed. "As you can see Commander, they must have used a metal object to break these boards and remove the door bolt. I don't understand how your guards in the caboose didn't hear or observe this."

"How is that possible?" Confounded, the Commander inspected the broken slats. Protocol demands all train cars, used for passenger transport, are inspected for any objects that can be used for weapons or escape.

"Apparently the Inspectors missed this one. It would take extraordinary strength to break through the steel supported slats."

Gebhardt shook his head, massaging the stress from his neck. "We need to find them now!" He barked.

"The trees are too thick to drive through Commander. I've order a few of my men to spread out on foot. It's my guess they disembarked in the Vistula River. If it pleases you Commander, we should use our vehicles to search the backroads along the river."

"Let's get moving! Have two of your vehicles come with me. We'll cover the East side roads of the Vistula. The rest of your men can search the West side. Don't forget, Hoss needs Chang alive. I don't care what you do with the others." Gebhardt's vexation with the General's blithe disregard of his loyalty to him. Years of thankless servitude emanated a nerve wrenching anxiety for his own survival. "Corporal, I need you to help me find them or I'm a dead man."

"We will find them Commander," he reassured him.

"We can't hide this plane forever Doctor Chang," the airplane mechanic insisted. "They need to get here soon."

"They'll be here according to plan," Doctor Chang inferred. He hid his distraught, knowing very well the most minuscule delay could obliterate the entire plan.

"If the Nazis are on to them it may be advantageous to start up the Messerschmitt engines."

"The engines are too loud. They would surely give our coordinates away."

"Too late now," the Austrian pilot said despondently. "We have company. Nazis at two o'clock."

About fifty yards from the road, two of Koch's men approached them with their rifles drawn. Doctor Chang shifted his stance and caught a glimpse of them in his peripheral. "Remember, you're flying me to Frankfurt to pick up chemicals on order of the Fuhrer."

"We've rehearsed it a thousand times Doctor. I just hope I'm as good an actor as you are a Doctor."

"Turn around and put your hands on the plane!" the soldier shouted, pointing his weapon at the two men.

"You're making a mistake, I'm Doctor Chang. I'm with the Wehrmachtgefolge under Doctor Mengele. I have credentials."

The taller soldier propped his rifle under his left arm and stretched out his right hand. "Show them."

Doctor Chang handed the papers he carried on the inside pocket of his jacket. The Wehrmacht infantry inspected Doctor's Chang's documents and handed them back to him. He motioned clearance clear and the other soldier also relaxed his weapon. "You look nervous Doctor. Where are you going?"

"To pick up medical supplies in Frankfurt."

"Why are you landing such a large plane as the Messerschmitt on a dirt road. Doesn't the Luftwaffe have an airstrip?"

"Convenience." Doctor Chang nonchalantly replied hiding his intense anxiety of the moment.

"You could be in extreme danger. We are looking for six Auschwitz prisoners who escaped off a train bound for Ravensbruck."

"We have weapons on the plane, if we see them we'll most certainly arrest them," injected the Resistance pilot. But his prophetic words came to fruition. Crunching of pine needles could be heard from the woods. The six prisoners emerged from the woods running toward the plane, determined, and with unfathomable speed.

The soldiers turned and remounted their rifles aiming toward the six escapees. "Halt!" But they were too far away to hear the soldier's directive. He shot his rifle into the air. This got their attention. Their perfidy mortified the soldiers as the six split up. Exigently running in all directions, with the intent of succumbing the shooters, they much rather a bullet than to going back to Auschwitz.

Doctor Chang's pulse quickened. He knew to save them he had to act. Was this also an opportunity to unleash the odyssey. Proving that his hypothesis and exponentially enhanced medical breakthrough was legit? Confirm that replenishing folic acid depleted blood with new PABA free blood was the missing part of the puzzle.

He was not a murderer, and recalled the trauma he suffered as a young man growing up in the Mongolian village of Khatgal. His Father killed for sport and would take him on hunting trips with his uncle in the Pamir Mountains. Snow leopard cubs had wandered into their camp. He fell in love with the three handsome cats. But the children were not alone and the mother soon discovered their location. Father swiftly grabbed his gun next to him, pointed and fired. The Large cat dropped, gave a helpless plea to her babies, who quickly mobbed her. His Father's brow wrinkled inward empathetically. Huey's Father, knowing it would upset his young son, also understood what the humane thing that had to be done. He reloaded and one by one killed each cub as young Huey screamed in protest. His Father was a kind man and holding back his own empathy for his Son, he gave him an insatiable reason for taking their lives. "It was for their own good."

The soldier's death would be for the good of his clients, his new family. He humanely understood that they would depend on him for years to come for their survival. He struggled with his Right to make that choice to thrust them into an immortal Nirvana without their consent. As the whizzing of bullets filled the air, he had no time to delay. He had been administering the same steroids to himself.

Standing close to the first shooter, he leaped onto his back, firmly wrapping his arms around him. The sound of cracking ribs and sudden loss of wind, confirmed to Doctor Chang, that he had become more than just a biologically engineered Hercules.

The German infantry couldn't maintain control of the rifle and dropped it to the ground. Sealing his lips over the coveted artery, Chang bit down hard, ripping into the soldiers solid neck muscle. Doctor Chang's mouth filled with the soldier's plasma. The soldier's scream turned to death's gurgling cacophony. He collapsed like a felled tree. Continuing to feed from the wound of the lifeless body, Doctor Chang's immune system attempted to reject the introduced blood. Soon, he developed a rhythm of swallowing that matched that of his prey's still beating heart. Was there an acclimating process and had his own body developed an insatiable hunger for it?

Panic raged through the second, more timid German guard. He aimed his gun at Doctor Chang, and placed his finger on the trigger. From behind him, the pilot tackled him to the ground. They struggled, both had their grip on the soldier's rifle. Years of beer drinking had caught up with the older pilot. They rolled together in the dirt and grass, the gun between them. There was a gun shot.

Face stained with the pilot's blood, the soldier rose quickly to his feet, aghast with horror at Doctor Chang's aberrant and monstrous behavior. "What kind of beast are you?" He raised his gun to take a fatal shot.

Heavy footsteps grew louder and approached from behind the soldier with explosive speed. Twigs breaking beneath their feet, the twins shrouded him faster than the soldier could turn to face his attackers. Fabien delivered an undercut, that connected with the soldier's chin. His helmet flew off and blood and teeth spewed from his mouth from the extreme force. Ludovic grabbed the barrel of the rifle and effortlessly took it away from him. The German soldier's eye's still wide open from the shock of his cohort's traumatic death, fell unconscious to the ground.

The other five escapees arrived seconds later, all with befuddled faces at Doctor Chang's bloody mouth. The German's neck Wound. Chang had some explaining to do.

Doctor Chang faced his clients. "There's no time to waste. They must be looking for us and the gunshots have alerted them to our position. However, we have a major problem. We have no pilot!"

"Perhaps I could give try," Giuseppe interposed. "My Father enrolled me in commercial flight school."

"How many hours did you log?" Doctor Chang asked apprehensively.

Giuseppe hesitated to respond, "Thirty."

"Thirty!" Heinz alarmingly protested.

"It's a commercial transport Piaggio P.23M, I have flown one of these."

"We don't have a choice! Jadwiga asserted adamantly. "Let's get out of here!"

"I trust you Giuseppe," Doctor Chang nodded reassuringly. "Either we risk falling from the sky or face Hoss's firing squad at the black wall. Let's go!" They climbed the drop steps into the Messerschmitt. Jadwiga pulled in the steps and closed the heavy door behind them. All but Chang and Ricci entered the fuselage and strapped themselves into the five of the eight available seats. Jadwiga allowed the others to select their seats while she looked for parachutes.

Doctor Chang took the co-pilot's chair in the cockpit and was baffled at the endless rows of switches on the control panel. "Are you sure you can fly this?"

"No," Giuseppe replied tenaciously looking for the power switch. "Please don't try to help me Doctor." Doctor Chang rolled his eyes with choked cynicism.

Giuseppe located a familiar switch and flipped it up. The Daimler-Benz DB 601 engines, mounted on each wing, began to roar and the variable-pitch four blade propellers started rotating.

Pang, Pang, bullets struck the rear fuselage. "Get this thing in the air!" Jadwiga caterwauled, "We're under attack!"

With an 88-foot wing span, the dead pilot picked an amiable road with wide open fields that use to be farmed before the Jewish farmers were incarcerated. "Buckle in!" Giuseppe demanded, his right hand thrusting the joystick at the center of the control column forward, steering the plane with his left.

Pang, Pang, Pang, bullets struck under the fuselage. "Are they trying to shoot out our tires?"

The plane bounced hard on the dirt road potholes. "They're solid rubber," Giuseppe shouted back, trying to maintain control of the plane. The plane began to reach lift off speed. Giuseppe kept his focus on the attitude indicator or artificial horizon and firmly gripped the steering mechanism to keep the wings level while achieving rotation speed. The nose raised to 15-degree pitch at 90 knots. "Come on baby," Giuseppe was not only concerned about the damage the bullets may cause but he only had about a quarter mile of road remaining. Pang, Pang, Pang. 120 knots. Pang, trees approaching. 130 knots. He glanced at the vertical speed indicator, or variometer. "Yes!" The plane lifted and cleared the trees by several feet. The unlikely crew celebrated.

"You're a genius!" Heinz wailed cheerfully, praising Giuseppe.

"We're not out of the woods yet," Doctor Chang stated speaking much louder to be heard over the propeller noise. He caught a glance at the compass. "We need to go Southwest and this compass indicates we're flying Northeast. We need to be heading toward Geneva not Moscow."

"Based on the density altitude, we need to reach an altitude of at least two-thousand feet before it's safe to turn this thing around. Thank God there's no headwind."

Doctor Chang looked dismayed, "Hope it's soon or there will be Russian guns aimed at us. Don't forget, we're flying in a German Luftwaffe market aircraft. Isn't that a navigation system behind you?"

"Yes, but we can rely on the compass until we get over the Alps."

"Do you know how to work it?"

"I've studied Italian instrumentation. We can only hope they're similar."

"Hope is all we have right now my friend," Chang stated under his breath.

Sunday, May 10, 1986
San Francisco –
Paul Coombs Residence

The royalties from his book, "Reverse Discrimination" added to Paul Coombs lavish lifestyle. Located in the middle of golf course heaven and overlooking Lake Merced, He loved his four-thousand-foot, John Muir Drive bungalow. Coombs worked less and golfed more. The New York Times refused to list his book on the top ten best seller List. He would never have guessed there were that many white men in America that shared his Supreme Race Elitist beliefs.

"You make him understand!" Rudi Helbard insisted emphatically from the other end of the phone line from his hotel room. "I am outraged. It's all over international news and the Krupp family does not want this to touch them directly or indirectly."

"I'll speak with Mr. Yarbrough this morning," Paul acquiesced, pouring himself a cup of coffee and pinching the phone receiver between his ear and shoulder. "Had I known he was planning the attack on the Synagogue I would have stopped it," Coombs answered tongue in cheek. He had to make Rudi believe he had nothing to do with the attack, even though he had planned the entire event as a show of homage to his out of town guests. The attack had brought attention to his movement, the result he wanted backfired. Now four of his men were dead.

"This Chang guy must have heisted a ton of money if they're that concerned," Paul retested Rudi. Perhaps Chang was worth more than what the Krupp family had offered.

"You worry about bringing Doctor Chang to me alive Mr. Coombs," Rudi rehearsed the agreement. "I have some good news that my team has learned. Do you have a pen so that you can write this down?"

Paul sat his coffee cup on the counter. Scavenging through his junk drawer, Paul found a pen. "Go ahead."

"My contact at the San Francisco Assessor-Recorder's office informed me of a business sale and title transfer from the Frank Sander's Family Trust to a Vaughn Muller. Muller is Chang's queer lover. He also learned that Muller and Chang opened a bank account together with a very large deposit. The address of the property is, are you ready?"

"Yes, go ahead."

"950 Gough Street, that's 9, 5, 0, G, o, u, g, h, street." Rudi spelled it out for him. "Use to be a Bed and Breakfast owned by the Sanders Family Trust. When the owners died their children turned it into a Hospice for AIDS victims. Muller and Chang have made renovations to the house and gardens, but the front is still overtaken with weeds and the Hospice sign is barely legible. Be careful who you select to do the job. You know what happened to your incompetent nut jobs at the Synagogue. Chang and his gang are very smart and dangerous."

"I'll personally oversee the Operation Mr. Helbard," Paul stated confidently and unabashed. "There won't be any screw ups."

"Remember I need Doctor Chang alive or the deal is off!"

"Does it matter in what physical state you get him?"

"Able enough to sign his name and talk to his banker."

"Have a nice day Mr. Helbard." The phone clicked off without acknowledgment. "Bastard."

Hospice – Same Day

"The house feels cold and abandoned," Vaughn deplored sipping his tea and flipping through the pages of the San Francisco Chronicle.

"Sorry, I should have told you," Doctor Chang pulled a patio chair away from the table and thumbed through the discarded paper for the international news section.

"Well?"

"They piled into the Limo early this morning to Stinson Beach."

"Why am I always the last to know?" Vaughn made a subtle vexed facial gesture.

"Unless we stop using, we'll always be middle aged men," Doctor Chang consoled. "At least at our age we're not losing our minds, our teeth aren't falling out, and certain body parts haven't called it quits."

He achieved the slight grin from his lover and forever friend that he found easy to amuse.

"I sure had a great night out with the, our," he paused, realizing he was about to be patriarchic.

"Our children?" Doctor Chang finished his sentence. "I know, I find myself believing we're all one big family. It's OK though. Oddly, it feels good."

"Is it?" Muller laid his paper down with a sour smile. His serious countenance warranted Doctor Chang's undivided attention. "Forever is a long time." Doctor Chang nodded affirmatively. "Forever has its problems."

"Are you falling out of love with me?" Doctor Chang turned his lower lip up in angst.

"I could never not love you. This whole redefining your family comes with complications."

"What family doesn't have complications?" Doctor Chang asked trying to qualm his anxiety.

"What will Jonathan do when Joey shows signs of mortal failings and inevitably leaves this world? How will Jonathan survive the pain? He's a very sensitive kid you know."

"He's an adult, and you don't have to remind me."

"Will Fabien look for a younger woman when Carol's hair turns grey? Or worse, how will we all survive when the world runs out of fascists?"

"Unfortunately, my love, there will always be a new crop of fascists. Hate is powerful and has always Trumped love. Unless a more intelligent and mature species rises up and conquers the human race, this narcissistic cancer will eventually destroy the world."

"Not if we can help it. But, you made my point," Vaughn asked still seeking solace, "Again, is Forever really a good thing?"

"I wish I could warp time and give you some encouragement. I'm almost certain that the mortals will, when the time is right, make the transition. It's inevitable. As far as Forever goes, there's almost nothing I couldn't endure as long as you're at my side." Muller managed a smile and the two men leaned in and kissed. "I need to pick up some items at the hardware store and pick up Giuseppe from Church. Would you like to go with me?"

"I'll take a rain check. I have some pruning in the garden that needs to get done. When did Giuseppe find religion?"

"Suit yourself. Mister Ricci finds his younger cohorts a little juvenile at times and I think he's just exploring his options. Nothing wrong with that."

"Bloody hell, who would have thought."

"When do we have to return the Limo?"

"We don't, Muller replied, "I bought it." Huey dipped a brow finding it oddly humorous. "Hey, don't make that condescending face. I like driving it."

"Really?" Chang challenged. "Or do you just like being the driver and being part of that whole juvenile thing Giuseppe referred too."

Annoyed, Muller shot Doctor Chang a contemptuous glare over his reading glasses. "Don't you have to something to do?"

"That's what I thought," Huey guffawed as he grabbed the keys of the Sedan from his pocket. "See you later."

"Love you."

"Ditto."

Johnson's Hardware Store

"I want to go into the ministry," Giuseppe announced unexpectedly from the passenger seat of the Sedan.

"Really?" Doctor Chang exclaimed. "Wow, how do I process this bomb shell?"

"Are we going somewhere?" Giuseppe notice that Doctor Chang had missed his turn to the Tenderloin.

"I've got to pick up some deck screws Joey put under the counter for me."

Giuseppe winced, "What's wrong with the hardware store on Polk street?

"I don't mind driving a little out of the way to support my friends."

"I'm at a crossroad in my life and this just feels right."

Doctor Chang turned onto Market Street toward the Castro District. A car, turning left into his lane, laid on their horn. It stopped a few inches away from striking the Sedan. "What the hell is your problem?" Doctor Chang berated him.

"Aaaa… Huey, she did have the green arrow," Giuseppe reproved nicely.

"And!"

"And that would mean she had the right of way."

The car sped past them and the pissed off female gestured to him with the middle finger of her right hand. Doctor Chang mouthed the word sorry. "Everybody is in such a damn big hurry these days."

"I'm going to stop using the steroids."

"It's funny, Vaughn and I had this very discussion this morning."

"I'm concerned obviously about withdrawals." He looked worried, in hopes Doctor Chang could placate his anxiety. "How bad will it get?"

"Well, first your hair begins to fall out, then your organs shut down, followed by jaundice, and finally you succumb to dementia." Doctor Chang turned in time to see his jaw drop and eyes open the size of avocados. "I'm bedeviled, it's not like that at all."

"Doctor Chang?" Giuseppe scolded, "I'm serious. You shouldn't take this lightly."

"Sorry," he sighed with an incorrigible grin. "There are no withdrawal symptoms related to going off the steroids, but your body may encounter some accelerated aging."

"What? I'll suddenly put on forty years?"

"No, but you'll start feeling the aches and pains of growing old."

"I'm all right with that," he sighed, somewhat relieved.

"Just do me one favor."

"What's that?"

"Don't go joining some radical cult and start renting space in your head."

Huey stopped at the red traffic light on 16th street. There was an awkward moment of silence. His thumbs twiddling in his lap, Giuseppe became melancholy. "My Aunt struggled to raise me and my two brothers. We had been traumatized by my alcoholic poor excuse for a Father. She worked two jobs and was never there to give us advice or stop my older siblings from beating the hell out of me."

Doctor Chang empathetically shook his head. "Whatever happened to your Mother?"

"She died giving birth to me. I think somehow my Father blamed me for her death."

"That's a lot of crap to put on a young man."

"It wasn't an easy childhood. But my Auntie did the best she could. I joined the Nazi Resistance as an outlet for my anger." He chuckled to himself, "Do you remember our last day at Auschwitz. The pilot was killed in the struggle and I was the only one that remotely knew how to fly the plane. Do you remember what you said to me? No one in my miniscule miserable life ever said to me, "I trust you." Do you recall?"

Huey nodded affirmatively, "I had no reason not to, you're a good man. My intuition and survivor instincts told me you needed words of encouragement at the time. I needed you to fly the damn plane. All our lives depended on it."

"No, it was more than that. It was the manner and sincerity in which you said it. You and Muller have been like real parents to me. Is it weird that I have this connection with you?"

"No, no, not at all. We're a family, define it as you may, there's no evidence to the contrary. Vaughn and I love you and wish only for your happiness." He reached over and grasped Giuseppe on the shoulder.

"Thank you," he smiled at Doctor Chang as a tear fell and wet his cheek.

The light turned green.

Market Street began to bend Eastward. Instantaneously, red and blue flashing lights lit up the buildings along Castro Street. "This does not look good," Doctor Chang stated unnerved.

As they passed the Castro and the Twin Peaks Gay nightclub, it was obvious to Giuseppe where the trouble was coming from. "Johnson's Hardware store is barricaded with crime scene tape!" Giuseppe pointed out. "Turn left on Collingwood Street and look for the first available parking space."

"This can't be good," Doctor Chang chagrined.

"Joey was with Jonathan this morning in the Limo. Didn't they say they were going to Stinson Beach?"

"That's what Vaughn indicated this morning. Look there," Doctor Chang pointed to a parking berth near the corner of 18th Street. "Do you think I can parallel park this beast? It's a tight fit."

"Doctor, I'm convinced you can do just about anything you set your mind to."

"Don't hold your breath." Doctor Change struggled. But after a few pull-ups, managed to fit the Sedan into the tight berth.

Covered with a white mortician's sheet, the cadaver was transferred from the mobile stretcher into the ambulance. Giuseppe and Doctor Chang had pushed through the moderate crowd to the taped perimeter. The press corps were mobbing the police chief, who was updating them on the guarded details of the apparent crime.

"Isn't that Alice in the back of that police car next to the entrance to Johnson's?" Giuseppe pointed her out to Doctor Chang.

"I've only been in the store once. She doesn't look familiar. You know her?"

"I've been introduced. I'm going closer to the building to see if I can get her attention." Chang followed him along the taped perimeter. Giuseppe picked a small pebble off the street and tossed it at the squad car rear door. Alice turned abruptly, looking out over the crowd for the culprit. She wiped back tears from her rotund cheeks with her shirt sleeve. Giuseppe waved profusely to get her attention. "Alice!"

Filling out his report from the driver's seat, Detective Stone was also curious as to who threw the rock at his squad car. "Do you know him?" He questioned her excitement over seeing a familiar face.

"He's Jonathan's roommate."

"I don't know this Jonathan guy."

"Joey's boyfriend."

"He has a boyfriend?"

"The note stuck to Freddie's body?" Alice was anxious to share what she knew with Stone.

"The one addressed to a Doctor Huey Chang?" Now she had his undivided attention.

"The Chinaman standing next to him is Doctor Chang."

"You're positive?"

"No, I'm not one hundred percent sure," Alice replied, impervious to his concerns. "I need to speak with Joey's friend."

"Don't get out of the vehicle, the press will mob you. Stay here." Detective Stone got out of the car and walked toward Chang. Stone wore plain clothes to distinguish his authority to that of the uniformed officers. He approached Doctor Chang and Giuseppe and flipped his badge close to their faces. "Are you Doctor Huey Chang?"

"Yes, in the flesh." Chang answered calmly. Although his nerves were beginning to flare up.

"I need to speak with you. Can you follow me to the squad car?"

"What's this about officer?"

"Homicide. I have something you'll want to see."

Giuseppe edged close to Doctor Chang, "I'll wait for you here."

"No," Stone grimaced. "I need you to climb into the back seat of that police car from the driver's side." Detective Stone pointed to the police car with the female occupant, Chang and Giuseppe had just spoken of minutes earlier. "The Lady has suffered some pretty serious trauma. She found the body on the office floor with a metal rod through him like he'd been roasted like a pig on a Rotisserie. She seems to know you and badly needs someone to talk to. Do you know her?"

"We've been introduced." Giuseppe claimed. "I might have met her once or twice."

"Do you mind?"

"Not a problem detective."

"Doctor Chang, if you don't mind, I'm driving that old brown Chevy El Camino next to the curb. The evidence I have to show you is in the car."

Detective Stone held up the yellow police tape as the two men ducked under it. They followed him back to the El Camino and the squad car and did as directed.

"Freddy is dead," Alice grieved. Giuseppe opened his arms and offered his shoulder. She immediately laid her head on his shoulder and began to sob. "How could anyone kill someone like that? God, they're sick mother-fuckers."

There was nothing he could conjure up that would console her. "I'm so sorry Alice."

Stone and Chang climbed into his El Camino. Detective Stone slipped on latex gloves and opened a folder on the front seat. Laying it out on the console in front of Doctor Chang, he admonished him, "Don't touch it without gloves Doctor. You'll want to read it." The note was blood stained. It had been pulled from the metal rod in Freddy's mouth.

Chang leaned in closer to read the note. "Geben Sie zurück, was Sie Doktor Chang gestohlen haben, sonst kommt dies in die Nähe von zu Hause." He repeated it in English, "Return what you've stolen Doctor Chang, or this will get close to home."

Stone looked cold face into Doctor Chang's eyes which were full of unequivocal fear. "These killers must think us idiots. We have interpreters. I'm not here to tell you what to do with whatever they believe you have of theirs. But these are brutal and serious killers. Let us help you." Doctor Change still taking it all in and trying to make sense of it, nodded. "People connected with you are going to start disappearing Doctor, unless they get what they want."

"I don't take threats lightly, sergeant," Doctor Chang responded recusant.

Detective Stone sighed, "I believe, and please stop me if You have contrary information, that the vampire killings, and this retaliatory murder are somehow related. It's my job to stop this war Doctor."

"I haven't a clue what you're talking about Detective," Doctor Chang didn't like his trenchant analysis.

"It was like I was chasing my tail in some serial killer vortex. Going after little crumbs of evidence. But this is merely a case of two rival gangs involved in a turf battle. It's clear to me now that one of the rival gangs are the Peckerwood Aryan Nation motorcycle gang. And until now, I was clueless as to who this other insane phantom gang might be. Forgive me Doctor. I mean no disrespect, but I think somehow your connected with these sick cult like Sons of perdition. In fact, this note implicates you as their Darth Vader. I take it you've seen Star Wars? Perhaps you might help me understand why you hate fascists so much?"

"That's absurd. What are you insinuating detective?"

"You don't have to be a forensic scientist Doctor to see that you've been implicated as a force behind the vortex."

"That's preposterous!" Chang defiantly stated. "May I ask you a question now?"

"Sure."

"Help me understand your admiration toward fascists?" Doctor Chang repeated his question with a loathing look of disgust. "Darth Vader?" Chang shook his head and paused. "You really need to stop watching so many villain movies."

Chang's question caught Stone off guard. "Trust me, I hate them too." Stone took a deep breath and shook his head. "My sources ran a background check on You Doctor. Seems your Visa expires in less than ninety days. I hope you're not planning on renewing it."

"Cut to the chase Mr. Stone," Doctor Chang assented stone-faced.

"There's some really bad players in town Doctor. I don't know if you're familiar with the National Alliance?"

"I am."

"I thought so. But what I couldn't figure out, that is until I got deep into the investigation of the Synagogue killings, just who was hunting who. I don't have a soft spot for Nazis either Doctor, but this is America. You know the whole First Amendment thing. I think you know Mr. Joey Sanders and possibly have close ties with him and his connection to our rotisserie victim, Fredric Garcia."

"They're acquaintances of mine, yes."

"Fifty-two people are dead or missing since this gang rivalry started Doctor. I'm sure you would agree with me that I would like to see it stay at fifty-two?"

"Detective, unless you plan to arrest me, I believe we're done here. And by the way, my Citizenship has been approved. I'm not going away."

"Right now, Doctor, there's little evidence to indict you. That's not my intent. It's obvious that you're involved and I'm hoping you would join my team and help me end this war. The District Attorney has dropped charges on Mr. Sanders for lack of evidence. I'm back to square one."

"That depends Detective on what side of history you're on."

"Enlighten me, please."

"These Peckerwood kids at one time I imagine were good people, born in bad situations. You don't have bad people detective, you just have good people who make bad choices. Minds are yearning sponges, and if exposed to sick ideology, they become poisoned and eventually become the poison. Whether it's the Christian Inquisition, Jihadism, Stalin's brand of communism, Hitler's fascism, Reagan's winner-take-all Capitalism, or Bill Pierce's Turner Diaries, the First Amendment isn't the antidote to stop this narcissistic poison, yesterday, today, or tomorrow."

"So, let me get this straight. You believe that if we kill all the white elitist gangs we all live happily ever after."

"Mr. Stone, you were born with two ears and one mouth, not the other way around. Don't put words in my mouth detective. This is an endless war between good and evil and ironically, it seems that laws always favor evil. The world just needs a better antidote, that's all."

"How do I argue with that Doctor," Stone replied indignantly. "You maybe right."

"No, I'm just on the right side of history, that's all."

"Unfortunately for me, I've sworn to uphold the laws of the land and I'm a man of my word," Stone replied sarcastically. "Unfortunately for you Doctor, I am going to monitor your every breath, every move, and even when you take a shit. I'll have eyes on you. Do you get me?"

"Great!" Doctor Chang answered facetiously, "Should I cancel the security guards I hired? Oh, and since you'll be on me like toilet paper, I like a good Port wine, preferably a Portuguese Port. Have a good rest of your day detective." Doctor Chang closed the file with the bloody note in it, handed it back to the detective, and got out of his car.

As Doctor Chang shut the car door behind him, Stone shook his head, disappointed with how the interview went, and stated out loud to no one, "Well that didn't go like I thought it would."

Saint Vincent Hospice

Driving home, Doctor Chang's mind was spinning out of control. The felicity and security of his redefined family was being threatened. Under attack by the very evil that once bound them in chains and tortured them irreparably, mind, body, and soul. The fascists had flocked to the City with the intent to annihilate, possibly their worst enemy of modern times, vampires. The magnitude of the threat meant that Doctor Chang had to act swiftly. How soon would they strike again?

The skyline constantly changed as Giuseppe starred out the passenger window. His eyes open but not looking, vulnerably unconnected to his thoughts, the palladia of his immortality versus the fatal option of the Ministry. "What was in the note Huey?"

"The Krupp family feels their donation to the Nazi Party is refundable," Doctor Chang's casual confident voice was different. "The Peckerwoods are the least of our problems. The entire Aryan Brotherhood are caucusing in San Francisco for world war three."

"What do you mean?"

"I mean we may be walking into a trap," Doctor Chang replied with despair. "It's about to get real messy."

"Are you suggesting that we may have to go back into hiding?" Giuseppe's stomach began to wrench. "Can we beat them?"

"I'm not sure." Doctor Chang realized the gravity of what Giuseppe had just said, "Oh, my God!"

"What?"

"Vaughn," Chang's demeanor changed to sudden paranoia. "The note ended by saying the fight was going to get close to home. We must get back to the Hospice quickly!"

"But why Freddy?" Giuseppe asked nonplussed.

Doctor Chang thumped on the steering wheel of the black Sedan, "Come on, come on light turn green!" Glancing over at Giuseppe, he realized they were both unarmed. "That spear was meant for Joey. They believe that Joey's one of us and most likely killed those juvenile Nazi creeps." The left turn arrow turned green for Van Ness Street. "About damn time."

Giuseppe was processing what Doctor Chang had said about Joey. "Good God, that would have devastated Dylan."

"You don't think Joey will be devastated to hear his best friend was shish kabobed?"

Giuseppe starred into his lap defeated. "I'll never be able to run from this will I Huey?"

"Open the glove box," Doctor Chang demanded. "Under the owner's manual you'll find my Beretta ARX 160 handgun and one extra 5 round Magazine. Check the safety make sure that it is on. We're going through the back way."

"What about you?"

"You're a better shot than I am."

"I have a trench coat full of weapons," he looked concerned. "You'll be unarmed."

"They're not going to kill me. They need me alive."

"I don't understand."

"The Krupp family is more interested in the money, they need me alive to get to it."

"Park on the next block," Giuseppe insisted. "They'll pick up the sound of the engine if you turn in the alleyway."

"Side door or back door?" Doctor Chang mulled over.

"Neither! We'll go through the wine cellar door. Giuseppe strategized with the element of surprise in his mind.

"The stairs are to squeaky."

"Look we don't even know if an attack is even eminent. The bushes will shield us from any window view if there is."

Doctor Chang slammed the gear shift into park and opened his door. "Let's do it."

They approached the corner chain link fenced perimeter with normal gait, trying not to solicit unwanted attention. As they approached the bushes and pavers, leading to the basement wine cellar door, both men jumped the fence into a gap between the thick bushes. Speaking sibilantly, Doctor Chang leaned into Giuseppe's ear. "Look the door's been forced open. There in the basement."

"They know we're on to them," Giuseppe vexed.

"Please be OK Vaughn."

"We're playing into their trap."

"Poor Vaughn," Doctor Chang said distressed. "We need to re-think this through."

Giuseppe gave Huey back his handgun, "You're no good to me unarmed." Giuseppe motioned with his hand for Doctor Chang to remain back.

"I don't need this." Doctor Chang insisted.

"God you're a stubborn man. The only thing you're going to do is get yourself killed."

"Give me two dragon beards." Doctor Chang insisted. "You're better with firearms."

"Suit yourself. Wait for me to clear the room before you enter." He reached into an interior pocket of his trench coat and handed Doctor Chang a dragon beard hook weapon. The DBH, as they it was referred to, consisted of two 33-centimeter razor sharp iron rings with a retraction rope attached. Dragon beards were used by the Song dynasty like a rope dart in hand to hand combat. "Stay low in the bushes by the door. If I don't signal you within a reasonable time, do what you need to do."

Doctor Chang had taught Chinese Kung Fu to his dilettantes and was a master at the art. "Go."

Approaching the cellar door, scoping potential targets with his gun raised, Giuseppe disappeared into the dark basement room. He was not alone and had the element of surprise in his favor. The dim incandescent light, through the open door, illuminated the heavy dust particles in the rays of the sun. They cast a shadow on the two Peckerwoods sitting on empty wine crates, guzzling wine directly from the bottle. Immediately they were startled by Giuseppe's entrance. Wine and glass shattered on the cement floor as both men dropped their wine bottle and reached for their machine guns. Giuseppe fired a bullet to the head of one Peckerwood who was wearing a fur collar leather vest, touting huge biceps. He fell instantly. Blood spattered against the foundation wall and the wine racks attached to it.

The second, younger, and much thinner Peckerwood, managed to get his finger on the trigger and released a round before taking Giuseppe's bullet to the chest. The round missed Giuseppe who hit the floor rolling. The Peckerwood released his gun and grabbed his chest. He fell on top of his fallen comrade. Heavy footsteps, on the floorboards above him, alerted Giuseppe that it was about to get real ugly.

Doctor Chang was about to leap out of the bushes when he caught an average built Peckerwood in his peripheral. He had his gun raised and was running towards the cellar door. Doctor Chang opened the dragon beard hook and held it steady in his palm. Chang's adrenalin kicked in at sight of the swastika tattoo on his neck. The sight of it stoked a renewed fight in the Doctor. Before he could turn to enter the cellar, Doctor Chang powerfully pitched the Dragon Beard which wrapped around the Peckerwood's neck. Giving the string a strong tug, the razor-sharp ring sliced through both jugulars. Blood erupted into the air with each remaining heart-beat. The Peckwood shook spastically. He dropped his gun and fell into the foundation wall.

"Nice throw," Giuseppe extolled. "Take this," Giuseppe said handing him the dead Peckerwood's machine gun. "You do know how to operate it, right?"

"You're kidding me," Doctor Chang shot him a demeaning glare.

"Great, it just became a fair fight. Any guess how many we're up against?"

"No clue. Let's not take the stairs," Doctor Chang calculated. "They're expecting us to come that way."

Giuseppe nodded affirmatively, "Front door, let's go. Cover our backside!"

They heard heavy footsteps pounding down on the wooden porch steps. "You two go that direction, David and I will head toward the cellar."

"In the bushes," Doctor Chang imposed in a softer tone. They crouched and aimed their new guns toward the front of the Hospice where inevitably Dave and his buddy would emerge with whatever fire power they were sporting. But the spray of bullets didn't come from the Peckerwood guns, but from the guns stolen by Giuseppe and the Doctor. Both Peckerwood gangsters dropped dead.

"Wait," Doctor Chang blocked Giuseppe from leaving the bushes. "There's at least two coming from the back. I'll watch the cellar door you keep your sites on the rear of the Hospice."

"Gotcha." Both men postured themselves low behind the bushes. Light footedly a youthful and frail looking Peckerwood followed behind the more emboldened husky gang member. Both armed with Colt automatic rifles, the two men stepped carefully toward the cellar door. "Hit the older Pecker, We need a blood-letting, I'm taking the cute momma's boy out at the knee."

Doctor Chang squinted his brow, befuddled at his sudden change of heart. "What about the ministry?"

"I've already uttered grace on the food," Giuseppe humored spontaneously.

As the Peckerwoods turned their backs to enter the cellar, Giuseppe's finger settled on the trigger. His site at the end of the barrel aimed at where the Peckerwood's blonde part line ended at the back of his skull. POP! POP! His face was blown off and splattered around the cellar entrance, he went limp as his gun dropped to his side. He collapsed forward, his body blocking the entrance to the cellar.

Before the body hit the ground, with unparalleled speed, Doctor Chang had taken the colt from the younger-looking traumatized Peckerwood with his right hand. With his left hand, Chang pinned his throat against the cement foundation wall and pressed his palm firmly over his mouth. "If you wish to see another day, you had better spell out how many more of you we have to kill." Chang released his hand over the boy's mouth.

"I'm a dead man either way!" he cried, tremoring profusely.

"OK, fine." Giuseppe pushed the nozzle of his gun under the chin of, in his mind, just another Nazi terrorist.

"Wait! Please!"

"Talk!"

"Paul Coombs, he's it. Has the old vampire chained up in a room that looks like a library."

"He's the only one?"

"I swear."

"Look up at the sky. Now!" Giuseppe barked into his face. Gradually, the young Peckerwood obeyed as tears and fear flooded his cheeks. Adolescent Pupils, locked in Giuseppe's hypnotic glare, afraid to look away as his chin lifted upward, exposing his small fleshy pedestal from which his memories rested. A short life expunged of proms, nightly baths, tooth-fairies, and Christmas trees. Giuseppe breathed in his salty stench of sweat and lack of oral hygiene. But oddly, it was a sweet aroma that stole his senses and crossed over his heterosexual preferences. He gently covered the boy's eyes with the palm of his hand and felt his long soft eye lashes brush against it. Giuseppe's humanity felt the boy's soul, void of love, but full of poison that inundated his heart. It beat hard for mercy, but there would be none. He was irreparably damaged.

Doctor Chang pressed his body tightly against the adolescent. Also aroused by the smell of his wrinkle free youthful core, he pressed his lips on the soft lobe of his ear, kissed the boy's cheek softly, and nibbled gently on the defining bone of his chin. Closing his eyes, Chang licked the rancid nectar from Peckerwood's neck until his tongue found the hard-pulsing feeding cannula. Opening his jaw wide, displaying the breadth of his bite, Chang chomped down hard. Blood swirling around his tongue, he swallowed with each robust youthful pulse, choking back the defiant heart. The blood-letting feast began. Oxygen deprivation of the brain gradually rendered the adolescent faint. His head fell back against the brick wall. Giuseppe moved his open lips next to Chang's, and anxiously took part in the sacrifice, losing but a few drops of blood in the exchange.

"Don't be overindulgent, we have to go in for Vaughn soon before the cops get here." Doctor Chang desired to finish the blood-letting, but with renewed strength, his only appetite was to save his lover."

Giuseppe sucked the life right out of the Aryan Nationalist. Stepping away, belly full of his blood, the Peckerwood dropped to the ground like a discarded robe. "Crap, I liked this shirt too," he complained of the blood-stained white Bellamy shirt.

"Vaughn!" Doctor Chang reminded him.

"Lead the way," Giuseppe collaborated. "Isn't Coombs the owner of the White Owl bar?"

"The one and only. Somehow I believe he may know where Jade is." Doctor Chang surmised. "Back door?"

"Agreed. They're expecting us to come through the front now."

San Francisco is anything but flat. The Hospice was built on a small incline. From street level, the basement was the first floor with a large impressive grand stairway leading up to the main floor. But the basement floor, with tiny windows near the top, disappeared into the hill on both sides of the Hospice. The main floor led out into the infamous rear gardens, where once a thriving restaurant with covered gazebos, topiary of perennials, and foliage, encompassed fine dining experiences. Vaughn Muller had restored all but the tables and constructed an enclosed back porch, where breakfast was usually enjoyed together with the Creed.

The grass muffled their footsteps up the small incline to the rear of the house. The glass walls of the enclosed porch made them easy targets from a sniper's view from the kitchen window. There was no easy or safe entrance into the house. They had no other choice but to take the risk, even though they gave no credibility to the dead boy's account.

Giuseppe darted to the corner of the enclosed porch with his aim focused on the kitchen window. He motioned for Doctor Chang to make his move. Together they entered through the rear door into the main-floor hallway.

The old stained wooden floors creaked under their soles as they proceeded toward the office, clearing each room they passed by for Peckerwoods.

Taking no chances, Paul Coombs had wrapped a heavy-duty, steel chain, around Vaughn Muller and the desk chair several times. He then locked the chain tightly with a keyed padlock. Muller was gagged with crinkled up documents from Doctor Chang's desk and secured from being spitting out with a Peckerwoods bandanna, tied at the back of Muller's head.

The office door hinged into the office and was intentionally left open. Giuseppe abruptly entered the room with a stolen machine gun mounted on his shoulder ready to release the remaining rounds.

"Drop it!" a female's voice shouted, emerging from behind the office door and forcibly pressing the nozzle of her hand gun into Giuseppe's temple. The door had swung closed. Doctor Chang stepped back into the hallway trying to surmise what just happened.

Paul Coombs held a gun to Muller's head, "Don't be stupid, drop your gun. We don't want to kill anyone. We just wish to leave with the good Doctor. We need him to sign some papers. Very inconvenient task," Coombs patronized, clicking the hammer and pushing the nozzle of the gun hard into Muller's ear. Muller's muffled protests pricked Doctor Chang's attention from the hallway as he listened intently with his ear against the outer wall.

"Vaughn," Chang agonized under his breath.

Giuseppe gradually lowered his gun and laid it on the floor. "I was about to call you a smart young man. But then, I realized you're most likely one of the Doctor's medical freaks and old enough to be my grandfather," Coombs humored himself. His voice changed from a natural conversational one and bellowed loud enough to be heard by the neighbors. "Don't keep us in suspense Doctor Chang, please come in and join us. Now!"

Keeping her gun wedged into the side of Giuseppe's head, his captor tugged on his trench-coat, moving him a few feet from the door. He caught a glimpse of her and realized it was Sandy, the bartender and manager of the White Owl bar. "Awe, how are you Sandy?"

She smacked the side of Giuseppe's skull with the nozzle of her gun, "How does he know my name Paul?"

"Relax, he's just trying to get into your head." Coombs became impatient and pissed off. "Chang! Get your goddamn ass in here or I'll blow your butt buddy's brains out."

"Your pretty girls like school?" Giuseppe continued, picking up on her vulnerability. "What future do they have as Peckerwoods?"

"Coombs, I'll kill you myself if they harm my daughters!" Deep within her soul she had always known there was no way out for her.

Doctor Chang entered slowly and with his automatic rifle poised to fire. He pointed it first at Paul Coombs, then at Sandy, then back at Coombs. "Let him go Coombs and I'll go sign your damn papers."

"Sandy, you seem like a respectable person who just wants the best for her kids," Giuseppe continued to work on Sandy's loyalties.

"I said to shut up!" Coombs demanded. "Enough! Doctor, you have ten seconds to shoot your freak here, or say goodbye to your lover. One! I'm not fooling around Doctor. Two! Three! Four! Doctor Chang began to panic. He turned and aimed his gun at Sandy. Five! Six! He closed his eyes and shifted his aim at Giuseppe, tears forming at the corners of his eyes.

"I understand Huey," Giuseppe attempted to make the decision easier for him.

"Seven! Eight! Nine!"

Pop!

A single shot rang out. Everyone in the room closed their eyes, waiting for the pain of a bullet entrance wound to inflict them. But the only eyes that would never open again was Coombs. The single bullet penetrated Paul Coombs between the eyes, followed by a trail of his blood splattering on the bookshelf behind him. He released the gun and dropped dead to the floor. Unexpected jaw-dropping shock filled the survivors as they faced his killer, still holding her smoking gun at her fallen boss. "Please don't hurt my daughters," she plead with Doctor Chang.

"Doctor!" Detective Stone's voice called out from the front entrance to the Hospice.

"Put your gun down," Doctor Chang negotiated with her. "We would never hurt a single hair on their pretty little heads. That's not who we are."

"We're coming in Doctor!" Stone was hoping for a clearance from the Doctor's voice before busting down the door with his entourage of law enforcement behind him.

"I can't go to jail," Sandy began to weep.

"You can trust me. As far as they need to know, you're with us and this was all self-defense," Doctor Chang reassured her.

"It's safe Detective," Doctor Chang called out. The hallway filled with heavy foot traffic.

Detective Stone and several police officers entered the office. Stone walked over to Doctor Chang, "When the call came over the radio and the address was the Hospice, I finally deciphered the meaning of the note. How many?"

Doctor Chang, still shaking from nearly having to kill his dear Giuseppe, replied, "Two in the cellar, four on the North side of the house."

Stone noted Giuseppe's blood-stained shirt and chin, "I'm not even going to ask how that happened." He shook his head in disgust and turned to Sandy, "Who's she?"

The Doctor managed a momentary grin, "She's a friend."

Monday, May 18, 1986
Brown Street – Presidio District
Large four-bedroom duplex rental

His trenchant mind was always present in the Creed's future destiny. Weighing current crisis and commandeering solutions, Doctor Chang suddenly, without notice, moved the Creed from the old Bistro, as it was commonly referred. Besides, the old mansion was now a taped off crime scene.

The four-bedroom duplex on Brown Street, in the Presidio District, would serve as a temporary base until the growing caustic threat was eliminated. Staying together as a large group was becoming antithetical to their survival.

They were told only to bring themselves and avoid any clue as to where they were going. "And for God's sake, make sure you're not being followed. And that means your brother, Joey," Muller adamantly forewarned Dylan.

The home was fully furnished. Even the constant fumigations of scented air freshener couldn't camouflage the cigarette smoke permeating from the cloth couch and walls. They were not happy about the temporary move, but realized the necessity of it.

Perplexed by his indecipherable feelings of compunction toward the young white supremacist he shared with Doctor Chang, Giuseppe saw an opportunity to confront him for answers. He seized on the opportunity, spying him alone in front of the kitchen sink filling a glass with water.

"I'm having nightmares Huey," Giuseppe cut to the chase, his back against the counter as Doctor Chang drank from his glass facing him.

"You're having second thoughts about entering the ministry?"

"No," he said, not sure where to start. "Do you ever have a connection with the mortals during the blood-lettings?"

277

Chang sighed and raised his brow in reflection. "If you call feeling empathy for their damned disposition, I have on occasion. That boy got to you, didn't he?"

"It was like I was looking into his soul and saw his innocence. Oddly, I saw a victim, but not of my doing. He suddenly was a beautiful boy in my arms, begging me to free him."

"It was already too late for him. Speaking to you, not as a Christian, but to a Christian, we were his salvation. The blood of Christ had never, likely would never, touch his tongue." Doctor Chang rested his left hand upon Giuseppe's chest, feeling his heart beat. "You freed, not only his soul, but spared the virtuous souls that inevitably would someday be his victims."

"He still cries out to me in my sleep," Giuseppe stirred, still troubled, still unnerved by his ignorance and sensitivity.

"Giuseppe, you saw the boy before his brainwashing, before the xenophobic influences poisoned his mind, still challenging his own jaded perceptions of good and evil. You see, there are no bad people in this world, only good people who make bad choices. You tasted his final cry for help and sheltered his soul in your renewed strength. The boy had not only rented space in his head to the fascists, he wielded his soul to them. They have the power over him."

"And Sandy?" he asked, taking a deep breath of hopeful vindication.

"Ah, you feel a strong similarity. Perhaps the real hidden cause of your dreams. The greatest power on earth is to wield another man's mind. The greatest weakness it to allow it."

"Lord," Giuseppe cried out, even more nonplussed. "How am I to interpret that?"

"Your feelings toward Sandy are no different from that of the boy. Compassion, empathy, love, even sensuality. The only difference is Sandy isn't weak and very much alive. She may have found a kind and gentle giant to help her take back her soul."

"Giuseppe smiled intensely. Doctor Chang's words rang true and lucid. "I know what I need to do."

"I'm sure you'll make the right choices. Let's go join the others."

Giuseppe took the empty space next to Dylan who was flanked on the opposite side of the couch by Jonathan. Tommy's arm wrapped over the shoulders of a much smaller Macias, who was comfortably leaning into him on the love chair. The Dubois twins, Fabien and Ludovic, sat crossed legged on the great room white carpeted floor. To the left of the fireplace, where dried drift wood crackled and spat embers into the cast iron triple screen, Doctor Chang's leather Boss Wingback chair sat empty. He was standing close to Muller, seated on a matching chair to the right of the fireplace. "I deposited most of it in their account this morning," he whispered into Muller's ear.

"It's done then? The executer of the Will is a respected man is he not?"

"She is," Doctor Chang corrected. Muller's lip and eyebrows lifted in unconventional surprise.

"She?" Muller asked grinning.

"She. You'll like her. I'll tell you who when they're gone."

Doctor Chang returned to his chair. "Thank you for explicitly following my instructions." He could tell by their confused facial expressions they were ready to hear more. "I don't have to tell you that the Creed and our way of life is under attack, again. It is only an assumption, but we believe that Jade is alive, most likely being tortured, and being held as ransom."

"By whom?" Tommy asked, being somewhat new to the situation. "Why isn't Heinz and Estella here?"

"It's a possibility," Doctor Chang glanced over to Muller, "That she is being held in Colorado Springs or Coeur d'Alene, Idaho. We went through Jade's things and discovered an arrant list of Fascist movements and organizations active in the world today. Jade had mentioned to us earlier that she had such a list. She has red lined each fascist that she has killed since her research ended. Members of the white supremacist group called the Order are Dzido's recent targets. Speaking of Heinz and Estella, Muller has made contact with them three days ago. He insisted they check out Jade's leads to the Order's headquarters in Coeur d'Alene. It might lead us to her."

Muller continued, "The other target was Colorado Springs. The defamation League has supplied me with information as to the headquarters of the Neo-Nazi White Nationalists there. David Duke, maybe attending a Klu Klux Klan rally in Colorado Springs on Friday. I have booked tickets for Tommy and Macias on Continental Airlines at 10:20 a.m. on Wednesday leaving from SFO."

Macias interrupted, "Did it ever cross your mind that we may not want to go?" His resentment of Muller's lack of respect didn't move Muller to ask for forgiveness.

"No, If I'm being honest. You're either with us or against us." His defiance of Macias's assumption was clear to everyone but Macias. Macias shook his head in contempt but remained silent, knowing his debt to Muller outweighed his angst.

Doctor Chang jumped in, "Our problem isn't the shit for brains Peckerwood Gang, or the skin heads from Idaho. The Krupp family trust has learned of our whereabouts and believe that their contribution to the Nazi's Auschwitz Project, which is now in my possession, is rightfully theirs. They want it back. The Krupp family is using these White Supremacists as their muscle. Jade maybe the only card they have to play."

"Why don't vee gives it to zem?" Ludovic insisted, not fully understanding the consequences. "Does Jade's life have no value?"

"Bloody hell over my dead body," Muller rebuked in his best English accent. "Mr. Dubois, do you believe we get the steroids free from the pharmacists? Besides, Jade's life depends on us getting to them before they get the money. They plan to kill her either way. She's their ransom ticket."

"Who's them?" Dylan inquired.

"Sandy, the White Owl club's manager, has had a come to Jesus meeting and is supplying us with intel. She informed us that Coombs was escorted by a very powerful organization to the Double Tree Hotel for a lucrative business deal. She didn't have a lot of details concerning who or why, but stated that he was obsessed with finding Huey."

"Why should we trust her," Dylan skeptically persisted.

Giuseppe looked hard at Dylan and asserted stoically, "Because three of us would be dead right now had it not been for her." Dylan shrugged off his concern.

"Nonetheless," Doctor Chang continued, "Sandy saw Coombs take Jade away in steel shackles. Which means they know enough about us to not to use regular handcuffs. Jade has most likely been transferred to Colorado Springs for a ceremonial execution, Coeur d'Alene to answer for a bloodletting there, or is held up here as bait. I'm hoping for the later. Tomorrow is judgment day. With Coombs gone there will be in-house fighting for Peckerwood leadership. They won't see it coming. Giuseppe, Jonathan, Muller, and I, will pay a visit to the Double Tree on Bayshore. Dylan, and the twins will converge on the White Owl. Its doors are currently closed for business. But I believe they are using the warehouse behind it for routine operations. Any questions?" He scanned the determined faces. "Good. Four A.M.. Sharp! We meet here. Make absolutely sure no one is following you. And for their sakes, I hope you've relocated people close to you. Next to David Duke and Bill Pierce, Coombs was high in the echelon of white supremacists. They are angry and they are hell-bent on retribution. Anyone who has been seen with you isn't absolved from their wrath."

"What about Sandy and her daughters?" Giuseppe asked. He had a personal debt to her he wanted to make good on.

"We still need Sandy to be our eyes and ears," Muller acquiesced his fear for her safety, I would advise you from becoming attached."

"I hate to disappoint you Vaughn, but I'm afraid I already have," Giuseppe admitted to Muller's discontent.

"Like in good friend?" Muller plead, hoping it wasn't more.

"Like, I've been seeing her," Giuseppe stated emphatically.

"You know her creepy older brother is living with them, right?" Muller's voice became firm and irreconcilable. "Their father is one of Duke's boys."

"She mentioned that."

"Sandy must be naïve then," Doctor Chang insinuated. "Or, perhaps we misjudged her."

"What do you mean?" Giuseppe glared at Huey.

Doctor Chang continued, "Donald Junior, a.k.a. Junior, is a registered sex offender in the State of Mississippi. He was arrested at a massage parlor with an underage girl. A sex trafficking sting that sent two high profile businessmen to jail. Junior got off with a hand slap and six months of probation. A sweet deal I'd say. Helps if the District Attorney is a card-carrying Klansman."

Giuseppe's aversion drained from his face and was replaced with disappointment. "The girls."

"Giuseppe?" Muller interrupted. "We need your head in the game. You're in deep now. Nothing can change. Do you understand me? You have to keep the romance alive and everything you've learned today from her. We're not sure she is truly on our side yet."

Giuseppe nodded affirmatively. "OK, OK, I get it."

Doctor Chang popped the cork from a bottle of seven hundred-dollar Armand de Brignac champagne and filled the nine empty glasses on the coffee table. "To the downfall of fascism!" Muller waited until all nine glasses were in the air before taking a very expensive sip.

"Hear! Hear!"

November 27, 1978
575 Castro Street
San Francisco Superintendent,
Harvey Milk's Camera Store

"Yes Mayor, I am coming into the office today…pause…He'll be a great replacement for Dan White…pause…I don't agree with Feinstein, but if that's who Dianne wants, I have no problem with it." Harvey Milk was on the phone with San Francisco Mayor, George Moscone. The short phone cord kept Milk pretty much tied to his desk behind the counter. "Oh, and George, thanks for your support for our anti Anita Bryant campaign, that means a lot to my Castro Constituency… pause…Well if you can pull off getting the Alice B. Toklas Memorial Democratic Club to support us I'll buy you dinner…pause…laughs…Rick Stokes had too many electroshock therapies to cure his gayness. I think it affected his nerve…long pause…Yes, you can count on me to be there and I promise to leave Jack at home…pause…I understand it's not about him being gay. His drunken ass has embarrassed me on more than one occasion too…pause…We'll talk about it further when I get to City Hall…pause…I will…later."

"Harvey, was that the Mayor?" Milk's lover, Jack Lira, inquired.

"The one and only," Harvey replied.

Milk placed the phone receiver in the saddle and picked up the small mic to his cassette tape recorder and pressed record and play. "November 27th, 1978, eight o'clock a.m. If a bullet should enter my brain, let that bullet destroy every closet door." He pressed the stop key and took a short respite to digest his spontaneous brilliancy.

"Play that back!" Milk's lover, Jack Lira, demanded, distracted from helping a client at the cash register. "That was crazy good!"

The customer was annoyed at Jack's outburst. "Look can we just finish here."

283

"Sure," Jack apologized and counted her change back to her. "Two dollars twenty, three quarters and a nickel make three, and two dollars makes five. Thank you." Jack placed the film into a paper bag and handed it over the counter to the customer, anxious to be somewhere.

Harvey Milk's attention quickly turned toward the large pane glass store windows. His ex-lover Scott Stills, holding hands with a tall, very handsome, athletic looking, young man, were dodging traffic as they crossed Castro Street. "Shit! Milk chagrinned. "What the hell does he want now."

"Who cares," Jack admonished. Jack censored Scott's validity in Harvey's life. But he was suddenly enthralled with the hot lad holding Scott's hand. "That kid he's with is hot."

"Dime a dozen," Milk lied. He couldn't take his eyes off the kid.

Scott entered Milk's Camera store like a giddy child who got everything they wanted for Christmas. "Hi Jack, Harvey."

"Scott," Jack acknowledged. "What brings you here?"

"Hi Scott," Harvey intruded. "Who's your hot boyfriend?"

"Jack, Harvey, meet Dylan Sanders, Dylan, Jack and Harvey," Scott's pinky finger pointed at each respectively.

"Nice to meet you," Dylan cordially replied, hiding his excitement of being in the presence of a local hero of human rights. Dylan recognized Harvey from his news briefings on the television. After all, he sensed he was the target of their lust, which counted for something.

"Can you guys breakaway for lunch?" Scott suggested. He caught Jack's eyes roaming about Dylan's bulging crotch, drooling to a fault. "Hey, focus, eyes up here." This drew an embarrassing smile from Dylan.

"What will you and Jack do?" Harvey's attempt at humor was not received well by either Jack or Scott. On the other hand, Dylan loved the attention and flashed his brow at Harvey flirtatiously.

"Seriously," Scott pressed on.

"Can't, have to report to City Hall this morning," Harvey resigned from the invitation.

"Call in sick," Scott insisted. "You did all the time when we were a thing."

"Let me think on it," Harvey paused to deliberate on how he could get out of the photo shot with the Mayor and Feinstein. "Well, Dylan's Dimples are making me a little weak in the knees."

"Pervert. We'll meet you at the Patio café at noon," Scott confirmed.

Jack hadn't eaten breakfast yet. "Why not eleven o'clock? They open at ten."

"Na, let's make it twelve thirty," Harvey had reconsidered his obligation. "I'll let the Mayor know I'm taking a longer lunch."

"That doesn't give you much time at the office," Jack educed. "You'll be on Muni longer than you'll be in the office. Why don't you call in sick and then go in this afternoon?"

"Don Horanzy is a friend of mine and I want to be in the picture when the Mayor announces that he's Dan White's replacement."

"I thought that fascist pig wanted his job back," Dylan interposed.

Milk was impressed that this cute jock had a brain to go with his looks. "Wow, rare, a jock with more than half a brain."

"It doesn't make any sense that you're going to work for such a short time," Jack continued to argue the point.

"Time isn't the issue here," Harvey convened. "I have all the time in the world. This photo shoot will only happen once."

"Twelve thirty it is," Scott was happy with the fact that Harvey would be joining them. "Patio boys. See ya."

Dylan smiled at Harvey bodaciously prior to leaving with Scott, "It was great to finally meet you Mr. Milk. Nice to meet you to Jack." Jack felt slighted at Dylan's less enthusiastic endearment.

"Same," Milk replied smiling, eyes roaming Dylan's erotic form.

"Can you be more obvious," Jack complained.

12:47 p.m. Patio Café – Castro Street

"It's not like Milk to be late," Scott chagrined sipping on his second glass of Syrah red wine. "You follow politics?"

"I pick up the Chronicle from time to time. Usually second hand. You?"

"Not really."

"Would you like another?" asked the slender middle-aged waiter who picked up the empty beer bottle off the table. Dylan was intrigued that his waiter's horseshoe mustache covered an overbite.

"Do you know, you look like…," Dylan hadn't finished he question when the waiter interrupted him.

"Freddie Mercury, lead singer from Queen. I get it all the time.

"Right! And Yes please I'd like another."

"I like a man who drinks beer," Scott, twelve years Dylan's senior stated.

"I drink based on occasion usually."

"What do you mean?"

"Beer when I want to keep my senses about me, wine at a white table cloth dinner, and whisky before sex."

"Good thing I've stocked a supply of JD at the apartment." Scott's humor got the reaction from Dylan he wanted. "Perhaps after lunch we could spend the rest of the day drinking whisky."

"That would be nice but I'm meeting my brother for dinner."

"Shame, perhaps tomorrow?"

"Sure, I'd like that."

Scott shrugged off the erotic talk. "You're the straight guy that queers know they'll never conquer. You throw gaydars off track. Do you mind if I get personal?"

"There's not much to talk about," Dylan avoided talking about his traumatic childhood as a general practice.

"Sounds like you don't have a lot of self-esteem," Scott perceived the angry victim in Dylan's eyes. "You're somebody's Son."

Dylan's flamboyancy drained from his face and he rested his eyes on the fork he twiddled in his right hand. "My mother died of cancer." His eyes swelled with tears, his voice cracking, "I miss her a lot." He regained his composure, "My dad started drinking incessantly. My family owns a Bistro that only serves brunch and is a bar at night. My brother and uncle pretty much run it now. I wait tables Sunday through Thursday. I make good tips I guess. Dad and I have an estranged relationship since I was outed."

"You were outed," Scott shook his head in disgust. "That's just wrong."

"It's not what you think," Dylan was not enjoying retelling his story over and over. "My Junior year I had some colleges interested in offering me football scholarships."

"See, I knew you were a jock," Scott interrupted. Turned on by his high school fantasy.

"There was this kid," Dylan continued, trying to keep a long story short. "My girlfriend's brother actually."

"It's always the girlfriend's brother!"

"We thought if we locked the janitor closet door no one would walk in."

"Janitors have more keys than there are students, hello!"

"Don't patronize me, please," Dylan managed a stupid grin. "We were such horny stupid kids."

"I don't judge you. Lucky janitor."

An air of panic, like a black cloud of deadly black widows, followed the terror-stricken food server approaching their table. Something was very, very wrong. "You're Scott, right?" He had previously served him and Harvey Milk.

"That's me."

"Come with me," he asserted with a sense of emergency. "You have a phone call."

Scott looked at Dylan with a grave but unflappable expression, "This will just take a sec."

"I'll still be here," Dylan stated the obvious.

Dylan's mind was all over the place. He rated which men, even those not sitting with other gay men, that he would have sex with. He even redesigned the restaurant to let in more sun which he believed would alleviate the cold shivers he felt from time to time.

But he wasn't prepared for the sickening shrill scream from behind the office door. "Scott?"

A patron emerged through the door to the inside bar and yelled at his boyfriend, sitting at their table with a female friend. "Hurry! You have to see this! It's on the Television in the bar!" His statement peaked the curiosity of other patrons. There was a mass migration to the bar.

Scott appeared from behind the office door at the other side of the Patio with tear stained and traumatized crimped cheeks. The painful news too much for him to endure. He stood beside Dylan, begging him to hold and comfort him. "That fascist pig killed my Harvey."

"Oh my God!" Dylan equally as shocked stood and embraced him. Consoled him.

"White shot Harvey and the Mayor. I need to do something!"

Dylan took his hand and headed to the bar. On the television where a clearly distraught interim Mayor, Dianne Feinstein, delivered the news to reporters. "It is my duty to make this announcement. Both Mayor Moscone and supervisor, Harvey Milk, have been shot and killed." There were screams from onlookers and one man cried out, "Jesus Christ!" After the crowd was quieted, Feinstein continued. "The suspect is supervisor, Dan White."

Stunned faces watching the news flash began to weep and cry out their pain, "Why? No! No!, What now!"

"That was Jack on the phone. He wants us to meet him at their apartment," Scott said.

"Let's not stay here, let's go," Dylan lead Scott by the hand and out of the restaurant.

Harvey Milk became a martyr for gay rights and would be immortalized as the person who fueled many human rights movements. His assassination gave life to the Stonewall movement that would eventually give LGBT persons a face in society.

Dylan would forever be haunted by Harvey's insistence not to call off sick. Somehow, he felt oddly culpable for his death.

Later that night – 5:52 p.m. – Intercontinental Hotel
The Roof Restaurant.

The Roof restaurant was a Sanders family favorite. Located in the lower Nob Hill District, it overlooked the bay bridge behind the not too distant pyramid shaped, Transamerica building.

The youngest of three children was not pleased with the moving elevator and screamed bloody murder, starting with the first floor. The elevator doors opened and the small Hispanic parents struggled to get their three small children out before the doors began to shut. Dylan's right arm caught the door as it began to close and gave the overwhelmed young parents a much-needed hand. "Gracias," the young father expressed his gratitude as he managed to get the baby stroller over the elevator lip. It must have been a special occasion to bring small children to the Roof, a fine dining experience where management surely would not tolerate colic babies. His bolo string tie hanging over his white wrinkled shirt was too short for his tall stature. Mom had the older siblings in each hand.

"You're welcome," Dylan smiled understanding of their situation. He sighed a sigh of relief as they turned down the long hallway to the banquet room. Directed by a sign with a pointed finger that read, "Sanchez Wedding Banquet Room 2."

Dylan scanned the restaurant, from the host podium, until he spotted Joey waving from a window booth. The maître d' had seated him early.

"Your shirt is stunning. Did you valet?" Joey taradiddly asked, raising from his seat far enough to kiss him on the cheek.

"I tried but the muni bus driver wouldn't wait." Dylan humored sarcastically. He scooted in on the other side, trying not to take the white table cloth and all the condiments with it. "I still love the view from here."

"What a terrible thing the Mayor getting assassinated," Joey announced, as if Dylan wasn't aware.

"You don't know the half of it. My day has been shit," Dylan complained picking up the menu. "You won't believe this, but I saw Harvey Milk this morning right before he was shot."

"How's that?"

"This guy Scott, that I hooked up with last night, told me he was Milk's old boyfriend and asked if I wanted to do lunch with him."

"No way!"

"Way. He took me to Milk's Camera Shop this morning and I met thee Harvey Milk in person. If he didn't have some big political event today, he would have called-in that he wasn't coming in to City Hall."

"That's crazy," Joey said shaking his head in disbelief.

"I swear on our Mother's grave," Dylan stated emphatically. "It's bizarre, but I think he had a thing for me."

"Who doesn't?" Joey rolled his eyes. "Jesus, I'd do you if you weren't my brother. You were just turned on by the attention, right?"

"Of course, He's Dad's age for Christ sake," Dylan's obliquity was a cover, for he was too embarrassed to admit he'd been with a few older men. "Have some respect for the dead for Christ sake."

The prudish greased back hair waiter noticed Dylan had arrived and approached the table. Primly dressed in a proper white tail coat, dipped slightly and inquired. "What would you like to drink sir?"

"Do you have any Portuguese imported Ports, perhaps a ruby?"

"Is Sandeman OK?"

"Fine, thanks."

Joey made an abhorrent face, "How can you drink that for dinner? It's an after dinner sweet wine."

"Just do," Dylan shrugged. "How's dad?"

"That's what I wanted to talk to you about." Joey paused and took a deep breath, "I don't know how to say this, but you know his health is going to shit?"

"Has he stopped smoking and drinking?"

"He told his doctor it was the only thing that made him happy."

Dylan lightly pounded the table, still angry at his Father, "He's such an ass!"

"Ironic," Joey paused.

Dylan shot his brother a perplexed scowl. "What?"

"Your attitude toward Father has done a one eighty."

Still confused, Dylan's brow turned inward, "How's that?"

"I wish I had a nickel for every time you told me to stop flaunting my gayness at him," Joey replied with a one up smile.

Dylan quickly changed the subject, "So his doctor believes he's had a series of small heart attacks?"

"The last one landed him in the hospital. If you ever came home at night you'd know that. I need you Dylan. John wants to retire. It's too hard for him to keep driving from Sausalito. If you were one of the employees, you'd been fired a long time ago. You can't keep calling off. I've pretty much had to hire an extra waiter to cover for you."

"I'm sorry," Dylan confessed his harum-scarum lack of responsibility. "I'm young still and so caught up in the thrill of nightlife." His head drooped, disappointed in himself. "I haven't been fair to you. You deserve a life too. You're my older brother. I take you for granted I guess."

"I would like to get my degree," Joey begged. "I have dreams too. I haven't had a day off in nearly three weeks!"

"Maybe we should just sell the place," Dylan pushed back being careful not to seem defensive.

"I don't know how much time Father has left," Joey considered his proposal. "But I know the Bistro holds some connection to Mother. He believes it holds our future."

"Not mine," Dylan interrupted, vehemently opposed to being tied to a food servers job.

"Not to change the subject, but you've managed to piss John off. He's nearly talked Father into cutting you out of your allowance and putting you on the payroll."

Dylan massaged his temples to relieve the migraine he felt developing. "OK, I get it! He snapped at his brother. "Just tell me what you need me to do."

"Good bartenders are hard to find and can't live off minimum wage."

"You want me to learn how to tend bar?" Dylan sighed. His consternation added to his growing migraine.

"Yes!" Joey responded adamantly. "You need to take over the damn bar, yes!"

"You want me to kiss my nightlife goodbye?"

"How selfish of you. You don't think I deserve a nightlife? John said he'd cover Saturday nights," Joey placated.

"Do I have a choice? I mean I'd rather manage the Bistro."

"You can't even manage yourself, let alone thirty-six employees," Joey castigated. "Besides, you can't cook. I need to control what goes out on the plate."

The waiter returned with Dylan's port wine. "Are you gentlemen ready to order?"

"Can you give us just a minute more, sorry," Joey responded.

"Sure, do you need another cocktail?"

Joey wasn't going to get drunk, "Sure, why not?"

"I'll do it," Dylan announced under his breath.

"You're being serious?" Joey hadn't expected Dylan to cave. Dylan nodded. "I love ya brother," Joey reveled. "Now I can register for night classes."

"One condition," Dylan held his index finger center table.

"What's that?"

"I want John not Dad to teach me."

Joey was still frothing, "Won't be a problem. Father will be in recovery for a while."

"God, I miss the days when we all went to the Delta fishing," Dylan reminisced.

"Nothing's stopping us now."

Melancholy returned to Dylan's mood, and he set his wine glass back on the table, "It's hard to be in the same room with him anymore. The way he looks at me, sometimes I think he wishes I hadn't been born."

Monday, May 16, 1986
Coeur d'Alene, Idaho –
"The Order Headquarters"

"Muller said to look for a Confederate flag painted on a rock at the corner of the dirt road leading to the warehouse," Estella Agsteribbe recalled. "He did say it is about a mile and a half on East Fernan Lake road once you left the residential area."

"Keep looking for the Confederate Flag then," Heinz Alt affirmed from behind the wheel of the rental. "We'll need to find an inconspicuous place to hide the car."

"We should find a place like this to settle down." Estella's senses absorbed the fresh mountain air, thick green pine trees, and the sun's reflective light off Fernan Lake as it descended behind the silhouetted ridge. "Reminds me so much of the Alps." She often felt the painful void, once filled by her murdered husband Samuel's soothing voice and touch. She remembered seeing hopelessness for the first time permeating his beaten brow as the Nazis led him away to the showers. Never to be seen again. She owed her life to Doctor Chang and the guy who now loves her unconditionally, Heinz. The sun's remaining light disappeared behind the Mountain and it got suddenly dark. The darkness renewed her anger toward the Nazis.

"Jadwiga said there is a large fascist population here," Heinz squeezed her hand affectionately. "We certainly wouldn't go hungry." She smiled felicitously, tenaciously scanning for a painted rock on the side of the road. "There it is!"

"I see it," Heinz confirmed and covered his brake. He checked his rearview mirror to assure that they were alone. Passing slowly by the dirt road, he could make out the warehouse about five hundred or so feet away. There were no cars in the dirt parking area, visible only by the incandescent lamp light above the entrance door. "Let's find a place to ditch the car."

"There's no one at the warehouse. I'm only packing a handgun." Heinz and Estella didn't care much for the trench-coats that Doctor Chang had made for them. However, in situations like this, they were more than happy to depend on the weapons creatively pocketed in them.

"Agreed."

"There," Estella pointed to tire tracks off the main road. "I wonder where that leads?"

"We're about to find out." The warehouse light was barely visible through the thick brush and trees. A small shed became visible in the headlight spray. "Check it out!"

"It's gotta be used for storage. Too small to live in," Estella added.

"Let's find out." Heinz brought the rental car to stop about fifty feet in front of it and put the gear shift into neutral. He pulled on the parking brake lever next to the clutch.

They approached the shed cautiously. Their path visible in the car's headlight spray. Heinz led with his gun drawn and ready to use if need be. Much of his military training he received when he was a member of the Resistance. After escaping with Doctor Chang, he elected not to flee to England, but rather joined the Nazi Resistance regime, Widerstand gegen den Nationalsozialismus. His accuracy as a sniper, bequeathed Heinz a feared reputation throughout the Nazi ranks. Hitler put a bounty on his head.

The door to the shed was padlocked. "Stand back," Heinz warned. He aimed at the padlock and fired one round into it. The echo rang through the forest. The lock shattered and only a partial remnant hung in the metal latch. Removing the mangled lock ring, he flung the door opened and quickly repositioned his gun toward the dark orifice.

"Rats!" Estella covered her mouth to muffle her scream. An entire family of them ran frantically out of the shed and through their feet toward the trees, startled by the gun shot. She feared them more than the Nazis. Concentration camp prisoners were tortured with, fed, and stalked by rats. "Oh my God," she caterwauled. "Jesus, I hate rats!"

"Ammunitions!" Heinz said, scoping the contents of the shed. "At least two different classes of explosive materials."

"Those drums contain bulk salutes," Estella noted the sticker on the barrels. "Look up there Heinz," she further identified a shelf of flash powders. "This stuff isn't stored here for target practice. These crackers are planning something big."

Heinz lifted a box off a nearby palette and set it on top of one of the drums. "Dynamite." He opened another box next to where he found the first. "Dynamite," he repeated. He removed a few sticks of the wrapped Dyno Noble manufactured explosives and filled his trench coat inside pockets. "We may need these later."

"You'll need this." Estella handed him a small roll of fuse cord.

"There's enough explosives here to knock down the entire forest," Heinz noted disgustingly. "Let's get back to the car."

Estella set the explosives on the top of a tree stump and got into the rental car. She maneuvered the vehicle so that the headlight spray shone on the larger warehouse through the trees.

"OK, now let's get done what we came here to do!" She reminded Heinz. "I have a gut feeling Jade isn't hold up there. Let's go find out."

"Lead the way," He said pointing toward the warehouse. "I'm coming back to rig the storehouse with ballistics as well."

Breaking the lock on the warehouse was an amateur level skillset. They carefully checked inside the warehouse corner to corner, including restrooms and a small storage unit attached to the warehouse. No Jadwiga.

"She's not here," Estella confirmed.

"Now what?"

"We rig the warehouse and we wait."

Kicking dirt over the fuse cord to each of the sticks of dynamite at each corner of the warehouse, Heinz and Estella would return to the rental car and wait, and wait, and wait.

"They couldn't have all gone to San Francisco, could they?" Estella asked with frustration. "Unless she is being held somewhere more remote, Jadwiga is not in Coeur d'Alene."

"Doctor Chang did say he was convinced she was being held captive in San Francisco," Heinz reminded her. "This is just to check that box off."

"Wait," Estella exclaimed, pointing to three sets of headlights turning onto the dirt road leading to the warehouse. "We have company."

"My God, they're wearing Klu Klux Klan robes and hoods."

Estella inspected the Occupants closer, "I count three in the first car, four in the second, and two in the rear truck. It appears that the two back seat occupants of the second car are not in costume."

Heinz studied the rear occupants of the second car closer, "Well, I can tell you that neither of them are Jadwiga."

"How's that?"

"They're both black. They look young."

"This can't be good," Estella acknowledged. "It looks like they're armed with semi-automatic rifles." Estella popped the plastic light cover from the overhead light in the car and took out the light bulb. They watched as the vehicles parked in front of the warehouse. All, but the two black young men emerged and surrounded the second car.

"Feeling Hungry?" Heinz stated, her clue to move.

"Let's get a closer look," Estella affirmed and slowly opened her passenger door. She didn't own a dress, and because she kept her hair short, from a distance she was often mistaken for a man. She was stronger now than when she won the Olympic gold.

The detonator was hidden beneath broken branches that most likely fell in a recent storm. Heinz and Estella were both adept in sniper tactics, masters of stealth, were sprawled on their stomachs, eyes in their scopes. The had attached silencers at the end of their guns.

The black prisoners were pulled from the car and tossed to the ground. Handcuffed, feet shackled, and blind folded, escape would be impossible. One by one, five of the seven Klan members took turns kicking them. They curled up into the fetal position to protect their face and groin. Two black men in their twenties on their way to explore Canada, missing. That would likely be the headlines in their hometown local rag. But they were adults and police would most likely lose interest in finding them.

"Those two-standing guard at the truck, leg wounds," Heinz whispered plan A in Estella's ear. They would be reserved for the blood-letting. But their hearts must still be beating. The blood still blue.

"The explosive concussion could kill the prisoners," Estella stated an obvious glitch in Plan A.

"Shit, Plan B won't work either. Plan C."

Confused, Estella inquired, "We have a plan C?"

"Fire fast and hope for accuracy, on three. Ready?" Estella nodded affirmatively with a sneer. "One, two, three."

Two muffled pops followed by painful screams from the hooded men keeping watch. Both fell to the ground grasping their injured leg. The coned shape hood slipped off one of the two men and exposed the same hunched back old man that Jade encountered in the line to the restroom, Leonard. "We're under attack, take cover!"

The few seconds it took for them to deduce the mortal consequence of the attack, two coned hoods turned red, filled with blood. A testament to the accuracy of Heinz and Estella's marksmanship. Both Klansmen, dropped their weapons and fell to the dirt, dead.

"Take cover!" cried out a fifth Klansman diving behind the first car. The other two Klansmen dove behind car one and car two, as Leonard and the other injured Klansman rolled under the pickup truck for protection. Both prisoners remained frozen, still moaning from their excruciating beatings.

"It's coming from the area around the munitions shed," a female voice screamed out. They had all removed their cone shaped hoods. Three white supremacists were crouched behind car one, an orange Buick Grand National. "Hold your fire. One stray bullet could spark the munitions shed and kill us all!"

"They're not going to run for it as long as they're blind folded," Estella stated of the two prisoners still frolicking in pain in the same fetal position and in the same spot. "They're dead meat either way."

"We have no choice, plan A," Heinz said, a gut-wrenching knot formed in his stomach from knowing there would likely be collateral damage. His hand rested on the detonator handle.

"You're right, a shoot-out is too dangerous." That was the confirmation he hoped to hear from Estella that would free the knot in his stomach. "The trees are thick and the covered shed should protect the munitions from shrapnel from the warehouse."

He nodded and pushed the handle of the detonator. The concussion from the blasts sent the Buick rolling into the air. It landed on top of the black victims, stifling their screams. The blast also lifted car two, a black Lincoln Continental off the ground, shattering the windows of all three vehicles. The mangled, debris eviscerated bodies of three dead Klansmen, lay several yards from the center of the blast. The air was teeming with dense smoke and ash.

"I can't hear," Leonard screamed, holding his head. The explosion had pushed his white ford pick-up, several feet from him. The blast also thrust the other wounded Klansman on top of him. "Get your fat ass off me Horace!" Leonard's wound had already drained much of what strength he had left. But with that little strength he managed to roll Horace off him. Then he saw it. The shredded rain gutter protruding from Horace's shoulder. Leonard exuded a sickening scream. Horace was dead. There was a high thin bright blue and red flame bellowing from a pipe leading to the where the gas meter use to be. A few sparks fell from a severed electrical line as they bounced off a large piece of metal roofing. The ground was becoming muddy and saturated with water from severed water pipes.

Heinz and Estella still lay tightly together on their stomach's, arms covering their heads. They quickly bounced up and brushed off the dust from their clothes and hair. Heinz immediately assessed any damage to the munitions shed. That's when he noticed part of a door had penetrated the roof of the shed. "Crap, that was close!"

"We have to act fast. This place will soon be inundated with first responders. The echo from the blast had to be heard from miles away." Estella reminded him with a sense of urgency.

Without the porch light from the warehouse, they had only the light from the stars to push through the brush and trees to arrive at ground zero. But their eyes soon adjusted and they maneuvered faster. Their first priority was to refuel their need for new blood. They realized that their opportunity for a blood-letting was exacerbated by the wound they inflicted in Leonard's leg. He was nearly bled out when they reached him.

But what they didn't realize was that Leonard had managed to get to his gun. He was weak and shaking profusely. Supporting his automatic rifle on Horace's dead body he took aim at anything that moved. As the silhouetted figure emerged through the thick smoke, his finger touched the trigger. He knew that this female figure was his nemesis and it was her life or his at stake. He took one last alignment with his scope. Had her in his sights. Leonard hesitated, "Come on, just a little closer bitch." Estella was not aware. She was a sure target. This might have been her last day of immortality.

Still deaf from the concussion of the blast, Leonard couldn't hear Heinz approach from behind him. There was no need for Heinz's stealth approach, but he did cautiously. The first lesson of combat, don't attack in clusters. He leaped on top of Leonard and pinned his arms to the ground. Leonard's finger pulled back on the trigger at the same moment Heinz's pounced on him. The gun fired. Estella felt the sibilant wheeze of air as the bullet passed a few inches from her head. She instantly fell to the ground to avoid the possibility of another.

"Shit! That was close," she chafed, still lying prostrate in the mud.

Heinz waived frantically for her to relieve him from sucking Leonard's blood while his heart was still pumping. Leonard's body convulsed under Heinz's powerful grip. He had managed to bite easily through Leonard's thin decrepit skin. Heinz believed, that he could actually feel Leonard's artery in his mouth, similar to that of a thin organic straw. It tickled his tongue which annoyed him. Maneuvering her lips close to his, Estella relieved Heinz. His pulse nearly stopped. She sucked hard as Heinz pressed deep and hard on Leonard's chest, with a pace similar to the rhythm on Leonard's chest. There was no color left but Leonard's hazel pupils, bulging out as the blood was literally drained from every visible and subterranean cell of his body.

"It tasted like lead," Estella complained. "I swear I'll never feed on anyone over thirty again."

"Sometimes, preference isn't a convenience," he said. "I'm going to check on the victims and then we must get the hell out of here."

"I'm right behind you."

"I will remove the car, you pull them from under it," Heinz volunteered. With his left hand, Heinz lifted the car and tossed it backwards on its top.

As she pressed the young man's carotid artery to feel a pulse, she was overwhelmed by how innocent he looked. Perhaps a freshman or sophomore, maybe younger. She checked him head to toe for injury, but found only bruises on his arms and face.

Heinz rolled the second youth, who was face down in the mud, onto his stomach. It was apparent to him that the car's tire had crushed his chest. "This one is gone," Heinz said.

"He has a pulse." She said exuberantly. "Help me get him to the car." As desperate as she felt to take his life and suck every ounce of blood from his body, her integrity mattered more to her. The oath she had taken to honor the code, and only take fascist blood, was paramount to revenge her dear husbands murder.

Heinz assessed the terrain. "Go, I got this. I'll carry him over my shoulder." He reached for the keys in his front pocket and tossed them to her. "Here's the keys. Start the car."

Estella nodded and took advantage of the head start. Putting her left arm out to block low hanging tree branches, she stepped quickly over fallen limbs and brushwood. Slipping the key into the ignition, she turned the engine on. Climbing back out of the car, she opened the rear door, then got into the front passenger seat. Heinz leaned down and rolled the black unconscious youth onto the rear car bench seat. His head struck the opposite door with a thud. "Shit!" Heinz wrenched his face, imitating the pain it wouldn't have caused the young man had he been conscious. "That's going to bruise."

There was just enough trees cleared in front of the munitions shed to make a three-point turn. Once back at the road, he turned off his headlights and headed away from town, not knowing where Fernan Lake Road may take them. After traveling for about three minutes, he turned his headlights back on.

"I'll look for you," Estella insisted, as the Fernan Lake Road was dark and windy. "You should see the convoy of red, white, and blue, lights moving toward the warehouse. We got out of there just in time."

Heinz pointed at the folded-up map sitting on top of the dashboard. "Can you confirm there's a turnoff North to Lake Hayden?"

Estella flipped the dome light on and unfolded the map. Running her finger along Fernan Lake Road she found the road and looked for the name of it. "Canfield Loop Road. It looks like a dirt road." She followed it with her finger until it ended at a private residence. "We can take this back to interstate 90, but it's about an hour's drive and there will be road blockages everywhere. There's a gun range about seven miles up the road. We can hang out there until the dust settles."

Monday, May 16, 1986
Half Moon Bay

"My thirteen-year-old, Tanya, hasn't been her normal self since Junior arrived," Sandy admitted, still trying to exculpate her brother's pedophilia conviction in her mind. "How long have you known about this Giuseppe?"

"Doctor Chang informed me this morning," Giuseppe replied, squeezing her hand gently. Walking on the sandy beach barefoot, the hot sand was becoming too uncomfortable. "There's an empty bench, let's sit down."

"It gives me the chills that he would do this kind of in-depth research on me?" She asked, finding it peculiar that she would be a person of interest. "I've only met the man once."

"Huey leaves no rock unturned," Giuseppe was quick to respond. "He's a very good man. Always one step ahead of his nemesis."

"You're going to have to stop using big words if this thing between us is going anywhere," Sandy humored. "I think that means he considers me a threat?"

"Sorry," he apologized, "Never considered myself a scholar. Trust me, He does not consider you a threat. So, do you feel comfortable talking about Tanya's feelings? She's thirteen you mentioned?"

"Yes, she's only thirteen, and no I don't have a problem talking with you about it," She answered, the fear coming back to her. "I just assumed she didn't like him. He's very hard around the edges. Somewhat self-centered. His southern drawl is very profound like my ex-husband's."

"Do you mind if I ask what happened to the children's Father?"

"He was murdered." Sandy's chin dropped to her chest to hide resurfacing feelings. "The case is still cold."

"I'm very sorry," Giuseppe stroked her hair. "Look, I'm not the type of guy that would ask you to forget about him."

"I know," she said managing a smile. "I wouldn't be sitting here with you if you did. He was a good man."

"So, what are you going to do?"

"Junior is leaving for Mississippi after the KKK Rally," Sandy said thinking out loud. "I don't believe he'd hurt his own family. He's always had a problem keeping his penis in his pants. Dad whipped him real good once when I was a small girl. I think I was seven or eight. Junior had just reached puberty, pulled his pants down, and asked me to touch it. I think I had more sense then, than I do now. I screamed for Dad who was outside mowing the lawn. Beat him to an inch of his life." She shook her head with a smirk, "My brothers and I use to crack up every time my other brother would tell the story. Doesn't seem so funny now."

Giuseppe leaned toward her and softly kissed her lips. "If I'm moving too fast."

"I don't feel any pressure," Sandy smiled with afterglow. "I'd let you know. I'm starting to really really like you. Perhaps I like you a lot more than just like you."

He kissed her again. "Then I'm a very lucky guy."

She sat up with renewed enthusiasm. "I'd like you to meet my daughters! It's time."

"I would love that," Giuseppe said. "Right now?"

"Right now." She said nodding affirmatively. "Yes, I have to pick them up from school in about forty-five minutes. I'll meet you back at my apartment." Sandy searched her purse for a pen and paper. Discovering an old business card, she had planned to discard anyway, she wrote her address on the back of it. "Are you familiar with the Sunset District?"

"That's North of Lake Merced Park, right?"

"Yes."

He glanced at the address on the back of the card and nodded, "I'll find it." He leaned toward her and kissed her again. "You should go so you're not late."

"Give me an hour and a few minutes," Sandy exclaimed. She left him standing at the bench, starring at her with elation.

Monday, May 18, 1986
San Francisco, Home of Captain Jack

"It won't be a problem," Thomas said, from the driver's seat of Jack's pickup. "You don't have to keep apologizing."

"It's just for a few days," Dylan explained. He felt embarrassed to ask Thomas's grandfather if he could stay at his home. What didn't resonate with Dylan was his assurance that Jack had no problems with him. "The Supremacists want to eradicate the Creed. Doctor Chang has warned us that they are being financed by a very powerful foreign syndicate, and we just need to disappear for a while."

"What about the others?"

"Carol is still recovering at a family members home in Sausalito. The twins are staying with Tommy and Macias and Jonathan is hanging out at my brother's apartment. Giuseppe is temporarily staying at the Rector with his new Pastor's family."

"Doctor Chang and Muller?"

"We promised them we would keep their whereabouts unknown," Dylan said with a visceral concern for their safety. "The Creed is a bad force to reckoned with. But these Fascists are bad asses. I've only seen fear in their eyes one other time, when Jade came up missing."

"They're very intelligent men," Thomas stated. "They'll figure this out. What I can't figure out is that of all people, Giuseppe strikes me the least to find religion."

"Most people who can't find love often find religion to fill the void," Dylan grinned tongue in cheek.

"There's a lot of ladies that would fancy him. He just needs to put himself out there."

"I don't know," Dylan contended, "His personality is somewhat nondescript. But there's a rumor he's dating that lady that managed the White Owl. I think her name was Sandy. Supposedly she flipped and is providing important intel to Muller."

"He needs to lose that obnoxious uncle Lurch grin though."

Dylan smirked, "He's even talking shit about leaving the Creed. I support whatever makes him happy."

"Do you support whatever makes me happy?" Thomas asked soberly candid.

"I'm not sure where this is going." The abysmal anxiety returned to his stomach. The detoxing withdrawals and excruciating pain as his muscle growth accelerated. He recalled the gut-wrenching adrenal highs when the steroids kicked in and the natural folic acid overwhelmed his PABA inhibitors. But the pain would return with a vengeance without the blood-letting, returning him to his dying condition of mortality. Did he want this for Thomas? Yet, the idea of having him forever always stirred, reveling in the back of his mind. Doctor Chang and Muller would help Giuseppe back through the change. A change he wanted to protect Thomas from having to endure.

"I want to join!" Thomas announced confident of his conviction.

"The Creed? Not happening," Dilan stated decisively.

"I watched spellbound as a wound repaired itself on Muller's arm that he snagged on a rose thorn. I've witnessed the super-human strength you used to throw that biker through the door of Pearl's. I've done some homework, Estella Agsteribbe, is a gold medalist. In the 1920's?" Thomas stated in the form of a question. "I also learned that Doctor Huey Chang worked under Doctor Karl Brandt. Performed medical experiments on Auschwitz prisoners?" His voice raising. "You're vampires. Am I right? Well?"

Dylan's voice had a tinge of anger, "I don't know if the term vampires is accurate. What am I saying. You don't know what you're asking for. I can't discuss this with you right now. Just let it go."

"Jack left the front door open," Thomas said as he steered the pickup into the driveway. "That's not like Jack." He slammed the gear stick into first gear, pushed hard on the emergency brake, turned off the engine, and released the clutch. His heart racing to get out of his chest. Whether it was Alzheimer's or an intruder, Thomas was bent on finding out.

"Wait!" Dylan grabbed Thomas's faded plaid shirt as he quickly swung his door open to leave. "My instinct tells me we might be walking into a trap."

"I have to get to Jack!" Thomas said, his face parched with fear of believing the worst.

"Thomas, listen to me," Dylan plead. "I don't trust these bastards. Considering everything that's happened we have to assume the worst. We can't know for sure that we're just overreacting. But it's not worth the risk."

"Jack," Thomas spoke his name with rueful realization that Dylan was right. "What do we do?"

"For starters, whether Jack is alone or has company, they had to hear us pull in the driveway. If the later, they know we're here. Secondly, we have to clear our heads and think clearly."

"God," Thomas aggrieved, frustrated with the situation. "To hell with this, I have to know Jack's OK!" Thomas darted from Dylan's grasp and darted toward the front door.

"Damn you Thomas!" Dylan yelled angrily at him. He got out of the truck, and took cover behind the neighbor's boxwood shrubbery which served as a barrier between their home and Jack's.

Thomas screamed, "Nooo!" But his scream, which resounded through the open door, ended abruptly. Silenced by a blunt object to the back of the head, he only caught a glimpse of Jack's bruised and swollen face. The Peckerwood's had broken into Jack's home and caught him off guard, tied him to a kitchen chair, interrogated, and beat him within an inch of his life.

"I'll kill those bastards," Dylan said painfully enraged. He removed a small handgun from one of the pockets in his trench-coat and released the safety. He then counted three razor sharp boomerangs in another, and a concussion grenade, which doubled as a smoke bomb. He was ready for battle. Not knowing how many or what type of weapons they were armed with, put him at a disadvantage. He had to act swiftly and with a keen sense of his surroundings. As much as he complained to Muller about wearing the trench-coat, it was situations like these that made any debate to the contrary invalid.

Dylan's heart pounded heavy in his chest. He uncapped the container with his steroids, and popped one into his mouth. He only needed one Peckerwood to complete the SR Process.

He carefully, and with ease, hopped the neighbors hedge and fence, which separated the rear from the front yard. He was grateful there were no dogs to contend with. He didn't know whether Thomas or Jack was still alive. He knew if they were alive, their survival was dependent on him. An empty void twisted his stomach in knots. He recalled feeling the same anxiety and anger the day his father broke the news of his mother's stage four cancer. Dauntless and driven to rescue Thomas, he pushed himself into the life and death challenge. He wished he could have faced his mother's cancer with the same odds of beating it.

He counted three motorcycles parked in Jack's backyard. A black Harley FXS, flat gray XLCR, and a beat-up blue Honda CL450. The Honda's kick stand had sunk into the grass and was a quarter inch from tipping over. Most likely three Peckerwood subjects held out in Jack's house. Dylan still didn't know what weapons they had in their possession. The lavender growing in Jack's garden was playing havoc on his allergies and dulling his senses. He held back a few sneezes.

Picking up a large boulder out of Jack's neighbors garden, he hurled it at the Honda motorcycle, which made a very loud echo off the metal gas tank. It was all the help the Honda needed to fall into the Harley's. Like dominoes, the bikes tumbled.

Thomas's head hurt. He could make out the image of a ripped six pack stomach as his eyes began to focus. He moaned, "Jack." He opened his mouth wide to call for help, but was met with a splash of cold water and the sound of someone spitting a warm sticky substance in his eye.

"The bikes!" the muscled interrogator exclaimed. "Mohawk, check it out!"

"Alone?" Mohawk, the younger, and less fit of the three, cowered. He flinched, and avoided a hand slap to the back of the head from an acne faced Peckerwood standing over him. Mohawk rose from the kitchen table where Jack was tied to an end chair unconscious. "Knock it off Frank!" he protested. Thomas, still in a daze, thought it coincidental until he heard him speak. It was the skinhead bully from last week's basketball game.

"Then go check on the bikes asshole, before I knock you out!"

"Leave him alone Frank!" barked the behemoth gangster. "Shoot that freak if you see it. Now go!"

Thomas's head was pounding. As much as it hurt to think or speak, he needed to get into their heads. "That gun won't help you Mohawk. You know it. He's one blood thirsty vampire."

"Shut up fag!" Mohawk yelled, knocking over a lamp. "RJ, I'm not going out there alone. You saw what they did to Mike's boys at the synagogue!" Mohawk's nostrils flared, his breathing accelerated from fear.

"Maybe there's some garlic in the fridge," Frank teased with a harassing smirk.

"You believe you're dealing with mystical vampires?" Thomas painstakingly managed to speak, antagonizing them. "These vampires are the real thing. You dicks couldn't have come at a better time. He has the need to feed."

RJ drew his hand hard across Thomas's face. "Shut up punk. Thomas went dark, his chin fell to his chest. "Frank, go with him, NOW!"

Frank glared at Mohawk with contempt, "Pussy."

"Go!" RJ shouted.

They hadn't taken two steps toward the mud room and rear door when the sound of footsteps from the roof stopped them cold in their tracks. "He's on the roof RJ," Frank pined.

RJ reached for his gun on the table and aimlessly fired three rounds into the ceiling. "Show yourself freak or I'll kill them both!" RJ pointed his gun at Jack's heart. Standing frozen, afraid to move, their heads turned left then right, wishing there was some barrier between them and the vampire. RJ's finger touched the trigger of his gun. "I'm not playing games!" he yelled loud enough for someone on the roof to hear him. There was a short pause. Nothing. RJ fired a deadly shot. Jack's body seized and went limp. He was gone. "One Indian dead. Your homo boyfriend is next!" RJ became impatient and angry. "Just tell us where we can find Chang and I'll let him go! Don't be stupid! I've already killed the old man!"

"We're screwed!" Mohawk wailed plangently.

RJ had zero tolerance for Mohawk's cowardice. No room in the Aryan brotherhood for weak minded cowards. Without hesitation,

RJ fired off one round which accurately hit it's intended bull's eye, Mohawk's forehead. The Peckerwood never saw it coming.

Frank stood over Mohawk's lifeless body. Blood and brains splattered the yellow wallpaper where Mohawk's head once cast a shadow. "Have you gone mad RJ!" Frank screamed.

The air was sucked out of RJ's response as sheet rock rained down on him from the ceiling. Dust and debris filled the small kitchen. RJ instinctively raised his right arm to block the falling ceiling debris. In the midst of the cloud of dust, and shrouded by his flared-out trench coat, Dylan landed on both feet. Crouched from the impact, one hand holding, then tossing the concussion grenade toward Frank. The deafening thunderous blast jolted Frank and RJ off their feet. The house immediately filled with thick blinding smoke.

Frank felt around the floor to find his gun that he had dropped. He couldn't find it. He felt around and found a wall instead and crawled into the bathroom and shut the door behind him. Frank secured the lock and wedged the metal towel rack under the door knob.

Laying on his back, RJ cupped his ears, still ringing from the concussion. His head leaning against the cabinet doors below the sink. He couldn't hear or see anything within an inch in front of his face. His right hand still holding onto his handgun. He fired a random shot into the air. "I'm going to kill you, you son of a bitch!" He fired another random shot. It ricocheted of the tile backsplash and a piece of the bullet struck a pendulum of the grandfather clock in the living room. It gave off an ear-piercing ring which echoed several times as the pendulum swung into the adjacent one. The echoed died.

No sooner had RJ managed to get back on his feet, that Dylan had grasped RJ's right wrist from behind him. Unmatched strength RJ had never encountered in all his days as a champion competition arm wrestler. But this unfathomable power, shook the gun out of his hand, turned him like a top, grasped his other wrist and lifted him up until his feet couldn't touch the floor. It happened so fast he had no time to react. RJ was pinned against the wall. His last memory was an angry, bluish crimson complexioned face with subconjunctival red eyes. The creature's upper lip raised, exposing two long white scissor teeth, like a wild animal about to bite down on Its prey. RJ had never known such fear, a taste of his own medicine. He felt the sting, like ten nurse's needles pricking his neck. He was pinned against the wall with such force that he was unable to squirm or push off. Weaker and weaker he became as the oxygen rich blood never reached his brain. What sounded like a baby slurping on Its bottle, RJ had no breath in which to scream, knowing from wence it came. RJ faded into an endless sleep called death.

The pain in his head was excruciating as Thomas awakened from unconsciousness. His right eye swollen shut. His face, still on fire from the beatings. But it paled in comparison to the beast like ritual he was witnessing. The memory of their first romantic encounter in the garden of the Hospice. He too was nearly a victim of this creature's insatiable dependency. The blood-letting, as his lover described it. Steroids transformed his body to prepare for accepting the new blood. A condition he was doomed to submit to. Thomas had never imagined it would look so abhorring and frightening. Is this really what he wanted? This immortal life dependent on the mortality of others? Was he so in love with this young man, many years his senior, that he was willing to kill for it? Now he understood why Doctor Chang was not in favor of the Creed mixing with mortals. This psychological pain was what Chang tried to protect him from. But it was too late. He loved Dylan unconditionally.

Not prepared for what he would see next, Thomas glimpsed upon Jack, pale and hunched over. His lifeless body still tied to the kitchen chair. A bullet wound to the chest had penetrated Jack's heart. The pool of Jack's blood had already begun to coagulate on the tile floor. Jack was dead!

"Jack!" Thomas wept. "Why? Jack! No! No! No! Help me!"

RJ's cold body dropped to the floor as Dylan released his grip and bite. Thomas's disconsolate cries of agonizing sadness, over the loss of his grandfather, was breaking Dylan's rejuvenated heart. There was nothing he could do to bring Jack back. He quickly freed Thomas and held him tight in his arms. Dylan wiped the residual blood from his lips with his tongue and kissed the top of Thomas's head. "He's gone Thomas. I'm so sorry."

"I couldn't help him," Thomas choked on his tears.

"There's nothing you could have done short of getting yourself killed," Dylan consoled.

"He didn't deserve this. They will pay! I promise you Jack," Thomas said with indignation.

"This is not a person Thomas," Dylan said, realizing there was still one Peckerwood in the house and he was hearing all of this. "This is a disease called hate. It has many names. Plagues even the holiest of places. We are powerless against it because it lays dormant in every mind, waiting for a reason to infest." Dylan bent his head down and began to whisper in Thomas's ear. "Now you must listen to me, and you must do as I say. There's still one locked in the bathroom." Dylan felt Thomas's aggression and held him tighter and covered his mouth. "I know you want to destroy him, but you're not thinking clearly." Thomas sighed and relaxed his anger. "Let me handle this. I'm going to let you go. Don't say anything, just sit back on the chair. I got this. Promise me." Thomas nodded.

Thomas pointed at the gun laying in the hallway where Frank had dropped it. Dylan nodded and kicked it down the hall toward the rear door. "I believe your name is Frank." Dylan stood motionless to the right side of the bathroom door. "Isn't that what RJ called you?". There was no answer. "Open the door Frank, we want to talk to you."

"I didn't kill anyone!" Frank cried out frantically.

"No one said you did Frank. The way I see it Frank, you're better off working with us than the Peckerwoods. I mean look what happened to your friend Mohawk."

"He's not my friend. He's a loser. I'm going to wait for the cops, go to hell!" Frank's voice was panic-stricken. He sat on the closed toilet lid shaking. His eyes looked up at the small window at the top of the shower. He knew with his girth, escape wasn't possible.

"Frank I'm losing patience with you," Dylan baited him mawkishly.

"Oh God, I'm screwed," Frank said under his breath. Horror-struck, he began to tear up, his breathing accelerated.

"Frank, Frank, Frank," Dylan paused to consider what options he had with Frank. "We could work out a deal."

"Fuck your deal!"

"Why don't you come out. I don't want to kill you Frank. We can strike a deal," Dylan was making a game out of it.

"I'm screwed either way. How do I know you'll keep your word?" Frank was taking the bait.

"Who's running the show? Who sent you? Have you ever heard of the Krupp Family?"

"That would be a death wish. You have no idea who they are!"

"Wow Frank, you disappoint me." Dylan turned and faced the bathroom door. Raising his foot to waste level, as if pulling back on a sling shot, he kicked in the door. Wood shards flew everywhere, as did the metal towel rack.

His heart racing, Frank shrank against the toilet tank, bawling like a child in trouble. "Please, I'm begging, don't kill me." His nemesis stood in the doorway, traces of RJ's blood on his chin and still noticeable between his teeth. A bluish hue shade of Dylan's blood pulsed hard through his temples and cheeks. Frank didn't believe in Vampires. He mocked the talk that frightened the neo-Nazi gangs and kowtowed them off the streets. But the Titan towering over him was not his imagination.

"Now you're going to tell me who's calling the shots and from where. Or I'll have you for lunch."

"OK, OK! Frank acquiesced, wiping the sweat from his brow. "Man, you've managed to piss off a lot of people because William Luther Pierce is in town."

"I don't know the guy, who is this Pierce guy?"

"He's the guy that wrote the Turner Diaries, today's version of Hitler's Mein Kampf. America's Hitler man. Him and this Krupp lawyer call all the shots."

"Where can I find them?"

"Man, you don't want to find them. They're protected by some heavy-duty fire power. They have moles in every law enforcement agency you can think of."

"Where can I find them!" Dylan demanded. His voice deeper and impatiently furious. He grabbed Frank's collar and lifted him six inches off the toilet. "Where!"

"Alright!, Double Tree close to the airport. They've pretty much taken over the entire Hotel."

Dylan released his grip and Frank slid off the toilet as the toilet lid snapped off from his weight. Frank regained his balance and managed to stand up. "One last thing. They have a hostage. Have you heard of her?"

"Chang's friend?"

"That's the one."

"She's why we're here." Frank paused with a quizzical look of being used. "My God, this is playing out just like they planned."

"Where is she!" Dylan yelled in his face, but he seemed unaffected by it.

"They threw us under the bus," Frank mumbled like a madman. "They expected that we would deliver their ransom message to Chang and that you would kill us. Destroying any leads for the Cops."

"Frank, concentrate, tell me where she is," Dylan said more tempered. He was losing Frank somewhere in the anger of betrayal.

"They have her," Pop, his head exploded. The bullet from his own gun penetrated through his left eye socket. Pieces of skull, blood, and brains, dripped down the shower curtain. Frank's corpse collapsed into the bathtub. The blood-soaked curtain ripped from the rings holding it to the bar and shrouded Frank.

Dylan stepped backwards, reacting to the blast. He looked perplexed and empathetically at a very angry young man standing in the doorway, still pointing the gun where Frank once stood. "Thomas, what did you just do?"

"That's for Jack," Thomas said with some gratification. With Jack's blood on his shirt and tear stained cheeks, he handed Dylan Frank's warm still smoking gun.

"Let's get out of here," Dylan took Thomas by the hand. "We can't take Jack's truck. The bikes!" Dylan let go of Thomas's hand and searched RJ's pockets. "Jackpot, he owns the Harley."

"Can you drive it?" Thomas questioned.

"Are you kidding me?" Dylan managed an elated grin. "My dad's favorite toy."

The passenger of the Mercedes 450L had fallen asleep. His head resting against the window. "Gary, wake up!" the driver barked loud enough to get his attention. "We're moving. They've stolen RJ's bike and are on the move!"

Parked across the street from Jack's place, the two white supremacists had been staking out the house, hoping and waiting for this opportunity. "Don't lose them!" Gary Yarbrough insisted, fully alert and tenaciously determined to locate Doctor Chang. The car sped off the curb and toward the direction Dylan and Thomas fled on RJ's bike.

Headquarters, San Francisco Police Department
Same day.

"We have some visitors, Feds," Detective Roberts said, poking his head through the glass door of Sergeant Stone's cubical.

"Well? Invite them back," Stone insisted, rummaging through police reports and polaroid evidence on his desk. Sam Stone was ready to throw in the towel on the case known as the "Bite" Case. The precinct employees simply referred to as the Vampire Case. "This is making me want to retire early," he stated under his breath. It would be impossible to work on anything clandestinely, as the walls of his office were all glass. He could see three suits walking behind detective Roberts. He marched them right into Sam's office.

"Sergeant Sam Stone, FBI Special Agent, Wayne Manis," Roberts introduced the two heads.

"This is Agent Ferris, and Agent Cooper," Agent Manis, pointed to the men behind him in crisp steam cleaned blue suits, white shirts, and solid color ties.

Sam extended a cordial handshake to each of his visitors. "Welcome to San Francisco, the City of love, drugs, and liberals." Agent Manis chuckled at his description of the City. "What brings you here?"

"The Federal government is taking over the Bite Case Sergeant," Agent Manis announced.

"There is a God after all!" Stone reacted with a fabricated sense of relief. But his pride was screaming from inside, "You bastards, I'm not a failure. Get off my turf."

"In light of the attack on the Thilim Synagogue, Attorney General Meese has ordered the Department of Justice to fund the war on white supremacy. My team has been working for some time on Neo-Nazi cases with some success. You may recall recently the Mathews case."

"Mathews was the nut job you guys fried in the Puget Sound fire at that National Alliance compound. Didn't he start that fascist terrorist group called the 'Order," Stone said with a condescending stare. "Any connection to yesterday's assault on the Klu Klux Klan in Coeur d'Alene? The District Attorney called me and asked about my investigation. He believes there is a connection as one of the Klansmen was bitten. Said the Order is very much alive and with more members than ever. Wants my help."

Agent Manis didn't like the direction the Sergeant was taking. "We were investigating the Alan Berg homicide Sergeant. The reason we're here is we have it on good source that Luther Pierce is in town. The other reason is to stop the Nationalist Alliance from an ideological over throw of the government and," he paused. "I can't believe I'm saying this. To bring some killer vigilante vampires to justice."

"Wow, even God can't stop hate. What makes Ronald Reagan think he's greater than God? History has taught us, you can't destroy an ideology. And the consensus around this precinct is that as long as we have vigilante vampires roaming the streets feeding on gangsters, our work is done."

"How's that Sergeant?" Agent Manis asked with some distain, but mostly curiosity.

"Shit!" Stone paused and walked over to a map, taped on the glass wall behind him. "The red dots represent all homicides related to the Bite case. Now here's what I'm talking about. Notice the blue dots? They represent crime events in the second quarter of this year." Stone touched a black dot with his index finger, "These black dots, which are significantly more, represent the first quarter of this year. That's an 87 percent decrease Agent Manis. Word on the street is "You need a dollar, give blood at your local red cross." Criminals are running scared, fearful of their own shadows."

"It's against the law Sergeant, even if you're a vigilante," Agent Manis castigated. "It's our job to enforce the laws."

"But we do a lousy job Agent Manis," Sergeant Stone stated soberly. "I've never seen results like these in all the years I've worn this badge. I'm torn as to whether or not it would be in the best interest of the community to arrest them."

"It's not your choice Sergeant," Agent Manis had heard enough. "I need copies of all your files related the Bite case," he looked sternly at Stone. "I'll send an Agent to pick them up in one hour.'

"One hour?" Stone protested. "That's impossible! I don't have that kind of manpower!

"You said yourself your work load is light now, make yourself useful." Agent Manis and his suits exited Stone's office. "One hour!"

"Damn FBI," Stone mumbled to detective Rogers.

"My ears work just fine Sergeant," Agent Manis hollered back from the corridor to his office.

"Sergeant!" the desk clerk summoned from across the room. "Code 245 Tenderloin, four dead, gun-shot wounds, one meets the vampire MO."

"Let's roll," Stone beckoned. Clipping his munitions belt around his waist, Stone grabbed his Fedora hat from atop the coat rack.

Agent Manis had picked up on the call and stopped to confront Sergeant Stone. "I'm riding with you. The FBI has been monitoring your frequency and is sending a small posse."

"Bring a barf bag," Stone said facetiously as he passed Agent Manis. "Nothing can prepare you for what you're about to see.

Sandy's Apartment

Giuseppe won Sandy's daughters over with his huge Uncle Lurch smile. Unlike the men mom normally hung around with, He didn't use profanity, spit tobacco, smell like a brewery, or have pestilent tattoos all over his body. Sixteen-year-old, Natalie, secretly told her mom, "He seems nice."

Sandy had decided that she didn't want to spend their time in the kitchen and decided to order Pizza. "Dominos Pizza OK?"

"Let me run and get it," Giuseppe insisted.

"I'm unemployed, I'm not poor," Sandy replied with an appreciative smirk. "Thanks, but let this be my treat."

"No seriously, I would like to do this."

"You're a real gentleman," Natalie interposed. "Most of the men mom brings home usually boss her in and out of the kitchen for beer and snacks."

Sandy's brow dipped inward from the unsolicited critique. But she couldn't shake the smile knowing it was true and that her daughter approved. "Oh, I'm not that naïve."

Natalie rolled her eyes, "Whatever mom."

"Giuseppe can speak five languages," Sandy said proudly, still selling Giuseppe to them.

"I can speak two," Natalie fired back, "English and Spanish."

Giuseppe grinned back, "That's great! It will come in handy someday, trust me."

"What languages do you speak?" Tanya asked timidly.

"Italian, that's my primary language, English, German, French, and Spanish."

"Wow," Tanya reacted, coming out of her indolent mood. "You must be really smart."

Boots clacking on the cement sidewalk outside Sandy's front door grew louder. "Sounds like Junior's got company," Natalie abashed, her face formed a disconcerted distain. Tanya looked troubled.

A sculpted middle-aged man wearing motorcycle chaps with a neatly groomed beard followed Junior through the threshold. Junior's facial features matched that of his sister's. Same larger than life nose, a little overweight, and stubble from days without shaving.

"Sis, this is Tank, Tank, my sis Sandy," Junior jumped right to introductions. Sandy smiled and acknowledged him. He grinned back at her. "Is this the lucky guy who's dating my sister?" Sandy was right, his Southern drawl was heavy.

Giuseppe's intuition was sounding the danger stranger alarm. He was apprehensive about shaking Junior's hand but acquiesced when Junior put it out for him to shake. Giuseppe clenched it firmly, tightening it only after Junior attempted to one up him. "Wow, that's a pretty strong grip you have Mister."

"Giuseppe," He said looking down at him with an insincere grin.

"Will you dudes be joining us for Pizza?" Sandy interjected, breaking the tension between them.

"Love to but, I promised Tanya a ride on my motorcycle," Junior beamed at Tanya. "Didn't I princess?"

"The dealer left a message on the machine Junior," Sandy castigated. "Either buy it or return it."

"I just need it for a few more days," He argued flippantly. "Besides, I need to make good on my promise to give Princess a ride on it. Ain't that right Princess?" Tanya nodded, not sharing his enthusiasm. "OK, I'll take it back tomorrow. Come on Tanya, before it gets late. You have school tomorrow." Tank formed a perverted grin that chilled Giuseppe to the bone. She was being coerced through fear. It was apparent to him that she no more than wanted a ride on his motorcycle than she did jumping into a vat of hot grease.

"I don't think so Junior," Sandy said, short of seeming pertinacious. "I brought Giuseppe over to get to know my daughters."

"It's OK Sandy," Giuseppe exclaimed, managing to bemuse Junior. "I'll run and get the Pizza. I'm sure this motorcycle ride shouldn't take much longer than it would for me to return with the Pizza and then Junior and Stank..."

"His name is Tank," Junior interrupted with disdain.

"Tank, I'm sorry," Giuseppe apologized insincerely. Tank's eyes squinted at Giuseppe with indignation. "Then Junior and Tank can join us."

"We had planned to take highway one down the coast to San Jose and back," Junior stated acrimoniously.

"Hey," Giuseppe exclaimed, throwing up his arms. "Work with me. Compromise with your sister a little."

"Do you know where the Dominos is located?" Sandy assented.

"No, what's the address?"

"South on the avenue then take a left on Sloat," She explained. "It's in the corner of the mall just East of Sunset."

"I'll find it," Giuseppe assured her. "Two large combos?"

"That's fine," Sandy agreed, walking to the kitchen table to get her purse.

"I told you I got this," Giuseppe said adamantly. He turned and walked out the door in an attempt to get ahead of Junior and Tank.

"Giuseppe!" She called after him. "Dang it!" Sandy complained. She turned to Junior and Tank who were also anxious to leave. Tanya was walking between them less enthused about going. "Do you want to go with them Natalie?"

"No," she responded with angst.

"Hurry back Junior," She stated firmly.

"You did good Tanya," Junior praised her performance, speaking to her like she was his prisoner, rather than his niece. He lifted her at her waste with both hands onto the back of the motorcycle and forced his helmet over her head. He threw his leg over the seat and grasped the handle bars and kicked up the kickstand. "Now hold on to me tight you little whore. You hear me." Tears welled up in her vulnerable eyes. He turned and threatened, with a sinister glare, "Tank paid good money, don't you dare let me down or I'll kill you. Do you understand?" She nodded obediently as her tears wet her cheeks.

Tank sped away, with Junior following closely behind, South on forty-second avenue. Giuseppe had parked on the West side of the street across from Saint Gabriel Catholic Elementary School. He slowly merged into the traffic lane when the bikes were about a half a block away, trying to remain covert. The one-way tinted windows of the black sedan made it impossible for Junior or Tank to see into the vehicle. "Let's see what you're up to Junior," Giuseppe sighed as he had caught up with them at the stop sign on forty-second and Sloat. The loud hunger complaints from the elephants could be heard from across the street in the San Francisco Zoo. He had vaguely remembered visiting the zoo last year with the twins and seemed sure of himself that across the high fence and rocks in front of him were the open bear cages. It was a nefarious thought that crossed his mind, but he filed it in his memory lobe.

Tank made a right on Sloat Street. Junior cut off a pickup truck trying not to lose him. Looking in his side mirror Junior could see the angry motorist with his hand out the driver side window with the middle finger pointing at him.

"You're a real idiot Junior," Giuseppe berated him from behind the steering wheel of the Sedan. The pick-up truck passed the intersection putting distance between the Sedan and the bikes. Honking profusely at Junior, the raging motorist tailgated Junior. Tank suddenly turned right on forty-fifth Avenue on a green light, ending the road-rage incident as Junior followed Tank close behind.

The sedan turned right just in time to see oncoming traffic lock up their brakes as Tank and Junior passed on the left side of a delivery truck. Traffic cones were set out at each corner of the utility truck and the landing ramp was extended to the pavement. The vendor was stopped to service the Irish Cultural Center. "Where are you going Junior?" Giuseppe thumped hard on the steering wheel in frustration. "This isn't the way to the coast highway." He too was cussed out by the elderly woman, whose arms were flaying above her head. She had locked her brakes again to avoid a head on collision with Giuseppe, knowing she had the right of way. She couldn't see Giuseppe apologizing through the tinted windows. But he would've surely lost them had he waited for her to get past the delivery truck.

The bikes turned left onto Wawona Street without signaling their intent. He expected nothing less from these two derelicts. "What the hell," Giuseppe stewed as Tank and Junior pulled into the drive-way entrance to the two story one-star motel called "Safari Motel." He slowed then made a right on forty-six Avenue across the street. He turned into a short drive-way of a yellow painted stucco two story house and got the car turned back around. He stopped the Sedan in front of a similar track home close to the intersection behind an old seventy-seven Chevy four dour wagon. He was blocking the home owner's drive-way.

Tanya followed Tank up a flight of stairs and into a motel room at the end of the platform. Junior followed them in and closed the door behind him.

Giuseppe had just shifted the transmission into drive, when he ascertained to his chagrin, that he was trapped by a muni light rail train. "Oh my God! Are you kidding me! Oh Shit!" He vaguely recalled seeing the train stopped at the platform around the corner on Wawona Street.

He hadn't taken notice of the tracks and wished he had parked closer to the curb. The crunch of metal on metal was loud. Glass shattered and showered down the left side of the sedan. Giuseppe opened his eyes and realized he had lost his left side mirror. "Damn, I'm a lucky bastard!" he exclaimed, grateful that the train only struck his mirror.

The incident didn't stop him, he released the brake and merged into the traffic lane. Broken glass crunched under his rear tire. He quickly scanned Wawona Street and ignored the stop sign. He parked closely behind the motorcycles, blocking their exit. Removing his Kevlar supple leather trench coat from the head rest of his seat, he slipped into it. Kevlar is an anti-ballistic carbon fiber material that protected him from gunfire to his torso. Feeling in an inside pocket, Giuseppe confirmed that he had an ample supply of Thomas and Betts three-foot Ty-Rap flexible zip ties.

Crouching low, Giuseppe soft toed it up the flight of stairs to the second floor of Motel Rooms. He ducked under the first Motel window and stood poised at the front door. Gently turning the knob, he sighed with relieve. The brain-dead Nazis had left the door unsecured. He grasped a Chakram in his right hand, in the event either Tank or Junior were pistol packing.

With the door knob turned to the open position, he charged through the door to find Tanya sitting on the edge of the queen size bed in only her panties and training bra. Her school clothes had been discarded on the floor where she stepped out of them. Tank was still fully clothed facing her with his back to Giuseppe. Junior sat in a desk chair stroking himself.

It happened all too fast. Tank turned to see Giuseppe's right hook connect with his jaw. He had taken a punch to the jaw prior, but the power that dropped him to the floor, on this occasion, felt like being hit by a muni bus. He was out cold. Tanya quickly scooted back to the headboard, still traumatized and not sure if she was out of the woods.

Junior realized he left his handgun in the bike's saddle-bags. His heart was racing hard in his chest. Giuseppe was hoping for that effect. "Get dressed Tanya and get into the black sedan downstairs. I'm taking you home." She didn't hesitate and slipped quickly back into her school uniform and ran out the door.

"I know who you are. You're one of those vigilante vampire freaks," Junior lambasted. "You're using my sister for information. You know I'm right." The sweat began to drip down his forehead to cool his body and calm his incessant shaking. "They'll find you and kill you." Junior's tone became less threatening. "Look I can guarantee your safety."

Giuseppe didn't waste words on the pervert but took slow and calculated steps toward him.

Junior kowtowed into the corner of the room and slowly slid down with his back against the wall. "Dude, my sister needs me," he plead and wept like a child. "Please. I'll pay you well." Junior made a mad dash to the door. He didn't get far. Giuseppe clenched the back of Junior's shirt collar and yanked him backwards. Junior's feet flew out in front of him. He attempted to swing at Giuseppe as he fell. Giuseppe's trench coat flared open and over Junior as he descended upon him. As the room seem to go dark in Giuseppe's shadow, Junior felt Giuseppe's fangs, like scissor teeth rip into his neck. The sting of death and lightheaded deprivation of oxygen, softened the concussion of his head hitting the hardwood floor. He struggled to breath as blood inundated his throat. Attempting to cough up the blood and clear his throat, his efforts were stifled as Junior gurgled on his own blood. He lost control of his limbs. His life literally drained out of him.

This wasn't the end to Giuseppe's troubles. He had an unfamiliar set of circumstances to deal with and he had to think quick and act fast. A dead body, an unconscious pedophile, and a traumatized thirteen-year old. He took hold of Junior's wrists and dragged him onto the throw rug next to the bed. Pulling one end of the carpet around him, rolled Junior's body up in it like a hotdog roll.

Taking out the zip ties from his inner pocket, Giuseppe tied Tank's hands behind his back. He added two additional ties to ensure Tank's strength wasn't as behemoth as his stature. Crouching down at the end of Junior's carpet casket, Giuseppe pulled one end over his shoulder and easily raised it over him like a bag of potatoes. He managed to get the three-foot zip ties secure at each end. But because of Junior's beer girth, he couldn't get one connected around the middle.

Navigating the stairs with the weight of Junior's lifeless carcass, it suddenly become even more complicated by the untimely presence of a small man child. Sitting on a small pedal bike, the child was sporting an overweening ten-year-old smirk.

Trench coats, minus the hardware, were on back order at most clothing stores as the popularity of the vigilante vampires grew. They had become, to their dismay, super heroes. The boy was void of fear or loathing. "I heard my daddy tell mom that you are Angels sent from God. I don't believe in God or Angels. But I do spider-man."

For all of fifty pounds, he struck Giuseppe as very brave. "Hello young man. Just taking the rug to be cleaned. This one's particularly dirty."

The lad was persistent, "There's a dead body in it, isn't there?"

"What makes you think that?"

"Carpets don't bleed," the boy replied matter of fact.

Giuseppe didn't have time to clean up the residual blood. He hurried and loaded Junior into the rear of the sedan. "Young man, do you think I'm spider-man?"

"No, you're a vampire." His blatant response and stalwart lack of fear caught Giuseppe off guard.

"Can you keep a secret?" Giuseppe patronized him.

"Sometimes." Giuseppe shook his head bewildered by the kid. "Do vampires have kids? Is that your daughter in the car?"

"Look, I'm on a very top-secret mission and I don't have time for questions," he plotted. "If you can keep this top secret, I'll come back and make you an honorary deputy Vampire. How does that sound?"

The boy finally showed some sign of emotion and smiled, somewhat mocking him. "I'm not three Mister. Don't worry, I won't tell anyone. You better hurry the other bad guy is still in the room."

"You're right, your also too smart for your age," Giuseppe smiled back at him and headed back up the stairs.

When he got to the door of the motel room, Tank wasn't lying on the floor at the base of the bed. "Shit!" Giuseppe exclaimed, scanning the room as he attempted to enter. Knowing he would have seen him had he left through the front door, Giuseppe was confident Tank was still in the Motel room. "I don't have time for hide and seek Tank," He called out, slowly entering. Hands still zip tied behind his back, Tank stumbled out of the bathroom leading with his head. His skull was pounding with pain and his brain suffering from vertigo from the blunt trauma he suffered at Giuseppe's punch. Tank charged for the door, breathing like a race horse with saliva dripping from his mouth. Giuseppe moved out of the way, "Here let me help you," He patronized, raising his foot, he planted it on Tank's buttocks. Tank lost control, from the additional help, and tumbled over the balcony railing, landing on the motorcycles a story below. Both machines toppled over with Tank sprawled over them groaning.

As Giuseppe raced down the stairs, the boy on the bicycle commented, "I would have chosen the stairs. Bad people are stupid."

"Our secret!" Giuseppe reminded him not losing stride. The boy made a zipping motion with his fingers across his mouth to let Giuseppe know he was still on his side.

"Can anyone tell me the typical life span of the Grizzly?" the petite female zoo tour guide inquired. Volunteering at the San Francisco Zoo earned her extra credits toward getting her degree as a Zoologist. The light green vest, with her name tag, "Your Guide Today is Michelle," was covered with pins depicting her favorite animals. The open Grizzly Bear cage was separated from the humans by a second and higher fence. The fences were separated several feet apart to protect little fingers from becoming bear finger food.

"I'm going to say fifty years," blurted out a freckled cheek eleven-year old. By the boy's appearance, his rich Canadian parents needed to feed him fewer McDonald hamburgers.

"Any other guesses?" Michelle scanned the group looking for another child to answer closer to the correct number.

"It's fifty!" the boy stated with a smirk. Michelle was patient, but quickly becoming annoyed with this little monster who had an answer for every question.

Finally, emerging from the Canadian tour group of twenty plus, nine-year old Kaylee Beal of Calgary shyly stated. "Thirty?"

"You're the winner!" Michelle announced, with emphasis on winner. The little boy shot Michelle a disgruntled unsportsmanlike glare. "The correct answer is fifteen to twenty years."

"I was close," the little boy emphatically stated to his papa for his approval.

"Yes, you were Alfred," his father corroborated to keep him happy.

Michelle continued, "The Grizzly in the water is named Friz, because, as you'll notice, the guard hairs on his shoulders are longer than most Grizzlies. The Grizzly is one of several subspecies of brown bears. They weigh up to 800 pounds and can stand up to eight feet tall. You would be no match for a Grizzly. They can run up to thirty-five miles per hour and have claws that can grow up to five inches. They also have grinding molars and piercing canine teeth."

"You haven't told us what they eat," Alfred demanded prematurely.

Michelle shot a contrived and officious smile at him. "Be patient, I was just about to go there."

"I hear that they like to eat freckled face children," teased Kaylee's teenage brother. Except for Alfred's parents, the rest of the Canadian tour group thought it amusing and fitting.

Giuseppe squeezed the gate padlock in his curled fist. The lock mechanisms broke and the U-shaped shackle pulled away from the lock. Removing the gate padlock, he opened the gate to the controlled employee entrance at the rear of the zoo, and drove through it. Surrounded by trees, he was confident no one saw him.

"Where are we going?" Tanya asked from the back seat, breaking her silence.

"She speaks!" Giuseppe patronized. "I don't know about you, but Mr. Tank here is becoming un b e a r able." He snickered at his own humor, pronouncing the syllables slowly suggesting Tank's demise.

Tank began to regain consciousness and heard parts of the conversation. He tried to sit up, but the zip tie around his neck and chair head rest restrained him. Another zip tie securely held an old dirty rag, Giuseppe found under the seat, as a gag in his mouth. His eyes opened wide with fright as he scanned vigorously for answers to his whereabouts.

"Well, look whose awake Tanya, Junior's friend Stank."

Tank's protests were muffled by the gag in his mouth.

"I promise Stank I'm not going to hurt you. Well, OK, not directly. I hope you don't mind, but I want to introduce you to an old friend of mine I met here at the zoo last year. Maybe you could share some of that grease in your hair and some beauty tips on how to slime it back. That's how he got the name Friz, if I recall right." Giuseppe caught a glimpse of a forced grin from Tanya in the rearview mirror. The sedan passed by several "Danger, No Trespassing" signs on the back road that circled the zoo. Giuseppe read the tags posted on each door as he slowly passed by them. He believed the bear cages were located in the area. He finally stopped. The door tag was labelled, "Grizzly, Authorized Personnel Only". Handwritten on a card insert, was the name Friz. Giuseppe was elated, "I can't believe I actually remembered his name, Friz."

Tank impulsively began to kick the floor board and squirm impetuously. His screams for help were again muffled by the rag.

"Don't be rude Tank. You and Friz have a lot in common." Giuseppe stepped out onto the dirt shoulder and walked around to the front passenger seat. Lifting the zip tie from off the head rest, with little effort, pulled Tank out of the car. Tank coughed and gasped for air as Giuseppe twisted the zip tie around his neck and yanked him backwards toward the cage door. "Give Friz my regards, will ya Tank?" Giuseppe turned the door knob, slightly opened the heavy metal door, and pushed Tank into the bear cage.

"As omnivores, they eat a variety of plants and berries, insects, fish," Michelle paused to add humor, "Like me, Grizzlies love sushi, especially Salmon." She suddenly realized there was something wrong as once happy audience faces were now contorted with horror and shock. "Carrions, rodents and large mammals. In fact, I believe it's almost Frizz's dinner time." With her back to the bear cage, Michelle was unaware of the mayhem about to happen.

"Is this some kind of sick joke," Albert's father demanded, enraged and in disbelief.

"What is that man doing in the cage?" Kaylee's Father asked flabbergasted.

"He's not an employee, he's not allowed in the cage area," Michelle stated with anxiety and confusion. She pulled her two-way radio from its saddle and pushed the clip to talk. Women began to scream for someone to help the man, who was apparently bound and didn't want to be in his situation. "I need security now. Code Red! Bob, we need a lethal restraint team. Do you copy!

"On our way."

"Call for paramedics, hurry!" Michelle banged on the exterior fencing with her radio to get the Grizzly's attention away from the intruder. "Friz! Friz!" But the bear was more interested in the human franticly kicking at the back door. Friz gracefully demonstrated for his horrified audience, his adroit skills that Michelle had earlier described. Quickly climbing the rocky slope, Friz was happy to prove that he could stand eight feet tall on his back legs. Pointing his snout in the air the grizzly let out an ear shattering growl, just like Michelle had so eloquently explained. "Friz, Friz, don't do it Friz, they'll put you down," Michelle yelled emphatically to no avail.

"I think you care more about that bear than you do that poor man," Albert's Father protested. "You need to do something quickly or he's a dead man."

Michelle had had enough. "She faced him and demanded, "I need you to shut the hell up and get these people out of here! Do you understand or by God I'll feed you to Friz myself?"

Emergency sirens and red flashing lights, on top of the electric golf cart like response vehicles, were closing in on the location. A security officer stood at the back of the lead vehicle with his gun pointed and ready to fire the tranquilizer filled dart loaded in the guns chamber.

Crying like a baby, Tank had crouched down at the base of the door. The power of the paw, endowed with the five-inch claws, left the crowd breathless. Blood spirt from the ripped flesh of Tank's face as he was tossed down the rocky slope. Unable to block the impact of his skull and bones against the rocks and concrete mortar, he rolled into the small cooling pond at its base. The water gradually turned blood red. Tank lay face down in the red water, dead from a broken neck.

The gunshot echoed off the stone walls. Friz took the dart in the hip and raced off angry toward the shooter. Friz slowed to a slow prance and then collapsed into unconsciousness as the lethal poison made its way to the bear's brain.

"I'm sorry Michelle I had no choice," the bronze skin Korean condoled. Michelle had turned away from the horror and slipped down the fence and wrapped her arms around her knees and wept, burying her face in her clipboard.

Same day, minutes earlier.
Brown Street, The Presidio District

"Jesus Christ!" Gary Yarbrough was enraged. "You're losing them!"

"Do you want to drive asshole!" caterwauled the Krupp PMC, a private military company security officer. There was a stark difference between the two men. The PMC was as professional in his demeanor as he was dressed. Steam pressed blue shirt formed to his strapping physic. The suit coat which concealed his side arm, hung over the back of his seat. On the other hand, his infirm passenger, newly appointed kingpin of the Peckerwood gang, had only one notch left on his belt to keep his Levi trousers up.

"They just turned onto fourteenth street!" Gary exclaimed. He caught a glimpse of the Harley making a right turn. The bike appeared briefly from between a high-profile utility van and a compact car, then disappeared behind a corner building.

Thomas was hanging onto the luggage rack over the rear wheel. They had no clue they were being followed. With steely determination, they caught up to the Harley, three cars in front of them, as they waited impatiently at a red light.

Gary's nerves were nearly spent. He didn't let on to the PMC that he admired his deft driving abilities, "That was close. Wish I knew where the hell they're taking us."

"Hopefully to Doctor Chang," the PMC spoke for the first time since leaving the murder scene. The light turned green and they were on the chase again. The Harley crossed Lake Street and then took a right onto Wyman into Mountain Lake Park. They could see the golf course lake up ahead. The Harley made a quick left onto Brown Street and stopped at the curb in front of the second beige duplex in a line of many. An Island of trees and shrubs to the left side of Brown Street, separated the duplex from a printing shop.

"There!" Gary pointed to the printing shop. "Pull around and park behind those trees."

The PMC impressed Gary further and backed into a parking berth adjacent a loading dock. They could both clearly view any activity at the Condo through the windshield of the Mercedes.

Thomas dismounted the bike at the same time Doctor Chang emerged through the front door. Chang had a scowl and quickened pace as if he was about to chase them off. But his contracted brow bent the other direction after learning of Jack's fate. Chang embraced and consoled him. The Doctor's displeasure returned to his face and he began to chastise Dylan. Thomas climbed back onto the Harley and it sped away. Doctor Chang stood at the curb shaking his head until the bike disappeared. Doctor Chang returned into the leased condo.

"This is going to be easier than I thought," the PMC said. "Keep your mouth shut and let me do the talking, got it?"

"Whatever," Gary chagrinned.

The PMC placed a handicap placard on the dash, "It's time." Both men exited the Mercedes and went to the trunk. The PMC released the latch and the trunk sprang open. He then handed Gary a Pacific Gas and Electric employee jacket with the name Ted embroidered on the pocket. He then put on a similar jacket with the name tag, Mike, and lifted a small tool box with a PG&E logo sticker on the top. Before putting on the PG&E jackets, both men attached shoulder harness munitions belt around them and screwed on the silencers to the 9mm Winchester Magnums. "Remember, no Doctor Chang, no cash. Got it?"

"I understand," Gary replied.

The PMC stood on the side of the door that opens and knocked twice. He raised his index finger to his lips, vehemently reminding him to keep quiet.

Doctor Chang glanced through the peep hole on the entrance door to confirm that it wasn't an adversary or law enforcement. The chain lock allowed the door to open about five inches. "Yes?" Chang asked their business through the small opening.

"This is Ted, my name is Mike, we're with Pacific Gas and Electric. We're here to inspect your power box for the retrofit."

"I'm not aware of any retrofit," Doctor Chang recoiled suspiciously.

The PMC made an apologetic face, "I'm sorry, we were scheduled to be here last month to inspect the box. Did we come at a bad time? It appears the Association didn't make you aware. We're attempting to look at all the boxes on Brown Street today. It will only take five to ten minutes."

Doctor Chang glanced up and down the street but saw no utility truck. "Where's you truck?"

"It's parked around the corner. We started there."

Doctor Chang was suspect of Ted's pretend smile. "I have no idea where the box is."

"This is floor plan B, so it should be in your laundry room in the upper cabinet," the PMC had done his research.

"Very well, come in," Doctor Chang released the chain lock and opened the door.

"I promise it will just take a few minutes," the PMC stepped over the threshold. He made mental notes of the layout of the condo and any home accessory that could be used as a weapon.

"Please do so quietly, my roommate is in his bedroom sleeping."

That was music to the PMC's ears. "Do you mind escorting us to the laundry room," the PMC said raising both eyebrows apologetically. "Company policy. Uppers trying to avoid liability in case anything goes missing. Sorry."

"No problem, right this way," Doctor Chang stepped in front of the two intruders and led them down the hallway to the last door on the right.

"I hate to ask you for one more favor?" The PMC stopped short of opening the laundry room door. "We've been at this all morning. I'm feeling a little dehydrated. Could I bother you for a glass of water?"

"Certainly," Chang glanced over at his co-worker and read off his embroidered name badge. "How about you Ted?"

"Yea, sure, thanks," Gary awkwardly affirmed.

As Doctor Chang turned toward the kitchen, the PMC nodded toward the closed door across the hall. Gary clandestinely turned the knob on the door and disappeared inside, closing the door slowly and releasing the door handle mechanism into the doorpost as quiet as a church mouse. Once inside Gary scanned the room. Fortuitously, it was the right bedroom. Sleeping on his right side, facing away from Gary, Muller lay in the fetal position. He approached the bed argus-eyed and cognizant of not allowing the heels of his cowboy boots to touch the hardwood floor. Picking up an extra pillow closest to him, Gary withdrew his Magnum from its holster. He held the pillow above Muller's head with his left hand and steadied the gun with his right. The PMC had warned Gary of the enormous strength Muller and Doctor Chang possessed. They were no match physically, but a bullet to the head or directly into the heart would have mortal consequences.

With brute force, Gary smothered Muller's head under the pillow. He shoved the barrel of the gun into the pillow, hoping it was a direct hit into his skull. As Muller woke with a vengeance, Gary fired a shot, the silencer muffled the thunderclap, and Muller went limp. Blood pooled from the sides of the pillow as Gary lifted it from Muller's face. Muller's eyes were opened wide with fear and locked in death's finite moment. He cringed at the sight of the entry wound and the exposed inner workings of flesh, tendons, and crushed bone. The bullet entered high enough to cause instant death. Muller was dead. Gary felt his nervous stomach knot up along with the burning pain of pre-vomit acid. He blocked the volcano erupting in his stomach and swallowed the burning taste of his lunch. He dropped the blood drenched pillow to hide the gruesome sight and walked back to the door for his cue.

The PMC had set the toolbox on the counter next to the stacked washer and dryer and released the paddle latches. He quickly grabbed the steel shackles, closed the lid, and set them on the lid. The clicking of hard rubber soles on the hardwood floor alerted him that Doctor Chang was seconds away from show time. He pulled his magnum from its holster and hid it to his side.

Doctor Chang appeared in the doorway holding a glass of water in each hand. Sudden jaw dropping confusion and apprehension overwhelmed Chang with fear and realization that he had been duped. He felt derision toward himself. How could he have let his guard down. He felt sick. "Where's your friend?"

His fate was now discernible as the metal barrel of Gary's gun pressed against the back of his skull. Glass shattered as he released the water glasses he was holding. "Keep your hands high where we can see them or you're a dead man," Gary barked his ultimatum.

The PMC raised the steel shackles and clamped one on each wrist. "Very slowly lower your hands and put them behind your back," the PMC directed. Doctor Chang knew he was powerless in steel shackles. The PMC quickly padlocked the two shackles and pulled on the lock to ensure that it had engaged. Crouching down he secured a shackle on both of Huey's ankles. A very short chain was connected between them to assure he couldn't run. Returning to face Doctor Chang, he picked up his magnum he had set on the counter and pointed it at the Doctor. He then pointed his gun at the floor, "Sit down. Pull the car around to the front," he instructed Gary. Gary took his gun away from Doctor Chang's head and re-holstered it.

"I knew this day might come," Doctor Chang lamented, his head drooping.

"If you believe your friend is coming to your aid, you're gravely mistaken. We've taken care of that problem," the PMC nonchalantly stated as if Muller meant nothing to him.

Doctor Chang's worst nightmare had come to fruition. He felt as if the wind had been knocked from him. He was forever alone. They had murdered his best friend, his lover, his world. "Vaughn!" he screamed out his name to no avail and began to weep profusely.

Later that night, Sutro Caves, Pacific Coast Line

Starring out the pickup truck's passenger window, Thomas's mind was not on the spectacular purple sky as the sun disappeared into the Pacific Ocean. Still traumatized and in mourning over Jack, he didn't feel in the mood to make light conversation.

Dylan turned right off of Point Lobos Avenue onto a dirt road toward the Sutro Baths. Built in 1896, along the coastline at Land's End, the public salt water baths burned down in 1966. The word on the street was that the owners torched the facility to cash in on the insurance benefit. The foundation still remains. The historical site has the appearance of an archaeological dig. A few curious tourists visit the site during the day but it is pretty much abandoned at night. Dylan parked Jack's truck next to the black sedan. There was also a rental car and a Nissan Skyline 2000GT parked on the other side of the sedan.

"I don't want you to do this because you're in a state of rage and just want revenge," Dylan said emphatically. "This is life changing."

His forehead wrinkled inward in protest, "Stop trying to talk me out of it," Thomas reaffirmed his determination to join the Creed. "This is what I want. Jack was the only real family I had. Now the Creed is my family."

"Suit yourself," Dylan acclaimed his last effort to persuade him to give it time. "This will be very painful. Normally Doctor Chang would be here to administer an anesthetic. I imagine it may be equivalent to child birth."

Thomas was too numb to care but cohesive enough to understand the consequences. "Please help me through this," he plead wistfully.

Dylan nodded, "OK, let's do it." He rested his hand on Thomas's shoulder, "I never thought I'd fall this hard for anyone." Thomas managed a smile.

They followed the paved footpath, down a flight of brick steps to where the path split. One path leading to the bath ruins, the other to the caves at the cliff's edge. The pathway to the caves was chained off with a sign that read, "DO NOT ENTER!" Underlined, "Area closed for your safety." Dylan held up the chain barricade for Thomas to duck under. With one hand on the fence post, Dylan catapulted effortlessly over the chain barrier. It was becoming clear to Thomas why public works declared the caves unsafe. A section of rock foundation under the pathway had given way to erosion and fell into the sea. The broken metal handrail bent outward. Thomas hesitated, unable to look down at the three-foot void and the cliffs below it.

"Oh my God," Thomas vacillated, unable to move.

"You didn't tell me you have acrophobia," Dylan said in a coddling way.

"In the worst way," he answered, his voice jittery. "I don't think I can do this."

"Let me get ahead of you." Dylan squeezed past Thomas and easily stepped across the crevice, and held out his hand for Thomas. "Take my hand."

"Lord, I can't," Thomas cursed.

"Don't close your eyes you have to see where to land your feet."

"OK," Thomas exclaimed and took the leap of faith in Dylan's grip.

Dylan suppressed his amusement, "See, that wasn't all that hard. We're almost to the caves." Thomas nerves flashed through his body at the sight of dirt and loose pebbles falling hundreds of feet before they hit the ground.

Four battery operated lanterns lit the cave at Its center where another small opening to the sea was fenced off with a parade gate. A sign on the fence read, "Danger, beware of sneaker waves." The one hundred fifty-foot cave was open to the surf on both ends. Eight silhouettes, cast twice the size of their owners, lined both walls of the cavern that was about twenty feet wide and equally as high. As Dylan and Thomas approached their awaiting friends, they noticed a man size burlap gunnysack twitching between members of the Creed, a shoe box, and a folded trench coat. The calm sea breeze menacing their long trench coats about their feet, the trending hallmark of their mantra.

The first words out of Thomas mouth were oddly, "What's a sneaker wave?"

"A rogue wave which is disproportionately large and unpredictable," answered Heinz. He was the scholar and a well read one at that.

"They say these caves are haunted," chimed in Tommy.

"That's crap!" Macias interrupted him. "Stop trying to scare him."

"I'm not a child," Thomas injected with disdain. "I've heard that rumor too."

"If you listen carefully, ever-so often, you can hear a faint human cry in the howling winds of the sea."

"Never heard it," Macias continued to be skeptical. "But people have died from these sneaker or sleeper waves."

Tommy quivered, "I'm sorry but that just gives me the weebie jeebies."

"Boo," Fabien pinched Tommy from behind. He jumped, which drew cackles from everyone.

"Let's get down to business," Estella said, instilling a sense of urgency with her ironclad demeanor. She tried to speak, but her lips began to quiver, as she attempted to hold back tears and keep from breaking down emotionally.

Dylan placed his hand on her shoulder for support, "It's OK, if you need to let it out."

She shook her head, "No, there will be a time to mourn. If this is our final battle with the Nazis, then so be it." The prey in the burlap sack, exhausted from the futile struggle to escape, got his second wind. "As next in line in the Creed's manifesto, it is my responsibility under the Code to lead in the event that Muller, Doctor Chang, or Jadwiga, is dead or unavailable. Sadly, all three conditions have been met. Is there anyone who feels that I am not worthy to lead the Creed."

"Doctor Chang is not dead," Macias objected without malice. "I would prefer we wait to confirm his fate. I'm sorry I just don't know you that well."

Dylan, more feared than other members of the Creed, stepped into the circle. Macias's pretentious defiance drained from his face. "But Doctor Chang is unavailable. Muller was a better father to me than my own. He is gone. We have no clue where Jade, who would be next in line, is either. Doctor Chang would be here if he wasn't incapacitated. We can only hope he is still breathing. No one knows Jade's demise. This is what Huey would want. As I see it, if you can't give your loyalty to Estelle, then you are an ungrateful traitor to the Code."

Muller loved the Royal family of Great Britain. Following the end of the war, he contrived the concept of the Creed while touring Windsor Castle. He later wrote the Code and pitched his nomenclature to Doctor Chang. It took some convincing. What started out as mere bagatelle became less trifle as the indictment on fascism became an alibi for murder and their necessity for the blood-letting. The pecking order was determined by seniority of entering the Creed.

"Amen," Jonathan stated firmly and took a step into the circle.

"I'm in," Fabien nodded and stepped into the circle. Ludovic nodded affirmatively and stepped into the circle as well.

Giuseppe walked over to Estella, kissed both of her cheeks and remained in the circle. It was a given that Heinz would follow his eternal partner.

Tommy stepped into the circle, "For Muller!"

Dylan smiled his approval, "Thank you Tommy, Macias?"

Macias caught the patriotic spirit emulating from the people he loved most and acquiesced, "Fine."

"Fantastic!" Dylan ruffled Macias's hair, everyone had codified the Code. "Estella, I think you have our undivided attention."

Estella took Heinz's left hand, a sign for the blood oath. They took hands and formed another circle at arms distance and repeated together the oath of the code. "Ewig leben von das Glaubensbekenntnis ist layalitat zu das Code. Tod zu Faschismus." (Eternal life of the Creed is loyalty to the Code. Death to Fascism.)

"Thanks to our mole, Ms. Sandy, we have credible intel on who's who and where they will lay their heads for the last time. We begin tomorrow night," Estelle declared.

"Why not tonight?" Jonathan asked. "Every minute we wait maybe Huey's last."

Giuseppe responded, "There's a meeting tomorrow at the Double Tree. Sandy says it's big. They believe that she is picking up where Paul Coombs left off and re-opening the bar. They have cut her in on the deal. Sandy has it on good source that they are keeping Doctor Chang alive for a reason. She believes it is to get the money Doctor Chang embezzled from the Nazis. She can get invaluable information on a much broader fascist network, like the National Alliance and where David Duke is taking their political interests."

"That's a great question though Jonathan," Heinz added. "Before he was abducted, Doctor Chang had set that plan in motion."

"The meeting is at eleven o'clock tomorrow," Estella continued. "We will meet at Robert Woolley State Park at the Anza Lagoon, ten o'clock sharp. After we take possession of Huey and Jadwiga, we will split up in groups of three. There's a rear entrance near the elevator shaft. We exit the seventh floor, one floor below the King Suite where Krupp's lawyer, Rudi Helbard, is staying. The Krupp Family has hired an army of private military professionals. The Hotel will be crawling with them.

Our traditional weapons won't be enough. Bring fire power. Again, Woolley State Park, ten sharp. The park is about a quarter mile from the Hotel on Anza Boulevard. This is a picture of Sandy for you who don't know her. Keep her out of harm's way and don't let on that she is in any way affiliated with us. Any questions?"

Heinz reached in one of his trench coat pocket's and pulled from it a silk bag with a draw string tied at the top. "Thomas," he said, turning and facing him. "In keeping with the Code of the Creed, you have chosen this eternity of your own free will. Is that corect?" Although the ritual was more trifling than necessary, some grinned amused, but all believed in it as they did in Karma.

"I understand the consequences and have so chosen," Thomas stated undauntedly.

Heinz handed Thomas the silk bag. "There are enough doses to last you six months. Dylan can fill you in on the particulars. Are you sure this is what you want? Once your body adjusts to the blood-letting, the pain, that your body will endure, will make child birth seem like a walk in the park. But adjusting to the SR process will have growing pains as well." Giuseppe's head drooped as he filled with anxiety after Heinz reviewed the withdrawals. He tried to hide his face from being judged by the others. But he knew that they all knew and never so much as deigned a glance at them.

Thomas took a step toward Heinz and took the silk bag from him. "I understand. Let's do this." There were no blurred lines in Thomas's decision to join the Creed.

Heinz nodded affirmatively for the others to prepare the prey for the blood-letting and propagation of the Creed. Dylan embraced Thomas, "I'll be here if you need me to help you. One last time, are you sure?"

Thomas glowed as he grasped Dylan's head, pulling it toward him and kissed him on the mouth. "I'm ready."

Dylan took the silk bag from Thomas and inserted the SR cocktail on his tongue. "After you swallow, you'll need to bite into the donor's carotid artery as if you're biting into Jack's burnt Bar B Queued Trip-tip steak. Don't be fickle or skittish. The transition is contingent on blue blood. Ready?" Thomas nodded. "Swallow."

Pivoting to face his destiny. Thomas could feel the fire below his skin, his heart racing, and an eccentric eroticism in his power over the subdued victim. The Peckerwood's youthful shirtless torso was spread as if to be quartered, held back at each limb by a member of the Creed. His mouth filled with a dirty rag and secured with vinyl tape wrapped several times around his head. Tattooed over his left breast, the Peckerwood tattoo, donning uncle Sam's top hat with the racial epithet Peckerwood spelled out over it. Meant to install fear in non-whites and Jews, it was now an inconvenient death wish. His nose was crooked like it had been broken a few times. Thomas was salivating for a taste of this bad boy's flesh and blood. Testosterone levels off the charts, he lunged like a lion on Its kill. Fabien grabbed a fist full of black greased back hair, holding the Peckerwood's head back, exposing the pulsing carotid. Thomas angled his head over his mark and bit down, puncturing hard through the metallic sweaty neck muscles. With a vengeance, the blue acid and odor free liquid filled Thomas's mouth cavity. He knew the second he broke the seal of his lips around the soft tissue of the neck, oxygen would taint the blood and bacteria would begin to grow. Tonight, he would not be sharing. His transition phase demanded every drop.

The color had drained from the Peckerwood's face and so had his life. But new life had been given to a vampire. Foisted and bloated with non-depleted natural folic acid blood, the Sulfanilamide Rejuvenation had begun. Thomas screamed with agony as his muscles bulged and ripped. Dylan's strength was no match for Thomas's adrenals repairing and rejuvenating them.

"Make it stop!" Thomas screamed hard and long from the excruciating pain. He rolled on the cave floor in the fetal position. Panting hard, the pain finally subsided. His flesh had ripped his clothing at the seams. He lay partially naked on the cold cave rock floor, exposed to the elements.

Heinz handed Dylan Thomas's new trench coat with an exuberant smile. "It's done."

Dylan wrapped Thomas in the trench coat and rocked him like a baby. "I'm so proud of you." He'd never felt closer to anyone other than his brother Joey. But somehow this was different. Thomas was now a part of him. He rocked Thomas in his arms, sitting behind him.

Giuseppe grasped both ankles of the corpse. Jonathan assisted, lifting it up by the wrists. Swinging it like a bag of potatoes, they tossed the body into the open crevice and into the sea. "Damn sneaker waves," Jonathan indulged himself with a little humor.

"We're out of here," Estella exclaimed. "Ten o'clock, Woolley State Park, don't be late!" Heinz kept stride with her as they exited the cave.

"Welcome to the Creed Thomas," Jonathan said as he walked past them.

"You're out of here too," Dylan responded.

"Yea, see you tomorrow."

"You did zis," Fabien said insouciantly. "Iz no easy zing."

Thomas glanced up at him but was too fatigued to respond. "How's Carol?" Dylan asked.

"I see her zis evening. Is bedder for her now." He turned to his twin, "Lez go eh?"

"See you guys," Ludovic acknowledged, and caught up to his brother leaving the cave.

"Where are you guys staying tonight?" Giuseppe asked, sitting on the cave floor in front of them.

"I don't know," Dylan agonized. "We can't go back to Jack's, my brother's apartment is too small, especially with Jonathan hanging out there. Perhaps we'll just sleep in the car tonight."

Giuseppe rolled his eyes at the unthinkable notion. His friends were not sleeping on the street. He wouldn't stand for it. "Look, stay at the church with me. There's a shower, and the monks will make you breakfast."

"You sure it won't be a bother?" Dylan asked, somewhat embarrassed.

"Not at all," Giuseppe replied empathically. "But you will have to practice celibacy, at least while you're in the church."

Same Night
Hospice

His life seemed disconcerted, notwithstanding new romance and enough money from the sale of the Hospice to fund his academic dreams. Jonathan had convinced him to carry a concealed weapon. Joey hated guns, but he admitted there was a sense of security and power. In defiance of being abandoned for the night, he was not going to stay home alone.

The low overcast was lit up by lines of street lights. He could still make out the downtown concrete skyline in the twilight. He had bought a beat-up green Volkswagen 1972 Beetle from a coworker and replaced the ripped vinyl seats with black leather ones. Jonathan tried to meddle in the decision to buy down, but Joey was unflappable. "I'm not cheap, I'm just frugal," He corrected him. He was going to roll down the window, but the cold breeze nipped at his cheeks. He was never lucky at catching the green lights, which added idle time for his mind to wander.

He missed his mother's comforting talks, his best friend Freddy's cheeky humor, and waiting tables at the Bistro. He would trade the large sum of money Chang paid, which he and Dylan split, just to have it all back. Joey knew there was a risk going back to the Hospice, still a crime scene. Nonetheless, against his better judgment, his mind was made up. But Joey couldn't help but believe that after all the hoopla in the news, Doctor Chang would have no choice but to sell it. He would lose a major part of his life. Besides his brother, it was the only connection to a life that was about to go extinct. He teared up from his anxious reminiscing. "This is crazy," he berated himself. It was prime real estate and oligarchs were champing at the bit to raze small mom and pop establishments and put profitable high-rise structures in their place.

He parked across the street from the Hospice, the perimeter still barricaded off with yellow crime scene tape. He hesitated from opening the car door until he had given the surrounding neighborhood a once over. There were no visible lights from within. It was totally dark. Even the porch light had been turned off. Doctor Chang had agreed to give Joey a key as long as Dylan was still a resident, and in fact had invited him to live there. Criminals usually don't return to a crime scene, so he had convinced himself. He had second thoughts more than twice about visiting the place of his childhood memories.

He lifted the yellow tape and ducked under it. Vaughn Muller hadn't done much repair in the front of the house, as not to draw attention to it. There wasn't much there to fix anyway. Some of the roses were making a comeback after years void of pruning and proper watering. He inserted the key into the deadbolt lock and turned it until he heard it click open. Then reinserted the same key into the lock in the door knob. It too opened. The door screeched. Nothing that WD-40 wouldn't fix. In the final days of his father's life, the house's upkeep took a toll on Joey physically. Those memories he didn't miss.

Joey knew where all the light switches were located. He flipped on the hall light, a frantic mouse made an escape from the living room down the hall and escaped into the kitchen. "You're lucky Toots is dead, miserable creature!" Joey yelled down the hall after it. Toots, the calico family house cat, was an avid mouse hunter. His enthusiasm usually resulted in a knocked over lamp, scratch marks on the hardwood floor, or disheveled rugs that posed as trip hazards for guests. But mother had trained him to take them to the side of the house to maul so as not too ruin guest's appetites.

The steps of the grand staircase creaked under his feet. Joey wanted to visit his old bedroom one more time. The Dubois twins shared the room and didn't change much of the décor or character. He cracked open the door and flipped on the light. His desk was still a light purple shade where he spent many late nights doing his homework. The poster of Baywatch TV series hunk, David Hasselhoff, still hung on the door to his private on suite. Strange that two straight men wouldn't find it odd. It would definitely take some explaining to a female bed friend who might think them gay.

"My God!" he said, reminiscing over his Ken doll, still in Its package on top of the dresser drawers. His grandmamma had gifted it to him for his ninth birthday. It was vintage collectable 1961 Ken Doll with original swimsuit with yellow beach towel wrapped over his shoulders. It was the object of his affection that caused the only argument he witnessed between his father and his grandmother. "It's a god damn doll mom," his dad lectured. "I'm not raising no queer." Those words, forever stamped on his mind, still hurt long after Frank's death. Into the closet went the Ken doll as well as his sexuality. Ken was his and he would reclaim him. He removed the box from the dresser. "You're going home with me dear."

The Dubois twins lived like typical bachelors. Dirty socks under their beds, a towel still hung on a bed post. Had the bed been made, he would have missed the shoe box meticulously stored under the head board. The temptation to open it overwhelmed him. He knew it was an egregious intrusion of privacy. But he would return the contents to their original state. No one would ever know.

On all fours, Joey reached under the bed for the shoe box. It was covered with dust that he immediately brushed off. He sat on the edge of the bed with the box in his lap. Indecisive as to whether he should listen to his conscience or cave in to his curiosity, he hesitated. But he gave into the queasy anxiousness in his stomach and opened the lid. Other than a few dollars in petty cash, the box was filled with unsealed letters. Thumbing through them, he discovered that most of them were from a woman named Clarice Dubois, most likely their mother or sister. The postmarks were dated from the 1940's and 50's. This person must have passed as there were no dates past 1958.

The front door screeched. "Shit!" he exclaimed under his breath. He was not alone.

"Police!" Detective Stone called out. "Anyone here?"

He quickly put the shoe box back under the bed and brushed the dust off himself. "It's just me Detective," Joey hollered out to acknowledge where he was.

"What are you doing here? Stone asked, yelling up the stairs. "This is a crime scene. You shouldn't be here."

"Hold on Detective, I'm coming down." Joey grabbed the Ken box from where he left it on the bed and headed down the stairs. He glanced at Stone pacing in the lobby scratching his head. "Just getting some of my things Detective."

"You still have a key?"

"My brother is still a resident," Joey looked at him, puzzled at his question. "Why?"

"We need to talk," Stone stated cordially. It was a softer tone than the last time they had spoken.

"Do I need a lawyer?"

"No, no, I just need to talk to you off the record," Stone assured him. "Confidentially, I promise."

"What brings you here this time of night Detective?"

"Routine check. Saw the light on."

Joey reached across the hall and turned the light on in the sitting room. A ceiling fan also began to rotate at a slow speed. Both men entered and sat across from each other on the leather sofa. Detective Stone broke the awkward silence, "God, I use to love to frequent this place. This is where the bar use-to be. Right?"

"Actually, it's in the room behind us. Jack partitioned the room off when we repurposed the restaurant."

"No wonder it looks smaller. Look, I'm hoping you can shed light on some stuff that's really crawled under my skin." Joey started to cut him off. "Please, just hear me out. OK?" Joey nodded affirmatively. "I don't believe in vampires."

"That's good," Joey replied sarcastically with raised brow.

"But I'll tell you," Stone said, unsure of his conviction. "Lately, I'm not so convinced anymore."

"What do you mean?" Joey injected without any expression of doubt or shock.

"See," Stone smirked. "Your reaction tells it all."

"I don't know what you mean," Joey responded. "What are you implying Detective."

"Please stop calling me detective. I was a friend of your fathers for Christ sake. Just call me Sam."

"Confidential, Saaam?" Joey's stalwart attitude drained from his face.

"On my mother's grave, "Stone reiterated.

"My brother was two shades from death when this phenomenon moved in. Now, he has to be the strongest man alive. Looks more attractive than he did in high school and hasn't a blemish or a mole on his entire body. I can't explain it. It wasn't until I fell in love with one that I began to learn why. He spoon-fed me a little bit at a time. I've researched the entire gamut of vampire nomenclature at every library in town. At first, I believed that perhaps they might be Dhampirs, half vampire half human. Balkan legend has it that, for the most part, they were just normal members of the community, with some kind of sorcery. But the more I read, the more ludicrous it all seemed. They're not the Bram Stoker Dracula's of fame that turn into bats or magically go invisible. But they are in every sense of the word, vampires. It's just that there really is a science to their existence. Doctor Chang is a real doctor of the sciences. You fought in Viet Nam, right?"

"I don't see the relevance."

"You kill anyone there because you had to?"

"That's different, we were fighting a war, and yes I lost count of how many of the enemy died at my hands. It was kill or be killed."

"There's all kinds of wars Sam," Joey leaned toward him with certitude. "This maybe the most important war of all time."

"And just what would that be?" Stone asked, determined to get to the bottom of it.

"The war on Human Rights."

"Joey," Stone said, searching for the right response. "We have laws in this land. You can't just kill someone because they're bad people. We let the system protect us."

Joey's eyes thinned in contempt, "So how's that working out?"

"That's not the point," Stone bolstered his position.

"The Chronicle reports that crime has dropped dramatically following the Synagogue incident. How did we do in Viet Nam? Oh, we lost that war!" Joey's voice elevated with frustration. "The entire fascist world has their eyes on this City Sam. And you know it. So, for once, be the hero Sam. I'm not saying that you have to get involved, just don't get in the way."

Sergeant Stone had nothing to say. Trying to absorb and justify the obvious truth to it all, he had no response. "It's out of my hands anyway."

"What are you insinuating?"

"The FBI has taken over the case. They've sent their best."

"One more thing Sam."

"What's that?"

"This morning the White Supremacists killed a highly respected leader of the Creed."

"That's what they call themselves?"

"It's about to get real ugly Sam."

"Where? When?" Stone's demeanor took a one-eighty.

"Even if I knew I wouldn't tell you because you are part of the problem."

"Come on Joey, people will die," Stone insisted adamantly.

"Seriously Sam, they're very tight."

Detective Stone rose from the sofa and began to pace. "You know Joey, if I had my way, I'd be fighting those fascist pricks along with them. But we have to draw the line somewhere. Hate ideology has no place in America, but they have a right to free speech."

"Unless that free speech turns violent and takes away another person's Rights!" Joey barked back.

"You're incorrigible," Stone exclaimed at the end of his rope.

"Then encourage me," Joey challenged. "Tell me how you and your broken system plan to make it better?" Detective Stone looked up at the ceiling as if asking God to give him the answer. "That's what I thought. I can see that you're a good man Sam. The kinda guy my father would hang with. I don't have the answers either. But I know the vampires aren't what you think they are. They're on our side."

"I got to go. I was supposed to meet my date ten minutes a go."

"You want to use the phone?"

"Sure, thanks." He calmed down enough to notice the Ken doll. "Where did you get that?"

"Hey, it's a collector's item. Probably worth a lot of money."

Detective Stone rolled his eyes. "I don't want to know."

Tuesday, May 19, 1986
Marin City. Crazy Horse Motel

The German SS guard covered Fabian's head with a burlap sack and drew the string around his neck. His hands were forced behind his naked body and restrained with steel shackles. A two-foot chain was fastened around each ankle. He wasn't gagged, but he couldn't speak either, as if he had no tongue. Before he could blink, he was standing in the midst of a man size cage with hundreds of rats. There were so many. Climbing over each other and running between his legs. But they ignored him as if he were invisible.

He dreamed in color and he perspired just the same. He recognized their faces. Some appeared and as quickly as they finished saying their beef with him, disappeared. Their condemnations wrenched at his heart, without empathy, choking him with their retaliatory digs.

Amidst the Rats in the cage, the red hair freckled boy he teased until he cried on the playground, "You think your better than the Nazis?"

Outside the cage stood a man who claimed to be his Father, "You were never worthy of my love, neither was your mother."

Standing but a foot from his face, the Catholic Priest he left behind. His flesh burnt and hanging on the bone. One eye missing from Its socket. "You are damned to hell for leaving me behind." Then they were gone.

As if Moses had parted the red sea of rats, the alpha rodent approached in the divide, stopping a few yards from Fabien's feet. Standing on his back two legs, a swastika tattooed on his stomach, he opened his fanged mouth and screeched so loud that Fabien felt his ear drums nearly break. Why could he see clearly through the burlap sack? They attacked him at once, tearing away the flesh from his feet, but it didn't hurt. First his feet were gone, but he didn't fall. Then his legs, but he didn't fall. Then his torso, but he didn't fall. Now it was just the alpha rat starring at him with malice. What was he waiting for? The rat's fury face oscillated from contempt to shame and finally to empathy.

"Wake up! Fabien, wake up," Carol shook him forcibly.

Fabien sprang up into a sitting position on the bed, perspiring like he'd just ran a marathon, "Oh my God!"

"You were having a bad nightmare. Fabien, for God's sake you're drowning in your own sweat," She sat up next to him, covering her bare breasts with the cotton sheet. "Are you OK? You must have dreamt something terrible."

"Shit," he exclaimed. "Whadza time?"

"6:15 am," Carol stated, reaching over the nightstand and turning off the alarm clock. It was set to go off at 7:00 a.m. "I wish you didn't have to go."

"I hope I not scare you." He apologized as he caught his breath. "I much like spend za day wis you my love," he kissed her and rolled his feet out of the bed slipping into this boxer shorts. "I muss go soon. Coffee?"

"Not right now," she said with suppressed felicity. Feeling melancholy that the short-lived ecstasy couldn't continue through the day, the blissfulness that they were together still filled her heart. "Will I see you later?"

Fabien tore off the top of the sugar packet, "Of course," he replied smiling affectionately at her.

"I still can't believe that Muller is gone," Carol said, starring up at the hotel room curtains. They were lit up by the rays of dawn's first light. "Sons of bitches. I hope the cops catch his killers."

He blew over the surface of his freshly brewed coffee cup, hoping it would cool some. It was still too hot to sip. Fabien sat the cup down on the nightstand and laid on top of the white comforter. "Zay will pay."

They lay on the bed shoulder to shoulder, staring at the ceiling, Carol under the covers Fabien not. "Fabien, there's something I can't keep from you any longer. Especially now that Muller is gone."

"Whazis?" he pried, turning on his side to face her.

"A few days ago, Doctor Chang paid me a visit. Did you tell him where I was staying?"

"No," Fabien professed defensively. "Really."

"Perhaps one of the guys told him," She rationalized. "It doesn't matter. Anyway, he had me sign some papers. He was very flattering. Said he trusted me completely. He stated that he had paid for a safe deposit box at his bank, Bank of America, and that my name would be a third signature on the account. He intended to put the sealed documents in the safe deposit box."

"Makes no sense," Fabien exclaimed somewhat stunned by her revelation. "Is like Doctor Chang knew that there was a good chance they might die. Did you read whaz you sign?"

"I did ask him what it was for? Huey looked discomposed and almost embarrassed to have to ask me to do this. He went on to say that it was a legal agreement that I would be named a partial benefactor, sole Executor, and Trustee. That in the event, and only in the event of both of their deaths, I was to execute and distribute the funds as was needed. But exclusively, only I, to protect against a rogue player, should distribute in small increments as needed.

"Zis crazy, why you?" Fabien's brow wrinkled inward. He was perturbed that she had been preferred over members of the Creed.

"I don't even know how much we're talking about here," Carol chagrined.

"Leez-half a billion, maybe more," Fabien replied nonchalantly like it was no big deal.

"You're pulling my leg, right?" She beseeched, sitting up against the headboard feeling unnerved and overwhelmed. "Half a billion dollars?" Carol stated as she swallowed hard. "Huey said that I would be a silent partner. I'm not sure what that means. But I do know that unless both of them are dead, my access to the deposit box is prohibited."

"Zay are, wuz you say in English, Cautious?"

"More like paranoid," Carol corrected and looked at Fabien forebodingly. "I'm getting the sense that something big is brewing. Something ugly is about to go down. Isn't it? This thing you have to do today, she paused. There's a chance I may never see you again, isn't there?"

"I promise," he said lifting her chin. Picking up on her forlorn feelings, Fabien scooted closer and embraced her. "You muz believe me."

"I'm just scared Fabien," Carol admitted tearing up. He kissed her forehead and held her firmly.

Tuesday, May 19, 1986
Double Tree Hotel

He had never witnessed the withdrawals before, his theories existed only on paper. Across the Hotel Suite room, Doctor Chang, still crestfallen over the loss of his soul mate, confirmed that his theories are accurate. Her skin had lost It's supple, fresh, and vibrant youthfulness. Exposed to the free radicals in the atmosphere that were damaging her cells, causing wrinkles and drooping of her skin. Even given her frailness, her captors were too afraid to release her from the industrial size hand truck. A thick, six feet tall, three feet wide, sheet of metal was welded to the back frame of the hand truck. Supports legs were also attached, allowing a forty-five-degree angle resting position. Her hands and feet were secured to the platform with metal claw like clamps. Doctor Chang was secured similarly.

Jade, under-nourished, managed, with what little strength she had, to raise her head to apologize to Doctor Chang, "I'm so sorry I let you down. I hoped there wasn't any truth to Vaughn's death. These fascists are scum Huey."

"It's not your fault," Doctor Chang assured her. "You need to hang in there. This will all be over soon."

"After the war ended Huey, did you ever in your wildest imagination, conceive that the next Fascist threat would come in the land of our liberators?"

Doctor Chang's acumen was clouded by his grief, but he still perceived that Jade had abandoned any hope of escaping. "My poor Jade," Chang replied in his gentle but resilient way. "It's far from over dear."

His statement got the attention of the high-ranking National Alliance members. They were socializing with two Peckerwood officers a few feet away. Ross Anderson, the only foreign white supremacist, a member of the German Republicans, left the conversation and stomped over to Doctor Chang. Nose to nose, he spit in Chang's face. "Oh, believe me, it's over you Bamboo Coon!"

"Get away from him!" demanded the PMC standing directly behind Doctor Chang. Two heavily armed Krupp PMCs had the duty of protecting the prisoners from, what they considered inconvenient second level threats. One standing guard near the hotel suite door, the other behind Doctor Chang's hand truck.

Anderson shot the PMC a contemptuous glare. "What are you a Chink lover?" A much smaller statured Anderson stepped in front of the PMC and had to tilt his head upward to look into his face. "Do you know who the fuck I am?"

"Should I?" The PMC stated without an inclination of fear. "Quite frankly, I don't give a rat's ass who you are or where you're from. But if you get within a foot of the prisoner again, I will break your fucking neck. Those are my orders." The PMC at the door couldn't help himself and cracked a defiant grin that drew disdainful looks from the Fascists in the room as the disdain was mutual. The German Republican shook his head in disgust and kowtowed back to his social circle.

Luther Pierce, Rudi Helbard, and Gary Yarbrough, flanked by two PMCs, emerged from a bedroom designated as an office for Helbard. "Just so we understand each other," Rudi continued their conversation from behind closed doors, "You will get the rest of your money when we return." Yarbrough nodded that he was onboard.

"You boys can handle this," Luther Pierce stated with a grin of satisfaction. "I'm driving back to my Hotel in Marin."

"It was an honor to finally meet you in person Mr. Pierce," Yarbrough obeisantly overstated. Pierce managed a fake gratuitous smile, then turned to Krupp and rolled his eyes.

"Ah, Doctor Chang," Rudi said enthusiastically. "You're a hard man to get in touch with. Sorry about your friend, Mr. Muller. I was hoping that could have been avoided."

"Who the hell are you?" Doctor Chang asked spitefully.

Rudi remained unaffected by Chang's loathing stare. "I apologize Doctor, I should have introduced myself. Rudi Helbard, Legal Counsel for the Krupp Group. I'm sure you're familiar with them. You did, after all, embezzled a fortune from them, remember. Unfortunate for you, they would like back what is rightfully theirs. I'm sure you would understand if that was your money."

Doctor Chang was reticent, "The Krupp Family donated that money to my research. You obviously don't know your history. How old were you? Two years old?" The other nine people in the room had frozen, waiting for Rudi's response.

Rudi pulled his sidearm from Its holster and pointed the barrel two inches from Jade's temple. "Wrong answer Doctor Chang. I'm sure your friend's life is worth more than a few million. Actually, I believe with the interest earned, that figure is somewhere in the neighborhood of a billion dollars. Would you agree Doctor?"

Doctor Chang nodded that he would surrender the money to save Jade's life. "So how do you propose this will go down Mr. Hell-turd."

Rudi grinned and shook his head amused. "Ahh, very funny Doctor. I'm glad you asked. The vice president of your local Bank of America Branch, Mr. Rockford, is on his way now to meet us in a small conference room on the first floor. You will join me, of course under heavy security, and sign the necessary documents. I hope we don't have to deal with any of your fanged friend's bullshit. Because if we do, we'll put a bullet in your girlfriend. Do I make myself clear Doctor?"

"Very."

"You don't have to do this Huey," Jade insisted. "I've had a great second life. I'm ready to go."

Rudi drew the back of his hand across her face hard. "Shut up bitch!" He walked across the room and faced Doctor Chang. "You make one false move and I'll riddle you with bullet holes." He stepped back and motioned for the PMC to release him. At the back of the hand truck, the PMC pulled down on a lever opening the clamps wide enough that Doctor Chang could pull his wrists from them and step off the small truck platform.

Doctor Chang rubbed each wrist, which had bruised from the metal pressing against his flesh. "After I sign your documents, what assurance do I have that you will let us go?"

"My officers will protect you until you leave the hotel. The Krupp Family only wants their money back. Killing you will only muddy the process. Trust me, we just want our money."

Doctor Chang ascertained the antipathy between the white supremacists and the Krupp thugs. "Let's get this done then."

"Ah," Rudi exclaimed delighted with his lack of resistance. "Lets." Two of the four PMCs stepped behind Doctor Chang as Rudi led them out the hotel room toward the elevators. The other two remained to secure the hostage.

Gary Yarbrough joined the group of fascists congregated opposite the door and toward the panoramic windows of the large suite. "Mr. Helbard, we're not leaving without our money," he said loud enough for Rudi to hear as he stood waiting for the elevator car to climb to their level. Rudi ignored him.

"God, I hate Americans," Rudi muttered under his breath.

The elevator doors opened and the four men stepped into the empty car. Doctor Chang knew it would not end well. His mind drifted to the life he once shared with Vaughn Muller. Gone was his euphoric world with Vaughn. He would miss him dearly. The nights cuddled in his arms as he fell asleep, gone. The morning colloquy on the patio over articles in the newspaper and sipping freshly ground coffee. Ah, the aroma of him. All gone. His heart was broken and he sunk into a deep sadness, "Have you ever loved someone more than yourself Mr. Helbard?"

"Doctor, I am very sorry whether you believe it or not. It wasn't my choice to work with these fascist low lives."

"Please," Doctor Chang mumbled, unimpressed with his disingenuous empathy.

The elevator door opened to the lobby. "This way," Rudi directed them away from the lobby and toward the conference rooms.

"The Shark Room, How apropos Mr. Helbard," Doctor Chang sarcastically read the room tag on the door.

Mr. Rockford, branch president at Chang and Muller's bank, sat officiously across the table next to a witness, bank employee, and certified Notary Public. Chairs screeched on the hardwood floor as the two men stood to welcome the entourage entering the Conference room. Mr. Rockford extended his hand for Doctor Chang to shake and then offered it to Rudi and the two PMCs that flanked them. "Doctor Chang, I wish it was better circumstances that we were meeting. We very much appreciated your business and I wish you and Muller good luck with your new life in Germany. Your Financial Advisor, Mr. Helbard here, has informed me of everything." Doctor Chang glanced at Rudi and rolled his eyes in disgust. "Deutsche Bank is a very lucky bank. Just to remind you, Bank of America does have a branch there, just in case you wish to keep investing your money with us."

"Thank you, Mr. Rockford, but no thanks. You have taken great care of our account, but we have had other ties to Deutsche Bank for many years there." Rudi exhibited a derided grin.

"I understand," Rockford opened the manila folder, exposing bank documents. "My assistant prepared these this morning for me. Would you like to read them over carefully before you sign?"

"Of course," Doctor Chang took the file from Mr. Rockford. "I'm sure Mr. Helbard would advise me to."

"Do we have time Doctor?" Rudi inquired, embittered that Doctor Chang was stalling the process. "Don't forget you have a plane to catch, SOON."

Doctor Chang thumbed to the last page of the document. He noted that indeed he had left the minimum five hundred dollars to keep the account open. "You say your assistant prepared this?"

"Is there a problem?" Rockford asked anxiously.

"No, that's the correct amount," Doctor Chang stated with a chicanery smile. "You did review this correct?"

"Actually no, but I trust my assistant prepared the transfer as requested."

"Let me see it," Rudi exclaimed, grabbing the folder away from Doctor Chang. Doctor Chang had set page four with the account total of five hundred dollars on top. "Is this some kind of a prank Mr. Rockford?" Rudi tossed the folder at the bank president, who looked confused and nervous. "Explain this!"

The color drained from Rockford's face as he read the sum amount in the account. "There must be some kind of mistake here. Last time I looked there was close to a billion dollars in this account."

"There's no mistake Mr. Rockford. Mr. Muller and I made some very expensive investments recently. A family emergency came up. I apologize for not communicating that to you first."

"What's going on here?" Mr. Rockford asked indignantly, cognizant of Rudi's sudden lividness and flushed red cheeks. "How dare you Doctor Chang insist that I meet you here over five hundred dollars! This is ludicrous."

"Mr. Rockford, it would be a good idea if you would leave us now," Rudi stated.

"Sorry Mr. Rockford," Doctor Chang apologized tongue in cheek. "Please, keep the five hundred dollars for your trouble. Next time Mr. Rockford, do your due diligence and review your documents first. Would have saved you a lot of trouble."

Rudi stood abruptly, his chair tumbling behind him, as Mr. Rockford placed the account folder in his briefcase. Without the usual professional endearments, he left the room with his Notary. "Stand up!" Rudi ordered. "Where is the money?" He pulled the sidearm from Its holster and pointed it at Doctor Chang's head. "No more games or you will join your friend Mr. Muller."

"You stupid sycophant," Doctor Chang starred into Rudi's eyes with contempt. "You've already taken from me the only thing that matters. Now you can only hope that you get out of here alive. My family will come for me, if they're not here already."

Rudi held his two-way radio to his mouth, "Kill her." It wasn't the reaction Doctor Chang had hoped for.

Doctor Chang closed his eyes in angst. Did he just give Rudi, Jade's death wish? "Wait!"

Rudi needed to prove a point to Doctor Chang, "leave the mic open when you pull the trigger. I want Doctor Chang to know his friend is dead."

"You got it," the PMC affirmed, and pulled out his automatic weapon from the holster underneath his jacket. His finger still on the talk switch, he aimed it at Jade.

"What the hell are you doing?" Yarbrough shouted from across the room.

The shot rang out over the walkie-talkie downstairs. Doctor Chang's head fell, overwhelmed at the thought of what he had just done. He felt the barrel of a gun in his back. The two PMCs stood behind him. Rudi led them back to the elevators, pacing impatiently. He was clearly angry as he watched the elevator floor indicator light drop from floor to floor.

There was a brief pause before the elevator doors began to open. The elevator car was fully occupied with fascists. Poorly, but effectively orchestrated, two Peckerwoods had dropped to one knee, and two remained standing, their semi-automatic AR-15 rifles aimed at their targets, Rudi Helbard and his two PMC thugs. Doctor Chang covered his face with his arms as the bullets hissed and moaned to both sides of him. The mammoth PMC, with his gun in Huey's back, managed to get one shot off. The stray bullet struck and killed one of the standing Peckerwood gang members. Rudi's body danced backwards against the rear wall as a barrage of bullets riddled his body. He fell to the carpeted floor, leaving a smeared streak of blood following him down the hotel corridor wall.

When the smoke from the gun powder settled, Doctor Chang was crouched alone, starring at Gary Yarbrough who emerged from behind his fire line. "Well, well, if it isn't Doctor Chang," Yarbrough regaled, "We meet again."

"How am I still alive?" Doctor Chang asked no one.

"You may have taken Mr. Helbard for a fool Doctor Chang. But now we're going to play by a different set of rules. You're going to get us our money."

"You are a fool," Doctor Chang belittled.

The black sedan pulled to the shoulder of Anza Boulevard, two blocks from the Double Tree Hotel. Flashing red and blue lights from emergency vehicles lit up the streets around the hotel. Muller's Limo pulled in behind them. Sirens indicated that more police and emergency responders would inevitably block major intersections and any road back to Airport Boulevard.

"We're too late," Estella exclaimed from the front passenger seat.

"We have to get out of here!" Dylan said unnerved, sitting in the seat behind her. "Stone will somehow find a way to implicate us. Trust me we have to become invisible. I say we turn around."

"Who's this Stone you speak of?" Heinz probed.

"SPD's finest," Dylan replied. "Whatever just happened, it can't be good."

Macias tapped on Estella's car window. She rolled it down enough to see his face. "Why have we stopped? We should get a closer look."

"We have to approach this pragmatically."

"Doesn't this vehicle have a radio?" Thomas asked presumptuously. His voice deeper, his muscular framework fuller, his Native American long black hair curlier and shinier. "If we park in the Embassy Suites parking lot, we'll just mix in with the other vehicles. We can lay low there. There's news media vans at the scene. This is breaking news."

"God, you're not only gorgeous, you're smart as well," Estella cajoled. "Turn on the radio Heinz and get us to the Embassy Suites parking lot." She looked up at Macias still waiting at the door for her direction. "Got it?"

"We'll meet you over there," Macias confirmed and walked back to the Limo.

Johnny Cash was singing Walk the line on 95.7 the bear country station. Adjusting the dial to Wild 94.9, Jimmy Page's electric guitar was in the middle of a famous riff.

"Go to the am dial," Dylan insisted. "740 am, KCBS is all news."

Heinz pushed the am key on the radio console and adjusted the dial to 740 fortuitously in the middle of breaking news. "Have said they believe the murders were gang related," the female reporter continued. "We have spoken with one police authority who stated that the FBI has taken over the crime scene." Heinz checked his left mirror and shifted the Sedan into drive. "Sources say that nine people are dead, including a German civilian and Krupp family lawyer. A hotel employee told authorities that it appeared that a local white supremacist gang had taken one-man hostage and disappeared in a green Lincoln Continental. There appears to be two separate crime scenes. A police spokesman stated that it is believed that a rival gang interrupted a sadomasochistic ritual that smacked of controlled substances. The second crime scene was outside a conference room on the main floor. A Bureau spokesperson stated that the person with whom the hotel suite was rented to was the Krupp lawyer. We will update our viewers as we learn more. Again, nine people dead at the Double Tree Hotel in San Francisco. This is Gloria Downs for CBS news. Back to Dan Rather and the CBS team."

"What do we do now?" Heinz asked, feeling benumbed and defeated. He always had a plan, an out, or if feeling inept, there was always Muller and Doctor Chang to lean on. But this time they were on their own. "It's very likely that the hostage maybe Doctor Chang or Jade."

Estella knew she had to step up to the plate and get her nerve back. "Dylan, what is Giuseppe's relationship with this Sandy chick?"

"Like he said, "She saved his life."

"I mean do they still talk?"

"I believe so," Dylan responded. "Do you want me to ask him?"

"Never mind," Estella said. "I'll be right back. Stay here and monitor the radio." She opened the passenger door and was on a mission. Walking back to the Limo, she opened the front passenger door and wasted no time demanding that Giuseppe follow her.

"Where are we going?" Giuseppe asked trying to keep pace with Estella as she marched toward the Marriott lobby doors.

"We need to get you to a phone," Estella replied not losing stride. "Do you know Sandy's phone number?"

"Sure," he responded still confused.

"Good," Estelle said relieved. "I want you to call her and see if she knows anything about a hostage."

"Who is they," he asked even more ambiguously.

"I have no fucking clue," She stated as she held the Hotel door open for him to enter.

"OK," He acquiesced. "There," He pointed to a niche in the wall with a sign over it which read, "Public Telephone." Their notoriety proceeded them, masquerading in leather trench coats, got them unwelcomed attention and admiration of hotel guests. They stared them down as they walked over to the phones. But the admiration wasn't mutual for three men sitting at the bar in the hotel lounge. Two of the middle-aged men wore Khakis and arm length dress shirts that tightly defined their muscular torsos. Pushing his empty beer mug toward the bar tender, the third man, in a full-dress suit and tie, with salt and pepper hair, stood and turned to monitor the two visitors.

"Let's make this quick," Estella whispered, not losing stride and aware they were being watched.

Giuseppe had little patience with rotary phones and was grateful the Hotel had push key. There was a ring tone. "Sandy?" ...pause... "Where are you at? Can you talk?" ...pause... "We know, we're just down the street. We were too late." ...pause... "Listen, do you know where they are taking their hostage?" ...pause... "Where's that at?" ...pause... "Do you know what time?" ...pause... "You're sure it's Chang? How many do you believe will be attending?" ...pause... "It's worth checking out." ...pause... "I know," ...pause... "They're going to know sooner than later. I don't think you and the girls will be safe." ...pause... "I will," ...pause... "I'm staying at the Rectory." ...pause... "I would like that very much." ...pause... "Hurry", ...pause... "Please be careful." ...pause... "See you soon, bye."

"See you soon? Are you taking a liking to this girl?"

Giuseppe, the man with steel nerves, seemed a little unhinged to her. "I just want to see where it goes."

"So, what does she know?" Estella asked impatiently.

"She believes that if they can't get Doctor Chang to pay his own ransom, they're going to lynch him."

"Did she say where?"

"At the Jim Crow Klu Klux Klan rally at the Hawk Campground, off the Bobcat Trail tonight at eight o'clock." He gave it a second to sink in. "Imperial Wizard will be attending. Full regalia."

"I guess we're having dinner tonight at the Hawk Campground, where ever the hell that is." Estella said winsomely. "Shit!" She grimaced. "Tell the others seven o'clock at the cave. The suits are headed our way. Go! I'm going to stall them. I had a feeling they were cops."

"Estella Agsteribbe, what a coincidence, I'm Agent Wayne Manis," he smiled cordially and put out his right hand for her to shake while flashing his badge with the other. "Let me introduce you to my colleagues, Agent Pursey and Sergeant Stone." He put his hand down after she refused to shake it.

"That's not my name Agent Manis," she said stoically, but had never felt more on tenterhooks. "Do you boys always stock the ladies while on duty?"

"Just wanted to get a signature from an Olympic athlete from the 1928 Dutch gymnastic team," Manis said with amelioration, straining the awkward moment even more for her. It was evident to Manis he was on the money as her face twitched uncomfortably. "Look, I'm going to cut to the chase."

Estella remained silent and unabashed. "Wouldn't have it any other way," she said with oblique malevolence.

"I'm on the same mission you are," he spoke confident of his conclusions. "Only I hunt and prosecute fascists legally."

"Welcome to the Team Agent Manis," Estella stated facetiously. "Do you want an award?" Agent Manis's flippant attitude drained from his face as Sergeant Stone covered the smirk on his face.

"Oh, It's hard to fathom, but I'm very much aware of Chang's charade."

"You've been watching way too many Twilight Zone episodes, Agent Manis."

"I'm sure the hostage cadaver's teeth is most likely that of Jadwiga Dzido, one of Doctor Chang's Auschwitz survivors. Don't look surprised, we're the FBI, the best forensic science on earth. What does baffle us is the sudden twist of fate. I think you know why the Krupp family want's Doctor Chang alive. So just come clean with us. Something went awfully wrong at the Doubletree today. And we're hoping you might be able to shed some light on just what went down between the Krupp family and the Peckerwoods."

"Again, Agent Manis, I have no idea what you're talking about," Estella smiled stalwartly. "Now, unless you tell me I need a lawyer, please excuse me I have to piss." She bumped shoulders with Agent Manis as she walked past him toward the restrooms. He massaged his shoulder, dumbstruck by her strength.

"Leave town Estella," Agent Manis shouted out to her. "Let us do our job."

Estella, stopped abruptly, turned and faced Agent Manis. "Even Jesus couldn't stop fascism, why do you think you can do any better?" She disappeared into the lady's room leaving Giuseppe standing outside the door.

"Sam, can you find out if these phones are being recorded? If not, at least we can find out what number was called."

"I'm on it," Sergeant Stone affirmed.

Noon, same day.
Joey Sander's New Apartment
Buena Vista Avenue

"Oh my God!" Jonathan ecstatically exclaimed, about to ejaculate inside of Joey. Clenching his pillow, Joey braced for the climax as the thrusts became painfully erotic. Jonathan grasped Joey's ass firmly, elevated it higher, and like a piston of a race car, pounded it against his pelvis. "I'm coming!" Jonathan inconveniently announced to Joey's chagrin. The massage oil and Jonathan's dripping sweat had molded Joey to the sheets. Joey didn't want it to end. "Yes, yes, oh shit!" Jonathan cried out in sexual intoxication, his body still seizing in uncontrolled rhythm.

"Leave it in," Joey demanded still rocking on Jonathan's erection. Releasing the pillow, Joey's right hand wrapped around his throbbing sex. Jonathan quickly removed Joey's hand and ebulliently swallowed and sucked the jism from deep in his loins. Joey's rigid body shuttered and went limp. They kissed less forceful for a good minute to savor the afterglow.

Jonathan rolled off him and toyed with a strand of Joey's blonde hair. "That was amazing," Jonathan relished, his panting subsiding. He suddenly froze, "Did you hear that? I swear that was glass breaking."

There was a thump against the studio wall next to the bed followed by the sound of more shattering glass and the muffled sound of an angry man's voice. "He's such an ass," Joey said loathingly. "She works the grave shift and as soon as she wakes up he's beating on her. I don't think he has a job. Such a loser. Speaking of jobs, I've got to get back before I lose mine."

"The Creed has business to take care of this evening," Jonathan announced somewhat distressed. "Most likely I'll be home very late. Please get some sleep and don't wait up for me."

"You don't believe he's still alive, do you?" Joey asked, professing that he was missing Doctor Chang terribly.

"I can't get into it Joey."

Joey looked concerned. "Please be safe."

"I understand Thomas is now a vampire."

"You won't recognize him now."

"How's that?"

"Estella believes the SR process is enhanced somewhat by his Native American gene pool," Jonathan explained as he climbed into his jeans and blue silk shirt. "That kid has become extremely powerful."

Joey listened arduously while buttoning up the last button on his uniform shirt. "If you see my brother tell him I need to speak with him. He hasn't called in days and I don't know where he's at or how to get in touch with him."

"You shouldn't worry about him."

"It's my job to worry about him, he's my younger brother," Joey snapped vehemently.

"I didn't mean it that way," Jonathan apologized.

Joey glared down at the floor, "I didn't mean to get upset at you. I just don't know how much more I can take. I've lost nearly everything, my mother to cancer, my father to alcohol, my uncle John to a heart attack, my best friend is murdered." His voice cracked. Overwhelmed with anguish, he took a brief respite. Jonathan embraced him. The kind of support he never got from his own Father. "I nearly lost him to AIDS, it would destroy me if something happened to him."

"Trust me, your brother is more than apt to take care of himself. He's going to be fine. I'll have him contact you tonight. Promise."

A hard thump on the floor from the adjacent apartment interrupted their moment. "I don't think I can stay here. I want to get involved and then I just think of how that could really complicate my already complicated life."

Jonathan kissed him. "You'd better get going before Alice writes you up for returning late from lunch." Joey pinned his name badge on his shirt, kissed Jonathan, and made his way to the door.

"Oh, I forgot to tell you, you have mail. It's next to the phone. Sergeant Stone is forwarding all the Hospice mail to me." Joey felt in his pant pockets for his keys. "Shit, where did I put my keys?"

Jonathan discovered them on the floor next to the bed post. "Here," Jonathan reached down and picked them up off the floor. "Must have slipped out of your pocket." Joey shook his head, somewhat amused and embarrassed at the same time. Not wasting a second of his short lunch break, he began shedding his clothes, not giving notice to where they landed. That's how his keys ended up on the floor.

"Better use the head, just in case I get stuck in traffic," Joey stated, disappearing into the bathroom.

Anxious to open the letter, he confirmed that it was addressed to him from the law office of Yates and Henderson. Jonathan sat down at the dining table. "What the hell could this be." He used his fingernail as a letter opener and pulled the contents from the envelope and straightened them out on the table and began to read it. "Dear Mr. Hughes, our law office has been appointed by the Texas Comptroller's Office as Trustees over your deceased father, Theodore Hughes's Estate. Texas Statutes mandate that any living descendants be notified as legal beneficiaries of all assets, including real property. Court records show that you are the only known survivor and next of kin. Please notify my office at 800-659-0023 prior to December 31, 1988, to claim your inheritance. Failure to do so prior to the deadline will result in forfeiture of your rights and your father's assets will become property of the State of Texas. The following is a detailed list of the Theodore Hughes Estate. Bullet one: Hughes Concrete small business valued at $2,250,000.00 Bullet two: 401K valued at $843,991.00. Bullet three: Real Property valued at $624,003.00. Bullet four: Personal Effects valued at $210,803.00. Bullet five: Petty Cash and Bank funds valued at $1,067,506.00."

Jonathan was numb with disbelief, "That loser got his shit together?" Jonathan's gut wrenched with mixed emotions. He had only tried to reconnect with his father to tell him that he was dying, but he lost the nerve. He loathed his father, yet he felt a void in his life and unable to fill it. How he wished Muller were here to advise him.

"You look like you've just seen a ghost," Joey asked concerned, emerging from the bathroom. "What is it?"

"I'm a millionaire," Jonathan stated starring at the letter in a somber trance.

"Really," Joey snickered. "You know those mail in sweepstakes are just a scam to get you to buy something."

"My monster of a father died," Jonathan said emotionless. He looked back down at the notice to verify he wasn't dreaming. "I don't want anything of his. I'm donating it all to charity."

"How much are we talking about? I mean don't jump to a decision too quickly. This could be poetic justice Jonathan."

"Five million roughly," he answered dolefully.

Joey swallowed hard, "You can't be serious." Jonathan handed Joey the letter over his shoulder without turning his head or speaking. "Holy shit! Please don't do anything stupid until you get legal advice. You hear me out?" Jonathan nodded. "I really have to go. I'm serious though."

"Fine," Jonathan acquiesced. "Go, or you're going to be late."

Joey stopped at the doorway and remembered what he needed to tell Jonathan. "Do me a favor will ya?"

"What's that?"

"I get that you have Obsessive Compulsive Disorder, and it is nice coming home to a clean apartment, but my underwear? Really? Just let me wash my own underwear."

Jonathan knew by the solemn gravity of his expression that he wasn't making light of it. "Fine."

The arguing next door escalated and grew louder and distracted Jonathan from his new fortune. It corroborated with bad memories of the day Jonathan's drunken father kicked him and his mother out on the street when he was fourteen. His Father's words still burned in his chest, "Get him out of my sight! I'm not raising no fag!" The three thousand plus square foot house belonged to his Father before he met his mother. Without a wedding ring on her finger, he was within his legal right.

The domestic dispute progressed into the hallway and Jonathan could clearly make out what they were shouting at each other. "If you quit your job I'll kill you bitch," the angry male barked at her.

She screamed back at him, "I want a divorce! I hate your lazy ass!" There was another thump on the hallway floor. "Don't touch me!" Her crying was the straw that broke the camel's back.

Jonathan opened the door to Joey's apartment to see a ballistic over-weight white male in his early thirties dressed in only his pajama bottoms and white undershirt. He glanced down at a younger Hispanic female lying on her back starring up at him, her face caught in the looming terror of the moment. This time she wouldn't wipe the tears and find an excuse for her clumsiness. Her linen robe barely covered her nipples. The pathetic wife, who always returned to her lying apologetic husband who truly loves her. Her left side of her face bruised, her eyes with a dam of tears ready to burst.

"But out Mister," the abuser warned Jonathan, whose curiosity was obviously piqued. "This doesn't concern you."

Jonathan shook his head in disgust and reached out his hand to help the female to her feet. "Wait in here," Jonathan imposed. She didn't hesitate and he closed the door of his apartment behind her.

"What do you think you're doing mister? This doesn't concern you." The husband challenged. "How would you like your ass kicked?"

"Nice, I won't have to order out for lunch. Home delivery, you're too easy." Jonathan stated unperturbed. The white of his eyes turning red from adrenals accelerating throughout his body. This strange phenomenon wrought fear in the husband's once testosterone overdosed demeanor.

"What are you some kind of freak?" the Abuser apperceived he was out muscled.

"Why don't we settle this in private, say perhaps in your apartment," Jonathan replied.

"Why don't you mind your fucking business," he answered, saving whatever was left of his manhood.

"Suit yourself." Jonathan wasted no time. Ducking under the man's attempt to swing at him, abruptly appeared behind him, grabbed a fist full of pajamas, and tossed him head first through the open door of the troubled couple's apartment. Unable to get his balance, the abuser fell into the coffee table. The legs collapsed underneath his weight. Jonathan stepped across the threshold and quietly closed the door behind him. "So, you like to beat on the ladies?" Jonathan approached him slowly as the man crawled away from him. "You're a real tough guy aren't ya?"

"Lorna! call the cops!" Scooting backwards on his butt, the now, not so tough wife beater, kowtowed in the corner, no place to go. Pathetic, perspiring, panic streaking down his brow.

"Oh, let's do," Jonathan regaled. "I'm sure they're going to have some questions concerning the shiner on your wife's face. Shall we call them?" He didn't respond. "See, cowards like you are all talk. Take it out on the wife and kids because you're a loser. I'm just not the type to let it go. You see, your type really get under my skin, literally." Kicking aside the broken coffee table, Jonathan pirouetted on his left foot and struck the side of the abuser's head with his right foot. It happened so quickly. His torso went limp and his head listed unconscious against the wall.

Showing no pity, Jonathan bent over him, raised his chin, but the loser's stench, from days without bathing, gave Jonathan pause. He coughed up a large mouthful of spittle and sprayed it at the intended entry point. Scanning the room for a clean cloth, he pulled several tissues from the box on the end table and wiped the neck bearably clean. Pressing his lips hard over the pulsing artery, Jonathan's bite carried the force of years of beatings and insatiable cries for leniency and love. His anger went beyond sucking the life from the abuser's convulsing body. The stranger's hair, tangled in his tightening grip, began to rip from his scalp as Jonathan began pounding his head against the wall, emotionally caught up in what seemed a retaliatory rite de passage and reconciliation. Jonathan began to weep and held the bastard's lifeless body in his lap as he rocked forward and aft until he felt the hidden emotional pain flow out of him with his tears. He cried out loud. The umbilical personification, as if this bastard was somehow his Father he was holding, came to light.

"That was for us Mother."

Walking to the rear exterior window of the second story apartment, Jonathan noted three large dumpsters, two with their lids open, directly under the window. One was empty, the other three quarters full of trash, mainly grass trimmings and boxes. He just got a break for a change. Jonathan dragging the corpse to the open apartment window. He poked his head out the window to make sure there was no one in the back alley to witness him getting rid of the cadaver. One last quick glance for bystanders and he swiftly steadied the body over the open trash bin, with the grass trimmings, and dropped it. "Bullseye!" It disappeared under the loose contents of the bin.

Dilapidated and in need of much repair, the apartment building was close to being condemned by the City. The door screeched as Mrs. wife abuser stood in the threshold with consternation and fear. "It got quiet," she stated nervously. "Where's my husband?"

"It's Lorna right?"

"How do you know my name?"

"Your loving husband flew out of here like the trash he is," Jonathan replied like a jester. "He cursed your name and stated that he never wanted to see you again. Ever."

Her jaw dropped. Her mouth agape, twitched with self-pity and her eyes filled with tears. "I'm pregnant. I start maternity leave next month. I can't afford this place on my own."

"And you think that loser was going to get a job?" Jonathan was dumbfounded with her benighted denial.

"How dare you believe that's any of your business," she shouted at him loathingly.

"Lady, you'll thank me later." Jonathan shook his head in disgust and walked passed her, retrieved his trench-coat from Joey's apartment and left the building.

"A police officer?" Dylan castigated Thomas for crossing the line with his latest blood-letting. "Are you out of your mind?"

"You weren't there," Thomas defended his actions. "If you saw how that Pig was talking to that elderly black man, you would have done the same."

"No!" Dylan followed Thomas from the bedroom into the kitchen for a cold beer after sex. "No! I wouldn't have." Thomas had dressed while Dylan had taken a shower. Except for the towel wrapped around his waist, Dylan was naked. "That's not how we operate." He grabbed two beers from the fridge and popped the seal off both. He handed one over the Kitchen table to Thomas, who removed a chair and made himself comfortable. "We don't play with Cops. This is going to bring the heat on us. You have to exercise better judgment."

"There are Cops and there are Pigs." Thomas reiterated vehemently. "This officer was a Pig. The old man's only crime was parking in a handicap parking place and being black. He tried explaining to the Cop that he had left his handicap placard home. The Pig accused him of being argumentative and then pulls him out of his car and pushes him on the ground. This frail old man had to be somewhere in his early 80's."

"So, you had to get involved?"

"Honestly, I did try and ignore it, but the Pig took a lot of liberties with the "N" word and threatened to arrest him. The black man begged him to let him move his car. I told the Pig I was in a hurry and needed him to move his police car. Hey! he was impeding traffic." Dylan rolled his eyes in disbelief. "When I got into his squad car to move it for him, he came after me. I had to defend myself, right?"

"When Stone, hell! the FBI, sees the marks on that cop's neck, they're going to be knocking our door down for answers!" Dylan exclaimed rubbing the stress from his forehead. "Were there any witnesses?"

"Just a kid, probably six and likely the old man's grandson. I admit I was feeling a bit of concern, him being a police officer and all. But when I looked up and saw that little boy in the rear window of his grandad's car with a huge smile and his little thumb pointed up, the shame disappeared." Thomas completed his story nonchalantly, his lips drawn back showing his pearly white teeth and his elation. He popped another steroid cocktail into his mouth and washed it down with his beer.

"You need to slow down on taking that shit," Dylan insisted. "You keep abusing and that dope will make your heart explode."

Thomas glared at him for the first time that Dylan could recall. "I don't need you to tell me what's good for me. You're not Jack."

"And you believe Jack would approve?"

"You obviously don't know who Jack was," Thomas scorned. Also, for the first time, Dylan felt the weaker. Thomas's voice sounded deeper and older. He had grown larger and much stronger in a very short period.

"I don't understand you anymore."

"Jack took care of me because his Son was too shit faced to take on the responsibility. He gave up a lot, including his life because of me."

"You can't just randomly start killing people Thomas. It makes you no better than the Nazis. And it's not your fault Jack is gone."

Thomas's face flushed with anger, "How dare you judge me!" He slammed his fist on the kitchen table and pointed an accusatory finger at Dylan. "How many executions have you carried out? A hundred? A thousand?"

"You're not thinking clearly!" Dylan pleaded. His heart feeling the pains of Thomas's love strings pulling away from it. "In the Creed, we depend on each other. Each blood-letting is calculated and systematically planned. You have to adhere to the Code. Period!"

"Creed! Code! Fuck all that shit!" Thomas swept his hand across the table. Condiments flew across the room and shattered against the cabinets. He stood abruptly, grabbed his trench-coat off the back of the adjacent kitchen chair and walked out toward the front door of the house.

"Where are you going?" Dylan called after him.

"Don't follow me!"

Dylan, still propped against the fridge door, felt helpless and afraid. Afraid that he was losing Thomas to some monster who possessed him. He lifted the wall phone off It's cradle and dialed Estella's Hotel room. "Hello," pause… "It's Thomas, he's out of control." …pause… "He left on the skinhead's Harley." …pause… "He's gone rogue… pause…How would I know?" …pause… "Do you know where this place is?" …pause… "I'll wait for you to get here."

30 Minutes Later
The Cactus Bar, Market Street

"I swear that's RJ's Harley," the brawny salt and pepper haired Peckerwood exclaimed, lightly smacking another younger Peckerwood on the shoulder to get his attention. Both men had already mounted their bikes. They took their bike helmets off and watched as Thomas kicked the bike-stand down with his foot and swung his left leg over the seat.

Thomas was defiant of the helmet law, and was mindful that he was being observed. "You boys have a problem?"

"As a matter of fact, we do," the older challenged. "Where did you get that bike? It belongs to a friend." Both Peckerwoods dismounted their bikes and began to approach Thomas.

"Not anymore," Thomas dismissed them. "It belongs to me now." Nonchalantly, Thomas released the strap securing his trench-coat to the bike rack, and draped himself in it. Both Peckerwoods stopped a few yards from Thomas when it became apparent that the he resembled that of the vigilante vampires. A sudden nervous chill caused the hair on their arms to stand up, concerned about the modus operandi of recent murders.

The elder of the two managed to keep his gangster posture, "You're the vampire freak that killed RJ."

"Honestly, I wish had, but, nope, that's strike two," Thomas replied, impervious to their threat. Thomas took note that both men were wearing iron knuckles. He gripped the laser gun in the left lower pocket of his trench-coat.

Raising both arms in a combat position and cupping the iron knuckles on his right hand with his left, the older Peckerwood wanted to save face with the younger. "Pete, I think we need to teach this child a lesson. What do you think?"

"Sure," Pete, his sycophant apprehensively agreed.

Thomas said with a sarcastic smirk, "Damn, I'd say that's strike three you're out." With haste, Thomas drew the laser and pulled the trigger, pointing the hot blue light at the Peckerwood's iron knuckles.

Smoke and stench of burnt flesh escaped from under the iron rings. "You're on fire!" Pete cried out!

"Mother Fucker!" the behemoth wailed out in excruciating pain, trying to shake the melting iron off his fingers.

The elder Peckerwood vehemently shook his hand. Instead, it caught his beard on fire and burned away part of his mustache and greasy long hair. With third degree burns on his face and burnt away finger flesh still hanging on the glowing red iron knuckles, he turned away from Thomas. "Son of a bitch! Oh my God! Let's get the hell out of here Pete." Both gangsters hurried to their bikes, drove over the gutter, knocking over a letter-drop-box and news stand. Their helmets fell from their bikes and rolled until they were stopped by the curb.

"Sorry you couldn't stay for the party," Thomas muttered under his breath.

The entrance door to the bar flung open. A goliath of a man, wearing only a leather jacket, cut at the sleeves, stepped out with suspense written all over his face. His female hustler was hanging on his shoulder wearing leather pants and a tight crop top shirt, exposing the lower half of her breasts. He surveyed both directions down the sidewalk and fixed his stare on Thomas. "We heard a man yell. Did you see anything."

Thomas pointed to his right ear with his left hand and made a grunt sound as if he were deaf.

"Figures," the behemoth beast smirked. Thomas started to walk past him into the bar. The doorman put out his arm barricading him from entering. "I. D." he demanded exaggerating the pronunciation of each letter with his lips.

Animus toward his grandfather's killers intensified the SR chemistry running through his veins. Before the doorman could take his next breath, Thomas raised his knee hard into the man's groin, clenched his extended arm, and swung him head first into the brick wall. David had shellacked Goliath, now sprawled bleeding out on the concrete sidewalk. His whore stood, like petrified wood, with her mouth frozen open in shock.

"Sorry about your boyfriend miss," Thomas responded with farcical empathy. "Let me make it up to you." He embraced her, pinning her arms at her side with his eyes on the spot of his next blood-letting.

"Pervert, get off me," She tried to scream but his robust compression around her rib cage allowed no oxygen to enter or escape. The lavender fragrance of her perfume was sweet and entrapping. He couldn't control his attraction to it and tasted it with his tongue. His lips pressing a tight seal over her pulsating artery. Thomas bit through the tender flesh hard and began to imbibe the metal fluid pumping in rhythm from Its source.

Thomas decanted her rather quickly. He found it odd that her pulse was rapid and hard, as if her heart was being squeezed. Then the world around him began to spin. The light spray from the neon sign was blurry. Every object in his environment, out of focus. Thomas began to feel nauseated, then vertigo. "What's happening to me," he slobbered the words mixed with drool from his mouth. He was losing consciousness. Suddenly, not so untouchable, rather vulnerable and scared. "Dylan!" he cried out, then blackout. He released his victim.

Both Vampire and whore fell to the concrete. She was a user. Needle marks riddled her forearms. She had just shot up. Her drug of choice, most likely heroin. He would have known that had he kept with the Creed. They would have seen the warning signs. They would have stopped him.

Car horns blaring at rubberneckers impeding traffic, who slowed to watch the debacle. "Awe, the vulture has fallen from Its nest," exclaimed Bruce, bartender and owner of the Cactus Club. A small group of bar clientele gathered around the crime scene. A small contingency of Peckerwood clientele and members of other aligned gangs.

"Monica!" cried out a petite female at the sight of her pale lifeless friend. She immediately knelt beside her and held her head in her lap. Grieving tears inundated her cheeks.

"Get him inside!" Bruce demanded of two male regulars. "Wait, he maybe faking it." Bruce cautiously moved toward Thomas's outstretched body and kicked the point of his cowboy boot into Thomas's rib cage. He didn't flinch or move. Slowly Bruce knelt beside him and felt Thomas for a pulse. "He's still alive. Carl! You and Stan help me with this one. The rest of you help put Don and Monica in the cooler. I'll worry about what to do with them later. Now! What are you waiting for, the Cops!" Bruce, normally second string to Paul Coombs, was feeling more like the local Kingpin.

"Do you want me to notify Yarbrough?" Barbara asked timorously as she knew Bruce detested him. Her wine bottle figure didn't sell well for lap dancing. But she was good with the books.

Bruce knew the dire consequences of not informing Gary Yarbrough. "Fuck him! Second thought, tell him I have a gift for him."

"Will do," she replied obediently and disappeared through the crowd of Peckerwoods.

Bluegrass banjo's brazenly boomed from the ceiling speakers in the bar. But the small bar crowd was silent. Dice cups were no longer slamming the bar top. The topless ladies had covered up and were standing rather than sitting on their boyfriend's laps. The bartender was no longer pouring beer from the taps. All eyes were on the limp young Native American youth, cloaked in a black trench-coat his captors had dragged him in on.

They had felt safe in numbers. Sheltered between the walls of the Cactus Bar. The past month, they had felt the pain of losing friends, the same reprobates they had shared their brutal adrenalin kicks with. No one was too thrilled about being on the streets alone at night. But more importantly, they were running out of money. Purse snatching profits, business security fees for operating on their turf, drug profits, all dried up. Hell, even the pimps were afraid to be on the streets. It was a damn shame, but the big guns were in town to remove the problem.

Barbara reappeared from the office with a sedative evil grin. "Gary says to put a bullet in his head before he comes to and kills every one of you dumb mother-fuckers."

Bruce's head dipped as he grimaced and said under his breath, "I wish that son of a bitch would go back to Idaho." He raised and shook his head in disgust, knowing well that Gary was right, had managed to shame him once again.

"Go on do it!" Barbara emboldened him. "Get your gun and shoot the bastard!"

Bruce walked behind the bar and reached down below the register and pulled out his Glock 18 handgun from the shelf. He released the safety and held it to his side. He had only used it once to stop a fist to cuff from becoming a bar brawl. The hole in the ceiling was proof and a reminder to the clientele that he would use it again. "Carl, Stan, drag him in the back room."

"Back room." Thomas heard only those words as he faded in and out of consciousness. But he was still dizzy, head pounding as hard as his heart in his chest. His left eye managed to open slightly to the light. "Dylan," he muttered.

"Shoot him!" Barbara cried out. "He's coming to Bruce! For God's sake shoot him!"

Sudden apprehension caused Carl and Stan to take a few steps back. Thomas managed to get his right eye opened only to see the barrel of Bruce's Glock poised between his eyes. What had he done? Had he let his uncontrolled temper get himself killed. He was feeling very disappointed in himself.

"Get him up!" Bruce demanded. Carl and Stan kowtowed and raised Thomas up, an arm over each shoulder. Head fallen, his chin pressed against his chest. "Pull his head up so he can see me." Stan complied and clenched a fist of Thomas's licorice black hair and pulled his head back. Bruce drew the back of his left hand ruthlessly across Thomas's face. His ring sliced his cheek from ear to mouth and left a streak of blood. "That was for Paul Coombs." Still holding the handgun in the direction of Thomas's forehead, Bruce raised his knee like a sledgehammer into Thomas's groin. His face wrinkled inward with unbearable pain. They released him and Thomas collapsed on the floor. "That was for the

Klan, Geronimo." Bruce extended his arm and moved his index finger over the trigger. "And this is for…"

"No!" Dylan's acrid scream filled the bar as the entrance door flew off its hinges, shattering into shards of wood as it crashed into the pin ball machine. Bruce turned abruptly and fired the shot aimlessly. Before him, the phantom of his fear, now nose to nose, eye to eye. Dylan slammed him to the ground with brute force, grasped his wrists and shook the weapon from his right hand. It spun on the floor and stopped under an empty table. "And this is for Jack."

"Fuck you." Bruce glared at Dylan with contempt. Wrists pinned above his head, he released one hand and connected Bruce's jaw with a sucker-punch. The blow knocked him out. Tempting as it was to feed on him, he knew there was a bigger threat yet to deal with.

It was thirteen against one, against two, against three, four, five, they kept coming until the large Italian filled the doorway.

A nonconforming, tanned, middle aged male, with no tattoos, reached into his nylon windbreaker for his gun. He was the only other Peckerwood carrying. The vampires weapon of choice was the Chakram, used by the Xena Warriors and Japanese Ninjas. They were effective weapons for incapacitating their enemy and still not killing them if they so desired to be fed. And since they needed a panicked stricken victim with a fast beating heart for the blood-letting, that was their intentional weapon of choice.

Ludovic released the Chakram which shredded the maverick's windbreaker and sliced his arm open to the bone. React to the pain, his fingers squeezed on the trigger. The weapon discharged into the chest of a long-bearded Peckerwood sitting next to him. His friend fell off his bar stool dead. Barbara darted into the back room for cover. The bar room became a blitzkrieg of Chakrams and screams, some meant to kill, some meant to maim.

Lying on his stomach, a Chakram lodged in his gluteus maximus, the once towering furry white supremacist crawled to Bruce's Glock under the table. Grasping it in desperation, turned and fired a shot toward Dylan. The bullet tore through his shoulder. The action was met with a reaction from Heinz who released another Chakram with such force that it guillotined through the Peckerwood's neck. His head, hanging by a few stretched tendons, finally broke free and dropped to the floor. Sprawled under the table, blood gushed from his neck wound, inundating the bar floor.

The blood-letting began. Heinz cornered a trembling younger patron crouched in the corner. He was an easy target and gave himself to Heinz without struggle. Ludovic seized the frantic female lap dancer, still distraught over her dead friend in the cooler. He attacked her from behind. She never knew what bit her. Estella preyed on the frantic, podgy, twenty-something daughter of the Peckerwood who was shot off his bar stool, collateral damage of a miss-fire. Giuseppe caught the fleeing freckled boyfriend of the daughter in a choke hold, and conveniently snacked on him. Fabien disappeared into the backroom and found Barbara crouched behind a broken refrigerator. He slowly approached her like a leopard Its prey, deliberately and tactically. Her brazen contempt of the killer evaporated with each closer step he took. Barbara wished she had listened to Paul Coombs and packed her weapon. His quickened heart beat turned his pupils red, spiking her fear.

"They will find you and kill you," Barbara forewarned him. "You're making a huge mistake!" But her warnings didn't deter him. Nor did he look upon her with pity. She swung and kicked profusely without aim. Fabien caught an extended kick and flipped her on her stomach. Her scream muffled as he fell prostrate over her and twisted Barbara's head to expose his mark. Her body twitched as the ebullition of her heart forced her blood through her wound into Fabien's siphoning draw. Her last thought was Fabien's unimaginable mechanical like strength that rendered her helpless.

Jonathan focused on Dylan's plight. Scanning for a clean cloth, he realized there was nothing clean about this bar. He settled for the bar towel drooped over the register and pressed it against Dylan's wound. The blood had already begun to coagulate and the wound to heal as Doctor Chang's SR remedies performed their magic. Jonathan extended an arm and helped him to his feet. Dylan refused the dirty towel. "I'll be alright. Can you help me with Thomas."

Jonathan knelt beside Thomas and cradled him in his arms, then lifted him off the floor.

"Let's get the hell out of here!" Estelle demanded. They fled through the unsecured threshold and one by one, climbed into the Limo.

Fabien exited the back room to find his friends had left without him. He raced to get to the Limo and took note of Tommy and Macias parked behind the Limo in the black sedan. "The caves!" he shouted at Macias with his elbow out the passenger window.

"We know, see you there!"

Earlier that same day
Sandy's Condo 2:00 p.m.

Sandy's life had been hard. Growing up in Beaumont Mississippi with two skinhead brothers and a widowed Father, Donald. The white supremacists draped the confederate flag on the side of his double-wide trailer house. Donald referred to himself as a Nationalist. He owned a small garage in downtown Beaumont and had a reputation for cutting corners. He never cared much about anything after Sandy's mother unexpectedly died from an aneurism. Don was a proud member of the Klu Klux Klan and dragged his boys to local chapter meetings.

Sandy met Terrance, two years her senior, a high school jock, with no ambition or dreams. She got pregnant with the first of their two daughters at the age of sixteen, dropped out of school. Terrance worked at Don's garage on Beaumont street. But he couldn't support his young family on the wages Donald paid him and they moved into an already crowded home with her Father and two siblings. It was a tumultuous household.

Terrance kept his liberal bias to himself, but didn't miss out on the opportunity to question Sandy's scrupulous skepticism of her family's racism in private. "Sandy, the color of their skin maybe different, but their hearts are the same color and break just as easy."

"You're preaching to the choir," Sandy whispered across her pillow. His face kind, handsome, and honest. "You have to keep your ideas to yourself Terrance. I'm afraid if they found out you like the Coloreds, they'd kill you." Her prediction came to fruition when Terrance secretly moved his family to San Francisco. Donald asked his boys to leave it alone, but they drove to San Francisco anyway to bring their sister back to Mississippi. Terrance was found with a bullet wound to his head sitting in the Pontiac station wagon his brother loaned him.

Paul Coombs, an old acquaintance of the Family, and a childhood friend of Donald's, gave Sandy a job as a cocktail waitress at his bar, the White Owl. Coombs took a liking to the new widow and upgraded her and her two daughters into a furnished condo in San Mateo.

She knew it was a stupid idea, but the girls had personal items they begged their mother to retrieve from the condo. Some feminine products and picture albums. Giuseppe had warned her that it wasn't safe for her to get within a mile of the place. She hadn't been in touch with Peckerwoods since their last meeting, announcing the arrival of the Klu Klux Klan ranking file. She played it safe and called an old bar patron, that was fond of her, to learn of the rally at the Hawk Campground.

Taped to her condo door was an eviction notice from the bank and a repossession notice to sell. She tore it off the door and stuffed it in her Louis Vuitton purse. "Shit!" she exclaimed despairingly. Since Coombs death and the White Owl closing, she had no job and no income.

She located the house key on her key ring and inserted it into the door knob, terrified the bank may have changed the lock. But it still worked. Oddly, she felt anxious stepping into her own abode. A place where normally she could destress and let her guard down, suddenly, she was feeling apprehensive about being there.

"Hello Sandy," a familiar voice calmly said from behind her. Most likely he'd heard her approach and hid next to her door. In her peripheral, she caught a glimpse of Mike Tate, an Owl regular and muscleman of the Peckerwood Gang.

"We missed you at Sunday's picnic," Gary Yarbrough stated from the lounge chair in the living room. "I was looking forward to your potato casserole. Damn Shame you know."

"So, I had a family emergency," Sandy shrugged. "You're going to pay me a visit and pull a gun on me because I didn't feed your fat face Gary?"

"Wow," Gary said starring at the floor and shaking his head disingenuously. "Coombs had a way of surrounding himself with dangerous women."

"You'll never be the leader Paul Coombs was," Sandy shamed him.

"Sit down!" Gary shouted infuriated at her comment and pointed to the leather chair across from him. "You have no idea who you have double-crossed Sandy." His voice gradually getting louder with each syllable.

"What the hell are you talking about?"

Yarbrough removed a small audio recording cassette tape machine from his shirt pocket and pushed play. Sandy swallowed the acid reflex from the sudden fear she felt for her life. Had they tapped her phone? The recorded voice was hers. "Hi, Giuseppe, is Doctor Chang hurt? He clicked off the recording.

"Sandy, Sandy, Sandy," Yarbrough chagrinned, displeased with her betrayal. "We knew we had a mole, but I must admit, you really had us duped. But now I know it was you that tipped Chang off. You cost me millions Sandy. How would you feel if you were me?" He patronized her. "Now this. Oh, the joke will be on your blood sucking friends. The ceremonial cleansing will go on."

"You mean the lynching Gary," She rebuked.

"It's God's wrath for crimes against his people. But now you'll get to witness it first-hand because you'll be joining them." He paused and pinched her chin between his fingers and held her head up so she could look him directly in his eyes. "You know what the penalty is for being a mole? This is on You Sandy." He stood and began to walk toward the door. "Sedate her and take her to the warehouse."

"They're going to kill you Gary!" Sandy frantically warned.

"Oh, them," Gary stopped again and smirked, "Lucky You, you'll get to see the ambush tonight. Oh, something else. I spoke with your Dad this morning. Told him the bad news about your unfortunate accident. He wasn't aware that Junior was missing. Did you have something to do with that too? Your other brother will be here in two days to pick up your girls. Your daughters will be great white Nationalist someday, Sandy."

Sandy's eyes widened with new fear, "You leave my girls alone, you hear..." The chlorophyll-soaked rag was pressed hard over her mouth and face. She collapsed into Mike Tate's arms.

Sandy's Apartment
3:10 p.m.

"Is this Giuseppe?" He immediately recognized that she was hysterical.

"What's wrong Natalie?" He appealed from the other end of the phone call.

"I don't know where my mom is," she began to cry. "She went to the condo to get some of our things and hasn't returned."

"Are you at home?"

"Yes."

"I'll be right there. Lock the door."

"I hear a motorcycle in the drive way, hurry."

"I'm sure your mom will be back soon. Calm down, I'm on my way."

"Please hurry."

3:27 p.m.

"Slow zis down you kill us before we gezair," Fabien demanded from the back seat of the black sedan.

"Thank you for coming Carol."

"It's not a problem Giuseppe," She reassured him.

"I would have asked Estelle to come, but she is overwhelmed right now." Ludovic sat quietly in the front passenger seat, not sure what to expect once they arrived at Sandy's apartment. "I just don't do well with kids."

"I think under that tough manly façade there's a gentle giant."

"I hope I get to meet that guy someday. This is it," Giuseppe stated pointing at the apartment and bouncing the sedan over a speed bump. "That's Junior's motorcycle all right, his brother must be in town. This is someone else, I have a bad feeling about this."

"I hate this guy already," Carol repulsed.

Tanya heard the sedan pull into the parking lot in front of the apartment and ran out sobbing, hugged Giuseppe as he emerged from the car. "Where's my mom?"

Giuseppe held her close. "I'm sure she's fine," he tried to suppress her fears.

"But she's always here when we get out of school."

"Who's in the house with your sister Tanya?"

"Uncle Rusty." Tanya answered loathingly. "I hate him Giuseppe. Can you take us away from here?"

"Sure," he reassured her. He took her hand and began to walk to the front of the sedan. "I want you to meet some friends of mine. They've come to help us.

She hesitated, taken back by their Albinism, she pressed closer into Giuseppe. "Hi, I'm Carol," Carol smiled and extended her hand. Tanya hesitated and then offered an anemic hand. "This is Fabien and his twin brother, Ludovic."

"Are you a vampire too?" Tanya's childish veracity took Carol by surprise.

"No dear," Carol suppressed an intrusive chortle. "Are you?" She attempted a little humor to lighten the moment.

Tanya grinned between the tears and sniffs, "No."

"That's good, I have too many of them already in my life." Fabien shot her a puzzled squint.

"Let's go check on your Sister," Giuseppe cut their small talk off and headed into the apartment. The others followed behind.

Tanya had left the front door open. Giuseppe caught a glimpse of Rusty, who, other than having a pony tail, had familiar family resemblances. Through the screen door, standing behind the couch, where Natalie was sitting by the phone, Rusty was running his fingers through her hair. "Keep your hands off me," She insisted, vexed by his incessant molestations. But he didn't drop the strands he had running through his fingers. Instead he grasped them tightly in his fist, slightly forcing her head back.

The screen door flung open, slamming into the wall behind it. "Take your hands off her you piece of shit!" Rusty tightened his grip then flipped her hair over her face. Natalie darted from the couch and ran to Giuseppe's side. He turned to Carol, still waiting to enter the apartment. "Carol, take the girls and wait for me in the car please."

"Come on dear," Carol motioned for Natalie to follow her.

"You little bitch, your mother's not coming home!" Rusty wailed out words meant to cut deep and hurt. "She's a god damn mole!" Rusty's voice got louder the further Natalie got out the door.

Giuseppe looked behind him to see that Natalie had collapsed in Carol's arms.

Rusty didn't like his odds and presumed it would not end well for him. He bellowed one last dagger as Giuseppe closed the door. "They're going to kill her just like they killed your father!"

"Now that's not a very nice thing to say about your sister Rusty," Giuseppe patronized, with a disingenuous grin.

They were alone. Suddenly Rusty's defiant attitude turned to fear. "You must be my Sister's creepy boyfriend. You're all dead. The Klan has come to town." Rusty looked around for a secondary escape. A door, window, or some type of object he could use as a weapon. Giuseppe took one step toward him and opened his trench coat. Rusty took two steps backwards in unison.

"Thanks to your sister, I won't have to wait for the Klan. I'll get to meet these creeps first hand tonight." Giuseppe took another step toward Rusty. Rusty dashed for the bedroom. But he didn't get far as Giuseppe blocked his entrance. "Leaving already? We didn't get to finish our conversation. I was hoping to explain the unfortunate death of your brother Junior."

"You bastard." Rusty was visibly shaken, and took a swift step backwards from him. Stumbling, he grabbed onto the back of the couch, bracing himself from falling backwards. "Look dude, you don't want Sandy to find out that you murdered me and my brother."

"I wouldn't be too sure. She might thank me after she learns that her own brothers were sexually abusing and prostituting out her daughters." Giuseppe's playful humor turned to raging indignation. His voice deeper, "Scum like you are the lowest and most repulsive living creatures. I think I'm about to do you both a favor." Giuseppe slowly approached Rusty, now pinned against the wall. Not breaking eye contact, Giuseppe pulled two zip ties from an inside pocket of his trench coat.

"What, you think I'm going to just let you kill me?" Rusty scoffed.

"Why would I think that?" Before Rusty could respond, Giuseppe poked two fingers into Rusty's eye sockets. As he raised his arms to block him, Giuseppe grasped his right wrist and twisted it behind him. He then pinned the other arm behind Rusty's back and secured one zip tie around both wrists. Rusty screamed with excruciating pain as Giuseppe pulled the zip tie tight. Blood oozed from where the zip tie cut through his tan sun baked flesh. Raising Rusty's bound arms up high behind his back, he forced Rusty forward into the kitchen and tossed him onto the floor. He slammed his foot into Rusty's gut. He coughed.

Giuseppe's eyes roamed the spice rack on the counter and pulled the small glass cinnamon spice bottle from the rack. "Open your mouth!"

"Fuck you!" Rusty screamed defiantly then began to sob.

"Fine, we'll do it the hard way," Giuseppe tightly pinched his nose closed. Rusty's lungs became depleted of oxygen. He caved in and gasped for air. Giuseppe had unscrewed the cap off and shoved the entire bottle into Rusty's mouth. He tapped hard on the bottom until the bottle was empty. Giuseppe released his fingers from Rusty's nose and covered his mouth so that he couldn't spit the cinnamon out. He coughed the powder through his nostrils and began to choke.

That was Giuseppe's clue. With his left forearm pressed against Rusty's chin, he forced his head back, exposing his hard-pulsing arteries either side of his Adam's apple.

"I commit you to hell," Giuseppe stated as if performing an exorcism. Rusty's eyes opened wide with terror, as Giuseppe's lips drew back over his gums and exposed his razor-sharp scissors. The sting of Giuseppe's fangs ripping through Rusty's neck wasn't as painful as he had imagined it would be. Unable to breath, Rusty felt numb. He became light headed, a waxen pale shade, and finally the lights went out. Locked in the imbibing blood-letting, the metallic thick blood rolled like a rushing brook over Giuseppe's tongue and down his throat. He left the carcass for the landlord. Rent wasn't due for three weeks. Plenty of time for the local rat and mice community to oblige.

Johnson's Hardware Store 5:00 p.m.

"Freddie's memorial is Friday, are you going?" Joey asked Alice, the new interim store manager.

"I don't think so Joey," she replied struggling to reconcile the day shift receipts on the office desk. "I really don't do well at those things."

"Freddie would want you to be there," Joey insisted without empathy.

Alice unintentionally ignored Joey as she wrote in the currency and check amounts on the day shift deposit slip. "Another slow day," she chagrinned. The pen ran out of ink. "Can you hand me a new pen. They're in the second drawer," she said pointing to the cabinet against the office wall.

"Blue or black," he asked taking note of the two different boxes in the drawer.

"Blue, always blue for identifying originals from copies."

"Makes sense," Joey nodded, still the student. He punched his card out right at five o'clock and hung his name badge on the hook above the punch clock on the wall.

"Is your friend Jonathan still interested in working at Johnson's?" Alice asked, zipping up the bank deposit bag. "There's still an opening on swing shift."

"He does, but I'd rather he not work here," Joey grimaced. "I don't need tensions in our relationship."

Alice rolled her eyes with a smirk, "Yea, working with you has it challenges."

"Really?" He winced knowing she was having fun at his expense.

"He seems like a really nice guy. I think he'd do well at Johnsons."

"He's a flake."

"Says the guy who is madly in love with him," She cajoled.

"Besides he doesn't need the job," Joey defunct her persistent query. "He's come into a lot of money."

"Rich Daddy," Alice taunted raising her brow with a simper from ear to ear.

"Something like that," Joey played it off.

"Lucky You. You better hook this guy."

"Mind your business," He replied adamantly as he kissed her cheek and left the office.

"Bye."

The access to the employee parking, located in the basement of Johnson's Hardware Store, is a narrow alleyway to Hartford Street. During the winter solstice, the only light to navigate safely to your vehicles are the two lamps attached to conduit from the power box on the main level. It's especially dangerous if one of the lamps is burned out. Regardless of sunlight, the basement is still dark without both lights, as it was this day. Joey was driving Fabien's 65 Mustang he had loaned to Jonathan at Jonathan's request.

But Joey wouldn't be driving back the mustang to their new apartment, where Jonathan had been pacing anxiously for him to come home. Jonathan was entertaining bad thoughts of terrible things that could be delaying Joey. Dwelling on the thought that perhaps Joey had to work late. "But damn it, he at least could have called him by now. He's nearly an hour late.

Finally, the phone rang. Jonathan ran to pick it up. But it wasn't Joey.

"Where the hell are you?" Dylan stressed from the other end of the phone call. "We're all at the cave but you." Dylan and Giuseppe had driven the Sedan to the nearest phone booth closest to the Sutro Baths located on Point Lobos Avenue.

"Joey hasn't got home yet. I'm worried about him."

"Did you call Johnson's?"

"I know, it seems like the reasonable thing to do," Jonathan replied.

"Da," Dylan mocked at his lack of common sense.

"I just don't want him to feel smothered."

"We have to be at the campground before six o'clock," Dylan continued to castigate. "We're leaving soon. You better get here!"

"Alright!" Jonathan acquiesced, "I'll call the Hardware store right now."

"You had better get your butt over here now!"

"Alright! Just give me a few." Dylan hung up on him. "Shit!"

Jonathan removed Joey's business card, which was pinched between the wall phone casing and the sheetrock. He pushed the key on the phone pad relevant to the number on the card. It rang.

"Johnson's Hardware," an unfamiliar female voice answered.

"Is Joey there?"

"Umm," there was an uncomfortable moment of silence. "You'd better speak with Alice. Let me get her."

"This can't be good," Jonathan thought anxiously to himself.

"Is this Jonathan?" Alice's voice sounded anguished and weak.

"Yes."

"Something has happened to Joey," Alice tried to explain.

"Say he's alright Alice!" Jonathan asseverated.

"They don't know, he's missing," Alice became despondent.

"What do you mean he's missing? Who's they? How do you know? Talk to me Alice!

"He left just before I did," Alice explained. "I saw that his car was still in the garage. The driver's door was left open. No signs of a struggle, but the police found his keys under the Mustang."

"Are the police still there?"

"Just forensics. They're sweeping for fingerprints," Alice's voice was broken with grief and began to lose it. "I'm scared! Who are these people? First Freddie, now Joey, who's next?"

Jonathan's nerves wrenched his stomach with anger and heartsick fear. "Look Alice, we don't know what's happened to Joey. But, we have to hope for the best. I can't explain right now, but I need you to do something."

"OK," She strained to hold her emotions.

"This may sound somewhat insensitive, but I'm not coming down to the Hardware Store. I need you to call the San Francisco Police Department and ask for Detective Sam Stone. Make sure he is aware that Joey is missing."

"I don't understand," She answered puzzled.

"And secure my friend's car. I'll have to pick it up tomorrow. Now don't forget to call Detective Stone!"

"Why can't you call him?"

"I can't explain right now. There's something I have to do," Jonathan demanded with compunction.

"I will, I promise."

"Thank you, Alice," Jonathan extoled. "I'll be back in touch real soon."

San Francisco Police Department
Bite Case

FBI agent Manis stood to the side of the six-foot high, clear plexiglass mobile board, designated for the Bite Case time line. A second board was wheeled in to accommodate the volume of related activity. There were pictures of male and female victims with their names written with erasable black marker. Down the first row, under the title "White Supremacist Victims", were the names of Vaughn Muller and Jadwiga Dzido.

Manis had insisted on referring to the White Supremacists as Terrorists, fueled by his strong sentiment that these hoodlums were not worthy of being classified as law abiding citizens. After all, he'd been tracking The Order, or Silent Brotherhood, as they preferred, for just over five years. His experience was that they met the legal definition of what a terrorist is and inevitably were behind the nefarious crimes.

A second category was labeled "Collateral Victims" where the pictures of Fredric Garcia and Carol Turley were posted above their names, also hand-written with black erasable marker. These were individuals not classified as being members of any group or cause.

A lone person was featured under the third category, which was labeled "Missing," Dr. Huey Chang. Many of the names provided to the FBI by Detective Stone.

On the supplemental board, a list of suspects under both titles, Vigilantes and Supremacists.

"I'll post today's nine dead Peckerwoods as soon as forensics confirms their names," Agent Cooper stated, facing six feet in front of the primary board and to Agent Manis's right.

"We have to get ahead of this war, damn it," Agent Manis cussed quiescently, staring at the board of casualties. "Any progress with the Peckerwood in custody?"

"We now know that Jason is the Son of this guy," Agent Cooper pointed to the picture of Clive Anderson on the Suspect Board.

"Jason Anderson," Manis repeated his name for no reason. "Still no leads on where his o'le man is?"

Agent Ferris, sitting in front of a small desk, wrestled with documents in a manila folder. "None, but surveillance has produced a video from the KFC across from the White Owl showing Clive greeting two men before going into the bar. The three men walked down one block and got into this red jeep. The video is too grainy to make out the vehicle's license plate number."

"Do we know the MO on the two men Clive met with?" Agent Manis inquired.

"Again, the video is not clear, but one of the men we believe is Bud Jenkins," replied Agent Ferris.

"What is the Grand Cyclops of the Birmingham Chapter doing in San Francisco?"

Agent Ferris held up a tattered old picture from the folder taken in 1968, "Jenkins is this young George Wallace campaign worker standing behind Wallace. This was a speech Wallace gave in Nashville."

"That would explain the sightings of three other high-profile Klansmen in the last week," Cooper added.

"Something big is going down," Agent Manis chagrinned. "I hope we're not too late."

Agent Cooper removed his glasses and rubbed the fatigue from his eyes. "Wonder if the press knows anything."

"I'd rather join the Klan than kowtow to those sleaze bags," Manis snapped.

A mammoth black Agent entered without knocking, "He's talking. But he wants immunity for his Dad before he tells us anything."

"Well he's not getting it," Agent Manis said adamantly. "Remind me what the circumstances are behind this kid's arrest?"

"He's one of the two survivors of today's massacre at the Cactus. Stone and his men found him hiding in the walk-n cooler with the two stiffs," Ferris responded.

"Did you say how old this kid is?" Manis inquired of Agent Ferris.

Ferris flipped through his documents and found the profile for Jason. "twenty-three."

Agent Manis deliberated for a few seconds, "Old enough to know too much and young enough to break. I need to talk to this kid now. Is Stone still interrogating him?"

Agent Cooper sighed, "Speaking of Stone."

Detective Stone entered the makeshift office on a mission and walked over to the case board and grabbed an erasable marker, "May I?"

"This is your house," Manis shrugged.

Stone wrote the names of Joey Sanders and Sandy Montgomery. He then removed Joey and Sandy's pictures from the suspect column and reposted them under the names he wrote in the "Missing column." "This one," Stone explained, pointing to Sandy's picture, "A Catholic priest reported her missing an hour ago. We found her car and purse at her condo. I'm curious as to why she's temporarily living in an apartment. The landlord stated that she had moved and owed on the last month's rent. I believe she's been shacking up with one of the vigilantes, this guy." He pointed to Giuseppe's picture. Many of the pictures were taken by surveillance teams as they entered and left the Hospice. "She's the one that Doctor Chang claims shot her boss in self-defense. Stone then pointed to Joey's picture. "Joey moved apartments as well. We still haven't located it as he usually takes the BART. The manager at Johnson's Hardware called 911 with a 10-65 a couple of hours ago. My detectives responded and found his car still parked in the garage with the driver's door left wide open and the car keys laying on the cement floor next to the vehicle. He had just finished his shift. The vehicle is registered to a Fabien Dubois. This guy." Stone pointed to Fabien's picture in the Vigilante's column. "Strange that no one will cooperate naming these Vigilantes as suspects." Stone turned up his bottom lip in sarcastic rebuke, "But they sure in the hell don't hesitate calling us when they need help."

"Come with me Stone," Agent Manis demanded. "You know this case as well if not better than anyone. We need to interrogate this kid again. Is he still in there or have they taken him back to his jail cell?"

"He's still there. I was planning on returning for round two."

Manis smiled, "Great, we conjured up an aiding and abetting charge to arrest him on if he doesn't talk."

"My lips are sealed," Stone said with raised brow with a sarcastic grin.

Interrogation Room

Jason Anderson wasn't the cocksure person that followed his merciless reputation with his Dad's fellow Peckerwood gang members. His sweat dotted his forehead. Moments of shaking from Stone's hours of harassment. His normal dauntless and crude attitude, drained from his core as he heard and later saw the horrific blood-letting as police marched him out of the Cactus Bar.

Aside from the cameras, lone desk and facing chairs at each end, the cement interrogation room had no windows, only a one-way observation glass to the adjacent room.

"Jason, I'm FBI Agent, Manis, and you already know Detective Stone."

"Unless you meet my demands, I have nothing to say to you. Anderson became defiant."

Manis was the best in his field when it came to interrogations. "We're considering your demands, which quite frankly confuse us. I presume that Clive Anderson is your Father right?"

"Why do you want information on him?"

"Your Father isn't being charged at this time with a crime. Unless you know something that might implicate Clive in a crime we know nothing about." Detective Stone stood silent with a grin, amazed at Manis's natural talent of bullshitting. Agent Manis walked behind Jason Anderson and patted him on the shoulders. "Jason, Jason, Jason, we believe your Father and his associates are walking into a trap."

"What do you mean?" Jason responded with unexpected concern.

Manis walked back to the empty chair facing Jason and sat down with both elbows on the table and his fingers laced together under his chin. "Do you believe in vampires Jason?"

Jason paused to answer then swallowed hard, "No."

"Are you sure?" Manis patronized. "You took a moment to answer my question. I mean, you saw what they did to your buddies. Your friends are some pretty tough guys, wouldn't you say?"

"They're freaks of nature. They out gunned us that's all," Jason insisted, still trying to rationalize what he saw.

Detective Stone tossed a confiscated Chakram on the table. "With this?" Stone guffawed. "How do you explain the neck wounds Jason?"

Agent Manis leaned forward toward Jason. "You see, Detective Stone and I, have conflicting opinions about the vampires."

"Vampires?" Jason challenged. "You're both as crazy as they are!"

"Oh! they're real," Stone interrupted, playing along with Manis's chicanery. "The difference between Agent Manis and I, is that I like 'em because they keep perps and criminals, like you, off the street."

"Now Detective," Manis continued with his subterfuge. "Both Mr. Anderson, and I, know you can't go around killing people just because they're different from you. Don't we Jason?" The similarity of the Supremacist's racist cleansing struck a nerve with Jason. He didn't respond. "We're running out of time Jason. There's a rumor on the street that the Klan has come to town and something big is going down. There's been no petition for a rally, so it's gotta be something else. Like an Initiation ceremony." Manis paused, "Or a Cleansing ceremony. We also have from a reliable source that the Vampires are planning to crash the party. It's going to be another blood bath, just like the one at the Cactus today. A lot of people could die Jason. One of those fatalities could be, most likely will be, your Father."

"What will happen to him if you stop it?

"That's a fair question Jason," Agent Manis said empathetically, knowing Jason was about to spill his guts. "We could plea with the judge that your Father was helpful to us, and you and your Father walk."

"They'll find out, no, they'll kill him," Jason argued despondently. "Besides, you having nothing on me."

"Come on Jason, Aiding and Abetting, it's all in the report." Manis lied. "Your Father serves a few days in jail to make it seem like he did time, they'll never suspect anything. And we'll drop the charges against you."

There was a short-lived silence as he contemplated their offer. "What do you need to know?" Jason Acquiesced.

"You're doing the right thing Jason," Stone chimed in.

Jason shot Stone a cold glare. "I'm only speaking with the FBI."

"Can you leave us Detective?" Agent Manis insisted. All part of the scheme.

7:30 p.m. Marin City
Suite at Traveler's Hotel

"The police just announced that the body found at Lake Merced was Junior's. The newspaper also states that the body was discovered by three teenagers playing near the Merced Bridge." Luther Pierce turned the cover page of the San Francisco Chronicle to page A-3. "Cause of death, Exsanguination from a human bite wound to the neck." Pierce tossed the paper onto the coffee table in front of him. "Exsanguination! Pierce shook his head in distain. "Why can't these Liberal journalists speak English."

"It means, to drain a body of all It's blood," Danny added without Malice. Danny was Luther's body guard, six foot three and highly educated.

"I know what the fuck it means," Pierce castigated.

Danny couldn't decide what he detested more, his job or having to listen to his imbecile boss all day. He rolled his eyes at Pierce's comment.

"It's unnerving Luther," Danny sighed, pretending to care.

"It's like these sicko freaks have it out for us. They have no idea who they're fucking with," Luther replied from behind the paper.

Standing at the panoramic window of the Hotel Suite, Danny scanned below for possible threats and for Gary Yarbrough's armored Suburban. Yarbrough, and members of the Peckerwood gang, would be escorting Luther to the Klan Meeting.

"He's late Danny, we should have just drove there ourselves," Luther cursed.

"Here they come now Mr. Pierce," Danny informed Luther.

"It's about Damn time!" Luther rubbed out his cigar in the ash tray on the coffee table and started toward the door. "Danny, grab my suitcase with my ceremonial robes."

"Yes sir."

Gary Yarbrough, along with the Grand Dragon of the local Realm of the KKK and two of his Hydras, were waiting in the Lobby to greet them. William Luther Pierce, author of the Turner Diaries, another fascist manifesto, was regarded as the architect of white supremacy.

Two men exited the elevator, Gary immediately recognized Pierce from his picture on the back-jacket of the Turner Diaries. The book that always traveled with him in his luggage. "Mister Pierce! What an honor it is to meet you," Gary held out his hand for Pierce to shake.

Luther snubbed him as Gary clumsily, somewhat embarrassed, dropped his hand back to his side. "You must be Yarbrough," Luther inquired, annoyed with formalities and the late pick up.

"That would be me. Welcome to San Francisco."

"We'll talk later," Luther insisted and pointed for Gary to lead the way.

Three Suburban SUVs exited US-101 onto the Rodeo Avenue off ramp which immediately changed to dirt road. The vans spaced themselves as dust from the lead car blocked the driver's visibility. The dirt road was not maintained well, and at times, proved to be a rough ride, bouncing the occupants as tires hit washed away road. "Stay to the left," Yarbrough instructed the driver from the middle bench seat of the lead car. "Then two quick right turns onto Bobcat Trail. You'll stay on that for a while." Yarbrough was flanked on both sides by two high ranking Peckerwood gangsters. "We'll need to arm up somewhere at the top." All seven available passenger spots were occupied. The two following Suburban Vans transported hierarchy of local and visiting Klan. Pierce and Danny sat in the middle bench of the second car.

"Pay attention there's a small turn off that will take you over the hill and to the campground," Gary Yarbrough informed the driver, a medium built twenty-seven-year old, named Mike. "I had to spend six hundred dollars of club funds to reserve this shit hole the County calls a campground."

The Peckerwoods were charged with securing the clandestine ritual where four people were to be executed for crimes against the Order. In the rear compartment of the Suburban, eight AG-043 were stashed. The AG-043 was designed in 1974 by Russian designer, Sergei Gavrilovich Simonov, as a fully automatic assault rifle. The weapon was an improvement of the AK-47.

"Stop here Mike," Yarbrough stated. "Let's arm up boys." The motorcade stopped as they crest the top of the hill. All eight occupants of the lead vehicle got out and commanded an assault rifle and two extra clips, then climbed back into the Suburban. The Peckerwoods were a well-armed militia with enough fire power to challenge any local law enforcement threat.

"Aren't we sitting ducks if we're all in the same vehicle?" Clive Anderson suggested from the rear of the lead Suburban. Clive had just learned that his Son Jason had been arrested at the Cactus bar earlier and his anger was surfacing. His protests to immediately retaliate had fallen on deaf ears.

"Stop worrying about your Son Clive," Mike assured his friend. "We'll get him out. We have connections to the second district judge."

"That's if that whore is right!" Clive redressed. "They could be on their way to Romania for all we know."

"Clive, shut the hell up!" Gary chastised him. "This is no time for debate or dissention." Clive sat directly behind Gary.

"Up yours Gary," Clive excoriated with growing animosity toward him. "Coombs would've thought it through better."

Angered by Clive's constant grumbling, Gary flipped the safety of his rifle off, flung it over his shoulder, and without turning his head to aim, pulled the trigger. Three rounds pierced Clive's torso, one striking his neck. Blood splattered throughout the rear of the SUV. The back window shattered.

"What the fuck Gary," repined RJ, a respected long time Peckerwood. RJ's leather vest exposed his lower belly from years of beer drinking.

"Does anyone else have any objections?" No one dare answer. Their silence was uncertainty of who would or wouldn't corroborate with Gary and take a bullet. "I didn't think so."

Reaching under his seat, Yarbrough removed several sheets of paper containing a bird's eye view of the Hawk Campground and distributed them around. "Note on the map three strategic locations marked with stars. The stars represent bunkers that have been dug with concrete gun mounts we installed yesterday. From these three foxholes, you should have a clear sight on anyone entering the campground."

"Do I go left here Gary?" Mike interrupted, as the dirt road split ahead.

"Yes," Gary responded. "Once over the hill, you'll see several vehicles parked in a field to your right, just before the only trees in the area. Pass them and park behind the folding chairs. Cal and James, you guys take the right position. RJ, you and Stanley follow me. We'll be directly behind the platform where Pierce is speaking. Mike, you and Shorty take the position on the left side of the platform. Only use the foxholes if you're taking fire. Any questions?" There were none. "Good." Yarbrough beamed, "Keep your AGs to your side and look official and stay put until Pierce is finished and the executions are carried out. It's a proud day to be white in America boys."

Knowing it would get unwanted attention from the Klan, the stretch limo was the only vehicle that would accommodate them. As they approached the check point, a half mile from the campground, the sight of a small greeting party gave them pause and consternation.

"Hood up!" Heinz charged. He noticed that one of the three Klansmen caught glimpse of the Limo as they crest the top of the hill. The point of his white hood towered a foot above the other two Greeters, but he paled in body mass. He raised a handheld radio to his mouth. The other two hooded Klansmen had semi-automatics hanging from their shoulders, and one of them a clipboard to his side.

Heinz rolled down his driver's side window as the Limo approached. The taller Klansman with the radio leaned toward his window.

"Code?" The cone head barked.

Heinz reached out his left hand and grasped the greeter's left hand in a normal handshake. Sandy had adamantly warned that extending the right hand would get a bullet response to the head. Heinz then turned the hand of his tester until the back of the Klansman's hand was parallel to the ground, just as Sandy had coached them.

The Klansman locked eyes with Heinz through the small cut outs and stared askance somewhat suspect. "Aren't you forgetting something?" The challenge caused Heinz to panic. The Klansman slowly turned his head toward the other two Klansmen who immediately gripped their guns.

From the front passenger seat, Giuseppe suddenly realized that Sandy had mentioned that there might be a collection. "We have already settled that with Mr. Yarbrough," Giuseppe interjected quickly.

"Great, I'll still need to get confirmation. Wait here," he stipulated and took a few steps away from the driver's door. Unmounting their weapons from their shoulders, the other two greeters held their assault rifles across their chest in the ready for combat position.

"That won't be necessary!" Jonathan called out from the rear of the Limo and extended his right hand across Hein's shoulder and out the driver's side window. In it five crisp one hundred-dollar bills.

Snatching the cash from Jonathan's grip, he replied beaming under his hood, "Your invite clearly stated that we don't make change. You know that right?

"Of course," Heinz stated indifferently. "Consider it a donation."

"Much obliged," he stated blithely and waved them on.

As the limo moved out of earshot, Dylan sighed a breath of relief, "Shit, that was close. Giuseppe you need to think hard on every detail that Sandy gave you. We're lucky that Jonathan had cash on him."

"I don't know why that slipped my mind," Giuseppe apologized shaking his head at the roof of the limo.

Dylan's brow wrinkled inward incredulously at Jonathan, "Where did you get that kind of money? You been saving Muller's allowance?"

"No," Jonathan gave little heed, "Came into a little fortune is all. But don't get too chummy, it's my poor excuse of a Father's savings and I'm donating it to charity."

The Klan hood, designed to protect their identity, also protected the identity of their nemesis mingling with them.

"Don't act aloof," Estella cautioned. "Shake hands and blend in. If anyone asks, you're part of the European Fascist League Contingency. That will explain our accents. And don't be stupid and sit together. Perimeter seating, 360 if possible. Fascists won't allow women in their ranks, so I'm taking refuge in the Stretch."

"I see the gallows," Giuseppe bemoaned, "But I don't see Carol, Chang, or Joey."

"Stay focused Giuseppe," Heinz stated ameliorative. "Don't let your emotions get you killed."

Purple and orange Pastel shades of the dipping Summer Solstice into the ocean's horizon, meant that the bamboo tiki torches would soon be lit. Nightfall would give the Vigilantes the advantage.

The vigilantes were sweating profusely under their ballistic shields that lined their trench coats exacerbated by the second layer of KKK robes. Jonathan argued a medical condition to convince a Klansmen in the back-right corner to trade places with him. Tommy and Estella remained in the Limo to hide their minority condemnation and sure execution.

Armed with handguns and the usual weapons of choice, they sat mixed in with the crowd, masking their fear of the inevitable full-scale assault. However, the inconvenient truth is that their fire power is no match against the Peckerwood's AG-043 assault weapons. But it wouldn't deter their dauntless conviction. It was too little too late to turn back now anyway. Play along, chant along, pretend to be what you detest, and wait for that moment. Pull out your Chrakran and prey for precision skill as if your friends lives depend on it. Because they do. Live or die, tonight would make the history books and the ruse or heroic tale of many motion picture. Yes, Bite your tongue and play along. Had Chang tailored their training for this moment. Their swan song when right and wrong meet head on for perhaps the epoch and final battle.

"What a glorious day for the Klannishness," Luther Pierce stoked the audience. He stood center front of the two-feet high platform.

"Welcome to this impromptu Klonvocation. It's an honor to address you this evening." He turned to two ranking members of the Klan sitting on two of three white folding chairs to his right. "Your introduction was too kind Mr. Siegel. I'll do my best to live up to your expectations. Let me, for those attending from visiting Realms, introduce the two great leaders on stage with me this evening, Grand Dragon of the Realm of California, Doctor William Siegel, and the Klansman responsible for putting this altogether, your Kladd, Mr. Bob Stikes." Both stood hoodless in their robes, pretending to be excited to be before the small audience, now erupting in clapping and cheers. "As Mr. Stikes had stated earlier, I too would like to thank the Peckerwood Organization for providing security and acting as the Klarogo for this Klonvocation." Again, the small crowd cheered and clapped. "But let's get down to business," Luther's demeanor turned from celebratory to sober temerity. "Our Race, the White Race, is a chosen Race, so pure and blessed of God."

"Here! Here!," responded a few over-zealous, caught up in Luther's fire and brimstone.

"But I'm outraged to report," Luther fanned the flames of their indignation, "The chosen Race is under attack by a repulsive liberal media and forces strange to our pure way of life."

"Death to Liberals!" A few answered.

His voice elevated. "They threaten to turn our children homosexual and racially mix with our seed in an attempt to make us extinct."

"Death to Liberals!" they answered enraged.

Luther waited until the chanting calmed. "And your government has sold us out." Pierce continued, "The Pentagon is biogenetically breeding prodigious creatures with herculean strength to wipe out God's Race."

"Hang them all!" Hang them all!" The crowd erupted again to Luther's pleasure.

Dylan and Heinz tilted their heads slightly toward each other and simultaneously rolled their eyes through the tiny peek holes at Luther's nescience.

"We will prevail!" Pierce shouted above the cheers of White Supremacists. He waited for the crowd to settle back down. "But our Aryan Nationalist Leaders are not sitting on their laurels. While the liberal propaganda proliferates, efforts are being made to put a White Nationalist into the White House that represents our pure values. Someone who will call out the degenerate liberal forces for what they are, rapists, murderers, con artists, drug dealers, homosexuals, illegals, and perverts. We will have our day, our President, our Nirvana! It won't come easy. It will take everyone listening to commit to give all to the fight. We must fight like hell or we won't have a Country. It might take America electing a black man to be President to wake the people up. But, mark my words it will happen. America will elect a President who understands our values and will represent White Nationalist Agenda. Today's Klonvocation is a call to arms my brothers. Join David Duke, our supreme leader, to bring this to fruition." The small crowd erupted in cheers of new enthusiasm and chanting incessantly "Duke! Duke! Duke! Luther Pierce grinned ear to ear as he waited for the storm of anxious men to settle.

"A Nigger as president," Yarbrough dismissively stated to RJ, "Over my dead body." RJ nodded affirmatively.

Behind the platform stage, stood a four-feet high twelve-feet long wooden gallows, framed in with two by fours and sheets of plywood. Two upright posts supported a transverse beam with four nooses hanging to match the height of each criminal's neck. Shackled in thick durable metal, the four prisoners to be lynched sat behind the gallows out of the audience's view. Three would die for a crime against the Order, simply being born, the other insubordination.

Luther Pierce spewed his hate Mantra for a Painstaking twenty minutes. "It's time for the cleansing ceremony. The Order's Codes mandate that any person or persons guilty of espionage, being Queer, or indicted for being a traitor, shall be punished by hanging until dead. I present to you four offenders. A black man, whom employed as a journalist at a local rag, disseminated false propaganda against the Order. One of our own who turned into a mole, sharing classified information with the enemy, whom we believed murdered Paul Coombs." Aw's and death chants erupted from a flabbergasted Klan. "A Chink, the scientist, whose formula was used by the government to mutate human hybrids for our demise. And the final prisoner, a known homosexual with ties to the beasts." Luther turned and faced Gary Yarbrough. "Mr. Yarbrough, lead the prisoners to the gallows and send their souls to hell."

Gary postured his assault rifle, and carefully stepped around his fox hole and down the small oblique dirt grade. Once behind the gallows began to shout orders. "On your feet!" Poking the tip of his gun into the Black reporter's skull.

It was an arduous effort for the four famished and beaten prisoners, chained together hand and foot, to stand. Still in his satin blue business suit, now stained in dirt and his own coagulated blood from his beaten face, the middle-aged Black Journalist began to weep. He knew all too well his life would soon be taken. By now his estranged wife would have reported him missing after concerns from their teenage children. "Man up!" Gary deigned on his fears. "Come on move!" Yarbrough nudged him along with the barrel of his gun.

Attached to the businessman, Sandy was yanked along, covered only in an oversized man's T-shirt. Her clothes discarded as her captors took turns sexually abusing her. Gary shot her a contemptuous glare, "This is what we do to moles bitch."

Joey was emotionally and physically numb. Surviving only on the notion that Dylan and Jonathan would come through for him. But his hope had dwindled to almost nothing. Beaten down physically and mentally, He had come to terms with his fate. At peace with the thought that today he would join his beloved mother and father. But he was not a religious man and if there was a moment he wanted to be wrong, it was today.

Huey was beginning to feel the PABA inhibitors take over his body and the geriatric effects of aging. Infirm from days without the SR treatment, he knew the consequences. Even in his condition, he still had twice the strength of his captors. Doctor Chang struggled, with great restraint, to fight off the urge to sacrifice Joey and gain back the needed strength to break the chains that bound him. Joey's arteries pulsed hard from the realization that death was near. In his delirium, he rationalized the elucidating thought that formed into a potential strategy for escape. Perhaps his bite would cause less suffering than being strangulated by a noose. The Gag! It most definitely complicated things. Joey caught a glimpse of a vulnerable Doctor Chang with an afflicted manifestation in his eyes. His parched and cracked lips, formed in a pernicious grin, which chilled Joey to his very core.

Joey managed to get his plea out through the oily cloth gag to his conflicted friend, "Don't give up hope Doctor."

Shame overcame Huey and he began to weep.

"Come on, get moving," Gary vehemently demanded.

Giuseppe and Ludovic reached into the large outer pocket of their white robes and firmly grasped the Pop Snapper Smoke Bombs, previously inserted as part of the plan. As rehearsed. Their timing was crucial despite unknown circumstances that would transpire. Giuseppe's heart was pounding hard in his chest, anxious to confirm that Sandy was still alive.

And where was Dylan's head? His brother missing. All the while protecting his juvenile lover Thomas, instead. He was feeling shame that he hadn't done enough to protect his brother. He had to be strong for everyone. Thomas, too weak to join them and Jonathan, too full of revenge and fear of losing the love of his life. It was always Joey who encouraged him and gave him hope. It was his turn to be strong for Thomas and Jonathan. But who would be strong for him? "We have to believe he's still alive," he consoled his friend only hours ago in likely the darkest hour of his own life.

Though he appeared browbeaten, broken, and bruised, Joey rose from behind the gallows sparking a renewed resolve in Dylan and Jonathan to fight.

A four-foot metal step latter was chained to the gallows around a four by four footing support. The Black Reporter stood two feet higher than the platform as he climbed each rung to the top. An executioner, in the same incognito robe with an iconic skull and cross-bone emblem embroidered on it, impatiently motioned the Black prisoner to the last rope. Deliberate juxtaposition of each prisoner, predetermined to represented targets of the Fascist's hate. One by one the premeasured nooses were place over all four prisoner's heads and tightened around their necks.

"Don't let your emotion's kill you," Heinz's words played over and over in Giuseppe's mind as his heart beat uncontrollably at sight of

Sandy's bruised and broken body. There was no way he would be able to control his anger.

"Now!" Heinz cried, tossing off his pointed hood. He drew the attention of everyone, followed by panic and confusion. Chakrams filled the air toward the top beam of the gallows slicing through ropes, tightly secured around each prisoner's neck. The Peckerwoods security force dropped into their shallow fox holes to take cover, fighting to dismount, control, and position their weapons to take aim.

"Drop the floor!" Yarbrough shouted orders to the executioner. Swinging his assault rifle around he began to fire rounds toward the gallows. Pop, Pop, …Pop…Pop, Pop, Pop, Pop, His sycophants followed his lead and endless rounds were fired into the crowd.

The executioner had kicked the metal spike holding the swinging platform door open on its hinge, seconds prior to the Chakrams slicing into the top board and three of four nooses. Three had missed their mark. Joey hit the floor first. The wind knocked out of him as the Black Journalist fell on top of him. Joey tried to cough but he had no air, for the weight of two men was crushing him. The dust overbearing and filling his lungs. But only two prisoners were coughing incessantly, and Joey realized he was one of them.

His spine aflame from the sudden jerk that momentarily paralyzed the Journalist. But he soon regained feeling in his tingling arms and legs. He managed to roll Huey's lifeless body off him. Joey's face was pressed into the pool of bloody mud from Doctor Chang's exit wound from his chest. He closed his eyes hoping he would awake from this nightmare. The numbness quickly turned to excruciating pain in his disfigured and broken left arm.

"Sandy!" Giuseppe screamed her name out as he sprung from his chair toward her, slamming the smoke bomb into the ground directly in front of him. Sandy was not so lucky as the Chakrams, intended to set her free, missed their mark. Her neck was broken as she swung from the noose, as bullets penetrated through her.

Pop, Pop, Pop, Pop, Pop, Pop, Klansmen became collateral damage, killed by friendly fire. The Peckerwoods fired relentlessly into the crowd and through the thick blinding smoke from the smoke bombs and gunpowder. A few lucky Klan found cover behind their vehicles.

"You're a dead man Yarbrough," Giuseppe cried out loud. But his scream was muffled by the barrage of ear-shattering gunfire. He removed the handgun from his trench coat, and began firing in Gary's direction.

"Zake cover Giuseppe!" Ludovic hollered, exhuming all of the air from his lungs.

The campground had become a battlefield. The Peckerwood posse hadn't planned for the Vigilantes to be mixed in with the Klan. The Peckerwoods fired aimlessly into the crowd as bullets, returned from the Vampire's handguns, whizzed over them.

Giuseppe's body danced as round after round penetrated it. At last a flash of Sandy's lifeless bullet riddled body caught his eyes one final time. They seemed to be at peace, locked in death's open arms. He struggled to keep their final regard alive as his own life drained. The SR process unable to keep up with the mending pace as new wounds were inflicted. Then the fatal shot which entered his heart. He spoke her name softly, "Sandy? It doesn't hurt, I love you." He closed his eyes and fell limp to his knees and then face planted into the dirt. He was gone.

Danny, Luther's body guard, lizard crawled on his elbows onto the stage platform, and dragged Pierce off the stage. Bullets whistled over them. Luther was caterwauling like a child.

"Will you shut the fuck up and stay on the ground." Pop, Pop, Pop, Pop, Pop. Danny felt excruciating pain as one bullet nicked his shoulder. He managed to get Luther past the fox holes, through the trees, and kept on running into the adjacent open field. Once into the adjacent field, he dropped and pulled Luther into the tall grass out of view.

Using two collapsed metal folding chairs as shields, Dylan and Jonathan, lay prostate behind them, managing to get off a random shot. Pop, pop, clang, pop, they were out-numbered and out gunned.

"We need to retreat to the Stretch!" Heinz called out for them to abort. Pop, clang, pop, pop, pop.

"We're not leaving without Joey!" Dylan firmly insisted.

"Shit!" Macias cried out. "I've been hit in the leg." The SR chemicals attacked the laceration through the nerve canals, healing it within seconds, the wound closed up. The exact science Doctor Chang had promised Adolph Hitler in 1939.

Caught in the crossfire, Doctor Siegel became collateral damage. Bob Stikes wittingly dropped to the floor for cover and began to crawl to the front edge of the stage. Stikes, covered from the deluge of Siegels blood, grabbed the edge of the stage and tried to pull himself off. He didn't like what he saw, the angry face of Ludovic who had taken cover at the base of the platform.

"I know I suck," Ludovic mocked uncannily. "Sis is for Giuseppe."

Wrapping his arms around Stikes in a tight bear hug, the crushing force drained his lungs as ribs cracked like breaking tree limbs. Bob opened his mouth to scream, but nothing came out. A trim of nubby hair encircled Stikes's bald crown, leaving nothing for Lodovic to grab in order to pull his head back for the kill. Improvising, Ludovic's hand reached over Stikes's skull and pressed his fingers into his eye sockets for leverage. Yanking his head back, Ludovic wasted no time penetrating Bob's pulsing artery. A small dram would suffice his craving. He rolled Stikes off him and grasped his handgun. The rest of Stike's blood pumped like a broken fire hydrant into the pruned weeds.

The smoke had expanded and covered the foxholes. "Shorty, this is our chance to make a run for it! On my count run for the tall grass behind us," Mike insisted as he reloaded his AG-043 rifle. Shorty did not respond. "Shorty?" Mike looked back over his shoulder to his friend. He was hunched back, lifeless against the back of the foxhole. His head flopped back with a bullet wound to the neck. "God dammit Shorty!"

Laying prostrate in Huey's wet and gooey blood, Joey stared helplessly into Doctor Chang's insouciant listless stare. Bullets hissing above them. Joey cringed as another bullet tore through the plywood walls of the gallows.

"Just stay down," The Black Journalist insisted adamantly. He hovered over Joey in an effort to protect him from the falling debris.

"Gary, stop firing, we're killing the Klan off!" RJ protested.

"Fuck those bastards! I'm not leaving here until everyone of those blood sucking pukes are dead!" Gary yelled, discernably enraged and out of his mind.

Macias and Heinz took cover behind Yarbrough's Sedan, near the bushes opposite the parking lot. Dodging bullets from Cal and James's foxhole to their right. They began to return fire, but their smaller handguns were no match for the automatic blitz of bullets. "We're not going to make it!," Macias had vanquished any hope of survival. "We have to find a way to get back to the Limo!"

"Here!" Heinz pulled out a flashbang grenade from his trench coat.

"What the hell is this? You had explosives all this time!"

"It's not ballistic. On my command, toss it toward the foxhole," Heinz adamantly insisted. "It will give me a few seconds of cover."

"What?"

"Just do it damn it!" Pop, Pop, Pop, Pop, Pop, it seemed that the gunfire had tripled.

"All right!"

"Now!" Heinz yelled, crouched, and ready to leap. The strategy was immediately interrupted by two Klansmen running for cover between the foxhole and the Sedan. Both were struck with friendly fire and dropped dead in front of them.

"Do it!" Heinz demanded as Macias pulled the pin and tossed it toward the foxhole.

The shockwave from the blast cleared much of the smoke near the impact. Deafened from the concussion, Cal and James let lose their weapons and held their heads, screaming from the excruciating pain pounding in their skulls. No sooner had they emerged from their shallow fox hole, afraid of a second detonation, Heinz put a round in each of them. They crouched over at the impact and dropped dead to the dirt.

The blast gave pause to the battle.

Believing he and Jonathan were the only two Creed alive, Dylan grasped his hand tight, and stared helplessly into his eyes as tears fell. "I had prayed it wouldn't end this way."

But the silence never ceased, odd as it was. Was their executioners approaching through the smoke to finish the job?

As the heavy smoke began to dissipate, Dylan could see an approaching army of police cars and armored vehicles surrounding the campground. The rocks and dirt spraying behind their tires. They were at least one hundred feet away, a telltale of the speed of their operation. But there were no Peckerwoods standing in retreat.

The blast also caused confusion. Gary Yarbrough scanned the campground, looking for evidence that the advantage had changed hands.

"Drop your weapons!" the voice on the megaphone unexpectedly announced. "FBI!" Yarbrough turned to look behind him toward the direction that the demand was coming from. They were surrounded by an army of armored vehicles and countless S.W.A.T. crouched behind and between those vehicles. The special forces had their high-powered assault rifles aimed to kill. "We need to see your hands high in the air and weapons on the ground, or we will shoot with intent to kill," Agent Manis barked from the megaphone.

He had been stabbed three times, beat to an inch of his life, and suffered sexual assault as a young prisoner at the Washington State Penitentiary in Walla Walla Washington. Going back was not an option. He made, what seemed like a slow-motion sweeping assessment of the aftermath of the combat, and realized what his option would be. Gary Yarbrough picked up his weapon, slowly stepped out of the fox hole, aimed it at the procession of law enforcement, and began firing off rounds. But his psychosis would be short-lived as returning fire obliviated his body like a stuffed bag used for target practice.

Bureau Agents, and members of SWAT, were slapping handcuffs on the few surviving Klansmen. R.J. was right, they were blindly killing their own. And for what? They had failed miserably.

Macias and Estella were among those in the parking lot that had surrendered and were being handcuffed.

"Cut her down!" Agent Manis motioned to Sandy's dangling corpse to a SWAT officer near the gallows.

"I need a medic!" Detective Stone called back over his shoulder as he discovered the bodies in the shallow grave under the Gallows. "My God man," Stone reached his hand down to the Black Journalist, "Give me your hand."

Exhausted, the Journalist began to weep and reached his hand out to Detective Stone, "Thank God, thank God." Stone helped him climb out of the small pit.

"Joey?" Detective Stone was suddenly filled with disbelief.

"He's still alive Officer," The Journalist reassured him as he pulled himself up to ground level.

"Hold on I'm coming down to get you." Joey managed to turn his mud and blood covered face toward Stone. A sudden sharp pain raced through his broken limb as he attempted to move it.

"It's broken Detective."

Detective Stone jumped into the four-foot pit and took short inventory of the mayhem he was staring at. He recognized Doctor Chang and grimaced at the realization that he was a fatality.

"Ahhh! Joey exuded a painful sigh at his attempt to move his limbs.

"Stay put, don't move."

"Officer?" Stone called up to the SWAT member cutting at the rope around Sandy's neck. "Do you have a sling in your med pack?"

"Of course," he replied and shuffled through his med pack that was secured to his belt. He ripped open the plastic package with his teeth and tossed the sling down to Stone.

"Thanks" He slowly rolled Joey on his back. "This is going to hurt you more than me," Stone's attempt at jocosity, brought a momentary smile to Joey's cheeks.

"Please, it hurts to laugh."

"Bite on this Son," he insisted rolling up the sling holding it in front of Joey's mouth. He parted his lips and Stone pushed the cloth sling between his teeth. "Now when I…" before he could finish explaining what he had planned to do, it was done.

"Ahhhhh!" Joey screamed and locked his jaw down hard on the sling.

"…move your arm around, bite down hard. Well, never mind."

"Shit!" Joey moaned. "You didn't warn me."

"That was the whole idea," Stone explained as he fastened the sling under his broken arm and around his neck. He took his belt off and used it as a bind to stabilize the sling against Joey's body. "Now I'm going to put your good arm around my shoulder and lift you up." Two SWAT members stood at the edge of the pit, ready to hoist him up.

"Thank you Jesus," Dylan nodded toward Joey being supported to his feet. He shoulder bumped Jonathan, whose wrists were also handcuffed.

"Joey!" Jonathan called out elated that his lover had survived. Joey limped toward Jonathan, tears raining down his cheeks.

"Don't move!" FBI Agent Parvin exclaimed, stepping toward Joey to stop him as is protocol to secure the scene. But Agent Parvin was blocked by Sergeant Stone's outstretched arm.

"Let him be. They're the good guys."

The dead were counted, photographed, and being put into body bags by the Sausalito Coroner's office employees, including Doctor Huey Chang, Giuseppe, and the person he had hoped to start a new life with, Sandy.

"What the hell took you so long!" Joey cursed Jonathan and his brother Dylan, still in handcuffs.

"You're lucky we came at all for your ass," Dylan reproached with sarcasm.

"I am drenched in Doctor Chang's and the bitch's blood," Joey deplored. "I just need to get out of these clothes and get cleaned up. My arm hurts like hell. I wish they would hurry I need to get to a Doctor."

Dylan knew his brother wasn't aware of just who Sandy was and what critical role she played in their survival. "You should know, It's because of that bitch, that you're alive," Dylan castigated. "She has a name, Sandy."

Joey made a curious face at his brother, somewhat shocked at what he had just learned about the woman Luther had called a Mole. "The same Sandy that Giuseppe was dating?"

"She jeopardized her life to help us," Dylan stated dolefully. "Now they're both gone. We couldn't save everybody."

"We were out gunned," Jonathan consoled. "We did the best we could my friend. I prayed you'd be alive Joey," his voice cracking in benediction and grace that his love still lives another day.

"What does this scum bag want?" Dylan shot Stone a disdainful gaze as he approached them.

"Lay off him," Joey chastened. "Sandy's not the only person being misjudged. I trust him."

Detective Stone motioned for Joey to follow him, "There's a Med Tech in the second ambulance that knows how to set your arm. Follow me."

"Oh God, thank you Sam, I'm in so much fucking pain right now," Joey grimaced.

Dylan turned his nose up, "Sam? You're on first name basis now with the guy that wanted to see you fry in the electric chair? Please someone tell me what the hell is going on."

Due to the unexpected number of fatalities, only two of the six paddy wagons were needed. They circled around the parked cars in the dirt field that served as a parking lot.

City and County Forensic teams began to show up to assist the Feds. The death toll grew as response personnel located additional dead in nearby brush, fatally wounded as they fled. The question on the mind of Agent Manis was, just who shot who? Could he charge all of them? What was obvious is that he had just crashed a staged lynching. At first he believed that there were only four true victims. And to his chagrin, he knew a reasonable jury would likely be sympathetic to the Vigilantes and rule self-defense. He soon came to the conclusion that he had no case on the blood suckers, and only one homicide warrant, the dead Italian already cold in his body bag.

Agent Manis located Sergeant Stone attending to the victim with the broken arm. "Walk with me Sergeant," Agent Manis seemed unnerved. The two men walked out into an empty field. "We have to let them go."

"Let who go?" Stone pressed him for answers.

"Your Vampire Freaks."

"What reason?"

"We don't have a grand jury indictment for any of them, do we?" Manis challenged, already knowing the answer.

Stone stalled. "Just a bench warrant."

"For all of them?" Manis countered.

"Not all of them no," Stone began to explain.

"No!" Agent Manis reacted displeased.

"Look," Stone plead his case, "The Anderson boy could only identify the Ricci suspect. We thought we had one of the albino twins at an earlier Cactus Bar double murder, but several witnesses at a nearby restaurant corroborated his alibis."

Agent Manis was shaking his head petulantly. "We only have one God Damn warrant? Did we get statements from any of the other witnesses at the bar?"

"Dead men don't speak Agent, neither do Peckerwoods to authority." Detective Stone replied squeamishly.

"Let me get this straight," Agent Manis insisted, his head nodding up and down, his lips rolled inward with fury. "The only fucking bench warrant we have is for the dead vigilante? Is that accurate Sergeant?" Stone raised his brow and nodded affirmatively, capitulating without speaking. "Holy mother of Moses!" He paced, then turned and conceded, "As I see it then, we have no choice but to let them go."

"But you can't rule out the possibility that they might be suspects here, Agent." Stone argued, hiding his pleasure at Manis's declaration.

"I can't hold them in a Federal prison when the evidence is very clear that they were acting in self-defense Sam. A reasonable judge would argue wrongful detainment, and you know it!" he paused to gain composure. "Let 'em go."

"You want me to let them go?" Detective Stone hid his bliss. "What about the Klansmen?"

"Guilty by association! Accessories to a lynching."

"Very well, I'll release the Vigilantes under your recognizance."

"Why do I get the impression, this pleases you?" Agent Manis inquired perturbed at his indifference.

Stone turned away to hide his sudden amelioration.

Friday, May 21, 1986
Paradise Drive, El Campo California

"Thank God! No fog over the bay today," Dylan stated, admiring the pastel morning in front of the large pane glass window. "How much did you pay for this place Carol?"

"Way more than it's worth," she chagrinned from behind the morning newspaper, lounging in her new leather Bergere chair. "Listen to this Dylan. Andrew Lloyd Weber's Phantom of the Opera opened in London. Vaughn and Huey would have given anything to see it."

Joey emerged, still in his pajamas from the bedroom down the hall where Jonathan could still be heard snoring through the opened door. "I'm going to make breakfast. Do we have any food in the fridge?"

Boxes from the move-in were stacked down the long hallway and took up a small portion of the living room. Carol finished and folded the Life section, placing it on the end table next to her chair. Picking up and snapping open the World News, she caught Joey yawning. Joey entered the large living room which was open to the kitchen. "Good morning Joey. So kind of you to offer. There's two flats of eggs, milk, and cheese, in the fridge. Not sure where I put the pancake mix. Need some help."

"No I got it."

"What a bad year this has been," Carol dolefully stated. "Listen to this, the death toll from last month's Chernobyl Nuclear disaster in Russia is in the thousands. Poor Ukrainians. On top of that there's the Shuttle Challenger disaster to start the year off, what's next?"

"You have to stop reading the News Carol," Joey patronized. "It's too depressing."

"It takes my mind off more depressing things."

"Found it!" Joey chirped, discovering the pancake batter mix in a paper grocery bag at the end of the long kitchen counter.

The open concept of their new home in El Campo, was the selling point for Carol, who was the sole beneficiary of Doctor Chang's fortune.

Vaulted beam ceilings, five bedrooms, each with their own on suite, the perfect home for Her life with Fabien and his extended family. Carol was the right choice to handle the Creed's Capital. Doctor Chang knew that her maternal instincts would find a neutral, yet prudent management of the Creeds survival funds.

But there was another secret that she held from the Creed that Chang had taxed her with. One she wish he had charged to someone else. She didn't want the responsibility, but she loved her boys, her friends, her life.

"I've been waiting for this moment to get you to myself," Joey stated with acute apprehension.

"Oh?"

"I figured that, since we're the only two mortals in this family, I really want to get to know you better and perhaps create a bond between us." He blushed, "I don't mean, like, intimately, but you know."

"Sure," she replied with uneasiness and set the paper down in her lap to let him know he had her undivided attention. "What do you want to know?"

Joey placed the carton of eggs on the counter and walked closer, out of ear shot of meddlesome ears, still pretending to be sleeping in. He sat on the edge of the sofa closest to lounge chair. "Honestly, I'm scared for my brother. With Doctor Chang and Mueller out of the picture, well," he paused. "Don't they depend on some formula of Chang's? Aren't you worried about what will happen to Fabien if he can't get access to it?"

Carol's chin dropped to her chest as she paused to collect her thoughts and tried to find words to explain her juxtaposition. "I didn't ask for this, nor do I need this right now in my life." Joey's eyes strained with confusion as the conversation took a bitter sweet turn. "But unfortunately for me, I understand why Doctor Chang and Muller chose me."

"You lost me back at "I didn't ask for this"".

"The Note for Chang's millions wasn't the only item in the lock box he gave me a key for. There was an envelope with a letter and a manila folder. The letter explained everything."

"The short version please."

"You have to promise to keep this between us. I have a plan to divulge this to the others later this evening at the meeting that Estella has called."

Joey made a zipper motion across his lips. "On my Mother's grave."

"Thanks," She affirmed and took a deep breath. "Doctor Chang made me Sole Beneficiary of his Estate. There's close to a billion dollars. It's mind blowing. He was probably one of the richest men in the world. And I've been getting VIP notices from his new Bank constantly. It's overwhelming Joey." Joey's mouth was a gape as he couldn't find the words or make sense of what she was sharing with him. "Doctor Chang adamantly insisted that I put no one, even Fabien on the account and instructed me to use the funds to enhance my lifestyle first. But, there is a caveat." Joey edged closer to her, both eyes and ears wide open in anticipation. "He begged me to fund the Creed and only permit Heinz and Estella access to the contents of the manila folder."

"The Formula?"

Carol nodded. "Please, you have to let me tell them."

"Muller and Huey where good judges of character and integrity. There's a reason why they chose you."

"Thanks for the kind words, but truly I wished they hadn't."

"What about you and Fabien? Do you plan to start a family?"

Her lower lip curled back into her mouth as she tried to physically respond without any emotional drama. "Because of my assault, I can't have children."

"I'm sorry. It's not fair."

"Life isn't fair. But we don't give up and we find the strength to move on. Speaking of which, I have to tell you I was very angry that the Creed had put Fabien's life in jeopardy to save you and Doctor Chang. I didn't know either of you that well. But now I feel ashamed of those feelings. Thank God for the FBI, you would all be dead."

"Thank Frank Sanders, Carol, not the FBI," Joey adamantly stated.

"Is he a friend of Detective Stone," Fabien never mentioned him.

"You could say that," Joey postulated. "The two of them use to meet at the shooting range. Frank was his favorite bar tender."

"I don't see what that has do to with the Creed," Carol asked, still puzzled.

"Frank is my father," Joey replied with a slight grin. Finally realizing that for the first time his father's integrity had made a positive impact in his Son's lives. Their estranged relationship with Frank had eclipsed and obfuscated any hope of reconciliation.

"I don't think I've ever seen you smile ear to ear," Carol stated. She caught his sudden elation and become intoxicated with it. "What? Why are you so elated?"

"It's nothing really," Joey blushed.

"In that case, you'll have to introduce me, so I can thank him properly," Carol insisted.

"My Father passed on several years ago." The years, since Frank's death, hadn't really healed their tumultuous relationship nor acquiesced his resentment. But he realized for the first time that his Father's good reputation, inadvertently, had a positive impact on his Sons.

"Sorry to hear that," Carol condoled. "He must have been an esteemed gentleman."

"To most people," Joey said, cloaking the history between them.

"Well," Carol intuitively surmised, "We couldn't have been more fortunate that Detective Stone's respect for your father carried over to his Sons."

"I guess so," Joey responded, content to leave it at that.

"Do vampires always require this much sleep Joey?" Carol humored.

Joey opined, "Only before the weekend it seems."

"We better get the others going if we're going fishing on the Delta. That rental boat wasn't cheap."

Later that same morning
Paradise Drive, El Campo

"How's he doing?" Joey asked his brother as they loaded fishing gear into the back of the black Sedan.

"What happened to Dad's tackle box? Dylan asked, still peeved that it was no-where to be found.

"I have it," Joey assured him.

"Why do you have it?" Dylan seemed a little irked. "I've been looking all over for it."

"Do you want me to pack some chips?" Carol called out from the open garage door to the mud room.

"Yes please," Joey answered. "I salvaged some things of mom and dad's from the Hospice, right before Doctor Chang bought it." Joey finished explaining. "Help me with this cooler."

Dylan grabbed a handle and assisted Joey lift it up and into the Van. "The Heroine in Thomas's system, from that Peckerwood whore, nearly killed him. He's fine now."

"He's joining us, right?"

"He's taking a shower," Dylan put his hand on Joey's shoulder. "I was wrong about Detective Stone."

"No, you had good reason to doubt him," Joey acceded. "He took a lot of heat from the Feds. He says we owe him a favor."

"What's that?"

"He wants the blood-letting to stop," Joey stated firmly, knowing that demand had no chance of coming to fruition.

"That would be a death wish for most of us," Dylan laughed off Stone's arrogate request. "The world needs the Creed to safeguard them from fascists and haters."

"Some may argue that you're playing God," Joey challenged.

"Some just might," Dylan countered. "But I presume that those "some" represent the incompetence of governments and churches to do just that."

"But wasn't it the Feds that saved the Creed? Joey impugned with raised brow.

"Or more accurately stated, wasn't it the Creed that led the Feds to the arrest of Key Klan and White Supremacist leaders? We're equal opportunity haters Joey, we hate haters."

"Are you taking the girls with you?" Carol's question was more of a suggestion. "It might be a nice respite from their grief."

"Are you sure it's not too early?" Dylan appealed. "It's only been a few days since they lost their mother."

"Is it ever a good time?" Carol asserted.

"Touché'!" Joey capitulated, reminiscent of all the years since his own mother passed away. The pain never less. The knot in his stomach seem to always reach his throat at the very thought of her. "What's going to happen to them?"

"I don't know Joey," Carol sighed, lost for words. "I'm concerned that the authorities will soon be tracking down their whereabouts. Does anyone know if they have family that could take them in?"

"Sandy's father is a die-hard Klansman," Dylan answered. "Giuseppe filled the twins in on her history. We could always ask Giuseppe's parish to take them in."

"Orphanage?" Carol asserted, exiting the open garage with two sacks of potato chips. "Over my dead body."

"I didn't mean for it to come off that way Carol," Dylan recanted. "Do you have any better ideas?"

"Well for one, we can do everything possible to make sure their psychopath grandfather doesn't get them. Fabien and I, have discussed possibly adopting them." Carol's facial droop reflected an angst that was obvious to everyone.

"What's the matter Carol," Dylan asked, attempting to get to the bottom of her sour mood.

"Fabien got a call from Giuseppe's Minister. Child Protective Services will be picking up the girls in two weeks to process through the system."

Dylan formed a pernicious grin, "Perhaps the twins and I should pay grandpa a visit to get his blessing on the adoption then. Don't you agree?"

"I think that's a grand recommendation Dylan," Joey concurred with a devious smile.

Delta Rio Vista
3:30 p.m.

"How many days did'ju renz zis houseboat?" Fabien asked Carol.

"We have it for two nights my love," Carol answered, leaning over the top deck railing and taking a sip of her gin martini. Fabien couldn't tan and wore loose white Dockers and an egg shell colored silk shirt. It was an unusually warm day for May and the men wore swim trunks, cut-off levis, flip flops and Birkenstocks. Carol looked stunning in her light blue two peace swimwear under her white silk robe.

"I like sis very much," he held up his glass of beer to salute her. "I could get very use ta diz." Fabien was consumed by her and their decision to spend the day on the Delta.

"This fishing trip was a great idea," Carol remarked. "Did Huey always treat you guys this fantastic?"

Dylan had beached the houseboat after finding soft shoreline along the Steamboat Slough.

"Za Creed was his family," Fabien wrapped his free arm around her waist and gently snugged up to her. "Have you asked the girls yet?"

"I'm waiting for the right moment," she replied. She couldn't help notice the others fishing off the stern below their deck. Between them, Natalie and Tanya. "Joey is so good with kids. Look how he's demonstrating to Natalie how to bait her line. Kodak moment, I swear."

"huh?"

"It's a camera slogan," She replied, rolling her eyes.

"Ah."

"I think you might have a bite Thomas!" Jonathan cheered.

"Are you sure," Thomas said anxiously, staring at his line.

"I swear!" Jonathan got impatient with him. "Your line just tightened."

Thomas's pole dipped hard. "Pull back babe!" Dylan coached and grabbed the net.

"Yes!" Thomas shouted. "Here it comes." He rapidly reeled it in.

"Steady, don't lose it," Joey warned.

"What do I do when I see it?" Thomas naively beseeched.

"Bring it up over the boat," Dylan replied. "That's what the net is for."

"I'm not touching it," Thomas loathed. He found slimy, wiggly, things disgusting. Especially snakes.

"Striper!" Joey stated the obvious. "Good job Thomas."

"Thanks."

Dylan reached under the fish with the net as Thomas lifted it out of the mucky water.

Natalie stepped back out of the way. "Are you going to kill it?" She empathetically begged for clemency.

"It's our dinner Natalie," Jonathan avariciously licked his upper lip. "The best Fish Tacos you'll ever eat."

"That's so cruel." She complained, making a bitter expression.

"I don't want you to hurt it," Tanya appealed, also afflicted with pity for the fish, now fighting for Its salvation in Dylan's net.

"Ahh, come on girls, don't do this," Joey said, falling for their crestfallen cute faces of compassion.

"They'll cave," Carol predicted, whispering into Fabien's ear.

Fabien guffawed. "No, zay wouldn't dare."

"In ten," Carol began to count unbeknownst to the fishermen on the deck below.

Thomas shot Dylan a proprietorship glare, buying into Tanya's doleful tears.

"Nine." Carol said shaking her head.

"We're eating this damn fish," Dylan assured Thomas, digging down Its throat with tweezers for the hook.

"Eight."

"Stop it Thomas," Dylan admonished, annoyed by his turned-up upper lip.

"Seven."

"Tanya, doesn't fish tacos sound good?" Jonathan implored.

"Six."

"It's my fish," Thomas stated, raising one brow.

"Five, wait for it."

"Please tell me you're not going to release it," Jonathan sighed.

"Four, here it comes."

Fabien was smiling from ear to ear, trying not to bust a gut.

"It looks like we're going out for dinner," Jonathan acquiesced.

"Three."

"Shit!" Dylan held up the fish with his finger in the fish's mouth.

"Two."

Thomas nodded.

"Catch and release it is," Dylan stated disconcertedly and tossed the fish back into the slough.

"Bingo!" Carol humored.

"Oh, damn! you called zat one," Fabien implied, fascinated. "Duz zis mean we dress up for dinna?"

"Yep," Carol chagrined.

6:45 p.m. Rio Vista, California "The Point" Restaurant.

The houseboat monopolized half of the public dock. Four large ribbed marine fenders shielded their boat from being gouged by the metal trim on the dock. The surf had grown to one-foot swells caused by the late afternoon breeze. Dylan tightened the ropes on the dock cleats to reduce the amount of boat movement. The hull, only a few fathoms from river floor. Whereas a few feet out, the deep channel was dredged to over a thirty-foot depth, to accommodate merchant ships and barges on their way from the sea to Sacramento.

"Thank God we're here", Jonathan exclaimed as he stepped onto the dock. "I was about to barf."

"The deep channel can get pretty rough," Dylan added from his experiences as a boy.

The restaurant deck extended out over the channel.

"This place is amazing!" Carol said, gawking over the large covered deck.

"Wait until you taste the food," Joey assured her.

"Your Dad use to bring your family here?" Thomas joined the conversation.

Dylan managed an unexpected smile, "It was actually mom's favorite place."

The eight fishermen were sat elbow to elbow at a round table designed for six.

"I like the view," Carol approved of their table in the great room overlooking the deep channel of the Sacramento River. The Point Restaurant held many family memories for Joey and Dylan and was the obvious choice for dinner. Natalie, couldn't wait to model her new black wool Reefer coat and pant suit that Joey and Carol had picked out for her at Macy's. Carol could never have afforded brand name clothes on a waitress's salary. The four Creed members wore their trench coats, regardless the temperature change. Carol was stunning in the blue Venus flare pants that embosomed her female features elegantly. Fabien's shiny long white mane was freed from Its pony-tail and hung on his shoulders like a romance novel model. He was enamored by Carol's stunning beauty that was core deep. He believed he had found his soul mate.

"Drinks?" the host, in her white cruise ship like uniform asked, pen in hand, ready to take orders.

"Water for everyone," Thomas spoke up, looking around the table for unanimous approval. Everyone nodded or responded with "Please."

"Shall we gez a bottle of vine?" Fabien recommended.

"Beer for us," Thomas said pointing at Dylan. "Do you have Watney's Red Barrel bitter?"

"Zis man knows his beers," Fabien said, somewhat surprised. Dylan rolled his eyes.

"I will need to see your ID sir," the Host held out her hand for Thomas's ID.

"Damn, I must have left it at home," Thomas feigned, searching his trench coat pockets.

"I'm sorry sir, would you like a soda instead?" she graciously allowed him a chance to save face.

"Actually, do you have tomato juice?" Thomas obliged. "Thicker the better."

His request seemed somewhat eccentric. "Sure."

"And for you beautiful young ladies?" The host asked speaking to the children.

"Do you have root beer?" Tanya inquired.

"Root beer it is."

"That sounds good for me too," Natalie added.

Carol interjected, "The rest of us are going to share a bottle or two of wine." She gestured that she wanted feedback from the others. "House Cav? One red, one white?"

"Most definitely all red," Jonathan responded decisively.

"Great!" She delightfully exclaimed, gathering the drink menus and distributing the dinner menus. "Our specialties today are Cioppino, a fish stew for sixteen dollars, Shrimp scampi for nineteen dollars, and finally the Chev's specialty, Plateau de fruits de mer. It's a French seafood platter of raw and cooked selfish served cold on a bed of ice. That runs thirty dollars and some change." The host smiled, "Are there any questions about the specials or the menu?"

"Yes," Joey interjected. "What type of fish are in the Cioppino?"

"Dungeness crab, clams, shrimp, scallops, squid, and I also believe there are mussels."

"Thank you."

"Sure, I'll be back with your drinks and your waitress will be by shortly afterwards to take your orders."

Natalie, understandably doleful, had kept to herself most of the fishing trip. Tearing up from time to time. Missing her mom much. "Carol?"

"What is it?"

"What's going to happen to us?" Her lip quivered. "Please don't let them send us to grandpa's." Thomas put his arm around her with a heartfelt hug.

"I was meaning to talk to you about that," Carol said with formidable fear of being let down. "Do you know of any other family member that you girls could stay with?"

Natalie strained to recall anyone from her mother's side, other than their grandpa. "My grandpa's brother. Mom said that he's a drunk and never married. There's no way."

"How about on your Father's side of the family?" Dylan prodded.

"My dad was an only child and his parents died in a car crash before I was born."

"So, Natalie would you and Tanya consider moving in with us?" Carol blatantly tossed the suggestion to everyone's bewilderment. "Take your time. You girls can talk it over and give us an answer later."

"Us, as in?" Natalie responded puzzled.

"Fabien and Carol," She stated pointing to herself and Fabien. "You don't think I'd let these overgrown kids raise you."

Optimism returned to Tanya's face, "We wouldn't be a bother?"

"Zis would makes us much happy," Fabien assured her. His dimples grew wide with her excitement.

"We would be no bother," Natalie's voice cracked. "We promise."

"I wouldn't want you to be anything else," Carol vowed solemnly. "We would only want for you to be your beautiful selves."

"What about Grandpa?" Natalie asked with despair. "You know he'll come for us. He's a real bad man. Mom says he's Klan."

"I have a notion that your fascist grandpa will never be part of your lives," Dylan stated with a sanguine confidence. "You'll just have to trust us."

Joey rolled his eyes with a smirk, "I don't even want to know."

Tuesday, May 25, 1986
Beaumont Mississippi, Don's Garage

Don's Garage was dilapidated and in need of exterior paint and a new roof. Don, owner, manager, and now, since the loss of his Sons, the only employee, tried to keep up with the neglected roof leaks by catching the dripping water in tin buckets. A battle he was obviously losing.

Located on Bolton Avenue across from the Beaumont Church of God, the only other close structure was an abandoned post office building a block away. Just outside of downtown Beaumont, Don's Garage lost a lot of business to the larger monopolies that could afford prime real estate downtown. Without the help of his two Sons, Don was content to let business shrink. But the garage resembled a pick'n-pull yard rather than a fix-it station. Several abandoned, and some client vehicles Don was working on, were parked along the side and in the back of the garage.

"I think you just passed it," Jonathan pointed back over his shoulder.

"Too many trees," Dylan griped. "Hold on!" He looked into his rearview mirror and confirmed that there was no traffic behind him. He let off the accelerator, then drove the rented Hummer H3 Arkon off road slightly over the embankment and then made a U-turn. The Centrifugal force sent the occupants of the Hummer sliding over the leather seats and into each other and the passenger doors. "Sorry."

"Were you trying to flip this thing and kill us all?" Jonathan grilled sarcastically.

"Just wanted to see what it would do," Dylan unabashedly replied.

Ludovic chagrined, "How you say, Juvenile?"

"That about describes him," Thomas concurred.

"What?" Dylan dissented, trying to act innocent of the charge.

"Pull up to za garage door," Fabien insisted. This was his war and he was determined to get custody of the girls. Estella had drafted a writ of release and award of fiduciary duty and guardianship over Natalie and Tanya. As next of kin, Don had the power to release legal guardianship to the courts or to a third party. Their first priority was to convince Don to sign it. How they got him to sign it wasn't as important as the assurance that he didn't live to contest it.

The main garage door was three quarters of the way open. The humidity unbearable. One by one the Creed ducked under the garage door and waited just inside. The tail of their trench coats flailed about their ankles in the breeze through the open garage door. Dirty grease rags and a clutter of discarded tools and other trip hazards, were significant enough to warrant several OSHA fines.

"Anyone home?" Thomas bellowed.

"You have customers." Jonathan stated loudly. "Perhaps he's on the toilet."

The back-office door opened slightly and a partially bald silvery hair, slightly overweight, man in his fifties stepped out, fastening the Dungaree overall buckles back over his shoulders. "You boys can't be in here," he complained. "You all suppose-ta enter through the main office door," he continued to castigate them in his southern drawl.

"Our apologies Don," Dylan offered insincerely.

"How da ya know my name mister?" Don asked with contempt.

A pudgy short middle-age female, with colossal breasts pouring over her bra strap, emerged from the office behind Don. She yanked up on one side of the bra to cover one bared nipple and went after the straps of her Camisole leather vest top.

"Looks like we may have interrupted something," Jonathan inanely explained to Dylan.

"I need my car by tomorrow Donald," she exclaimed to her boyfriend, unobservant of the five men standing in front of the large garage door. "I'm gonna be in a load of shit if I don't get my brother's car back to him this weekend." She froze in her tracks at the realization that they were not alone. "Who are these men Don?" She asked timorously. "Ya all look like a bunch of damn Chippendale strippers. What's yer business?"

"Wow, I'll take that as a compliment mam," Jonathan patronized.

"Leave us Betsy," Don demanded adamantly.

"I'm not gonna leave you alone Donald. You should call the cops."

"Can I call you Betsy?" Jonathan pretended to ask permission. Her eyes narrowed and insolently glared at Jonathan. "As I was saying, unfortunately, you being here has complicated things a bunch. I'm afraid Don, Betsy is invited to the party."

"Who the hell you think you is?" Betsy threatened in her illiterate way.

"Shut the hell up Betsy and let me handle this!" Don riled, annoyed with her mouth. "Who are you? How do you know my name?"

They slowly enclosed in on them. Thomas walked over and blocked the door to the main lobby. Ludovic, and Fabien, remained at the large partially opened garage door. Dylan ducked under a green, wood paneled Ford station wagon suspended on a hydraulic jack. He walked over to the side door and closed it, standing with legs spread in a blocking stance. Jonathan, holding the Adoption papers in his left hand, began to take slow calculated steps toward Don and Betsy, and then explained. "We are close colleagues of your daughter Sandy."

"What do ya want?" Don asked sternly. His blood pressure elevated from sudden anxiety as the five strangers surrounded them, poised in a threatening disposition. "I have no daughter. My daughter is dead to me ever since she turned into a damn mole."

"Well, isn't that fortuitous for us," Jonathan patronized. "We'll be doing you a great favor then."

"Oh my God Betsy!" Don muttered faintly, suddenly alarmed. These were the vampire freaks Paul had tried to explain to him.

"I don't like your tone Don," Betsy's voice trembling. "I'm scared already."

"Let her go," Don begged, "She doesn't know anything."

"What's going on Don," Betsy begged, becoming hysterical.

"Just get behind me," Don urged. "They're them vampire freaks Betsy."

"Don, Don, Don, you don't need to be rude about it," Jonathan patronized him.

"Get back in the office Betsy and lock the door," Don demanded. Betsy obeyed and slipped back into the office. The click of dead bolt plunger confirmed that she had locked herself in.

Jonathan tilted his head, motioning for Dylan to foil her escape from an office window or a back door.

Once in the office, Betsy picked up the phone on Don's desk and dialed 911. Putting the handset to her ear a chill went through her body.

The line was dead. She threw the handset on the desk and began to caterwaul, "No!" her scream turned to sobs. There, in the opened glass shuttered office window, she caught glimpse of one of the young men with strong handsome features.

"Sorry," Dylan sympathized, holding up cut phone lines in one hand. "We really weren't planning on a large crowd." He slowly mounted and climbed through the window and into the office.

She cowered into the corner and shielded herself behind a tall filing cabinet. "Please, I won't tell anyone," she begged. "Please let me go." Starring into Dylan's eyes, she suddenly began to feel light headed, but not dizzy.

"Betsy!" Don yelled from the other side of the door. "Talk to me! What's going on in there?"

Dylan smiled innocently at her and licked his lower lip. Hypnotized by his dreamy piercing blue eyes, she felt her anger melt. He draped his trench coat over the office chair. An unwelcomed desire for his touch overwhelmed her. She tried to speak but she couldn't form the words. Betsy slipped into a catalectic trance as he locked eyes with her.

Approaching her cautiously, she went limp but managed to stand on both feet. How he swiftly crossed the room without stride was magical to her. She tingled with passion hoping he would take her, use her. She didn't fight back. She slowly raised her right hand to his face and ran a finger over his lips. Caught up in the musky masculinity of his fragrance, she became light headed with passion. Dylan opened his mouth as if to welcome her finger into it. She had never seen such white enamel. His teeth were perfect. Dylan drew back his lips even more. But she hadn't expected to see that natural selection had formed his cuspids into dog like fangs. Her stomach, suddenly burning with fear. But not as much as the burning between her legs for him.

With a firm grip of her hair, he snapped her head back violently and bit down hard into her neck, ripping through her creamy skin to find the jugular. Dylan suckled on the rhythmic surges of blood into his mouth, like a baby breastfeeding on Its mother's breast.

The office door was kicked open and swung hard into the wall behind it. Jonathan entered pushing Don to the floor. Don was aghast as he watched Betsy's seizing body giving new life to the vampire feeding on her. Fabien appeared, followed by Ludovic and Thomas, into the small office. One by one the five vampires satiated their Rejuvenation Synthesis. Thomas got sloppy fifths and managed to get Betsy's blood on his chin. Dylan, yearning to taste his boyfriends face, gently grasped the back of Thomas's head and drew it toward his mouth slowly. Like a lizard's tongue, Dylan devoured Betsy's blood from Thomas's chin and mouth. Thomas kissed him back affectionately.

"Now lez finish whaz we came her for," Fabien prompted.

Dylan and Thomas gripped Don at his biceps and lifted him up. His feet dangling a foot from the cement floor. He was sweating profusely.

Jonathan took a document from the folder he brought with him, and laid it on the desk. "We can do this the easy way or the hard way. But either way, you're going to sign at the bottom of this document." Smoothing the folded document with both hands, he pointed to the signature line, then took out a blue pen from his trench coat and laid it next to it. "Sign it."

"Stick it up your ass!" Don protested.

"Bad choice Don," Jonathan patronized, shaking his head. "Ludovic, I believe there was a free-standing metal work bench next to the hydraulic lift. Can you position it under the front tire of the wagon?"

Ludovic grinned, "My pleasure."

Dylan and Thomas clenched Don's wrist with one hand and with the other suspended him off the floor and into the Shop. Ludovic dragged the heavy metal workbench under the front tire of the station wagon. The metal legs of the table screeched across the cement floor with an ear-piercing sound. They spread Don across the table and centered his crotch under the front passenger tire of the vehicle. They positioned the table so that Don's upper torso was not under the vehicle.

Dylan pinned Don's hands, as did Thomas his feet, to all corners of the table. Jonathan laid the document by Don's face. "You've worked on a number of these station wagons Don. Am I far off the mark if I guessed that the vehicle weight rating for a Ford Station Wagon is close to four thousand pounds?" Don struggled to free himself, but he was no match to the strength of a vampire. His eyes opened wide with horror and rage at the prospect of having his manhood crushed. "This can be all over Don, just need you to sign," Jonathan explained. Don spit in his face. Angry, Jonathan wiped the spittle from his cheek and motioned for Fabien to lower the hydraulic lift. "I should have seen that coming. My bad Don." Don squealed and floundered helplessly as the tire inched closer to his crotch. "Duck Thomas," Jonathan signaled for Fabien to push the stop switch on the lift post. The bottom of the tire was approximately one inch from Don's crotch. His heart was racing like a race horse.

Picking up a greasy blue rag off the filthy shop floor. Jonathan pinched Don's nostrils tight. Don gasped for air as Jonathan slid the rag through his teeth and tied a knot behind his head, securing the gag, he pulled it tight against the back of his mouth.

Jonathan was still fuming from being spit on. "I imagine gradual pressure on the pelvic area is more painful than child birth Don." Stroking the carotid artery on Don's neck with the back of his index fingernail, Jonathan leaned in closer. His anger changed to carnal desire as he felt the rapid pulse pumping through Don's artery. "I'm sure somewhere in your office we'll find a document with your signature. I just don't want to work that hard Don, I'm sure you understand. Yes?"

Don turned his head away from Jonathan. "Dis should work," Ludovic entered the Shop from the office holding up a sheet of paper. Searching for a document with Don's signature, he had found one of many on Don's disheveled desk.

Jonathan set the document from Don's office next to the previously notarized affidavit, and slowly copied Don's lazy signature. He held them up for Don to examine. "What do you think Don?"

Dylan leaned over Jonathan and remarked, "Hard to discern which one is the authentic one." Don glanced at the two signatures and again began to thrash about to no avail.

"I thought you'd agree Don," Jonathan content with his work, again patronized him.

Lurking close, Fabien and Ludovic's satiated grins, implied they were anxious for the blood-letting to continue. Jonathan nodded that it was time. They slithered slowly against the metal table, partially under the lowered wagon and toward the terror-stricken white supremacist's head. Ludovic positioned his mouth over the Radial artery that ran through Don's right forearm, restraining it at the wrist and elbow.

Fabien knew his bite would have to go deep to reach Don's Brachial artery of the same arm. Fabien kept a finger on the lift switch. Dylan's first Radial artery penetration, had him a little peeved from fear he might choke on the small chicken like bones. Thomas would join lips with Jonathan against Dylan's liking. Thomas tried to keep his secret attraction with Jonathan a secret, but he was sexually aroused, and it was obvious.

Fabien pushed the Lift switch, the vehicle lowered until the tire pinned Don's midsection between the tire and the table. The oily cloth barely muffled Don's scream of excruciating pain. Like vultures on street kill, they converged on the horrified mechanic. Repulsive sounds of cracking bones breaking, tongues slurping and deep sucking with each inflicted bite. Don's carotid artery yielding most of his thick red fluid through the clenched lips of Jonathan and Thomas. Jonathan groaned salaciously as Thomas began to suck harder on his tongue than Don's artery.

"Thomas!" Dylan balked jealously. Thomas smirked at his jealous eyes and he and Jonathan disengaged. Blood surged in pulsating spurts from Don's exposed neck wound, pooled and dripped from the edge of the table. Don convulsed one last time and went limp. The lifeless corpse lay pinned under the weight of the car. Fabien engaged the Lift up switch and raised the car back to the original height.

"zis is yer mess," Lodovic chastised Thomas and Jonathan for their moment of careless debauchery and tossed them another dirty shop rag.

Dylan tried to remain unaffected emotionally. But his silence and deadpan discount of the matter, infuriated Thomas. "Can't you just admit for once that you get jealous?"

"Your insecurity tells a different story," Dylan stated matter of fact.

"Argue later!" Fabien chastened. "Clean! Leave no evidence."

Jonathan noted a large vat in the far corner of the shop with an OSHA warning tag posted on the front. "Danger! Acid wash, use protective gloves and face shield!" The chemical wash was used to clean grease from the metal pours of engine parts. "We're not burying them!"

"Why not?" Thomas questioned.

"We're going to disintegrate them from existence," he explained further. He pointed to the vat. "In that acid wash tank. Be careful not to get acid on you. It will eat through your skin."

While the others disposed of both bodies, Fabien folded the post-dated, notarized, and forged signature 'Release of Custody Form' into a pre-stamped envelope. Leaving the shop through the side door to the main lobby, he left the building to locate a mailbox. It was easy to detect. Tilted slightly in the dirt shoulder of the road next to the garage entrance. Fabien inserted the stamped envelope addressed to *Child Support Services, 617 Mission Street, San Francisco CA 94105.* Fabien smiled ecstatically knowing that this would make Carol the happiest female on the planet. She was now a mother.

May 1987
Lori's Bistro San Francisco

"Tanya, do you mind helping your sister clean the guest bedroom?" Carol requested. "Auntie Estella and Uncle Heinz are arriving this afternoon."

"Sure," Tanya acquiesced without objection, tapping her pencil in frustration on the desk under the grand staircase. The architect repurposed the space into a small library with a reading desk at the center. She turned off the desk lamp where she had been struggling with her algebra homework, and headed toward the office door. Carol sat at the new mahogany desk, in the center of the room, where she had been preparing the Bistro's budget for June.

"Tanya," Carol exclaimed. Tanya's head appeared back into the doorway.

"Yes?"

"Math was my forte," Carol stated as a suggestion.

"Please," Tanya sighed a sense of relief.

"When is it due?"

"Monday."

"It's only Friday," Carol reassured her. "How about you and I work on it tomorrow after we close for dinner?"

"Thank you!" Tanya was elated and ran to Carol and hugged her.

Carol kissed her forehead. "You're Daddy and I got approved for the adoption. We meet with the surrogate mother tomorrow. I would really like you and Natasha to come up with a name."

"You know what name I want?" Tanya stated adamantly, as if Carol should have already known.

After an awkward moment. "OK I give."

"Giuseppe!" Tanya exclaimed as if it wasn't contestable.

Carol nodded. "Alright then," she replied noncommittal. Tanya smiled and left to help her sister clean the upstairs guest bedroom. Being from a large family, Carol was relishing in being a mom.

Lori's Bistro was closed on Sundays and Mondays. Carol gifted the Paradise House to Joey with one caveat, that he would allow Her to occupy and bring back the Garden Bistro to Its original grandeur. The backyard gardens were showing dire need of Muller's many tedious hours of pruning and maintaining them. Dylan had begged that they let him carry on in Vaughn's stead. It was both therapeutic and in some small way ameliorated the pain of missing them.

Contractors restored the bar and industrialized the kitchen even more efficient than Lori could've ever imagined.

Restaurant Management was Carol's forte and she had decided to drop out of college to manage the Bistro.

The small enclosed patio diner was expanded and new iron tables and chairs replaced the old furniture that was stored in the basement. The boys had no problem convincing Carol to honor their mother and renamed the Bistro, Lori's Bistro. Dylan managed the bar, Joey the kitchen, and made Carol and Fabien made them equal partners. Carol balanced the books and Fabien became their marketing director.

In the first two months since the grand opening, the Bistro earned over two hundred and fifty thousand dollars in profit. But the real staple, besides Lori's family recipes, was the new neon sign that demanded the attention of a hungry passing appetite.

The guests began to arrive for the Creed's routine Sunday dinner at the Bistro. The Bistro closed Sundays and Mondays. Family and friends knew the code to the lock on the side gate to enter. Ludovic appeared on the stone walk-way from behind the corner tall Italian Cypress trees. He seemed lost without his Italian side-kick.

"Brother!" Fabien greeted, an arm full of red and gold Versace Medusa plates. "How are you?"

"Fine," He turned from the question to hide the honest truth of his depression. "Be careful with those particular settings, they're Versace."

The spring patio door slammed behind them.

"Chelsea traded David Speedie to Coventry for seven hundreds fifsy dollas," Ludovic remarked, changing the subject to sports.

"He'sa Striker, no?"

"Yes," Ludovic answered. "Zay needs him."

"Has Estella and Heinz arrived yet?" Carol inquired.

"Dylan and Jonathan wen zu picks sem up," Fabien replied.

"Joey gave Fabien a one arm hug. "Hear someone is going to be a Father."

"I very happy man," Fabien replied.

"Carol tells me you're meeting with the surrogate mother tomorrow."

"Yes."

"And I'm very happy for you," Joey stated with a euphoric cheer. A moment one realizes they've had an arrival moment of success or joy, and all is well. "Can I help you set the table?"

"Sure," Fabien replied. "I nearly fineesh."

Joey began to reset the silverware and move the crystal glasses to their proper place. "First rule, utensils are placed in the order of use. Second rule, forks go to the left of the plate, and knives and spoons go to the right. Third rule, water glass should be placed approximately one inch from the tip of the dinner knife, and wine glasses to the right of the water glass. Got it?"

Fabien studied the corrected setting. "I sink so."

Joey, hearing Ludovic's voice from the adjacent Kitchen at the back of the house, entered the patio to greet him. "Ludovic, when did you arrive?"

"Jus' a few minutes ago," He answered.

"Do we have an unexpected guest for dinner?" Carol asked nonplussed.

Joey stared for a moment at Carol with a facetious grin. "I want it to remain a surprise."

"We've quiz him all za day. Doe-nz wayz yer bress," Fabien injected.

"Surprise it shall be," Carol acquiesced.

Dinner

"What's he doing here?" Dylan castigated Joey in his ear, out of earshot of Detective Stone.

"Never you mind," Joey said without apology. "I invited him."

"You've lost your mind brother," Dylan shook his head realizing his concerns were falling on deaf ears.

"I expect you to be a gentleman," Joey lightly scorned him.

"Whatever," Dylan agreed to disagree about the guest being an extended family member.

"I'd like to make a toast," Joey announced, raising his wine glass. The guests thought it odd as Joey had never lead any of the dinner toasts. "I'd like to make a toast to Sergeant Stone." Joey stood and turned to face Sam sitting next to Jonathan at the center of the table. "Please give me your respect, because you owe it to me to listen to what I have to say." Sergeant Sam Stone, the surprise guest, was welcomed with mixed emotions.

Somewhat embarrassed, Sergeant Stone injected, "You don't have to do this Joey."

"Yes, I do," Joey relieved Sam's apprehension with an amicable smile. "All my life I have endeavored to slay the dragons that threaten who I am as a person. Hoping to find the smoking gun answers to right and wrong, good and evil, humility and confidence, hate and kindness. When I lost my mother to cancer, I lost my anchor, my go to person." A few chins around the table lowered in empathy. "Mother's last advice was meant to keep my train on the tracks. Never lose your integrity, she said. If you need direction, don't rely on people you love, but those you trust. Those you believe have integrity. It's better to be trusted than loved. Never forget that. When I first met Sergeant Stone, I most certainly didn't love him." Some at the table chuckled. "But under undesirable circumstances, I discovered that Sam was someone I could trust. I'm only standing here drinking with my family, because I followed my Mother's advice and because Sam trusted his friend, my Father. Sam is man of great integrity. So, here's to Sam." Some responded with the traditional here here, others just joined in clinking their wine glasses.

Carol stood at his seat at the head of the table. "To echo what Joey so elaborately expressed, I share those sentiments about Sergeant Stone. The Creed welcomes you into our family. This doesn't mean you have to become a vampire," Carol joked. This time everyone found it amusing. "We do owe you our lives Sam. And for this we'll be ever grateful. Your welcome to say a few words, because I'm starving." Again, those at the table responded with laughter and amens.

Carol took her seat as Sergeant Stone remained seated. "I'll be brief." He became somber and sighed heavily before speaking. "I'm flattered at your kind words. But please don't have any premonitions that I condone the taking of life without being subject to due process. With that said, I'm not entirely ignorant on the fact that your kind," He hesitated to not offend them. "Sorry, I mean, as you call yourselves the Creed, the media calls you Vigilantes, whatever. Nevertheless, you have had an unprecedented effect on bringing down crime in the City. I can't pretend that I'm not the least bit excited about that, I'm ecstatic. You make me look good. But I fear the consequences if one of you decide to go rogue." Many at the table took an unwelcome glance toward Thomas.

"What?" Thomas became defensive.

"The consequences of which I shouldn't have to draw you a picture."

"Mr. Stone?" Tanya asked in her sheepish, unpretentious childhood way.

"Yes, young lady."

"What's going to happen to those bad men that killed my momma?"

"Well," caught off guard Stone paused to gather his thoughts. "I imagine they're going to prison for a very, very long time,"

"That's not good enough." Natasha challenged adamantly. He could see the fire raging through her eyes from her heart.

Sam swallowed hard looking for a way out of the conversation. "Because these are pending cases, I'm really not at liberty to talk about them young Lady. But what I can tell you is that capital punishment is on the table."

"So, what you're saying is they could go free?" Natasha responded crestfallen and still enraged.

"And what about Luther Pierce?" Dylan was anxious to ask.

"Has an alibi," Stone replied, trying to avoid another debate.

"Maybe this Due Process thing needs due process of a different kind, Thomas interjected still steaming over Stone's Rogue label that he inadvertently pinned on him.

"You have all the witnesses you need sitting around this table," Dylan confronted. "That Nazi was the keynote speaker for God's sake."

"David Duke has corroborated his story that he was with him at a rally in Colorado Springs."

"Dis is notza time," Fabien interjected. "Can continue zis later, OK?"

"Let's eat!" Jonathan exclaimed, also over the impromptu toast and debate. "I'm starving."

For a few quiet seconds the mood turned somber. The tension was thick.

"Anyone heard from Tommy and Macias?" Dylan inquired over the clanging of silverware on the glass china.

"Argentina," Estella replied from one side of her mouth. The other side chomping on spare ribs.

"Argentina?" Thomas said, thinking it odd. "Why Argentina?"

"Adolph Eichmann," Estella continued after taking a second to swallow. "Heinz can elaborate after Dinner."

"Dzido's List," Heinz completed her statement. Carol has approved it. We will complete Jade's research, and wipe Fascism off the face of the Planet."

"You don't believe the world's most wanted Nazi is alive in Argentina?" Stone regaled. "He was hanged by an Israeli court in 1962."

"Yes, that's correct Sergeant," Heinz concurred. "Eichmann falsified a Red Cross Passport with the help of a Franciscan Monk in Genoa, Italy, and boarded a steamship with his wife and four children to South America. However, Israeli Mossad agents captured him and smuggled him out of Argentina to face prosecution. Afterwards, his adult children, with the help of Peron, established the Fascist Liberation Army, a secret covert political faction. Well at least the FLA was loud and proud back in the 60's and 70's."

"You spend a lot of time studying these people," Stone injected.

"Not as much as I should," Heinz chagrinned. "I found Jadwiga's diary in her personal effects. They were her next target after taking down the Order."

Thomas's eyes narrowed, "So why aren't we in Argentina?"

"I'm afraid I'm starting to give credence to your rogue concerns Sergeant," Estella stated in a deliberate hard tone. Her derisive glance at Thomas, spooked everyone at the table, except the one, who felt his fear and apprehension. He was going, with or without Dylan.

The Beginning
Chapter Two: ROGUE